Marva Cope

Also by Teddy Jones

Making It Home

Slanted Light

Jackson's Pond, Texas

Well Tended

Nowhere Near: Stories

Marva Cope

a novel

By

Teddy Jones

New York, New York

Published by MidTown Publishing Inc.
1001 Avenue of Americas
12th Floor
New York, NY 10018

Publisher's Cataloging-in-Publication data
Names: Jones, Teddy, author.
Title: Marva Cope: a novel / by Teddy Jones.
Description: New York, NY: Midtown Publishing, 2023.
Identifiers: LCCN: 2022951119 | ISBN: 978-1-62677-037-9
(paperback) ISBN: 978-1-62677-038-6 (e-book)
Subjects: LCSH: Texas Panhandle (Tex.)--Fiction. | Middle-aged
women--Fiction. | Small town life--Fiction. | Friendship--Fiction. | BISAC
FICTION / General | FICTION / Small Town & Rural | FICTION/ Women
Classification: LCC PS3610.O64 M37 2023 | DDC 813.6-dc23

Praise for Marva Cope

For the fortunate readers of Teddy Jones's beloved Jackson Pond stories, the engaging novel, *Marva Cope,* is now here, with the eponymous Marva as the new postmaster in town. She and her peppy aunt live under one roof, jousting with one another affectionately, and wrestling with their own demons.

At its heart, the book is how spirited, unconventional women find their way toward love—not a sappy, predictable love that entraps them in roles that stifle and imprison, but love that is big and free, engendering deep friendships and with luck, good partners. You will find the truth and bravery of lived life in these pages, and characters who will feel as real as anyone you know.   Eleanor Morse, author of *Margreete's Harbor*

The novel *Marva Cope* is a rarity— an artfully told "coming of age" story that morphs into a "getting on with life" saga that, in the end, celebrates the simple joys of human connection. Martha Burns, author of *Blind Eye*

In her trademark no-nonsense writing style, WILLA Literary Award Finalist Teddy Jones is back with a deeply reflective and rewarding new novel, *Marva Cope.* After two hard losses back-to-back during her youth growing up on a farm near a small town in Texas during the mid 1970s, Marva propels herself forward despite objections from friends and family who think they know what's best for a young woman determined to make her own way in the world. The story whips seamlessly back and forth between the past in the seventies and eighties to the present time —2017 and 2018.

At its heart, *Marva Cope* is a story about one woman's evolution as she faces one challenge after another, from learning how to manage a working ranch on her own as a single mother, to dealing with abandonment from those she trusted the most, to reconnecting with people from her past and forging new friendships. I enjoyed all the references to small towns in south and west Texas and eastern and northeast New Mexico. Teddy Jones captured the spirit of the plains and the caprock, but this story could be set anywhere because it's about the human struggle to create a good life despite the obstacles set before us. I'm counting on Marva to teach me how to be brave.

And if you've ever loved a dog, a dog as loyal as Bullet, you'll want to read this novel just for the chance to meet him. I highly recommend it.
Kathleen M. Rodgers, a 2021 WILLA Literary Award Finalist in Contemporary Fiction for *The Flying Cutterbucks*

Acknowledgments

Every person I encounter influences my writing in some way. It's inevitable that phrases spoken, anecdotes related, experiences shared, and unique aspects of friends and strangers alike affect me and are stored in memory because people fascinate me. Names also cling to me. Could I possibly list and thank each one for those contributions? Certainly not. But please know that I appreciate every opportunity to learn of and from you all.

Others who encourage and support me in other than that global way do merit specific mention. Martha Burns is my writing colleague, valued first reader, and candid critic who affects everything I write. Three mentors from Spalding University's MFA in Creative Writing Program shaped my approach to creating and revising fiction. They are Robin Lippincott, Eleanor Morse, and Philip S. Deaver (now deceased). Current long-time mentor John Dufresne generously guides me toward continued improvement with each manuscript. For this manuscript in particular, the workshop members at the 2022 John Dufresne Master Class in Taos, NM provided critique and support and many good times. They are Scott Jones, Peter Stravlo, David Norman, Karen Kravit, and Helena Rho.

Stephanie Jacobson and Sue Jane Sullivan lent their names to continuing characters in this novel as in the prior *Making It Home*. Cathy Shields, Postmaster, and Rhonda Wilkins, Justice of the Peace, both furnished essential background information for *Marva Cope*. Elizabeth Trupin-Pulli of Jet Literary provides continuing encouragement which I value. Michael Zealy, publisher at MidTown Publishing champions my work. Hearty thanks to each of you.

And finally, family and friends, please know that your continued reading of my fiction is vital to me. I appreciate your interest and your spreading the word to prompt others to read the stories I write.   Teddy Jones 2023

At the innermost core of all loneliness is a deep and powerful yearning for union with one's lost self." *Attributed to Brendan Behan*

Marva Cope

a novel

By

Teddy Jones

Jackson's Pond Leader
Inaugural Edition
Thursday, June 8, 2017
From The Editor

Welcome to the first edition of Jackson's Pond's hometown newspaper, the source dedicated to local news in our town.

Good journalism answers the questions who, what, where, when, and sometimes why and so what in regard to the topic at hand. So:

What and where: The first local newspaper in decades arrives today in all Jackson's Pond mailboxes. Readers can expect a new edition each Thursday reporting items of interest in the prior week or events scheduled in the near future along with regularly scheduled columns—Letters to the Editor; 'It's Your Health' by Claire Havlicek, Family Nurse Practitioner; Youth Sports Today; The Arts and Literary Scene; 'Good Words' by Sue Jane Goodman; Cooks and Cooking; and Around Town.

Why: Many enjoy reading actual print, and particularly enjoy local news. A community is best served by news gathered by local people and reported to serve the interest of local citizens.

Who: Editor and publisher Donald Scott invites your comments and suggestions and solicits your advertising and subscriptions. (Subscription form on following page)

CHAPTER 1

June 10, 2017

Game On

"Ha! Bingo!"

Marva Cope startled, looked up from staring at the SCRABBLE tiles lined up on her holder. Her aunt, Violet Steel, sitting across from her at the kitchen table, clicked down seven tiles across the center squares on the board. R E T R A I N laid out vertically, the R situated on the pink double word star. Violet said, "I'll keep score."

"That's *retrain* not bingo," Marva said. She looked back at her tiles. Q B N W I H X

Marva's aunt said, "I assume you know the rules of this game. If you need a refresher, there they are printed inside the box lid." Hardly stopping for breath, she said, "Fourteen points for the double word plus fifty for Bingo, all seven tiles used at one play. If you're going to live in this house, to coexist amicably with me, it's important that you play SCRABBLE. By that I mean that you do your best each game to beat me." She pointed at the board. "All champion players shout Bingo when they make that play."

Marva said, "Uh huh. Well." She spelled out *whine* connected to the e. "Whine, that's what you won't catch me doing in this game. Fifteen points."

Violet snorted a little laugh as she drew a new set of seven letters. "Glad to see you're up to it. The old gals in our weekly game will only play cards with me, not SCRABBLE. I always win."

Marva said, "Watch what you say. Could be there's a new sheriff in town." She drew four new tiles; J O E P, and smiled across at Violet who was busy making her next play.

"Thirty-four," Violet said. She'd made *grazing* using the r at the top of *retrain*.

She and Violet had worked out details of her renting a room, kitchen duties, sharing grocery costs, and other routines last week before Marva moved her clothes into one of the extra bedrooms and spread her toiletries in the guest bathroom. Violet had insisted that rent wasn't necessary, but Marva convinced her that there would be extra expense with her living there. Violet had emphasized that Marva should stay as long as she liked, but that she would understand if she chose to eventually find a place of her own. After that initial discussion, Marva felt their arrangement would work. Moving in with Violet was the perfect excuse for Marva to give her second-hand furniture to a women's shelter and travel almost unencumbered to Jackson's Pond.

It seemed like a perfect situation, at least for now. She spent the week opening a bank account, stopping by the post office to meet the retiring Postmaster, changing her address on her driver's license. She'd also gone to the grocery store, using a list from Violet and adding several items of her own—almonds, celery, pimento cheese. She'd also made a trip to Calverton to buy wine. They both enjoyed a glass in the evening. Until tonight, there had been no mention of SCRABBLE.

Violet made no comment as Marva connected b and o above the final g in *grazing*. "Four points." Marva said. She closed her eyes and drew two more tiles, then leaned back in her chair. "What happens if I lose?"

Without missing a beat or looking up from the board, Violet said, "I'll come up with some penalty. I have a great imagination." A second later she laid out *nauseate* attached to the n of *retrain*. "Bingo! Fifty for that and double word for fourteen. That's sixty-four." As she wrote the score on the pad at her left hand, she said, "The Official SCRABBLE Players Dictionary 5th edition is the authoritative source, in case you decide to challenge a word." Marva looked up from scouring the board for possible plays. Violet held the book up and pointed to the word Official.

When she'd been offered the promotion to the Postmaster job in Jackson's Pond, Marva was more than ready to leave Plainview, Texas. She'd been there ten years, and there was nothing to hold her. The fact that her aunt lived in Jackson's Pond wasn't the deciding factor; Marva would have taken the job regardless. She had occasionally been in touch with Violet over the years—she called her aunt a couple of times after her dad's funeral, and Violet had sent a note saying she wanted to come to Marva's high school graduation, but had a required event at the high school in Austin where she was teaching. Since then, they might have exchanged some Christmas cards and maybe there had been some phone calls. But just the same as with others she'd known or was kin to, Marva had let Violet fade into that space she thought of as The Past. That lack of contact didn't mean she didn't love her aunt. Thinking of her always gave Marva a positive, expectant sensation. If Violet had come to see her, even as a surprise, Marva would have welcomed her. She hadn't known that Violet lived in Jackson's Pond for the same reason she didn't know a lot things about her relatives. She had let life pass by at a rapid pace, her head down, doing what was needed to take care of her daughter and herself. That was what she told herself, anyway.

She ended up moving in at Violet's house because in a rare conversation with her mother a couple of months back, Marva mentioned she'd be moving to Jackson's Pond. That brought an immediate suggestion that Violet, her mother's only sister, likely needed help, that she was becoming frail. Later, Marva deduced that Violet let people believe whatever they wanted to, but she was far from frail.

At seventy-nine, Aunt Violet lived alone in a three-bedroom house on a large lot in Jackson's Pond. The house was in good repair, and the furnishings were a combination of antiques and some obviously new items in the den. She had a group of friends who gathered for card games each week, and she had a computer that she used mainly for email and record keeping. She had no pets, but enjoyed watching birds at feeders situated in some of the backyard trees. On Sunday, she attended the Methodist Church. When Marva declined going, Violet smiled and said, "I understand." Clearly, her aunt managed quite well alone.

She'd inherited the place from her parents who'd built it, along with several others, in the town's better days. According to Mother, Granddad had come from Tennessee with money in his pockets, and had owned a ranch, but lived in Jackson's Pond and dedicated himself to helping make the town grow. He'd been into lots of things—housing development, Electric Coop, School

Board, you name it, he was in on it. Marva's primary source of information about the family background was her mother, and only in the recent years when they'd begun speaking civilly to each other, and only rarely. So, she took it all with a grain of salt. Her mother's version was likely shaded in a lovely pink. Although with her mother, little in life was truly rosy.

Marva's two new letters, a and t, let her form *spate* onto the s in *nauseate*. Six points. Big deal.

Violet said, "How's it looking to you now, Sheriff?"

"I remember your being a really nice, understanding person," Marva said. "What happened to change you?"

"Memory is often unreliable," her aunt said.

In short order she filled the board with double digit plays against Marva's measly eights and threes and a single twenty-two. And then the game was over with Violet scoring 301 to her 102.

Violet said, "I haven't played in a while; my score is usually higher than that." She picked up a thin, folded newspaper, unfolded it. "Looks like we'll have local news for a change. *Jackson's Pond Leader*, not a bad name. Arrived in today's mail. I will subscribe. Obituaries are always good reading. And it could be the women I play cards with are less than objective in the news they report." She folded the paper and scooped the tiles off the board into their bag.

It was only 8:10 p.m.; Marva expected she'd be forced to play again. But her aunt surprised her.

Violet said, "About that penalty. While you were searching for a way to play your last n, I decided. You will tell me your story now, all that you remember. No need in my having to wait for bits and pieces to dribble out. And maybe one day, when you beat me, I'll fill you in on some of my tale, too. Living together, we need to know one another."

That would have been good advice a long time ago, Marva thought. She said, "Now?"

Violet peered over her bifocals and said, "Yes, penalties must be paid promptly. It's a rule."

She said, "I could use a glass of wine. How about you?"

"I'll pour," Violet said as she stood. "Red or white?"

"White." Then, after closing her eyes and thinking where to begin, Marva started with the worst year of her life, 1975.

CHAPTER 2

November, 1975
Should Have Been a Boy

The school bus driver made the turn three blocks from the high school, and the early morning sun struck Marva full in the face. She took that as a sign. From now on, nothing would be the same. Her brother promised, said he'd come back for her as soon as he passed the driving test. He aced the written part a week ago. "I'll do great. It's not like I haven't had any practice. And if they tell me to parallel park, I'll just make one try. Everybody says they won't fail you on that. No one has to parallel park in Dimmitt, Texas." He grabbed his algebra book off the seat between them when the bus halted in front of the high school. Just before he headed up the aisle to the front of the bus, he whispered to her, "From now on, we'll have wheels! Next weekend we'll be cruising Polk. Amarillo, here we come."

"You will. Mother's already told me I'm not getting a license until I graduate. Less temptation, she said. I thought about arguing but didn't."

"That's the difference between boys and girls."

Marva said, "I should have been a boy."

As Chance bolted off the bus, he said, "I'd have argued." Then he ran toward the high school entrance.

Her brother always kept his promises to her. So, she'd be ready to go by four o'clock, soon as she got off the bus at home. Dad was supposed to leave the pickup in town by two p.m. The coach already said he'd let Chance out of sixth period. Her job was to make an excuse about needing to go back to the school to get a book, having a quiz to study for. Dad would tell Chance, who would be back home by then, newly licensed, to drive her to the school. They'd make a few blocks while they were in town, maybe see someone to wave at. He promised. From her seat on the bus she watched him until he disappeared in the front door of the high school. She stayed on. Junior High was at the end of the route.

The first period bell rang as she opened her locker to look in her mirror. Her hair wouldn't do right this morning, and she was out of hair spray. Right. She looked like a wild woman and couldn't do a thing about it. Besides that, she had the cramps. Boys didn't have that to worry about that either. She slammed the locker and slipped into her classroom two doors away.

Chance always ate lunch with his athlete pals, ignoring everyone but the guys. But that day when he saw her looking his way, he gave her a quick chin-up, and then went back to shoveling food like the rest of them. She understood. He had to act like that—ogle the cheerleaders, make fart jokes, stuff like that. Fitting in. But she knew it was all an act. He was different, special. Had the grades to prove it.

Well, she was different, too. Next year, ninth grade, she'd be in high school, Chance would be a senior. She was going to run track, maybe play basketball. He'd been helping her; told her she was built to be a sprinter. He'd measured off fifty yards between the driveway and the farm implements and taught her about getting off the blocks fast. "Key to a good sprint," he said. "Practice out here five days a week. Run until you think you can't, then run one more, like coach makes the guys do."

She'd make grades good enough to get a scholarship to college, too. Whatever it took, she was getting off the farm and out of town.

Fifth period, Texas history, she half-listened to the teacher, a droner who read to them from the textbook at least once a week. Today was the day. So, Marva spent her time drawing her dream car, and when her first set of wheels wasn't recognizable as a Camaro, took up looking over the shoulder of the girl in front of her. That girl's page of notes consisted entirely of her name, Marie, along with the last names of various players on their high school football team. Who did she think she was? An eighth grader! When Marva sighted *Mrs. Chance Cope,* and *Mrs. Marie Cope* done up in fancy script near the bottom of the page, she thought about snatching the girl bald-headed. Cramps always turned her mean.

Sixth period she switched back to drawing. The pickup she sketched looked a lot like her dad's. The parking lot she drew in around it included the driving test markers for parallel parking. The pickup sat neatly between the poles. She'd seen the place plenty of times and knew that if anyone could parallel park on the first try, it would be Chance.

The bus loaded, minus Chance, and she spread her jacket and books across the seat so no one would sit next to her wanting to talk. She had less than thirty minutes to perfect her story, her lie about the forgotten book. *Texas history test tomorrow, have to do well to keep my A, left my book and notes at school. Not too many details. Excess words add up to obvious lie. Ask Mother to take me. She'll say I have to live with my mistake. Ask Daddy. He'll be too busy.* In fact, she had left the book and notes at school, and the teacher gave a pop test almost every day. So, it was a minor lie. She'd gotten away with bigger ones.

Satisfied she had the story and the plan together, she stared out the window at the passing fields of cotton ready to be stripped, others already shin high forests of bare brown stalks. Cotton lint littered the roadside, blown from tall-sided trailers that rattled their way to the gin filled with bolls. Daddy said this year might be his first decent crop in three years. Mother said, "One more like these last two and you'll be farming this place alone." That was only one of the mean things she said; they argued all the time.

Trudging toward the house from the bus stop, she put on her saddest face, which was hard to do because she knew Chance was having such a great day. Knowing how to drive is one thing—even she could shift the gears well enough to drive on the farm—but having a license meant the highway. And that meant freedom.

Chance would act cool about it, like it was no big deal. But she'd seen the pictures of Corvettes he cut out of car magazines, had watched his eyes following the senior boys who drove to school, no longer riding the bus. After today he'd be more like them, even if he wouldn't be allowed to take the pickup to school every day. That didn't mean he'd forget her, his best pal, his little sister. She wouldn't let him.

"You'll have to do the best you can without your book," her mother said. "Maybe you'll learn to keep your wits about you." The answer Marva expected. That was followed by, "Since you can't study, you can use the time to clean your room. It looks like a sty."

It would be easy for Marva to get a little cocky about how she could predict her parents' answers. Patterns. And their fights were predictable, too. One of three subjects usually set them off—

money—her mother spent too much or he didn't make enough; her father should get a job with steady pay—also money; and now and then about her or Chance. Never about their married sister, Carly. Married four years ago, right out of high school, Carly might as well be on the moon for all Marva and Carly knew about each other now.

Listening through the wall, them in their bedroom, her in the one next to it, Marva had been tempted plenty of times to turn up in their doorway, and say, "If you're both so miserable, why don't you get a divorce?" When she was younger, she'd worried her father would leave and they'd be stuck with their mother. Now that she was older, Marva could see that being his wife wasn't any picnic, either. She would never get married. She knew that for sure.

Her dad said, "I have work to do and Chance's not back with my pickup yet." She must have done a good job with the sad face and slumped shoulders because he said, "If he gets here in time, he can take you."

A couple of minutes later, Chance was back, grinning like a little kid. Dad told him to take Marva to town for the book. And he said, "Come right back. You've got that irrigation pipe to stack. Has to be done before dark."

She and Chance didn't look at each other. They would have laughed.

As they left the school, her book and notes in her lap, Marva said, "Can we stop for a Dr Pepper? I brought money."

Without a word, Chance sped to the convenience store and trotted inside. He came back with two cups, and just as quickly, they made three blocks down Main Street, turned the other direction, and headed home. They didn't see a single soul. If it hadn't been such a special occasion, she'd have pouted about not getting a chance to wave at anyone from school. Chance must have felt the same. He said, "We'll have more time later. Got that pipe to stack and phone calls to make." He winked at her as he drove one-handed and slurped his Dr Pepper.

After they passed the city limit sign, Marva said, "How fast will this go? Daddy never drives above fifty."

Her brother gave her a side glance and accelerated. Speed pushed her back into the seat like a hand held against her chest.

"Wow!" she said. "Good to know we can make a getaway if we need to."

He slowed a bit as they crossed the intersection of County Roads N and 21, six miles from the farm, then kept it steady. He said, "Getaway is right. I'm so ready to get out of town. One more year." He lifted his right index finger off the steering wheel as they met an oncoming pickup, the same way Dad saluted folks on the road. "If there was a way to graduate early, I would. I checked. I'll have enough credits by the end of first semester. But my chances for a scholarship are better if I finish the year, play basketball after football season's over."

Marva nodded. "In a hurry to play college ball?'

He shrugged. "Not really, I intend to study engineering at Tech, don't care if I ever play any kind of ball again. I'm just ready to be on my own, off this farm." He'd slowed to a crawl, then sped up a little. "I can tell you are, too."

She said, "It'll be hard without you here." She watched his profile, saw the slight frown, felt the acceleration again. Chilly wind whistled in the driver side window. He rolled it down farther and threw out his empty cup. She did the same on her side, and watched the cup take flight toward the ditch. She'd rolled her window back up halfway when she heard a loud pop. The pickup swerved to the right, tipping her toward the door. Chance said, "Dammit! Blowout. Hold on!"

She held the door handle with her right hand and steadied the left against the dash, not making a sound, watching three fence posts blur into one. The pickup bucked into the ditch; her head slammed against the roof. Still she managed not to make a noise. The pickup accelerated, swerved to the left, then settled upright on the road. Chance pumped the brake, brought them to a halt. She let out the breath she'd held. "You okay?"

He nodded. "I sure hope the spare's not flat." He might think he was okay, but his voice shook. Flinging his door open, he said, "Hop out. You need to learn to change a tire anyway."

Chance worked fast, talking only to explain what he was doing as he set up the jack, took off the bolts, removed the tire, and mounted the spare in its place on the rear of the passenger side. She wondered what he was thinking. It wasn't his fault. If anyone was to blame it was her for begging him to take her riding as soon as he had his license. He lifted the ruined tire as if it weighed only a couple of pounds. Pointing to the hole in the side of the tire and the piece of tread hanging loose, he shook his head and said, "This tire's a goner. Too torn up to repair." He pointed to the door, "Let's go."

The blowout and the tire change took less than thirty minutes. But by the time they got home, the sun was sliding toward the horizon. Their parents stood in the yard as they drove up. Marva could tell from their faces they'd been arguing again.

She picked up her books and notes from the floorboard and hauled them toward the house. Dad said, "You were supposed to be back right away. What else did you do besides get a soft drink?"

Chance said, "Had a blowout."

"Lucky you didn't kill anyone."

Marva said, "He did a real good job of keeping us out of the ditch." Then she kept on walking, but slowly so she could hear them.

Dad said, "Get out there and get that pipe stacked. I've told you three days in a row. This is my last time. Do it or get yourself grounded."

Chance took off toward the implement yard, head down. While Marva watched him walking away, her mother said to her, "You were in such an all-fired hurry to study, get in your room and get to it."

Marva took a couple of steps toward the back door, then turned to watch Chance again. When he reached the starting line he'd marked for her, he broke into a trot. She ambled to her room and spread her notes on her bed, pretended to study. A few minutes later, her mother called her to set the table for supper. They were in the kitchen, her mother frying hamburgers and Marva placing catsup in the center of the table, when a loud crackling sound, somewhere outdoors stopped them both. A bluish light rose from the direction of the implements, then disappeared. Her mother said in voice that sounded like she was choking, "That's something electrical. Run out and see if Chance and your dad are okay.

Marva had just stepped out the back door when she saw her dad running toward her yelling. "Go. Call the ambulance. Chance's been shocked." He panted between words like he couldn't grab a breath.

Marva screamed, "Mother! Dad says call the ambulance now; it's an emergency. I'm going to help. Out at the equipment." For once, her mother didn't argue.

Marva sprinted in the direction her dad had gone and passed him at the line Chance had marked for her.

Skidding to a halt beside the pipe trailer, she saw Chance lying on his back, arms and legs at odd angles, as if he'd been thrown there. She screamed his name as she fell to her knees beside him. His eyes were open, startled. His face a mask of pain. Feeling no pulse at his neck, she lifted his right arm, then dropped it when she saw the blackened hand with the thumb and index finger missing their tips. Through her tears, she lifted his jaw, pinched his nose and breathed into his mouth twice, saw his chest rise each time. Then she started chest compression the way she'd learned in first aid. Chance couldn't die. She wouldn't let him.

Then her dad was on his knees opposite her. He said, "Let me." He took over compressing Chance's chest and she continued puffing in a breath each time he paused. Her dad's face looked older, grayer, and more lined than ever before. The odor of burnt flesh clung to the three of them. She wondered if it would ever wash away.

After what seemed like an hour, but was only a few minutes, she said, "Let's trade," and she took up the compressions, ignoring the startled look in Chance's open eyes, vowing to herself she wouldn't stop until he came back. After a bit, they switched again.

One volunteer fire department truck and an ambulance paused on the driveway where her mother yelled directions to them, wringing her hands in her apron. Marva heard her say again and again, "This can't happen. This can't happen. Not to my boy."

Counting each compression, Marva blocked out everything but Chance, even when she paused for her dad to push in breath. She wouldn't stop. His life was in her hands. Even when an EMT appeared beside her, she kept on pumping. Then the EMT placed his hands in position at her next pause for air, and said, "We're here to help. Let me."

Marva leaned back, let him, but she'd forgotten how to stand. All she was able to do was to continue kneeling, crying, until Dad helped her up.

After a few minutes, more minutes, the EMTs called it to a halt. Three firemen stalked around the trailer half-filled with metal irrigation pipe and shined flashlights at the nearby power pole. "I can see what happened here," said one of them. "That piece of metal irrigation pipe on the ground there hit that power line, made an arc and he was electrocuted. Electricity going to ground. Made a circuit." He nodded as if he needed to convince himself. "Did the lights to the house go off when it happened?"

Dad said, "That line runs to the well pump only." He pointed to the well house. "Not the house. I heard the crackling sound and saw the arc." He shook his head. In a barely audible voice, as if he spoke from a long distance, he said, "Knew what happened right away."

The ambulance men took Chance's body. The firemen drove slowly out the way they came in. Marva tried to put an arm around her dad, but he said, "Not now. We have to go to town—the sheriff, the funeral home, see to Chance." They trudged beside one another toward the house. His voice weak, almost a whisper, he said, "It's all my fault. That pipe could have waited another day." When they neared the driveway, he said, "Hell, it could have waited until spring."

He seemed to be alone, unaware Marva was beside him. She wanted to lift his head, to help him bear the weight of what had just happened, but no one could comfort him. She wanted to say, "It was an accident." But the words didn't some out. If she opened her mouth, she might scream.

Her mother sat at the kitchen table with her hands wrapped in her apron skirt, staring at something Marva couldn't see, something far away. Dad said, "Y'all get your coats. We have to go to town. There's things to see to."

Marva went toward her room for her jacket. It didn't surprise her to hear her mother say, "I'm not going anywhere with you. Not ever again."

CHAPTER 3

November, 1977
A Broken Heart

Marva sat between her mother and Aunt Violet on the first pew at the Dimmitt Baptist Church that day in November. Her aunt, who had driven in that morning from Jackson's Pond, put an arm around Marva's shoulder. Her mother, inches away, could have been in another state for all the attention she paid to either of them. Dressed in black, her mother sat still as a statue and stared at the coffin. Her husband had died, and she took it personally. Anyone could see that.

The preacher had spent some time already going over facts about Marva's father, as if everyone there had never met him. But to give the preacher some slack, she'd admit some of the congregation might not have known he was born in Cookietown, Oklahoma, or that he had once worked as a baker for Mead's Fine Bread before coming to Dimmitt.

Fact was, she only knew he wasn't always a farmer because of an afternoon last month. The two of them had been sitting out on the back porch, staring into the distance. She was avoiding looking at the power line from the main that ran out to the barn. She couldn't tell if he saw anything other than a memory. He'd said, "I never should have bought this place from my cousin. He convinced me because there's two good wells here I could make it as a cotton farmer. I was tired of the smell of yeast, so I paid him everything I had plus ten more yearly payments." Then, when she asked about the smell of yeast, he told her about being a baker. And after that he said, "Your brother would still be alive. We'd probably live in Cookietown." Then he shook his head just a fraction, and cocked a thumb backward toward the house. "Don't think she hasn't told me that same thing."

She, her mother, now sat there, looking like she could exist without breathing. Marva saw that the expression on her face hadn't changed since they sat down, ushered into the first pew after everyone else was in the church. Just the four of them—Marva; her sister Carly, back in Dimmitt for the first time since marrying straight out of high school; her mother; and Aunt Violet—all that was left of the family.

After the congregation stood and sang "I'll Fly Away" and "Shall We Gather at the River," they sat again. The preacher began again, this time talking about resurrection and all those promises of life hereafter available to folks who had accepted Jesus and been saved—streets of gold, heavenly home, no heartache, no sadness. As if he knew her father, who'd seldom ever attended church with Marva, her brother, and her mother, the man assured everyone that Mr. Cope had been saved in the church in Cookietown at the age of twelve. After he said that, her mother exhaled through her nose, a rush of air audible to Marva and maybe even the man up front.

Aunt Violet hugged her a bit tighter. The preacher raised both hands and said, "Please turn in your hymnal to page 221, 'The Old Rugged Cross.'" Marva hated that hymn. Her mother didn't sing along. Next, Marva half-listened as the preacher offered up a long prayer. After those assembled echoed his "Amen," he announced there was a family graveside service immediately following and the family would be at home for visitors from one until four. Marva looked again at her mother and on past her to Carly. They were holding hands.

The pianist played some other music as the pall bearers, six farmers whose cotton wasn't going to make this year, just like her dad's, marched up the aisle ahead of the funeral director's men who pushed the casket toward the front doors of the church. The family, what little there was of it, followed. In rhythm with the slow cadence of the music, Marva thought, "Daddy. Would. Hate this. Daddy. Would. Hate this."

They stood near the casket in the little entryway as the congregation filed by to speak to them, mainly to her mother, words like, "So sorry," "If there's anything you need," "My condolences." A few hugged her mother. One of Marva's teachers patted her shoulder.

Then one by one they stopped to stare at Daddy's body in the open casket. One murmured, "God bless." Another said, "Such a pity." Some woman she didn't know stopped a long time, said softly, "Died of a broken heart." Then she blew her nose into a handkerchief and moved on.

Although it was only minutes later that the sanctuary was empty, already the day had lasted too long. Her mother and sister followed the funeral director to ride with him to the cemetery. Aunt Violet said to Marva, "I'm taking my car. Want to ride with me?"

The short ride from the church to the cemetery was long enough for the three people who stopped on the sidewalk with bowed heads to follow their passage down the short main street. Aunt Violet's nineteen-sixty model red Thunderbird attracted attention no matter what the occasion. All Violet said on the way was, "We'll talk later."

Marva looked straight ahead, said nothing. She'd stayed at home, wouldn't go to the funeral when her brother died. All she could do was cry and sleep, and sometimes cry and not be able to sleep. One night her mother pushed open the door to Marva's room and stood in the doorway. She said, "Since you couldn't be bothered to go to his funeral, the least you can do is pray for your brother's soul. So, get out of bed and get on your knees." Then she slammed the door.

Marva tried praying that one time. But it felt empty, like talking to herself with no one listening. After that, every night, she talked to Chance. Told him how much she missed him and how she needed him to help her get through the next years until she could get away. With her eyes open as she talked, she saw him the way he was—always smiling in her direction, sturdy, muscular, healthy. The image of him broken and staring at the sky, his body bent and twisted, his hand blackened and exploded, faded. Soon all that was left was him helping her, listening.

So finally, the tears came less often. Chance hadn't left her. He would always be there. But it was nearly three weeks before she bothered getting dressed; and by the time she finally went back to school, it took her until after Christmas to catch up on the homework.

The two years since had taught her some things. She had

gotten ready for Daddy's funeral without being told to. And she'd managed not to cry, not until Aunt Violet walked in the front door, came straight to where she sat in her navy blue dress, waiting for the funeral director, and hugged her. She'd said, "I'm so sorry. I know this is hard for you."

The graveside service seemed to last as long as the church business did. She knew better, but all she could hear were the thoughts in her head, and all she could see was her daddy the day he took her to town to the place people practiced parallel parking. It was November then, too, last year. He'd been patient and as sad as he'd seemed every day since her brother died. She managed to get the car positioned between the two poles and close to the curb. Then she'd sat there wanting to say what she'd carried around in her head all the time since that awful day. It was my fault, not yours. If I hadn't made him promise to take me riding as soon as he got back. If I hadn't lied about needing my school book. If Mother hadn't believed me because I lie so well. He would have been paying attention. He wouldn't have had to hurry because it was getting dark. He wouldn't have died. But she hadn't said it then, and her daddy had died blaming himself.

After the coffin was lowered into the ground, and the preacher said another prayer, he shook everyone's hands, and strode across the spare, bumpy grass of the cemetery toward his car. The funeral home man made a sort of shooing motion, heading them away from the green carpet spread over the dirt around the grave.

Speaking to Marva's mother, Violet said, "We'll see you at the house in a little while." She got away with taking charge, not asking permission. When her mother didn't answer, Carly said, "Okay," and got into the funeral director's car. Her mother, still seeming like a marble version of herself, got in next to Carly and stared straight ahead.

Violet turned her car north from the cemetery, heading toward Hereford. "We'll ride around a bit. I need a cigarette." She fished in her purse, driving with one hand. When she pulled out the package of Tareytons she offered Marva one. Then she lit them both, all accomplished with her right hand, steering with her left. "You smoke much?"

Marva took a puff and exhaled slowly, watching the smoke. "If I hang out with the guys, Chance's friends, they give me one or two."

Her aunt said, "Takes me a couple of weeks to use up a pack. But it's relaxing now and then."

After a few miles, Violet rolled down a window a couple of inches. "How are you doing in school?"

"All A's."

"Still playing basketball?"

Marva shook her head. "I quit and started running track, cross country."

"Some of us do better at individual activities. Not team sports."

Marva had quit basketball and some other things she didn't mention to her aunt because people acted like she had a contagious disease. The football boys, her brother's friends who'd always treated her like a little sister—joking with her, watching out for her—didn't talk to her in the halls. Girls on the basketball team weren't mean, they just didn't include her in anything besides practice and the games. Nothing was the same. She knew it was her fault. Maybe they did, too.

Marva took another puff on the cigarette and turned in the seat to get a better look at her aunt's face. She said, "Mother doesn't know, but the nurse at school kept me from getting anorexic. She saw I was wearing baggy clothes, Chance's shirts and sweats. I guess I looked pretty bad."

"When was that?"

"It happened kind of in stages. After I went back to school that December, I just wasn't hungry. After I lost quite a bit, I covered up by wearing the baggy things so Mother wouldn't notice. Maybe she would have. Anyway, in that spring semester, when I started running cross country, even when I did eat some, I didn't gain any weight. Kept losing."

She took another drag on the cigarette, then said, "If you'd rather not hear this… Not sure why I brought it up, even."

"Because you wanted someone to know. Maybe to see if it sounded as strange when you tell it as when you experienced it? So, how did the nurse get involved?" Violet stubbed out her cigarette in the ash tray below the radio. "Don't worry. I don't intend to tell anyone."

"She called me into her office and said, straight out, that she knew I had an eating disorder. Called it 'flirting with anorexia' and said it was extremely dangerous. Then she pulled out a chart and made me find my height and weight on it. I was already way underweight by then." She put out her cigarette. "I'll skip all the things she checked and things she told me."

She waved a hand like all the scary things that nurse told her and showed her pictures of were nothing. Then she went on. "She gave me a choice. Eat, hungry or not, and gain at least one pound a week for the next four weeks or she would call my mother in and recommend that I see a doctor and a psychotherapist."

"So, you started eating?"

"It was what she said after giving me the choices. 'There are faster ways to commit suicide. If that's what you're trying to do, I'll call your mother right now.'"

The nurse had also asked her if she prayed. Marva had told her she did sometimes. Truth was, she didn't. Aunt Violet didn't need to know that what she did was talk to her brother every night, saying how much she missed him, how sad she was, how she wished it had been her that died.

"Didn't really give you a choice, did she?"

"The only choice left was what day and time I'd report to her office to weigh in every week."

"You didn't want to talk with your mother?"

Marva shook her head. "She had her own things to deal with. But mostly I didn't want Daddy to know." She straightened up in the seat, looking out the windshield at a cotton stripper creeping through a field, doing what could be done with a pitiful crop. Violet slowed and made a turn to take them back to Dimmitt.

Violet said, "You don't look underweight now." Then after a few miles of silence, she said, "But you do seem very sad. Time helps, but I think you could benefit from seeing a therapist now, too. A few visits." Neither of them spoke until the city limit sign appeared just before the Reduce Speed one at the edge of Dimmitt. Then Violet said, "Think about it. Call and let me know what you decide. I'll help."

When they stopped in the driveway at their farmhouse, Marva didn't open her door. She counted eight other cars. One was Carly's, the rest, neighbors and people from church, she guessed. She said, "Are you going to tell Mother?"

Violet said, "Only if you want me to." A smile flitted across her features, then disappeared. "You've probably noticed we're not really close, your mother and I."

"Is there a reason?"

Violet hesitated, her hand on the door handle. Then she let go, leaned back in her seat. "Probably several. I'm nearly five years older. I think she always felt second best. I got a lot of attention for being smart. Looking back, I can see she had reason to feel short-changed as a child. Our own mother wasn't a warm person, always distant.

"Another thing was that I knew your father before she did. Went out with him a few times. Even though I was older, she thought I wanted him for a husband. He was a sweet man, but he wanted to settle down, have a wife and family. I didn't. Maybe she was able to be happy when they married. But she's been disappointed a lot. I don't know if it helps you to know it, but it's not you she hates. Or me, for that matter. I think she's been depressed most of her life."

Marva didn't know what to say. She got out of the car. "Thanks." She walked toward the house, Violet following. As they reached the porch, Marva said, "I'll call you next week."

Violet stood beside her. She nodded and said, "Take a deep breath now. Are you ready for this?"

"I guess so."

CHAPTER 4

May, 1980
Getaway

L ast September, when Kerry Galloway's family moved to Dimmitt, Kerry got a late start on the school year. Marva knew how it felt being out of place, not fitting in, had known it since Chance died and then her dad. So, she'd made an effort, tried to be a friend for Kerry. Even though, to tell the truth, Marva didn't actually know what being a girl's friend should include. Until he died, her brother and the guys he hung out with had been who she'd claimed as friends. Since then, she'd become a loner. Running cross country and studying all the time made being solitary simple. Or maybe it was the reverse. She was a loner and so she ran and she studied. Didn't matter which came first. That's who she was now.

Kerry knew how to be a girlfriend. She called Marva at night and talked about people at school. She found Marva in the cafeteria at noon. She cut pictures of clothes out of catalogs and magazines, brought them to discuss with Marva, and she wore lipstick. At Christmas, she had given Marva a pale pink scarf and a lipstick the exact same color. Marva gave her the Gloria Gaynor album *I Will Survive*. Marva tolerated all that gossip and beauty stuff because they also talked about going to college, being roommates.

This year, as seniors, they began in September poring over college catalogs during home room period. The counselor had covered a table in the library with piles of catalogs from schools all over, not only in Texas. They had decided they'd both apply to the same colleges—Kerry had good grades, too—and they'd room together, probably choose the same major.

And bit by bit, Marva occasionally took time to do more with her hair than a pony tail, and now and then remembered to wear lipstick. She should have known, when Kerry started dating, that things would change. More than once Kerry tried to get her to agree to double date with a friend of her boyfriend, both boys from Nazareth, a few miles east.

Marva's life was complicated enough. She'd save dating until college. And she hadn't given up cross-country. "No boy wants to date a sweaty girl," she told Kerry. Dating was the only thing they actually disagreed about. Had someone asked, Marva would have said they were good friends, shared a lot with one another. But Marva figured Kerry kept some things to herself, just like she did. In Marva's case it was about her brother dying.

Not that everyone in school, including Kerry, hadn't heard about his accident, now five years past, as part of the lore of the school—promising high school quarterback struck down by freak accident; football jersey with his number ten retired; enshrined along with his photo in the trophy case on first floor. The rest of that story, Marva kept to herself. And she'd walk the long way around to the classrooms to avoid passing that trophy case.

What Kerry kept back, Marva never pried about. But she was pretty sure Kerry's parents didn't approve of her boyfriend. And more than once, Kerry had hinted about being grounded a lot. Marva knew they did agree on one thing. Life for them both would be so much better when they graduated and left home.

That afternoon they'd stopped outside the school building and sat on a bench out front, facing into the sun, working on the first tan of the year. Another thing they agreed on was that they were both too pasty for words, all pale skin and mousy blondish hair. So, she wasn't prepared for what Kerry said that afternoon.

"I hope you won't get mad, but I've made a big decision and it affects both of us."

Marva opened her eyes, turned to face Kerry. "Both of us?"

Kerry didn't look her way, kept her face tilted toward the sun. "I'm not going to Tech this summer."

"Your parents?"

Kerry shook her head. Marva shouted, "Look at me! If it's not your parents, then what? You didn't even mention you were thinking about not going." She took a breath, held it. Maybe Kerry only meant not the summer. She exhaled, lowered her voice, and said, "If you're waiting until fall, that's okay. But I'm going now."

"We're talking about getting married. I have to stay."

"Getting married! You're not even eighteen yet."

"Don't tell. My parents don't know."

"Who would I tell? You're the only person I talk to. I thought I knew you." She stood and stared down at Kerry, still face up toward the sun, eyes closed, a tear running down her face. Marva sat again. "Why? Just tell me that."

Neither said a word for what seemed like a long time. Then Kerry turned and faced her. She said, "I'm probably pregnant." More tears dribbled down her cheeks. "I don't know what else to do."

"Yes, you do."

"But he says he loves me."

"And wants to get married?"

Kerry shook her head. "But he said he would."

After another long silence, because she knew a good girlfriend would say something, Marva said, "I have to go. Mother will wonder where I am." Her mother never wondered where she was. But Marva couldn't stand watching Kerry cry. She wanted to scream at her, "How could you be so stupid?" She'd thought she was her friend.

She said, "I'll see you tomorrow."

It had been so long, ever since her daddy died, since Mother had said anything to Marva other than telling her when meals were ready, that she didn't expect her to say anything. That afternoon, the day after she and Kerry had argued, she and her mother sat on opposite sides of the kitchen table. That's where her mother usually ended up each day, eating Oreos and drinking another of the many cups of coffee she downed like some long distance trucker. After Daddy's funeral, Marva had pushed herself to try making conversation with her mother about something every day. After a few weeks of vacant stares and mumbled single-syllable responses, she gave up on getting her to talk. Now she just sat with her a few minutes. At least her mother knew she was home, knew there wasn't some stranger pilfering around in the house.

Her mother put a meal on the table every evening and kept the house tidy. And Marva had heard her talking on the phone to Carly several times, so it wasn't that she'd quit talking altogether. It must be her, she'd concluded. For the rest of her life, her mother intended to punish her in the slyest of all ways, by ignoring her, pretending she had died instead of her brother and then her father.

Really, Marva had nothing to complain about. If a person wanted to live almost alone, this was the way to do it. She had a cook, maid service, and a bank account in her own name opened when her mother sold the farm and moved them to town. All Marva had to do was keep her room clean, take care of her clothes, and clean the bathroom once a week. There was even a phone in her room. She knew lots of girls her age who'd fight her for a chance to take her place. They hated their mothers. Marva's mother had all but disappeared, so there wasn't anyone there to hate.

Marva waited until her mother looked up from her coffee cup. Then she said, "I'm going to start college this summer right after graduation."

"Since when?"

"The counselor told me today I'll get two scholarships at graduation. One's for being in the top five in the class. The other's a Presidential Scholarship from Tech."

Her mother said, "Where Chance intended to go." After a long pause and another drink of coffee, she said, "Where will you live?"

"I have a reservation in one of the dorms. Already confirmed. I paid a deposit."

"When?"

"Like I said, right after graduation. No sense waiting. Summer school starts June second."

Her mother picked up another Oreo, examined it like it was a foreign object, eventually nibbled a bit off one of the chocolate sides. Then she nodded and didn't say more.

After she got to her room and changed into sweats and one of Chance's T-shirts, Marva called Carly. As soon as her sister answered, Marva said, "Well, I did what you suggested. Registered for the summer at Tech and got a dorm reservation. I told mother. She hardly said a word. And when I told her I'm getting two scholarships, I might as well have been reporting that it's a bright, sunny day here. Not a word. Not 'good for you,' how much,' nothing."

Carly said, "She's doing the best she can."

"Yeah. You've said." She was afraid to ask Carly if she was coming to graduation. So, the phone line hummed without words. Her sister said, "Marva? Good for you on the scholarships. I'm not surprised. You're the smartest one of us."

Marva heard Carly's baby crying. She said, "I know you're busy. The baby. I'll let you go."

"I'll be at your graduation. We'll go out to eat after. Okay?"

"Thanks, Carly." She intended to tell her sister she loved her, but couldn't get the words out.

After a six-mile run, Marva showered and sat through another silent meal with her mother. Fried pork chops and mashed potatoes with lettuce and tomato salad, the same as two days ago didn't surprise her. Her mother cooked, but often the same meal three times in a week. Didn't matter to Marva. Running gave her an appetite.

When she opened the box that was in the mail a couple of days later, a graduation present from Aunt Violet, she'd taken the suitcase in the kitchen to show her mother. A nod, and the word, "Nice," was her mother's only response. Marva waited a few seconds; maybe she'd tell her mother about the note enclosed with the gift— Violet telling her she hoped they'd see one another again soon, that she couldn't be at graduation because she was would be chaperoning a senior class trip to New York City from the school in Austin where she was teaching. But her mother's attention had turned back to her coffee cup.

In her bedroom, Marva returned the note to the zipper pocket inside the bag. Then, even though it was only May fifteenth, she folded her three good winter skirts and two sweaters into the plain navy-blue bag. Too full from supper to go to bed, she opened her English IV notebook to review for the final. The test would be easy for her. But the review could help prepare for the Credit by Exam test she'd take her first week at Tech. She could get up to twelve credit hours by passing tests in English, Government, and American History Before 1865. Her plan was to take twelve hours in summer school. If she got the extra credits, then she'd be close to being a sophomore by the time fall semester started. She and Kerry had planned all that together.

That was before. Each of the three days since they argued, Kerry had sat alone at lunch, and she'd been absent today. She might be waiting for Marva to apologize. But that wasn't going to happen. Marva wasn't the one who let herself get pregnant and spoil their plans. She wasn't the one . . . She grabbed the phone after the first ring. Kerry said, "I want to talk. Will you meet me?"

Marva knew where she meant, the elementary school playground. "When?" She heard herself sound like her mother.

"Fifteen minutes."

There was plenty of time before dark. It was only seven. "Okay." She debated about putting on lipstick, but settled for dragging a brush through her hair and leaving it out of the pony tail. She walked slowly toward the playground, determined that if Kerry wanted her to be a bridesmaid, she'd say no.

Kerry sat in one of three sturdy swings hanging from heavy iron pipe legs anchored in concrete. Sand beneath the seats showed paths of feet pushing to propel the swings. Daddy had built one with two swings out on the farm. Chance had taught Marva when she was small how to push herself high and then jump out at its highest point, the closest she'd ever come to flying. He caught her every time.

Marva took another swing, leaving an empty one between them. Kerry twisted hers around, winding the chains, lifting the seat until her feet barely touched the ground. "I'm not pregnant."

"That's good." Marva pushed against the ground moving up and away, then lifted her legs, reaching with her feet toward the sky. "Still getting married?" As her swing lifted her back, she pumped her legs, urging the seat to lift higher on its forward trajectory.

Kerry's chains untwisted, twirling her around. "No. He didn't really mean it. I could tell."

"How do you know?"

"He didn't call. When I called, he didn't answer."

"No, how do know you're not pregnant."

"My period. Started yesterday. Lots of cramps."

Marva slowed her swing, dragging her feet as she drifted

back. "Now what?"

Kerry twisted her swing a half-turn so she faced Marva. "I'll start school somewhere in the fall. Not Tech." She stood and moved in front of Marva. "I don't want to be your roommate. You only care about yourself. Never even told me you were sorry I was in trouble. Or thought I was. Never called. Avoided me at school. All you cared about was your plan." She moved closer.

Marva waited, thinking Kerry intended to slap her.

Splotches of red showed on Kerry's neck when she spoke again. "If I got married, I was going to ask you to be my maid of honor. I thought you'd stand by me, support me no matter what. I thought we were true friends. But it's clear we never were. You don't know how to be a friend." She stalked away.

Marva didn't say any of the things she thought—a good friend would tell you you were being stupid; a good friend would have made sure you didn't ruin your life by getting married. She didn't say anything because Kerry was right. As far as Marva was concerned, starting college, becoming someone other than the sister of the school's dead hero, the daughter of the man who died of a broken heart, the daughter of a woman who'd ignore her even if she was on fire, the girl who had no friends, was the most important thing in her life right now. She shouted at Kerry's back, now nearly a block away. "You're right!"

Graduation was scheduled at seven p.m. on Friday, May twenty-third that year. As had been the case every year since anyone could remember, the evening was humid and hot. Thunderstorms were forecast; a tornado watch was in effect. A full audience would tax the capacity of the air conditioning system, so the doors on both sides of the high school auditorium would stand open until the actual ceremony began. All Marva was interested in was having it over. On Sunday morning she would be on the bus to Lubbock.

Graduates were required to be at the school at six. Because her mother had given up driving—she still had a car—for who knew what reason, Marva walked to the school. If Carly made it from Junction in time, she'd do all she could to get Mother to attend. Otherwise—well, otherwise, Marva would walk back home when it was over. Didn't matter much to her, although it would be nice for someone to be there to applaud when the principal handed her the scholarship letters.

Marva didn't let Carly or her mother see the tears that surprised her when she found them waiting in the hall for her after the ceremony. By then it was nine o'clock, and Marva was starving. Maybe hunger was what had made her cry. Or seeing that Carly was pregnant again, and no one had told her, or that her mother had actually gotten up from the kitchen table to be there. Carly, who had come without her two-year-old or her husband, took them to the only eating place that was still open at that hour, the Dairy Queen. She said, "Order anything you want, little sister. I'm proud of you."

Carly had a Dude and french fries. Mother ordered coffee and a small dish of ice cream. A large cherry, chocolate Blizzard was how Marva rewarded herself. She focused on getting part of it in her before she took a breath and leaned against the back of the booth. Carly chattered a bit about some people she'd talked to there, families of some of her classmates. And then she said directly to Marva, a signal Mother already knew what was coming, "I'm going to start working next week. Bookkeeping for an oil company." Her voice sounded odd, uncertain, or like she had to concentrate to keep the volume up. She talked about the job—it wouldn't be hard since she'd made an A in bookkeeping in high school; it would be nice to have some money for little extras. Marva knew there was something else she wasn't telling. Then Carly stopped talking, like she'd suddenly deflated.

Their mother said, "I'm moving to Junction to keep the kids and help out. She found me an apartment close to her work."

Marva nodded and concentrated on the last bit of the Blizzard. Neither of them had mentioned any of that to her. And there was a lot more she hadn't been told; that was clear. Carly probably thought she was too much of a kid to understand about marriage problems. She knew for sure her mother thought very little about her, regardless. So fine. Now she had no family and no friend.

Then her mother kept talking, uncommon as that was. She said, "Tomorrow when you finish packing for school, pack up anything you want saved. I'll store it somewhere."

Marva scooped up the empty cups, spoons, a single-use catsup container, and one unopened salt packet, then carried all that to the trash container by the door. When she sat back down, she said, "There's nothing I want saved. Anything I leave can go in the mission barrel at the church." Then she looked Carly in the eye and said, "I'll be getting a job, too. Buying college clothes."

CHAPTER 5

Summer, 1982
A Summer Adventure

Marva had made friends with three girls on her hall since last fall semester. They were the first since she'd been at Tech, not because people weren't friendly, but because she kept herself so busy working and studying that she barely noticed the girls who clotted the lines in the dining hall and rushed to watch afternoon soap operas in the lounge. That past fall, the three who lived on her hall, all freshmen from Uvalde, invited her to sit with them at supper one evening. Marva had never been to Uvalde, or much of anywhere else, but she knew it was a small town in ranch country west and south of Lubbock. Small town girls, they were more like people she'd grown up with than the ones she'd met from Houston and Dallas. The girls from those towns invariably spent their time talking about sororities, clothes and hair, and boys. More than once, she heard the words, "I'm pledging in the spring." Getting in a sorority, snaring a guy, and getting married no later than the week after graduating were the top items on their agendas.

But the Uvalde girls actually studied. Their parents expected them to make their grades and end up making the nearly 300-mile trek home to teach school or do something else useful. One intended to be an agricultural extension service agent, another a high school speech and drama teacher, and the third, Stacey, the one taking ag economics courses, was the only girl in most of her classes. She expected to take over the cattle and sheep ranching operation her dad had built up. No brothers.

Stacey had been a barrel racer in high school and still talked about going on the circuit, maybe taking a year off. Those discussions always ended with her saying, "My parents would kill me." But she still managed to be in the bleachers or helping out in an alley at any rodeo within two hundred miles. If it hadn't been for them, Marva would probably have graduated without ever having a date.

Two months ago, the Uvalde girls had told her they wanted her to go with them, a group date, they called it, to a rodeo in Levelland. "I'm at least a year, maybe two, older than you. And I don't want to be the extra girl," she'd said. Not wanting to admit she'd never had a date before and had no clue how to behave had something to do with it, too.

One of them said, "Don't worry. We're taking care of that."

No one had claimed matchmaker credit so far. But Marva had gone and Cutter Gulley turned up, also unattached. So, they sat together, and he answered her questions about the score-keeping for the events. Since she admitted she'd never been to a rodeo, they all pointed at her—in the bleachers where the group sat—and shouted in unison, "It's her first rodeo!" Lots of people seated around them applauded.

Somehow, she hadn't died of embarrassment; she'd even pointed back at the group and yelled, "It won't be my last! Now where do I get a beer?" More applause! Whatever possessed her at that moment, she had no idea. It was her first beer, too. After that, she relaxed slightly and was fine until the rodeo was over. No one had told her about the dance. Another first for her. That definitely would have kept her in her room.

When he walked her to the dorm door, Cutter said he hoped he'd see her again. She couldn't imagine why; she'd trembled during most of the first slow dance, and she stumbled through "Cotton-Eyed Joe." But he did say that. And then he was gone. So, she didn't have to admit she'd never been kissed on a date before either.

Later that night, in Marva's room, Stacey sat on the bed and said, "I'm not sure, but I think Cutter's dropped out of school. He's talked about going on the rodeo circuit. And I haven't seen him in class in weeks. He's older than you. Probably ought to be graduating next year if he stays in school." She picked at a spot of mustard on the front of her shirt halfway between two of the pearl snaps, then spit on her finger and wiped at it.

Then she stopped and said, "You ought to be careful about him. He's got a reputation at home."

Marva, still feeling pretty good from the whole evening, said, "Bank robbery?"

Stacey laughed. "No, but I hear he leaves a trail—unkept promises, broken hearts. That kind of thing." She glanced down at the mustard spot again. "Not that I have first-hand knowledge. But at one time, an older cousin of mine was sure he was going to marry her. Right out of high school about five years ago."

"I doubt I'll have to worry about a broken heart. That's probably the only time we'll ever go out. And it wasn't a real date."

Stacey shrugged. "I've got to get this spot out. See you in the morning."

A lot happened in the next two months. Marva had told herself more than once that everything she and Cutter said and did was exactly what others had done before they graduated from high school—steamy kisses; hands all over one another, everywhere; bodies pressed together; breathless, embarrassed laughter from her; head shaking from him. But she hadn't, not before. Every sensation, every thought about being with him, evoked reactions that even she knew were exaggerated. Breathlessness became a minor affliction that began exactly one hour before a scheduled date. Sounds amplified, aromas and flavors exploded, almost overpowering—a simple hamburger and fries became a sumptuous meal and every song she heard pierced directly to her core.

If someone else smiled too much, laughed too loudly, and admitted to feeling the way she felt, she'd diagnose lust. In her own case, she'd add that the first-time experience of lust could be overwhelming. Even knowing from her anatomy and physiology classes enough about the effects of hormones to label all the parts and understand the chemical pathways, the part of her brain that knew all that had become disconnected from the rest of her body. So, she did what any intelligent twenty-year-old virgin should do. She rode the city bus to Planned Parenthood and got a prescription for birth control pills.

After the necessary exam, the nurse who handed her the prescription said, "You can fill this at the pharmacy here in the building. Remember, don't trust the pills until you've been on them one full cycle. And always use condoms even then."

Knowing she must be blushing, Marva said, "Thank you for that information."

The nurse nodded and handed her a paper bag. "If you have any problems with the pill, come back to see the doctor. I put some condoms in there for you."

Before Marva could get out of the exam room, the nurse said, "Tell him no condom, no sex. And if you aren't comfortable talking about it with him, then you don't know him well enough to be having sex with him. Just a little advice. Might save you some hard times later."

Numb and still embarrassed, Marva only nodded her head and buttoned her blouse as she walked past the nurse, out of the exam room.

Since she started the pills, there'd been none of the side effects mentioned on the package insert; she'd read every word. Her period should begin tomorrow—the first one, after which it would be safe to trust the pill. Not that she was planning to test it. But good to know.

They'd been to three rodeos and out to the movies twice, plus several quick meals in small town cafes while out for long drives around Lubbock. After the first rodeo, they had gone without the rest of the crowd. She learned to dance the Cotton-Eyed Joe without stumbling, and she'd stopped quivering when Cutter took her in his arms for a dance. Progress, as far as she was concerned. In between the times the two of them were out together, she'd managed to study, go to class, and keep her wits at work. She hadn't surrendered her ability to concentrate on school. Often, hours would pass without a thought of Cutter. But the thing that he'd said the past weekend threatened to make her lose focus. It had been on her mind almost full time the three days since.

That night, they had gone to the movie, seeing *E.T.* rather than *Rocky III*. After she told him she didn't much like fight movies and liked Stallone as an actor even less, he'd shrugged and bought the tickets. "Okay by me. I can see a fight any Saturday night. Two cowboys and enough beer ..." He looked away, then turned back with a smile. "If you don't have to study, we'll go somewhere after. Something I want to talk about."

"We can skip the movie if it's something urgent." That had come to her in a flash. It was bound to happen anyway. He was probably accustomed to faster girls, ones he didn't have to teach how to dance or anything else. She'd make it easy on both of them. When he came to the passenger side to open her door, she didn't get out. "Listen. I've had a good time going out, but don't worry about hurting my feelings if you're tired of it. No harm, no foul."

He stepped back, shaking his head. Then he laughed and said, "You beat all I've ever seen. That's not what I want to talk about. Come on. Let's go see a movie."

About halfway through, while the ten-year-olds in front of them were laughing, and she had relaxed enough to do the same, he reached for her hand and held it until the credits came up. The breathless feeling returned, and the aroma of popcorn made her mouth water.

"I can concentrate better on talking if I'm not driving." Cutter said that as he pulled into the empty parking lot at the Municipal Auditorium on the north side of campus. He turned off the lights and pushed back his seat. Marva turned toward him and waited. He said, "I'm going to give you some background first. When I got out of high school, six years ago, I told my dad I didn't want to go to college. They'd saved money so I wouldn't have to work while I was in school. We all knew I'd have to study. Even high school was hard for me. It's the reading. If I listen to something, like lectures, I don't forget. But if I read it, I might as well have not bothered. Never sticks. But Dad said, 'You'll need a degree someday. Right now, you want to be a cowboy, manage a ranch, work at things you know already. But when you have your own place, to make a go of it, you'll need more—business knowledge, scientific breeding, and lots of other things.'"

She said, "You get along with your parents?"

"Usually. I'm their only kid. They both graduated here at Tech. That's why I'm here. The plan was to take a minimum class load, get tutors, whatever I needed to pass. I managed to get a lot of my basics done then got into the ag courses. But at this rate, it's going to take me another year and a half to graduate. And that's if I can ever pass algebra and a bovine genetics course."

Marva didn't say anything, but she wondered where he was headed with this. Sounded like he was the luckiest person she'd ever met—new pickup, easy class load, not required to work, lived off campus in a house with two other guys. Easy street.

He took a deep breath, thumped a fist against the steering wheel. "Well, hell, I may as well just tell you. I don't care if I ever graduate. I'm not going to go to summer school, and I may not come back in the fall."

"Where do you intend to go?"

"Not sure. Probably follow the rodeos this summer, then get a job on a ranch after that."

She said, "I don't get it. Why not finish? Aren't you supposed to take over your family's place?" Her brother would probably have ended up running theirs. But now there wasn't even a place to run, even if she was capable of it. She shifted in her seat, looked straight ahead at the outline of the bubble-shaped auditorium building.

"Dad's having to take bankruptcy. Too many dry years in a row down there where it's dry to start with. Couple of the wells are pumping nothing but sand. And the cattle market's down. They've spent too much on me already."

"Have you told them you're planning to quit?"

He shook his head. "Only that I intend to work this summer, and they don't need to pay summer tuition or rent. At least I won't add expenses while they're having a hard time."

She said, "How did that go over?"

"We're supposed to talk about it again next weekend. At home."

She waited. Finally, because he'd apparently run out of words, she said, "I'll miss you when you're gone. I've had lots of fun since we met."

He said, "That's what I'm trying to get to. I want you to go with me for the summer."

That stopped the mental packing she'd been doing, putting away all the fun of the past few weeks, returning to her usual organized, study-drudge existence. "I'm registered for summer school. Dorm fee's paid." She took a couple of big breaths, then went on. "Besides, why would you want me with you all the time?"

He chuckled, shook his head. "You really don't know, do you?"

"Know what?"

"Being with you is like being with one of the guys."

She sat up. "Excuse me?" She leaned against the door.

"Wait," he said. "What I mean is like being with a pal, but way better because you look so good and make me laugh even when you don't mean to."

A sigh was all she could do. She'd never had an adventure, thought she probably never would. A summer on the road. Her mother would choke! She said, "I need to think about this."

Afraid to look at him because she wanted grab hold and not let go, afraid he'd see that need she felt. "If I don't go, will I ever see you again?"

"I hope so. But not this summer." He caught her hand again. "I don't know. All I know right now is I need to get off my parents' payroll and on my own. And I'd like you to be with me at least for the summer."

A rap on the driver's side window startled her and made Cutter sit up straight. A flashlight shone on his face, then hers. A heavyweight, uniformed man stood at the window. He said, "Campus Security. Sir, put both hands on the steering wheel." Cutter obeyed. "Now with your left hand, roll down the window." Cutter did as he said. "Have you been drinking?"

Cutter said, "No, sir."

Then the man asked Marva if she was all right. His light focused on her face nearly blinded her.

She said, "I'm fine. We were just talking."

"You'll have to move on. No parking here after dark."

Cutter drove slowly toward the other side of campus, taking a long detour down University, across Nineteenth Street for several blocks, not speaking. Marva hardly noticed where they were; her mind full of how impossible it would be to go with him and how exciting. He'd made it clear he wanted a pal, not some romantic attachment. She had no idea what she wanted.

He slowed as they eventually came to the dorm parking lot. "Still with me?"

She said, "Yes, well, no, it's just . . ."

He parked. They both faced forward staring toward the dorm, as if deciphering a message transmitted by the lobby lights.

Cutter said, "I'll leave for Uvalde after my exam on Friday."

"If I go with you, I'll need a job, too. I'd want to pay my own way."

"We could figure all that out."

She shifted to look his way. "You make it sound simple."

He turned toward her, smiling. "It's just the summer. No need for it to get complicated. Just think about it. If I don't see you before, I'll call Thursday, see what you've decided."

Opening her door, she said, "Either way, thanks for asking me."

"Hold up there, I'm walking you to the door."

A goodnight kiss, his arms pressing her to him would erase all her questions, send her to the registrar's office to drop summer classes, make her forget her plan for an early graduation. But she didn't bolt and run.

He opened her door, snugged her close to him with one arm, and walked with her toward the dorm lobby. She leaned against him, telling herself she'd think clearly when she was alone in her room. At the lobby door, she took a step away from him, manufacturing a big smile, and said, "Talk to you Thursday." She didn't trust herself to look back as she crossed the lobby.

Marva Cope

40

An hour or more later, nothing was a bit clearer. Talking with Stacey might help. But Marva had never allowed herself to confide, to tell a best friend everything, to learn what other girls seemed to know instinctively. It wasn't likely she'd learn it that night either. So, she went to bed and finally fell asleep around midnight. All she'd managed to do was realize that spending a summer with Cutter would be stupid and irresponsible.

The next day at work, she'd heard herself, as if she were another person, say to her manager, "I'm not going to be here for summer school. Needed at home. I'm really sorry."

The manager made sympathetic comments and told Marva she'd take her off the schedule after Saturday lunch.

Living in the dorm had more advantages than drawbacks for Marva. So, she'd stayed put since the semester she arrived at Tech. One of the drawbacks was underway that week in May. Next weekend was the end of semester, move out time. That afternoon the noise of people packing, friends crowding the halls, helping with the luggage and boxes, talking about summer plans sent her out of her room, walking as fast as she could. The library would be the best place to go; she could find something to read there until time to go to work.

Her job at the restaurant on Broadway, now as a waitress rather than dishwasher like that first year, kept her in spending money. Her mother deposited funds in her account each semester for tuition, room and board, and some incidentals. Marva had never spent that money for anything other than the tuition and dorm fees. So, she'd saved some. Marva knew her mother had enough; she'd sold that house in Dimmitt when she moved to Junction where Carly lived. But it was a matter of pride to Marva to have savings. Besides, she wasn't inclined to spend much on clothes and never a cent on cosmetics. The lipstick in her purse had been a graduation present from Carly two years ago.

Marva started up the library steps, then turned and walked back toward the dorm. No sense waiting, she'd already quit her job; already knew what she intended to do. As soon as she was in her room, she broke a promise she'd made herself years ago. She told her first lie since the day she'd vowed to always tell the truth, no matter how hard. When her mother answered the phone, Marva asked how Carly and her kids were doing, then listened to her mother recite a litany of childhood ailments and Carly's successes at work.

Then her mother said, "What's wrong? You'd never call otherwise."

Marva said, "Nothing's wrong. I'm calling with some news. No problems. Everything's fine. But I decided to give myself a break." She hurried on with the tale she'd concocted. "I'll be a nanny, well a baby sitter for a six-year-old girl, child of two doctors. You should see the house. You know, just spending the days doing what six-year-olds like to do. I'll move out of the dorm and live-in at their house, a little apartment they have out back." She knew as soon as she stopped talking that she'd said too much. Simple lies worked best.

Her mother listened and murmured the equivalent of nods during a boring conversation, never asking a question. Then Marva heard the sound of a child crying. Her mother said, "Don't hang up. I'll be right back."

The crying stopped and her mother was on the line again. She said, "You may think you're fooling me. But you're not. I know you, and I know lies when I hear them. You never babysat a day in your life. Don't even like little kids."

Marva knew better than to argue with her mother. Once she made up her mind, nothing changed it. She'd blamed her since the day Chance died.

With hardly a breath between words, her mother went on. "I don't know what you're up to. I hope to God it doesn't involve a man. But whatever it is, you have to make your own mistakes. You'll live with the consequences. As far as I'm concerned, you've seen the last of money from me for school. If you're old enough to stop, you're old enough to pay your own way if you ever go back." And then she hung up.

Marva stared at the phone which answered her with a dial tone. Her only thought was that she was glad she hadn't wasted money on a bus ticket to Junction to tell her mother in person.

She jumped when the phone rang. When Marva answered, her mother said, "And one more thing. If you've gotten yourself pregnant, don't expect any help from me. You should have sense enough to get birth control if you're sleeping around." She hung up again.

Cutter called a few minutes later to say he'd meet her in the parking lot, wanted to talk before he left for home. She saw his pickup several rows away from the front, and walked slowly toward it, trying to decide whether she'd tell him now or wait until he'd talked to his parents. She stuffed her shaking hands into her jeans pockets. Maybe they'd talk him out of stopping school; maybe he already regretted asking her to go with him. As soon as she sat in the pickup, he said, "Did you decide?"

She said, "If anyone here asks why I'm leaving, my answer's going to be that I'm going to work as a rodeo clown. And if they don't believe that, I'll say I'm going to hitchhike across the west. That way, no one can blame you for leading me astray."

He grabbed her by the shoulders, then hugged her, then kissed her. "I promise you we'll have a good time."

"No promises required. Let's just try not to do anything we'll regret, not much, anyway." She had no idea where any of those words she'd said came from. But now that she'd said them, there was nothing she wanted to take back. "I'll drop my courses and get my tuition and dorm fees refunded. Probably will take a couple of days. I'll have to be out of the dorm by or before next Wednesday." That breathless sensation urged her to inhale, to remember to breathe.

He looked at his watch. "I took my finals. Might have actually passed. I'll be back here Sunday evening if not before. Wish me luck."

"You'll do fine. Your parents love you."

"What did your mother say?"

"About what I expected. Didn't believe the lie I told her, doesn't care what I actually do." On the spot she decided not to tell him the rest. She'd made the choice; the consequences weren't his fault.

He looked at his watch again. "Better get on the road."

"Be careful," she said as she got out of the pickup. As she started toward the dorm, a single beep of his horn turned her around. He beckoned her to his side window.

"How about a kiss from a rodeo clown, for luck?" It turned into a long kiss. Then she stood back and waved as he left.

CHAPTER 6

Summer, 1982
Continuing Education

Because they'd stayed in a motel in Tucumcari the last two nights, not sleeping in their bags in a park, Marva had gone to their room while Cutter played pool with some guys he knew. Long, hot showers made her feel she'd gotten off a layer of grit that threatened to be permanent. Tonight, her hair suited her for the first time in a week, finally released from under the gimme cap she wore almost all the time. When she felt clean, she spent the rest of her evening lounging on the bed watching television and reading the Tech course catalog. And if she were to tell herself the truth, she'd admit she was waiting for him to come in because his holding her close when they went to sleep was the best part of her day. If he'd ever have come in drunk and obnoxious, she wouldn't have been surprised. Guys did that. But so far, even though his mouth often held a flavor of beer when they kissed, the nights made any thoughts about going back to Lubbock alone and living in the dorm with a roommate evaporate.

She pulled on her pajamas, which were actually her panties and one of his T-shirts, remembering the first night they'd actually seen one another undressed. It was the night they left Lubbock. They got as far as Fort Sumner, New Mexico, where a motel's sign advertised "horses welcome." The motel property adjoined a park where he backed up the trailer and led the horses into a small corral to stay for the night. The motel manager said the horses wouldn't be bothered there because the town police checked the park during the night.

Until that night, they'd never gone past heavy breathing and insistent hands, both of them exploring and eager but cautious. They'd had beer with supper and taken a couple to the room. It was barely dark when he said, "I think it's time we got to know each other better."

"Yes, there's a lot we don't know about each other." Some part of her she didn't even recognize spilled out what she hadn't imagined saying. "For example, no man has ever seen me undressed." Then she slowly peeled off her jeans and shirt, then her bra and panties, and stood across the room from him. When he didn't say anything, she went on, "And I've never seen a naked man."

He was out of his boots and clothes seconds later. In a voice that was almost a whisper, he said, "What else haven't you done?"

"Drunk beer without my clothes on."

He crossed the room, took a swig from a long-neck Lone Star, and handed it to her. "Anything else?"

She took a long drink from the bottle, then drew a big breath. "Never slept with, had sex with a man."

"We can fix that." He took another drink from her bottle, then put it on the bedside table. "I guess no one's ever told you, you look even better without clothes."

Her face heated. She resisted the urge to put her hands on him, everywhere. He wasn't handsome in the usual ways, no curly hair, no dimples. But intense almost black eyes; his strong jaw; a smile that suggested a lively, full-of-fun mind; and a lean, muscular body made him arresting. She wasn't about to tell him all that. She said, "Wait." After a few seconds of rifling through her purse, she handed him a condom. "You'll need this.'

He shook his head. "You're not on the pill?"

"I am. But that's not enough. There are diseases."

He backed away a couple of steps, shaking his head.

She turned, picked up her blouse from the chair by the bed, and said, "Your choice."

He didn't move. "You beat all I've ever seen. You sure this is the first time?" He took the condom from her.

"Would it matter?"

He pulled her toward him, pressed her to the full length of his body. She lacked only a couple of inches being his height. He ran his hands down her back, and cupped her buttocks, "As warm and smooth and beautiful as you are? No, not really."

Rising on her tiptoes, she reached her arms around his neck, then a hand behind his head, guiding him to her lips. They stood kissing, generating heat that melded them together until she leaned away, and pulled him toward the bed. When they finally slept that night, she didn't bother with pajamas. The next morning, she woke snuggled next to him, an arm across his chest. When she moved to get up, he said, "Don't leave. You're perfect right where you are."

She didn't know what to expect, whether they'd want sex every night, more often than that maybe, or if it would be something reserved for special times—his winning a roping or her deciding it was time. She should have eavesdropped more at the dorm. All she knew was that it took only a touch, a long, deep kiss, and she became shameless, using her body to urge him, them toward the sensations that shook her, forced her to sigh aloud, made her limp, yet fully awake.

Then about a week after that first time, again sleeping nude next to him, in a motel room in another rodeo town, she dreamed vividly that each time she touched him, her fingers tingled. In a room, in a bed that was familiar, she felt her body awake though she was unaware of any sights or sounds except her and the man she would not let go of, her body pressed to his. Then, in the same dream, she turned his face toward her, to kiss him, and saw him clearly. It was her brother, Chance. She woke crying silently, fearing the dream, afraid to think about it. Creeping across the darkened room lit only by a slice of light that slid in under the single window's curtain, she found Cutter's T-shirt. Pulling it over her head, she sniffed his familiar smell, and relaxed. Then she found her panties in the pile with her jeans, slipped them on, and crawled back into bed. Since that night, she hadn't gone to sleep without wearing something to remind her of Cutter and to protect her from dreams.

If anyone had asked right then, if there'd been anyone interested, which there wasn't since no one knew she was in Tucumcari, how she'd enjoyed her summer, Marva would have said, "It's been an education. Not that college courses aren't also, but these past nine weeks have taught me things I never even knew I didn't know." The trouble was, she knew it had to end.

The next morning, she sat alone in the café next to the motel. Until then, she hadn't mentioned getting back to Lubbock. But she had to register for the fall semester. With ninety credit hours, she could still finish a degree by the end of May if she took fifteen hours a semester. Then what? She had no idea. In fact, she'd have to piece together which degree those hours would count toward because she'd taken what interested her, not necessarily what some degree plan required. But now things were different.

All summer, she'd avoided thinking about anything past August thirty-first. Now, here it was the fourteenth. Anyone with any sense would get organized now. The past two months had been pure freedom, and she hated for it to end. She opened the Tech course catalog she'd brought along when she and Cutter pulled out of Lubbock headed west.

Her head down, she didn't see Cutter come into the café. She'd stayed there after breakfast when he went to fill the gas tank and load the horses. He said, "Ready?"

Marva looked up and said, "Sure." She tore a strip of paper napkin and stuck it between the pages listing human development degree requirements and those for a B.A. in English. After stowing the catalog in her purse, she followed him outside, caught up with him. She said, "I'm trying to decide what courses to take next semester. I can graduate in May if I can get what I need for some degree."

She knew he heard her because he nodded. But he didn't say anything. It was several minutes later and quite a few miles west out of Tucumcari when he finally said, "Has it quit being fun?"

She laughed. "Not at all. I'm still having the time of my life. But I have to think about later—not wasting what I've already done—what I want to do when I quit waiting tables, things like that."

"My parents would love you. A woman who thinks ahead."

"Probably not. They'd think I lured you away for the summer."

He kept his eyes on the road, occasionally looking in the rearview mirror, checking the horse trailer, then the side mirrors. He might be reckless in some ways, but he was a good driver. And, like her brother, he'd been happy to teach her things he knew. This summer, so far, she'd learned to saddle and ride a horse. And she'd even learned how to hook the trailer to the pickup's hitch and how to back the truck with the trailer attached.

Something he didn't know was that she'd spent quite a bit of time learning about the job of the rodeo secretary. While he hung out helping in the alleys or waiting for his turn to compete in the roping, she got acquainted with several of those women. A person could get work if she knew enough about the scoring and some bookkeeping. Not that she'd spend the rest of her life on the rodeo circuit, but if she happened to stay with him this next semester, she'd need to earn money. So far, they'd split what expenses there were, and she hadn't touched her savings which would now have to be her tuition money.

"I told you before I didn't bring you along for decoration. You've done your share. I'd set them straight on that score."

He'd called his parents every couple of weeks, concerned his dad was depressed, not just upset, but truly depressed about having to take bankruptcy. She said, "How are they?"

"Dad sounds a little more like himself. Mom's always the tough one. She'll keep him going." He fiddled with the radio, then turned it off again. "She got on the phone and told me she had money put away from when my granddad died, in my name, at a bank in San Antonio. Said it would be plenty to get me through school. So not to worry about that."

After a long silence and the right turn a few miles out of Santa Rosa that aimed them north, she said, "Want me to drive a while? You're probably tired."

He said, "I'm fine. We'll take a break in Las Vegas."

Rather than continue talking, she thought of things she needed to do in Lubbock, whenever she got there. Get more birth control pills, more condoms. Wouldn't need any of that if he didn't stay in town. Silence filled all the vacant space in the cab, but neither of them swept it away.

The sign they passed said Las Vegas twelve miles. They'd be on the short stretch of Interstate soon. Since there were no more rodeos for the summer, they were going to be sightseeing in the northern part of the state and then . . . well, it would be time to get back to the real world. That's how she thought of it. The only real plan they'd made for the rest of the summer was this trip to Red River she'd suggested. She remembered one of her brother's friends going skiing there. Chance had told her and said one day they'd do it, too.

Cutter had agreed. He'd never been there summer or winter, so they were going to sleep in parks on the way and then ride trails in the mountains when they got there. That was the plan. But she had a feeling, and that's all it was, a feeling, that something had shifted, maybe had oozed in with the silence. After a couple of miles on the Interstate, he said, "What would I have to do to get you to stay?"

"Nothing. I intend to go back and finish school. Get it over with."

"But does it have to be right now?"

She turned to face toward him, to watch his face when they talked, to speak to him, not at him. "When we left Lubbock, we agreed it was for the summer. You needed to decide what you're going to do. I wanted an adventure." She watched as he frowned. "That was the deal. No promises, no plans beyond that."

"I still don't know." The truck slowed as they climbed a hill. He checked the mirrors again.

"My being along won't fix that."

"Look, I'll marry you if that's what you want."

Another long silence gave her time to think, but instead all she did was fume. They passed the first exit for Las Vegas. He slowed again.

She waited a few more seconds for the urge to slap him to pass. Then she said, "That's an insult. If that's what you intended, you certainly accomplished it."

"Settle down. I didn't intend it that way."

She leaned closer to him, wanting him to see her anger. She said, "Don't you ever tell me to settle down. You made it sound like you're willing to do some whore a big favor. Make an honest woman of her."

He exited at the next Las Vegas sign and pulled to the side of the road. He faced her, pulled off his hat, and wiped a bead of sweat off his upper lip. "Dammit, that's not what I meant. I just thought . . ."

"You have no idea at all who I am, what I want, so you come up with that patronizing bullshit about getting married. For your information, that's the last thing I want. I've seen what marriage can do to people."

He exhaled. It sounded like a sigh. "I can't stand the idea of going back to school, and I don't know what else to do—shit or go blind." He shook his head. "I guess you hooked up with the wrong guy."

Her heartbeat still hadn't returned to normal. If she knew where she was, she'd be out of the pickup walking right that minute. He'd just spoiled the whole summer.

She said, "Take me to the bus station."

He didn't start the pickup. "I'm not taking you anywhere until you've settled down. We've got another ten days. Let's have a good time, then I'll take you back to Texas."

"I'd rather take the bus. Now." She wasn't about to let him talk her into staying. And she admitted to herself already that she'd made a mistake. She had thought he was smart enough, man enough, to figure out what he'd do next, that he'd come to his senses. But he was as lost as she was.

Cutter put his hat back on and started the pickup. "I'm going to stop at a convenience store and get directions and a Dr Pepper, and then I'll take you to the bus station."

He walked out of the E-Z Mart with two canned Dr Peppers. There was a newspaper under his left arm. She didn't say a word when he set the cans on the dash. He said, "Sure that's what you want to do? Red River was your idea."

"Another mistake I made. Yes, take me to the bus station." After driving several blocks, Cutter pulled up in front of the bus station. He'd barely stopped the vehicle before she was out her door, folding down her seat back, and pulling out her one suitcase. She flung her purse over her shoulder and slammed the door. She said, "Thanks for the summer. Everything I learned will come in handy sometime." Even to her the words sounded cold and sarcastic. She didn't look back until she was inside at the ticket counter. He was gone.

There was no such thing as a direct bus from Las Vegas to Lubbock. She'd have to wait an hour and twenty-seven minutes for the next bus. Its route was through Albuquerque where there was a layover. At six fifty-two, she'd board a different bus to go east two hundred twenty-two miles to Clovis. She'd arrive there at eleven p.m. From there she could get another bus for the one-hundred-mile trip to Lubbock. The ticket agent reeled off the route and schedules and then said, "That's if they're all on time, then after a two-hour layover in Clovis, you should make Lubbock at three-thirty a.m."

She'd been calm when he'd started reciting the information, but felt her pulse quickening again as she thought of the Lubbock bus station in the middle of the night. But she straightened her back and paid for the ticket and stood looking around the waiting room while the agent filled in blanks on the ticket. She should have made Cutter drive her back to Texas. But she'd run out of anger at him about the same time she slammed the pickup door and saw the woeful look on his face.

Sitting on a pewlike bench near the back of the waiting room, she told herself it was for the best. Now she could get on with her plans for school and then figure out what to do after that without someone else's problems, without woeful looks. As soon as she got to Lubbock, she'd get a job. It would all work out. She repeated in a whisper, "It's for the best." Then she wiped away the tears that tracked down to her chin.

When she stepped off the bus and into the station in Clovis, followed by a woman with two children who had sat behind her all the way from Mountainair outside of Albuquerque, Marva stretched and headed toward the vending machines lined up on the far wall. She fed change into the drink machine and waited. Just as the can fell into the tray at the bottom, she heard a familiar voice. Cutter said, "Could I offer you a ride, lady?"

Her first impulse was to whirl around and slap his face, but when she turned, he was standing beyond arm's length and holding his cowboy hat over his heart, looking like some old-time cowpoke meeting a stagecoach. She said, "I don't ride with people I don't know."

"If you've got the time, we could get to know each other. I hear Red River's real nice this time of year."

He followed a few steps behind her to the seat where she'd parked her bag. She sat. He stood close and said, "You were right. I don't really know you. Spend seven more days with me. I'll find out who you are and show you who I am. Then we can decide together what's next."

She took a drink from the can she clutched. Sleeping some on the bus had warded off the worst of her weariness, but anger and disappointment had taken the starch out of her. All she wanted right then was to sleep. She said, "I can't go another mile tonight."

He offered her his hand. "Then we'll stay here, and start over in the morning." When she stood, he picked up her bag, and they walked together to the pickup.

She said, "I'm not promising anything. One week. That's all. Then back to Lubbock."

"Got it. That's a start."

The next morning, a note lay on the pillow next to Marva. She must have slept so soundly she didn't hear Cutter leave. Maybe he was paying her back, leaving her there, after that fit she threw yesterday. Holding the note near in the pale dawn light, she read the back-slanted script. She knew he was left-handed, but she'd never seen his handwriting before. Not a scrawl like many guys', his words marched across the page in a straight line, every letter perfect and complete.

I've gone to get the horses at my buddy's place. It's 6:10 a.m. mountain time. Will bring coffee and doughnuts when I return.

He'd been gone close to an hour. She headed to the bathroom. A week, she'd told him. Nothing was likely to change her mind. But Red River would be a good way to finish out their adventure. Today was a new day, a start of a good final week. The sun was shining and she intended to do her part to make it a good day for both of them.

In the shower, shampoo dribbled into her right eye as her attention wandered between thoughts of exploring high altitude Northern New Mexico trails on horseback and mundane details of finding a job and getting back to dorm life. For every notion about what she had to do, a voice inside her said she didn't have to do any of it, not now, maybe not at all.

She twisted the shower handle marked COLD; the shock of icy needles against her scalp and body erased the argument between her dutiful nature and the carefree side that until this summer she'd forgotten had ever been part of her. She'd been that girl who would spin a lie to get away with following her brother anywhere she could. Who'd beg him for a soft drink and a fast ride. Not anymore.

Cutter walked in the door just as she came out of the bathroom, wearing a skimpy motel towel as a short sarong with her long, damp hair hugging her shoulders. As if an alarm sounded, they both stopped, absolutely still. He was the first to break the stare that held them each in place. "Didn't mean to scare you. Here's coffee. Doughnuts are out on the pickup hood. I'll be right back." He turned to go, then turned back. "Think the doughnuts might wait a few minutes?"

"Get them and get back in here. We have places to go."

She pulled her clothes on, towel-dried her hair the best she could, and jerked it into a pony tail. Between bites of first one, then a second doughnut, she jammed the things she'd taken out back into her suitcase. Cutter followed suit, and soon they were both packed, and the paper bag held nothing but bits of sugar glaze. She said, "That should hold us until we find a diner."

She felt him watching her as she moved around the room. Then after they were in the pickup, his movements were uncertain, tense. As far as she was concerned, yesterday's bus episode was past and should be left there. Maybe he wasn't sure. If she knew him better, his moods would be clearer to her, but a few short months had only revealed so much.

He started the pickup, but didn't put it in gear. She waited, then finally said, "Forget something?"

He shook his head. "No." He turned the key and the motor died. "Well, yeah. I need to say something. You were right. I assumed you were like other girls I've known. That was wrong. You're different, and I wasn't smart enough to see that. I'm sorry. I'll try not to let it happen again."

She'd give him a little credit; he wasn't stupid, just slow

figuring out not all girls are alike. She said, "Okay. It's over. Now let's go have a good week in Red River." She shifted in her seat to look out the windshield. She didn't need him to see her face right then.

As they left Clovis, they both went silent. A half hour later, when they made a turn north, she turned on the radio, volume low. They commented occasionally on the dry pastures, the cattle grazing, or lack of livestock entirely, with the music as background. She'd have been happy to ride along that way for days, thinking only about what presented itself beyond the windshield. Then Kenny Rogers started singing "Love Will Turn You Around," and she reached to turn off the radio. Cutter caught her hand and said, "Let's leave it on. I'll bet we'll hear Willie before long."

She leaned back and focused on the farthest distant point she could see, imagining it was the edge of the earth. He was still holding her hand, gently. After some more miles, he said, "You really scared me yesterday. I'd never seen you mad like that."

She moved her hand, pretended to study a ragged nail. She said, "I try not to get that way. I don't like arguments, fighting. Until Chance died, he took care of me. I seldom had reason to get upset. But after, I had to learn to take care of myself."

"Always on My Mind" came on the radio next. She reached to turn it up. "There you are. Willie, right on schedule."

He winked at her and said, "Willie knows me too well." He hummed along softly until the song ended. Then he said, "Maybe we'll find a place in Red River to dance. Would you like that?"

She nodded. "You know I would."

The road climbed steadily toward Las Vegas and past, and Cutter began talking again after they lost the radio signal. From there on, the trip uphill was the best part. As far as she was concerned, if they had to leave for Lubbock tomorrow, those miles and the conversation they had during those hours were enough. Hearing Cutter tell about his worries, his mistakes and regrets, and his hopes, speaking as if he'd stored those things for a very long time, so long that the words spilled and ideas tumbled, sometimes unhitched from logical connections, was worth everything that had gone before. She smiled at a couple of stories of misadventure, guy things with no one harmed, but mostly she listened, making no judgments, only learning more about him.

Then, as if he wanted to correct any mistakes, misunderstandings, incorrect assumptions between them all in one day, he asked questions about her life, about her aspirations. And he wasn't satisfied until she, reluctant at first, sketched her story. And he listened. She could tell he had because he asked more questions to push her beyond the outlines, urging her to expose as much of herself as he had.

They both turned silent as they left the grand, level vistas of the High Plains, passed through the tiny old town of Cimarron, and then a spot called Ute Park. Soon they were confined by soaring palisades on both sides of the road. She caught her breath and said, "Oh!" Nothing had prepared her for the sensation that they were entering a secret passageway. When they emerged at the other end of the canyon, at the village of Eagle Nest, she felt another clutch at her chest, this time at the sight of the serene open lake on the left and the mountains directly ahead.

The cabins they stayed in just outside Red River had been there since the 1920's. The woman who owned them would have entertained them with her stories and scrapbooks for hours if Cutter hadn't said they needed to get the horses taken care of. The corrals there were a big reason he'd chosen The Pines. The sun was edging down behind the mountains by the time they got themselves and horses settled in.

That week they packed in every possible activity the little town and its surroundings offered. They rode the easy trails that started just behind the corrals at The Pines; they hiked to Goose Lake and back, then threw themselves on the bed and napped for hours; they cooked in the cabin's kitchenette; picnicked at Middle Fork Lake; and at night they added their sleeping bags, zipped together to make one, to the quilt on the bed and slept close, holding on. Friday night, they went to the Bull of the Woods Saloon for supper and live music. The steaks and fries were excellent and the band was lively. At first, they were the only couple on the dance floor. But later, a crowed arrived. They laughed and joked with a bunch of Texans from Amarillo. She pretended they never had to leave.

Saturday morning, when she woke, Cutter was sitting at the kitchen table, about eighteen inches from the bed, drinking coffee, reading a newspaper. She said, "Is there room service here?"

"Yes, Ma'am. We have coffee ready. Anything else you want, place your order now." He folded the paper and left it on the table, then made the three steps to the tiny stove, brought her coffee, and sat next to where she lay on the bed.

She reached for his arm to check his watch. "I had no idea, ten-thirty! I only drank one beer."

He said, "I think it's the altitude. Makes a person hungry and sleepy."

She sat up and leaned against their pillows. "You have a plan for today?"

He shrugged. "Needed to talk to the woman I'm traveling with before making plans."

"Wise choice." She sipped coffee. "Where'd you find a newspaper?"

"Livestock Weekly. Got it in Las Vegas. Coffee hot enough?"

She nodded. "The only thing I had in mind for today was going dancing again tonight. Other than that, rest of the day is up to you."

He brought the newspaper to the bed and sat again. "I don't intend to make you mad again, but I want you to know I want you to stay with me, not go back to Lubbock. I've decided I'm not going. Not now at least." She sat up and swung her legs off the bed. He held up a hand. "Please don't say anything until you hear me out."

She pulled the sleeping bags over her bare legs.

He said, "Sometimes they have ads in here for couples to manage ranches. Absentee owners want someone on the place to take care of livestock and keep up the main house. Lots of them down near home. Sometimes they use the place for hunting or guests and when they do, the couple takes care of that, too. There's one of those ads in here this time. The ranch is east of Cimarron." He stopped talking. Then he said, "We could go and talk to the owner today. I called him."

"When?"

"That day you lit out in Las Vegas. Just thought I'd see what it was all about. They furnish housing, salary, a pickup."

She stuck out her hand. "Let me see the ad."

He pointed to the place on page three he'd circled in the help wanted section.

She said, "Married couple for ranch caretakers. We don't fit the description. And before you ask, I won't get married to qualify for a job."

"But we're a couple. We'd just tell them it's the eighties. Marriage isn't necessary."

"You know about taking care of a ranch. I don't. So, I wouldn't be worth as much on a ranch as you would. But I want a paycheck of my own. Not shared with you. I doubt they'd go for that. Or you, for that matter."

"We don't know until we talk to them."

Part of her wanted to stick with him no matter what. That was how she felt. But there were too many reasons why she should do as she'd planned. "I'll go with you, just to talk. I've told you my conditions. And even if they want us and agree, I'm not sure I'm ready to stay. I told you before. I want that degree. I like to finish what I start."

"I promise we'll go dancing again tonight. All we're going to do it talk to the man."

"You know you cheated."

"How's that?"

"Got me up here so I'd love it. Then asked me again."

He shrugged, watched something on the floor. "When you put it that way, I guess I did. But it wouldn't be forever, not for any longer than you want to."

"What time are we supposed to be there?" She had one clean pair of Levi's and one shirt she hadn't worn. But her hair would take some work.

"Two."

Cutter drove and Marva read aloud the directions he'd gotten when he'd called for the interview. Then, just ahead, she saw the sign for Skinner Road, and pointed. The unpaved road that led from the highway to the main ranch buildings stretched out straight and narrow. "Twenty-eight miles to the nearest town?"

Cutter nodded as he made the right turn. "Our place at home is twenty-two miles out."

When they pulled up at the main house, he got out, then turned back and said, "I'll go meet him first. If he asks, I'll tell him we're a couple, but don't believe in marriage, like you said. If he asks, I'm going to say we've been together two years."

She didn't answer. Now she knew he might be as good a liar as she could be. She opened the pickup door. "Call me when you want me to come in. If you do." She watched him stride up to the front door of the big house, which looked to be in good shape, as if he was a regular visitor. A red and white spotted cowdog trotted to where she leaned against the tailgate. He sniffed her, then leaned against her. She petted him on the head and said, "You live here?" He looked up at her like he might answer. Then he trotted off toward the other house, which appeared to be a one-or-two-bedroom place with a wide porch across the front. A woman came out onto the porch, waved at Marva, and walked toward her.

When the woman came near, she said, "Y'all here about the job?"

Marva nodded and said, "Maybe. Just an interview today."

Then the woman, who looked to be in her forties stood beside Marva. "I hope you take it. I'm ready to get back to town. Worked here long enough."

"How long?"

"Five years. These people are okay. Seldom around. It's not a bad place. Pays okay. But my husband's not that good with cattle, and I end up doing a lot more than taking care of hunters and keeping up the houses. So . . . well, I told him it's time." She leaned down and flapped dust off her jeans. "If we had kids, I'd have made him leave earlier. You're young. Your husband a good cowboy?"

Marva said, "Seems like it. He's ranch raised in West Texas."

"You?"

"Farm."

"You might grow a garden. I never had time."

The dog was back, nosing at Marva's leg. She said, "Looks like a good dog. Is he yours?"

"Belonged to the last people who worked here. Left him behind. Guess he'd be yours. Well, I've got stew cooking. Better check on it." She turned to leave, then stopped. She said, "That dog's good company when you're alone." Then she headed back toward the house.

It had only been a few minutes when Cutter and a tall, dark-haired man came out of the house toward her. While she'd waited, Marva listened to a battle in her mind. The twenty-year-old version of her pointed out that she'd be even more isolated than usual, that she and Cutter didn't really know one another that well, that either one of them could get sick and die before they'd be able to get help, that there probably wasn't any television reception out there, and she never finished that first-aid course after learning CPR back when she was in 4H. Her lying, reckless, life-is-short, adventure-is-for-the-young self argued that if she didn't like it, she could leave, anytime. And besides, the only thing for her back in Lubbock was a job waiting tables where the mostly college-age customers didn't tip that well. It was up to her. Nobody else cared what she did.

She walked toward Cutter and the owner. When they neared, she put on her biggest smile, raised her chin, offered her hand, and said, "Hi. I'm Marva Cope. Cutter's partner."

The owner nodded, said, "Jack Gorman." Then he led them to what he called the ranch pickup. He opened the passenger door and said, "We can all squeeze in here. I'll show you the place."

Marva hoped Cutter absorbed all the details because the tour of the place felt to her like a whirlwind. Different pastures, cattle, horses, hunter cabin, bulls, barn, hunting blinds all passed by at a speed too fast for her to even remember. She tried picturing herself waking up there each day, being partly responsible for keeping the place safe and operating. All she'd ever known at home were plowed fields, a tractor pulling sturdy implements, irrigation wells chugging in the night; pipe being moved, stacked, moved again, connected, constant repairs being made, and accidents. Foreign didn't half describe how this ranch felt to her. She didn't know the language or the customs; she would have to rely on a guide. The reckless, adventure-seeking part of her suddenly fell quiet.

Thirty minutes later, they were back at the main house. the three of them sat on rockers on the porch as the owner offered the job and explained the pay and conditions. He said, "We've been in the habit of making it a one-couple, one-paycheck job. But I understand from Cutter that you two are independent operators." He chuckled and repeated that phrase, independent operators, and looked toward the house. "My wife would applaud that idea, I know for certain. So, I'm willing to split the salary however you two agree to. We'll be without help this time next week. I need to know what you decide by tomorrow afternoon. Say three o'clock?"

Riding back toward the highway, Cutter pushed his straw cowboy hat back from his brow, wiped his face with his right hand. "Quite a tour of the place he gave us. I think he wanted to see how we reacted, if we thought we were up to it."

She said, "It looks like it'd be a lot of work. What did you think?"

He shook his head. "Nothing there with the cattle and the rest of the ranch stuff I haven't done before. Most of the land is in the hunting pastures. Wouldn't be too much trouble tending to thirty cow-calf pairs and two bulls. I'd need help with gathering and branding. But keeping up the house, taking care of hunters in the fall. That's another whole job. And that cabin the hunters stay in would mean more chores." He made the turn onto the pavement, going west toward Cimarron. "I see why they want a couple."

She raised an eyebrow and said, "Because men don't like to clean houses? Here's a flash—not all women do either. I don't."

Cutter gave her a solemn look, and said, "Good to know."

When they entered the Cimarron Canyon, the late afternoon sunlight's low angle cast alternating shadows and shards against the palisades and trees, creating an eerie, flickering display. Marva's eyes widened. "This could be spooky at night."

Cutter chuckled. "How about that ranch on a full dark night, twenty-eight miles from town and twenty from the nearest neighbor, the electricity goes off, the coyotes start to howl, and there's no television and poor radio reception? Think that might be spooky, too?"

"Guess I'd need to learn to shoot. Just in case." She didn't add what she thought, that she wouldn't be frightened if he was there and he was the person he seemed to be.

After feeding the horses as soon as they were back at The Pines, they set out for The Bull of the Woods. The place filled early with good-humored laughter and plenty of loud music. Saturday night in a place with nothing much else for entertainment. As soon as they polished off a steak and fries each, Marva and Cutter spent lots of time on the dance floor along with occasional breaks for beer. When the bartender yelled, "Last call," and the band struck up the beginning of Cotton-Eyed Joe, everyone in the place crowded into lines on the dance floor. Marva didn't stumble once.

Driving back to The Pines was when she decided. Something her daddy used to tell her when they played dominoes: "Play one and look at the other." That meant get on with making a choice. Either decision could end in regret. Stay with Cutter and things turn bad in some way, then regret that choice. Leave and miss the adventure, then regret that before she hit the Lubbock city limits. So, she played one— she would stick with Cutter if he wanted to take the job. When he asked, she'd tell him.

He opened her door for her and took her hand. "Let's watch for meteors a while." He led her to a space near the corrals where they had a view of the sky high in the southeast. He sat on the ground and leaned against a boulder. She took a space next to him, and when he opened out his right arm she leaned against his chest. As their breathing synchronized and one of the horses nickered, she leaned forward and pointed at a light streaking across the sky. He said, "Make a wish."

She did, but kept it to herself. He said, "You know what I wished?"

"Pretty sure."

"For a year? Two if it works out?"

She leaned back against him and said, "Granted." Both his

arms went around her then, holding her as if she were treasure.

Neither of them said more that night. The next day as they packed to leave, she said, "There are some things I need to do in Lubbock before we move to the ranch." That last phrase made her smile, especially the we.

Cutter said, "I should go see my folks and let them know." He folded a T-shirt into a neat square, tossed it into his bag. "Guess I could leave the horses in Uvalde. If we still have a ranch there."

"I should call my mother. Get another lesson on how much of a disappointment I am."

An hour later, they were headed back to Texas. She searched for a radio signal, hoping for something to distract her from thinking about her daddy and dominoes, and hoping she'd played the right one.

CHAPTER 7

August, 1982
On Our Own, In Charge

Cutter said, "Where do you want me to take you?"

They were about thirty miles from Lubbock. Marva had been so focused on getting an appointment at Planned Parenthood and going to the bank to close her account there that she hadn't dealt with that detail. She said, "That motel on 19th, Lubbock House. It'll do for tonight." She'd find someplace cheap after that. He didn't have to know. "I'll make sure to be outside there waiting when you come back. Saturday, right?"

"Yeah, about four. Takes me about six hours from home." He glanced at her, then said, "No sense you having to spend money on a room. I'll pay when you check in."

"I pay my own way, remember?" After she took care of her business, she'd see about picking up a few shifts at the restaurant where she worked before.

"Do me a favor. Just don't argue. We came back because I need to go see my parents. You won't go there with me, so . . . ."

"We already discussed that. Y'all have family stuff to talk about. I'd be a distraction—that girl Cutter's taken up with."

"Right. So just let me pay."

She looked out her window, her right foot twitching against the floormat, watching the familiar acres of cotton plants march toward the horizon, the irrigation pipe hemming the fields, the familiar sameness of the South Plains all but erasing the exhilaration of days at high altitude. "Okay. You win."

"It's not a contest."

She shrugged. He wore a serious expression and focused on the road until they were at the edge of Lubbock. As he turned onto Nineteenth Street, he said, "Are you sure you'll be okay without wheels?"

"I managed all the time I was here before. I'll figure it out." She said it as if she was certain. "I didn't take up with you just to have transportation." She added a little laugh to make that sound like a joke. She could always walk, even the couple of miles out to Planned Parenthood if she had to. Or farther if necessary—getting pregnant would definitely turn their high-altitude adventure into a nightmare.

When she opened the door and reached in the back for her suitcase, he said, "Let me." He carried the bag and walked ahead of her into the motel office. A few minutes later he led her to the elevator, then to the room on second floor, he said, "Two-thirteen. Second floor so the room doesn't open into the parking lot. This isn't too bad a neighborhood, but you never know. In both our names so no one would think you're alone."

He'd probably brought girls here before. She didn't ask.

He opened her room and handed her the key. "I'm going on. We'll stay here Saturday night. Get an early start Sunday morning. Be sure to lock up when you're alone."

"I'll be fine. See you Saturday around four."

He started toward the elevator, then turned and came back. He said, "I'll miss you." Then he hugged her, kissed her like he meant it, and left.

Speaking to his back as he trudged toward the elevator, she said, "I'll miss you, too." As she closed and locked the door, she wondered if he'd be back on Saturday.

Monday morning, she called and got the first available appointment at Planned Parenthood—Wednesday morning at nine. After that, she put on her cleanest jeans and shirt and walked over to the campus, intending to eat whatever was cheap in the cafeteria at the student union. She'd need her strength to tackle getting to the bank to empty her account and to the restaurant to beg for a couple of shifts.

As she passed the dorm where she'd lived, she thought of the girls from Uvalde, Stacey in particular, and wondered if they'd moved off campus as many did after the required freshman dorm year. Soon she sat alone in the student union at a small table, polishing off the last of the breakfast special—two scrambled eggs, toast, and coffee. Between bites, she watched students milling, some with food, many more apparently with no purpose other than to be where people congregated. Those would be the freshmen. It seemed far more than two years ago that she'd been one of them.

She heard her name called, and looked to her right, far across the room. As if she'd heard Marva thinking of her earlier, Stacey rushed toward her. Marva stood when Stacey neared the table. Stacey said, "You're back! My best friend's actually back!" By the time she got the words out, Stacey had wrapped Marva in a tight hug which, for once, she didn't back away from.

As soon as they sat, Stacey leaned forward across the table and said, "Okay, I want to hear the story of your summer. But first, are you already in the dorm again? My new roommate and I have rented a house on Twenty-eighth Street. You could live with us, help pay the rent. It's just two of us. We need one more." Talking so fast she hardly got a breath, Stacey hopped from topic to topic—telling about her own summer—long vacation on South Padre, a family reunion in Central Texas—never asking another question or waiting for an answer about Marva moving in with her.

Then Stacey stopped talking as if stunned. She leaned back, hands up, and said, "Sorry. I'm so excited to see you, I haven't let you say a word. How was summer?"

Marva gave a compressed version of the months she and Cutter had spent together. Stacey gaped when Marva first told her she hadn't stayed for summer school. But Stacey didn't say anything until Marva dropped the news about the jobs in New Mexico. At that, her friend grabbed Marva's hands and said, "Tell me you're joking. Not Cutter. Girl, I told you before, he's out for only himself. Always taking care of number one. I don't want you to be hurt."

"I can't be hurt if I don't expect anything. We're partners. That's the deal. Either one of us can call it quits anytime."

"So, when are you supposed to leave?"

Marva told her she'd be in town until Saturday evening. Stacey said, "So come with me out to our house. Maybe I can change your mind." When Marva shook her head, Stacey said, "Well, you can help us get the house in order while you wait around for Cutter to come back."

"I have a couple of errands today."

Stacey exaggerated a pout, then said, "Seriously, we could use some help."

"Tomorrow, then. But that'll probably be the only day. They may want me to work when I stop by the restaurant."

By eleven o'clock, Marva left the bank with a cashier's check for four hundred dollars zipped into a compartment in her purse and a hundred plus change stowed in her billfold. Her entire life savings.

When she walked into the restaurant on Broadway and asked to see the manager, the cashier said she was out, didn't know when she'd be back. Marva took the table for two she was offered. No sense going hungry. Not like she had an appointment. Stupid to expect she could waltz in and be greeted with a job offer.

She ordered the day's special and dawdled eating the tacos, feeling bad about taking a table when there were people waiting. Her server asked, "Is there anything else?"

Marva said, "Any idea when the manager will be back?"

"I don't know. I just started yesterday."

Marva left a tip under her water glass and headed toward the front. When she stopped to pay the cashier, she asked, "Could I leave a message for the manager with you?"

A nod was her answer as a customer edged in front of her to pay. Marva turned to leave; she'd come back later. The manager met her on the sidewalk out front.

The woman asked Marva if she was ready to be put on the schedule again. She seemed genuinely disappointed when Marva said she was available, but only for that week.

The manager said, "That'll help. And can you take this evening? Plus Wednesday, Thursday, and Friday evenings? It'd help us a lot."

Marva hesitated, thinking about how she'd get to the motel after closing time at ten. But she didn't delay long—evenings were best for tips. "I'll be happy to if you can pay me before I leave Friday night."

The manager agreed and said, "You're a lifesaver. A meal a day when you're here is on me."

By the next afternoon, she'd recalled why she'd seldom had female friends. She, Stacey, and the roommate had spent several hours unpacking boxes, cleaning the floors and bathrooms, and making a shopping list for household items. Because Marva had to be at the restaurant at two, Stacey called time out just before noon, and proposed they go to a pizza place a few blocks away. Minutes after they went through the buffet line and chose a table, Stacey said, "Please tell me you're going to change your mind. Stay here, even if you don't go to school this semester." The roommate munched her salad, then before Marva could answer, said, "Stacey told me a little about what you intend to do. I agree with her. It's a mistake."

Marva said, "I don't recall asking for anyone's opinion. I made up my mind before I got here."

Stacey said, "Don't get upset. It's what friends do. Keep each other from making mistakes."

Marva put her fork on the table. "If I'd asked, it would be different. But I didn't. Now, is there something you'd like me to give you two advice about?"

The roommate said, "Well, I can't think of anything."

Knowing she might regret it, Marva went right ahead and said, "I could start by saying that house is a mistake. You're paying too much for rent. The plumbing's bad; there are roaches everywhere; and the backyard's been used for a dump—you'll have to work for a solid week to even clear a path to get to the Dumpster in the alley." She took a bite of pizza, chewed a few seconds while focusing on the roommate's wide-open eyes. "I'm just trying to keep you from making a mistake."

The roommate situated her fork at an angle on her plate, and sat back. "Well," she said, "I like the house."

Stacey turned to her roommate. "You don't get that she's being sarcastic. Okay, Marva. Sorry I mentioned it."

They ate pizza in silence. Marva didn't regret her sarcasm. What she did regret was confiding in the first place. They were nearly finished when she said, "I'm out of practice. All summer, I was around guys only. I forgot how to talk to other girls. I didn't mean what I said about your house. Once you get those curtains up, it'll be great."

Stacey said to the roommate, "See, I told you she's different.

Keeps me on my toes."

Marva felt about an inch tall.

Later that afternoon, Stacey offered Marva a ride to her job, and when she let Marva out at the restaurant, she handed Marva the address of the rental house and her phone number written on a piece of blue paper. "I know you don't have an address yet, but when you do, please let me know. Don't forget I'm your friend. And please take care of yourself."

"I will. And thanks for the ride." She thought about apologizing again, but nothing seemed quite right. So, she said, "I'll stay in touch."

When Saturday arrived, Marva gave herself the day off. She ate breakfast and lunch at the café next door and spent the rest of the day using the laundry facilities of the motel, resting and watching television. She'd done all she came to do—got a year's supply of birth control pills, emptied her bank account, and worked enough to add close to three hundred dollars to the stash in her purse. She wasn't leaving anything behind in Lubbock.

Cutter turned up right on time. He said all he wanted was a burger, french fries, a beer, and about ten hours of sleep. Sunday morning, they headed west again as the sun rose behind them. Marva soon dozed, her head against the side window. Around Muleshoe, Marva roused and saw Cutter turn off the radio. He said, "If I had one more cup of coffee, I think I'd be decent company." After stopping in Clovis for take-out breakfast and a large coffee, Cutter said, "I missed you a lot while I was gone."

"Not tired of my company?"

"Not a bit. Did you get your errands done?"

She nodded. "I saw Stacey. She wanted me to move in with her and another girl. They've rented a house."

"Stacey probably told you I'm no good. She never did like me much. Not since a cousin of hers thought I was going to marry her."

"What made the cousin think that?"

Cutter looked her direction and raised an eyebrow. "Probably something I said." He shook his head. "It was high school. Guys that age'll say anything. You know—I'm sure guys you grew up with were the same. One thing on their mind."

"No, I don't know, I never dated."

"Never?"

"You're the first."

He gave her look that said he didn't believe her. She shrugged.

Past Fort Sumner, after miles of silence, Cutter said, "Here's how it went at home." She turned sideways in her seat, paying attention to his profile and his hunched shoulders. "They won't have to take bankruptcy, but over the next year or so, they'll sell the place and move to San Antonio. Years ago, Dad trained as a land appraiser, has promise of a job with a company there as soon as the Uvalde place sells. Mom can teach school again for a few years if they need more money." He glanced her way and shrugged. "They were worried I'd be upset. Tell the truth, I'm relieved. It'd take three years of good rains to make that place fit to graze anything more than a few stockers. And no one around there can remember ever having three good years in a row. So, I'm happy for them to do something easier than ranch."

Marva nodded and waited for more. After a couple more miles he said, "Mainly it'll be good for my dad. I remember when I was a little kid, Dad would get this look, like he hated everything and everybody. He never beat me, and I never saw anything to make me think he ever hit Mom. Mostly he'd go from gloomy to surly to belligerent. All words, hateful, paranoid. Then he'd leave. Just leave. Gone for days, weeks sometimes. He'd come back and things would be fine. It was like a different guy moved in and made everything dark and grim, and then left. Later, he'd come back and be normal again, my real dad would come home." After a long pause, he said, "Happened several times."

"Did you ever think he wasn't coming back?"

"Usually, I wished he wouldn't. I found out when I was older he'd been depressed and would go on drinking binges. As far as I know, that never happened after I was in high school. But you know, kids never know half of what's going on with their parents. And at the time, probably don't even care. I doubt I know all of it even now."

Marva sighed. Hers wasn't the only screwed-up family.

"Must have been hard on your mom."

"It aged her pretty fast."

She watched his face as he talked. She saw no hint of the lingering worry that he'd kept poorly hidden all the time she'd known him.

He said, "They want to meet you."

She said, "No rush. We can get to that when it's convenient." She showed him her best smile.

They pulled into the ranch outside Cimarron mid-afternoon. The small house was vacant, waiting for them. The owner and his wife were packing their pickup to get back to Texas. After Cutter talked to the owner, he came back carrying a big ring of keys. He said, "They'll be back next week when the first hunters come. After then, they'll be around once a month, maybe. Other than that, we're on our own. Treat it like it was ours, he said."

They unloaded the few things they'd brought along, and then together they made the bed with sheets from a cabinet in the bathroom. Finding that everything was clean—sheets, towels, pots and pans—and that the pantry and cabinets held plenty of staple items left Marva wondering what to do next. There were even eggs in the refrigerator. Her gaze lit on the telephone hanging on the kitchen wall. She hadn't called her mother when she was in Lubbock. Maybe she'd call Aunt Violet instead. Maybe later. She joined Cutter at the front door. They stood looking out the screen door as the owner pulled his pickup away from the main house, headed toward the road. Cutter waved and the man honked. "Well," he said, "here we are. In charge."

He told her he wanted to get a better look at the place, and take his time doing it. So, they loaded into the pickup. About the same time, the dog appeared from somewhere back of the house and jumped into the bed of the pickup. Cutter said, "If he's any good with cattle, he can be a big help. What do you want to call him?"

"Bullet."

"That was fast."

She said, "My dad had a dog when I was little. That's what he called him. Said it was Roy Rogers' dog's name."

"Okay then. Cowdogs are smart. He'll learn to be Bullet. If you're the one who feeds him, he'll protect you when I'm not around."

For the rest of their ride, neither of them said anything. The dog stood in the truck bed near the cab window, balanced perfectly on turns and over bumps, looking from one side of the road to the other as if he owned the place. Marva was happy to keep quiet while Cutter focused on the cattle they came across in the big pasture. Then, when they stopped at the barn, he walked slowly from one end to the other, pausing occasionally to look at tools hanging on the walls, the two horse stalls at the back, and a stack of bales of horse hay. Then, apparently still taking inventory and getting a sense of the whole place, he spent several minutes making a full circuit around the outside, stopping to check the water trough with its float bobbing gently on the top. She had questions, but she'd ask them later.

Two of the horses, both mares, ambled toward them from the corral. They ignored the dog and stood still as Cutter spoke to them, then rubbed his hands down their necks and shoulders. He beckoned Marva over and she held out a hand to each of the horses. They allowed her to touch them, and then soon they returned to the open corral. She visored her hand above her eyes and gazed toward the west. The sun edged down over the distant mountains and the few clouds scattered in the Technicolor blue sky echoed the late rays' coral, then gold, then faded as behind them on the east, the twilight rose. Marva's shoulders relaxed, surprising her as tension she hadn't been aware of melted.

When they got back to the house, the dog followed them inside, as if he'd been invited. Cutter sat in one of the two, big, worn leather armchairs in the front room, his feet propped on a hassock. She took the matching chair angled toward his. She said, "We haven't talked about cooking."

Cutter's answer was a puzzled glance. Finally, he said, "What about it?"

"You might have assumed I can cook. But I've never done much of it. And contrary to what some people believe, females aren't born knowing how. Can you make meals?"

"Haven't had a lot of practice. But I can grill burgers and steaks." He lifted his feet off the stool and leaned toward her. "What are you trying to tell me?"

"I'm not great at it and don't really want to be. I'm not saying you should do all the cooking. But I don't want to get stuck in here making every meal, being the one expected to figure out what we'll have every evening, all that. That's one reason I never learned. I can work outside. Just explain the job and show me how, whatever it is."

Cutter leaned back and smiled. "Maybe I should have asked earlier. But it never occurred to me that we might starve."

"No surprise," Marva said. She'd spent some of the time on their way there thinking about how to explain to him that he shouldn't assume she was there to be the domestic worker. "There'll be things on the ranch you'll do lots better than I ever could. But just so you know about the cooking." She watched his face, waiting to see if she'd started something that would end up with them sounding like her parents. Then she added, "And we'll need to talk about laundry before long, too."

He said, "There'll be plenty of times I'll need you with me taking care of things outside. We'll figure the rest out." He scooted to one side in the big chair. "Come on over here and sit with me. I like having you close. And I like hamburgers. Could live on them."

She snuggled into the chair with him and leaned against his chest. The last thing she saw before she fell asleep was the dog lying on the rug beside the chair.

CHAPTER 8

October-December 1982
Rough Patch

They became a team, the three of them. The days and then weeks passed. When they ran out of sandwich meat and steaks, and there were no Fritos in the cabinet, they made a trip to Las Vegas to the large grocery store. They bought ground beef and steaks and four chickens pre-cut for grilling to fill the freezer. She bought a cookbook and wished aloud that lettuce lasted longer. Cutter loaded a case of beer and a bottle of champagne on the bottom of the cart. He said, "For special occasions." She made certain they split the bill.

Over the next couple of months, they had settled into a rhythm—up before the sun, days outdoors working together; him teaching her how to mend fence, to shoot the twenty-two he kept in the pickup and the shotgun he'd moved into the coat closet in the house, checking the cattle once or twice a day, cleaning up after each group of hunters left, sharing most chores. She took over the laundry—she was better and faster at it. He agreed and he handled dealing with the hunters when they arrived and left. "No sense your having to put up with any b.s. from those Dallas types," he'd said.

Near the end of October, three of the guys he'd rodeoed with, one of them a high school friend, surprised them one Saturday afternoon. The phone seldom rang, so when Cutter answered it and said, "Sure, come on out," and then gave directions from Springer to the ranch, she knew someone was on the way, thought it might be his parents. After he hung up, Cutter told her who it was. "They hunted me down, got in touch with Mom for the phone number. They'll be here in an hour or so.

The cowboys piled out of the loud mufflered, long bed, red pickup, took off their hats when they said hi to her, then pulled a cooler out of the pickup bed. One of them said to Cutter, "Where should we set up the bar?" Then he gouged Cutter with an elbow and lowered his voice, but not enough to keep Marva from hearing. He said, "Gulley, you always could get the lookers. She's prime. Blond, green-eyed, made for Levi's."

Cutter cut a glance her way, rolled his eyes, then said to the two holding the cooler, "How about the barn?" He stepped off the porch to follow his friends, who'd apparently started their party before they arrived.

Bullet stood alert next to Marva near the screen door. She said, "I'll thaw some chili. If y'all get hungry, it'll be on the stove. Just warm it up. I'll put out our sleeping bags and some quilts out in case they want to camp in the living room tonight. From the looks of them I doubt they'll be fit to drive."

He nodded and hurried to catch up with the crew. Watching the four of them jostling one another, laughing, talking loud, she remembered Chance and his football friends. They'd close ranks that same way. Leaving her standing there with the dog wasn't intended to be unkind. When young males got together, they were simply unable to pay attention to anyone other than their own kind. She didn't like it. But she understood. She patted her leg, and Bullet followed her inside, sticking with her as she moved from room to room.

She ate a bowl of chili, went to bed to read a magazine, then fell asleep with Bullet on the rug on her side of the bed. She woke sometime after midnight. Cutter wasn't in the house anywhere. The pickup with the Texas license plates was gone. She locked the doors and went back to bed. He'd come back or he wouldn't. The next time she woke was around four in the morning—still dark—when Bullet growled low and stood up from the rug. The sound that woke them was a pickup motor and voices. Then a door slammed. The pickup revved and then its sound moved away. She said to the dog, "It's okay. Stay with me. Let him figure out where his front door key is."

When she got out of bed around seven, she found Cutter sprawled on top of the pile of sleeping bags and quilts, snoring, a red-turning-purple bruise on his right cheek. She and Bullet were at the barn checking the horses' water a couple of hours later when she heard the screen slam at the house. He drove the pickup to the barn where he stopped long enough to roll down the window and say, "I'm going to check cattle."

She said, "Hangover?" No answer. He probably deserved the headache, so she finished with the horses and went in the house to get supplies to clean the hunting cabin. She made sandwiches for two, wrapped his and put it in the refrigerator and ate hers. If he wasn't back soon, she'd walk to the cabin. Let him keep his bad humor to himself.

Seven days later, she'd counted, the bruise on his cheek had faded and the scraped knuckles on his left hand, which she hadn't noticed at first, had healed. Another group of hunters had come and had left that day. But in all that time, the only words he'd spoken were the few he had to when they worked together, which was seldom because they each mostly did chores that required only one person. She'd finished cleaning the hunters' cabin and sat in their little house watching the night bleed in through the open blinds. And that's when she decided. If he didn't say anything that night, she would leave the next morning, make him take her to Cimarron, catch a bus or a passing truck, she didn't care which.

As soon as he walked in, went in the bathroom, then appeared again headed toward the kitchen, she said, "Sit down."

He didn't answer, but he sat in the chair he usually occupied. She said, "I don't know what's going on with you, but I thought we were partners. You don't owe me anything. But I don't have to stay here and tolerate this silence. Either tell me what's wrong or I'm leaving in the morning."

His face like granite, etched with lines that made him look years older, showed her a future she didn't want to imagine. Finally, he said, "I don't know. But I know I don't want you to leave."

"Then talk to me. Talk about things that don't matter, about the weather, about the cattle, anything. Just don't do this."

He sighed. "I'm afraid to. The only things that come to me are hateful. I don't want to sound like my dad."

Bullet trotted in from the bedroom and stood near her right hand which was resting on the chair arm. She patted him and said, "I don't want to be my mother. So, we're even. But if I stay here like this, I know that'll happen."

He leaned forward, his elbows on his knees, head in his hands. He looked toward her and she saw a flash of the person she thought she knew. He said, "Please give me a few more days. I'm trying."

She sat silent for what seemed to her like a long time. Neither of them moved. Then she said, "I'm hungry. It'll be Frito pie tonight."

He nodded.

As she stood, she said, "One more week. Things get better or I'm gone. No harm, no foul, like we said." Walking toward the kitchen, without looking back, she said, "I'd hate leaving the dog."

For the first week it was daily; after that, frequently in the past six weeks, Marva had wondered if she made a mistake by staying. The doubts weren't because of anything that had happened since she'd threatened to leave. Instead, she wondered if her staying would make it harder to leave the next time Cutter's dark, almost mute, secretive other side turned up, if it did. Would she actually pack up and go, or would she become one of those women, the ones who stayed and ended up sad, or just old and grim, or dead? But the time she spent doubting, talking to herself when he was out working, and thinking without speaking when he was near decreased daily. He was the person she wanted to be with now, the one who understood her and who called her his partner, the one whose body fit next to her at night. He became more of that person each day.

They worked together cleaning the hunters' cabin after the final group left that morning. Marva said, "Since tomorrow's Christmas Eve, the store may be closed in Cimarron. So, I'm going in for a few groceries this afternoon. Do you want to go with me?"

He looked out the door, stepped out, looked at the sky. "I heard on the radio there's a snowstorm headed this way. I'd better check all the cattle before we move them back to the middle pasture, and I need to check on the hay. I can do it by myself. You go ahead. Bring me a surprise from the store."

Marva remembered saying those words to her dad every time he left for town—bring me a surprise. Usually, he brought back something small like bubble gum or a little bag of peanuts. They were prizes as far as she was concerned. "I will. And I'll tell you something now that'll surprise you. I'm going to make a real Christmas dinner."

They'd agreed there wouldn't be any gifts—both saving money—but a turkey and cranberry sauce could make the day seem festive. And for the first time ever, she intended to bake a pie. From the cookbook she'd bought, she'd already chosen pumpkin, best because it had only required one crust and very few ingredients.

Cutter said, "I love a holiday dinner." The smile he wore convinced her to put her doubts away.

After her trip to town, Marva unloaded the groceries as the radio played Christmas carols. Then she emptied a bag she'd gotten at a store that sold tourist souvenirs and, in the back, stocked locals' favorite craft materials. She hummed along to "The First Noel" as she searched for the right spot to hang the surprise she'd gotten Cutter. Without a fireplace and mantel, there was no traditional spot to use. The bar that separated the kitchen and living room would have to do. She laid out his sock, the red one; hers, a green one, and Bullet's, camouflage, side by side. Ten minutes later, she'd finished gluing on letters that spelled their names. She'd hang the stockings from the bar edge with thumbtacks and tomorrow night before bed she'd fill them with candy, gum, dog treats and other things she left in the bag. Plus, for Cutter's, there was a can of sardines she'd put in the toe.

She'd know next Christmas whether he got the gag. Her brother had started it, their weird little tradition. When she was seven, he put a can of sardines in her stocking. She hid it in his the next year. Back and forth each year, some years the ante was upped—two cans. Why was it funny? Maybe because it was nonsense that only the two of them understood as a reason to laugh. Something that was theirs without their parents' understanding. There was no reason Cutter would get it. But still . . .

From another bag came an artificial Christmas tree, no more than seven inches tall on its own tiny plastic stand, sporting spindly green branches decorated with colored plastic beads and a foil star on top. Marva placed it on the small table between their two chairs.

She thought for a second about calling Stacey like friends might do at holiday time. That paper with Stacey's number and address was still in her purse. But she'd be home with family, not in Lubbock. Marva looked at the phone, took a long breath, then shrugged and folded one of the paper bags she'd emptied. Then with no warning, sadness washed over her, an ambush she had no reason to expect. She went to the bedroom, lay down, covered herself with the spread. Without making a sound she lay there and cried silent tears, the kind people hide from others because there's no external wound to account for them, no insult or slight, no lost love, nothing except life. Sometimes it can be too much.

A knock at the door alerted Bullet. He jumped off the bed where he'd been lying beside Marva and ran barking, toward the front door. Cutter wouldn't knock. She hushed Bullet and said, "Who's there?"

"Mail," a woman's voice said.

Marva wiped at her eyes, then opened the door. She said, "Sorry, I was napping, didn't hear you drive up." Mail delivery was at a box outside the ranch gate. This was the first time she'd seen who brought it. "It's cold out. Would you like to come in for a cup of coffee?"

The woman said, "Can't stop, although I'd like to. This requires a signature." She held the box toward Marva. It was addressed to Cutter. She said, "Can I sign for him? He's out with the cattle."

"Sure. Right here," She peered over her bifocals at Marva and pointed to the line on the paper she held.

As Marva signed, she said, "I'm glad to see a woman on this route. It was always a cranky old man where I grew up."

"I'm the only one around here. But the Postal Service is recruiting more women, I hear." She backed away after handing Marva the box. "I'm Carol McQueen." She squinted toward the paperwork at the name Marva signed. "Marva?"

"Right. Marva Cope. Glad to know you. And Merry Christmas, Carol."

Cutter looked at the box when he came in, then put it aside, saying, "Clothes, I imagine. My mother." After supper he opened it.

He was right. Two pair of Wranglers and two sets of thermal underwear plus an insulated barn jacket.

He handed Marva a package from the bottom of the box. The tag had her name on it from "The Gulleys." Marva opened it, not sure why her chest felt tight. The holiday wrapping covered two sets of insulated long underwear, female version. They were her size. She discarded the boxes, keeping the address. A handwritten thank-you note would be the right thing to do, even though they'd never met.

Christmas day she and Cutter woke to find three or more inches of snow on the ground, with a steady fall continuing, beginning to pile small drifts on the lee side of fence posts. Her first impulse was to run outside into it, fling herself down and make a snow angel. Cutter said, "We have work to do. Better eat and get dressed."

When they went toward the kitchen, he stopped at the sight of the stockings lined up on the counter. She'd laid them out when she filled them after he went to bed. "I guess there's a Santa Claus after all." He grabbed her and hugged her, and Bullet jumped and bounced off her back. "Thanks for making it seem like Christmas."

He made toast as she scrambled eggs. She said, "I'll put the turkey in after twelve and we'll eat late in the afternoon. Gives us time to get the work done."

He nodded, then said, "Can I see what's in my stocking?"

"Sure."

"Wait a minute," he said, as he walked back toward the bedroom. When he returned seconds later, he said, "Close your eyes." A few more seconds later, he said, "Okay. Open them."

A lump in her stocking told her he hadn't forgotten. How could he with the socks hanging there? Some people would have. Without another word, Bullet watching intently, they poured out some of the contents of their socks. She took care of the dog first. "Oh look, treats for a good boy!" When she opened the package and held up a bone-shaped dog biscuit, Bullet sat. Drool trickled from his mouth. She gave him the treat, and he carried it to the rug he preferred, then bit it daintily into two pieces.

"Someone trained that dog," Cutter said. "I'm glad he stayed here." As he talked, he sorted the M & M, Snickers, and PayDay candies into one pile and the two cans of Copenhagen snuff into another. "All my essential items. Please tell Santa thanks." Then he pulled out the sardine can from the toe of the sock. A big smile turned into a laugh. He said, "You wait. Just wait till next year." He hugged her again. "Thank you for staying and making it Christmas."

Her stocking held two peppermint candy canes and a small white box. In the box was a delicate, silver heart dangling from a slender, silver chain. She put the necklace on and said, "I love this. Thank you for the surprise." Then she kissed him, hugged him tight, then kissed him again. Bullet sat waiting for another treat.

Decked out with her new thermals under her jeans, wearing every warm thing she could pile on and still be able to walk, she rode with Cutter to the barn. He let her out there to break ice on the water trough and put out feed for the horses while he went to check the hunter cabin for any leaks or other problems. Soon he was back and she and Bullet sat in the front seat with him as they rode to the pasture. As soon as they opened the gate to the middle pasture, Cutter let the dog out and said to him, "Bring 'em up." As if he'd been waiting to work, Bullet streaked across the pasture and got behind the cattle farthest out. With the dog at their heels, the cattle ambled through the gate, heading toward the earthen tank. It hadn't frozen, so there would be water for them. They each counted the cows as they passed by; their counts agreed, forty-four, each pregnant. The two bulls had been moved back to their pasture after they'd done their jobs.

Back at the house while Cutter checked to see that the bulls' water wasn't completely frozen, Marva touched her new necklace, then moved it under her thermal T-shirt, next to her skin. Soon she had the nine-pound turkey seasoned and ready to slide into the oven. "Here Comes Santa Claus" poured from the radio. She positioned the turkey mid-oven, checked the temperature a second time, and shut the oven door, then closed her eyes briefly and crossed her fingers, hoping her first turkey would taste like her mother's did.

She shouldn't have been surprised that thinking about how the turkey would taste would lead to a "you should call your mother" twinge, which ended with her staring at the phone imagining another conversation like the last one. She stood still, biting the inside of her lower lip, telling herself calling would be the right thing to do, when the phone rang. The ranch owner's voice sounded far away and weary as he said, "Just to let you know, we aren't going to make it there for New Year's. Too many in the family with other plans." Then he paused. She wondered if he'd been interrupted. Then he said, "Is everything all right there?"

She told him about the weather, the cattle all being in good shape, hunter's gone, cabin secure. He didn't ask any question. She said, "Do you want Cutter to call when he gets back from the bull pasture?"

"No, that's okay. I sure wish we could be there." He trailed off, like a stray thought had his attention. "Wouldn't seem right to come alone."

She was sure then it was sadness she heard in his voice. And she heard a sigh just before he said, "Have Cutter call if something important happens. Otherwise, y'all are in charge. Thanks for all you do."

When Cutter came in an hour or so later, shook the snow off his jacket and set his boots on the paper bag she'd put down for them to dry on, she told him about the call. He said, "Last time I talked to him he mentioned some problems at his company in Dallas. I wonder if he's going to have to sell this place."

They both went silent for a while until Cutter said, "That smells good. When will the bird be ready?"

Marva said, "An hour and a half . . . or that vicinity." Saying that aloud sent her directly to the kitchen. The pie! As she rolled out the crust, she realized the mistake she'd made—the turkey cooked at a different temperature than the pie would. Besides that, there wasn't room for both in the oven. Still not sure if they'd have to eat Snickers or candy canes for dessert by the time she had the pie oven-ready, she looked toward Cutter's chair where he'd nodded off and to the rug beside him where Bullet slept with his head on his paws. She rushed to prepare the green beans, dressing, and sweet potatoes, working quietly. Her daddy would have called that letting sleeping dogs lie.

Later she wished she'd thought about her daddy longer before she let herself dial Carly's number. Not sure what she wanted to say, she almost hung up when her sister answered. After Carly said hello, before Marva said a word, she heard a child crying. She said, "Carly, I'm sorry if I called at a bad time. Do you need to tend to that baby?"

"No, Mother's got him. He's just cranky. A lot."

"I called to say Merry Christmas. So . . .well, I hope your family has a good holiday."

The next sound Marva heard was Carly whispering and their mother saying in a loud voice, "No. I will not talk to her."

Then her sister was back on, with no mention of their mother. Carly said, "Thanks for calling. I'd been wondering if you were okay. Thought you'd get it touch if you weren't. Where are you?"

After explaining about the job on the ranch, mentioning Cimarron, in case Carly might know where that was, she started telling about how pretty the snow was. But Carly said, "Just a minute." Then muffled words and a voice she was certain was her mother's stiffened Marva's spine and stopped her breath for a few seconds. Doing the right thing shouldn't be so hard.

Carly said, "I'm in the kitchen now. I told Mother to hold the baby, who doesn't need holding, to keep you from having to listen to her. For heaven's sake, it's Christmas. Why can't she just be nice for once? Give me your number, and I'll call you back another time."

"I'm sorry."

"It's between you and her, but I don't want to hear it."

"I understand. Neither do I."

A three-breath silence made her think Carly might have hung up, but then her sister's voice, weaker and sad, was back. "It's hard. Just me and her and the kids. I threw Jimmy out six months ago."

"Oh, Carly, I'm sorry. Is there anything I can do?"

"No, I'll manage. At least he's not here chasing young girls, drinking up his paycheck and mine. She takes care of the kids, cleans the house. I just get really tired sometimes."

Marva gave her the phone number and the mailing address. And then they both ran out of things to say until Marva said, "I have to check on my turkey. Try to have a good Christmas. And tell Mother the same." She heard Carly breathing, so instead of hanging up, Marva said, "I love you, Carly." She didn't wait any longer after that. She hung up.

Cutter and Bullet slept on, so when the turkey was done, she put the pie in to cook. She set the timer again and sat staring at their tiny plastic Christmas tree while "Oh, Holy Night" played in the background. She touched the tiny, silver heart, a warm spot against her skin under her thermal shirt, and thought about choices and consequences until the timer's beeping intruded, prompting Bullet to run to her side.

"What would you be doing if you were home?" She asked Cutter that a couple of days later while they were out checking cattle.

Looking toward the cattle, he said, "Hanging around the house, wishing I was somewhere else, counting the days until it was time for school to start again, telling Mom and Dad how nice Christmas was, thanking them for whatever they gave me." He slowed the pickup and turned to face her. "Being an only child has its down side. Feeling responsible for making them happy. I'm grown, but a part of me feels like I ought to be there with them, like I'm a big disappointment. Mom in particular." He took a deep breath and pointed toward Bullet frolicking in the snow feinting at one of the feistier cows. "He's got nothing to worry about."

She scooted across the old pickup's bench seat and snuggled close to him.

That evening, as they ate hot turkey sandwiches and mashed potatoes, he said, "I'll be sorry to see that last piece of pie go."

"I saved it for you."

"How about I reward you for that? Take you out for New Year's Eve. If it's not snowing a blizzard. They have a party at the St. James Hotel, I hear."

She wondered where he'd heard that. Party meant drinking. She managed a smile and said, "That could be fun. Sure."

CHAPTER 9

January 1, 1983-September, 1983
Unintended Consequences

As the minutes ticked toward 1983 in the bar at the St. James, Marva watched, a stiff smile she could feel etched on her face, as all five of the guys who had wives or girlfriends along switched from beer to tequila shots. She'd stuck with the one margarita she'd ordered when they arrived. Cutter nursed a third beer (she counted) and danced with her to the jukebox music until tequila-fueled loud talking turned to arguing. A girl had smiled at, and then danced with, someone who wasn't her date. Cutter said to Marva, "All hell's about to break loose if the bartender doesn't do something. Ten to midnight's close enough for us grown-ups." He pulled her into a long kiss, then said, "Happy New Year!"

As they opened the door to leave, Marva heard a girl scream, glass breaking. In the pickup, she said, "Good choice. Happy New Year to you, too!"

As they turned off the pavement onto the dirt road to the ranch, she allowed the smile she'd strained to maintain slip away. Her face relaxed and her neck and shoulders went loose, and something genuine softened her, rising from the inside, warming her all over. The pitch-black sky, uninterrupted by any artificial light, illuminated only by a sliver of a moon and about a million stars, left her searching for words to describe the peace and calm that made her wish for the right things to say.

Cutter slowed the pickup as they neared the bull pasture. Then he stopped. "I have a surprise." He reached behind the seat and lifted a paper bag which he placed between them on the seat. "Remember when I bought that bottle of champagne for a special occasion?" He pulled the bottle from the bag along with two plastic glasses, stemmed and shaped like crystal champagne glasses.

"Fancy," she said. "Yessir, life with you is just one surprise after another." She held her glass, waiting while he cut the foil on the bottle with his pocket knife, and popped out the cork. After he half-filled each glass, she said, "I have a toast. To a good year. And many more good times!"

"I agree," he said. "I think we have the combination. Hard work, good food, no expectations." He refilled their glasses. "You warm enough?"

She said, "I am. Let's get out. See all the stars." Seconds later, side by side, they both leaned back against the truck's hood and stared up into the sky, a vision of vastness made vivid by the frigid night air. As the motor at their backs ticked, cooling off, she said, "Do you make resolutions?"

He raised the half-full champagne bottle. "Why yes, I resolve to finish off this bottle if you don't help."

"I'm serious. Real resolutions. Do you make them? Do you ever keep them?"

He shook his head, no, then said, "But I will if you want me to. What do you suggest?" He filled both their glasses, raising his in a silent toast, she didn't know to what.

"You could eat more fresh fruit. Or use less Copenhagen."

"Yes, I certainly could. I choose fruit. Starting tomorrow. A resolution for the year. Thanks for your help."

"Anytime."

His lopsided grin didn't mock her, simply said he enjoyed this harmless foolishness. He reached an arm around her, pulled her close. She said, "I can't recall ever making a resolution. What do you suggest?"

"Nope, trick question."

"I won't get mad. Promise." She held out her glass. He filled her glass and emptied the rest into his, then held the bottle upside down, and shrugged.

He blew across the top of the bottle creating a foghorn blast. "Okay, okay. Let's see. Well, you could be a little friendlier."

"Really?" She scooted away from his hug. "Get in the truck."

He roused himself slowly off the hood. "I knew you'd get mad."

"I'm not mad. No way. But you take me to the house right this minute. I'm about to show you just how friendly I can be." She made it to the passenger side door before he could catch her. When he did, she whirled around into his arms and kissed him with all the desire that had been buried by anger and then turned to dismay. He didn't back away. She said, "Friendly enough?"

"Maybe you need to show me again. Soon as we get to the house." She's never heard him giggle before. But he did then.

Sometime in the night, Bullet woke her, wanting to go out. Marva smiled as she stood, naked except for house shoes, at the front door waiting for the dog to come back in. She expected a headache in the morning, doubted she'd be the only one. The memory of that night would be worth it.

Spring arrived early. Marva had expected that the altitude would make the new season wait until mid-March at the earliest. But she was wrong. The last snow fell early in February and by the last week of that month, tiny shoots of green started showing at the bases of the clump grass. A seed catalog, addressed to Occupant, arrived in the mail, delivered one day by Carol McQueen. When she knocked at the door, the mail carrier said, "I had a few extra minutes, so I thought I'd hand deliver this."

Marva ushered her in and poured coffee for them both. As she handed over the catalog, Carol said, "These always make me want to plant a garden."

"My mother did that. I wouldn't be sure where to start."

"First step, find a spot that'll be sunny, and soon as the ground's warm, start digging." She pointed to the catalog. "You'll have time to figure out what you want to plant before it's warm enough for that." They chatted a couple more minutes during which Marva learned that Carol lived in Cimarron, widowed young and living alone now that her two children were off in college. As she stood and headed toward the door, Carol said, "When I saw you before, I was concerned you looked a little peaked, kind of sad. But I must have been wrong. Now you're almost rosy."

She'd never been called rosy before; the idea made her smile. As she walked with Carol to her pickup Marva said, "I'll consider that a compliment. I hope you'll stop again when you have time."

A few days later, while she was out back of the house, considering where she'd start digging when the time came, the pickup brakes squealed as Cutter skidded to a stop out front. He yelled her name and as Bullet came running toward her, Cutter yelled again, closer this time. She hurried toward his voice. "One of the cows is in labor, having trouble. I've got her in the pen, been watching her all morning. It's her first. She's young, doesn't know what's happening. I'm going to have to help her. Need you, too. Get your gloves and some dish soap and a couple of gallon jugs of water."

She ran into the house and he followed. While she searched for gloves, she heard him calling the vet. A short while later, in the pickup, he said, "The vet can't make it. He's in Raton."

Marva said, "What'll happen if you don't help?"

"They could both die."

Cutter said he'd turned a calf before, but it didn't always work. He skidded the pickup to a stop, bailed out, and ran to the calf. Marva followed with the jugs and soap. Bullet kept the other cows from clustering up too close while Cutter dropped to his knees, slopped soap and water under the cow's tail and then pulled on a long rubber glove. Then he pushed his hand and arm into the cow nearly to his elbow. The cow moaned with the labor pains, lying on her side, rolling her eyes. "Calf's head's not in position. I'm going to have to turn it."

Between the animal's contractions, Marva held tight to the its front legs and talked to her as Cutter pushed with one hand and worked inside with the other, gloved one. A gush of bloody fluid poured out with the next contraction. Marva closed her eyes and took several deep breaths. The cow moaned another pitiful complaint. Cutter said, "Here come the feet." He pulled out his hand and moved back, still on his knees behind the cow. "Keep hold of her. If it comes out like I hope it will, she might try to get up pretty quick."

With the next contraction, the calf's front feet and lower legs, along with its head, emerged. Marva watched from where she knelt, repelled by the blood and amazed at the process of birth.

Afraid she'd vomit, she inhaled through her nose and willed her arms to stop shaking.

With the next contraction, the calf slid out onto the hay Cutter had spread in the pen. He moved the calf, rubbing its chest, saying, "Breathe, breathe" as he wiped mucous from its nose and mouth. Then, as if awakening from a long sleep, the calf thrashed its head and moved it legs. At the sound, the cow wrenched her head from Marva's grasp. Cutter said, "You can let her go. Get back by the fence out of her way."

Standing beside her, watching the cow and calf, he stripped off the glove. Looking down as his bloody pants, he said, "I'll have to keep an eye on them for a few hours. See if the afterbirth comes out okay, and if she lets him nurse."

"What if she doesn't?"

"We'll have to bottle feed him. There are calf bottles in the barn and some colostrum powder. Same as the mother's early milk."

"You did a good job. I'm impressed." She stuffed her hands in to her pockets, head down. That word didn't exactly fit— what she felt went beyond the respect that implied. She couldn't remember feeling the way she did right then. It was some combination of pride in his ability and of being attached to him, a good person determined to save the animals' lives. And she admitted to herself that she was grateful he trusted her to work beside him, his partner in something important. If they ever reached the point of talking about love, if she had any real notion how it felt, maybe that moment out there in the pasture could be an example.

He shrugged. "Stuff you learn growing up on a ranch. Anyone could do it."

She shook her head. "Not just anyone. You're good at this." She caught a glimpse of his smile even though he had his head down, watching the cow and calf. She touched his shoulder as she walked into the barn to pick up the bottles.

When she dropped the bottles in the pickup bed, she said, "I'll walk back. There's a garden to stake out." A walk would give her time to get confused thoughts straightened out and put ideas about love back where they belong—in some romance novel. They'd agreed, no expectations.

Late that afternoon when Cutter came in, he brought the calf bottle and powder. He said, "We're going to have to feed him, at least until his mama figures it out. I started him on the colostrum, but he didn't take much."

"How often? If you show me how, I'll do it. You have other work."

"Yeah, I do. There are three more out there ready to drop calves any time now. If you're sure, that'd help a lot. You'll have to get him to finish that first bottle and then at least two more before tomorrow. Maybe by then the mother will take him"

He mixed two more bottles of the powder and hot water as he talked, running through a list of instructions about bottle feeding—the right liquid, the right temperature (warm), clean bottle and nipple, the right amount, raise the calf's head, stretch its neck as if nursing from an udder. Then he wrapped the warm bottles in newspaper and put them in an insulated bag they'd used to keep coffee warm in the pickup in colder weather.

She listened carefully, then repeated his directions back to him as she got her sleeping bag out of the bedroom closet. Then she put a couple of soft drinks in a small cooler along with a hunk of cheese, some crackers, two Baby Ruths, and a bottle of water. As she stuffed a wad of tissues in her jacket pocket, she said, "Ready to go."

Alone with the cow and calf, she set her gear in the hay near the pen's fence and moved slowly toward the cow, which was now standing, munching hay, facing toward the pasture, ignoring or maybe unaware of the calf. Marva stroked the calf and slowly scooted it on its pile of straw closer to the mother's head. After sitting a while, watching them, waiting for she wasn't sure what, Marva took out the unfinished bottle, helped the calf stand, and pushed the nipple toward his mouth, slowly, her own breathing shallow and quiet. Then she remembered to lift his head to angle it upward. A slurping sound rewarded her. Soon, foam dribbled from the sides of the calf's mouth as he swallowed, gulping noisily. The bottle emptied about the same time the calf butted his head against her leg. "You want more? Just hold on."

Half of the next bottle disappeared as quickly as the first. When the calf pushed the nipple away, Marva sat and the calf shuffled in the hay and then lay down near her. Meanwhile the mother rolled her eyes and stood still. Marva watched, wondering if only instinct drove the cow or whether that far away gaze had meaning. And what about the calf? Did it feel something missing, its mother distant? Marva rubbed her hand along the calf's side a while, and said, "I'm not your mama." Then she dozed.

Three hours later, according to her watch, Marva woke when the cow mooed and moved to the water trough. Her udder, stretched tight, showed she needed the calf to nurse. Marva eased toward her, stroked her back, leaned down, pulled on a teat. As a thin stream of pale milk dribbled into her hand, she shrugged as if responding to some question. No, she didn't really have an idea if it would work. But she quickly expressed a little more milk into her hand, then smeared it on the calf's face as she urged him to stand. Moving him close to his mother, she repeated the milking and smearing. After a couple more cycles, when the calf's tongue sought the liquid on her hand, she pushed him close to his mother. The cow stood still, her head turned watching the calf. Marva backed away, slowly. She whispered softly, "That's your mama. Now get your breakfast."

As the sun rose the next morning, she rolled up her sleeping bag and finished off a Baby Ruth, and right after, Cutter and Bullet pulled up outside the pen. The calf wobbled to his mother and began nursing again. Cutter said, "Well, partner, looks like you're going to make a hand. We'll keep you on if you want the job."

"Unless I get a better offer, this'll do."

Late in March, she knew she had to tell him. She hated to spoil the best string of weeks she could remember. Not a calf had been lost. All the cows were fine. The pastures were greening up, and Cutter had helped her prepare the garden plot for planting.

But it was time. They sat on the porch admiring the two-leaf tomato plants she'd started from seeds in pots on the south-facing porch. They'd go in the ground before long.

Still focused on the terra-cotta pots, her pulse throbbing in her neck, she said, "I'm pregnant."

After a few silent seconds, Cutter said, "How could you be? Maybe you're just late."

"No. Not late. No period at all for the last two cycles."

How could that happen? You quit the pills." Those last words weren't a question.

She shot up from the chair. "You stay right there." She slammed the door going into the house and let it slam again as she came out. Standing directly in front of him, she held out three flat, circular plastic containers. "See these pill packets. Every single one, taken in order. December, January, February and until a week ago. Remember I told you. They're not a hundred percent. I said we always have to use condoms even with the pill."

"I always do. So, it wasn't me."

She wanted to slap the suspicious glare off his face. "It's for sure I didn't get pregnant by myself. And as you well know, there aren't any other suspects."

He stood and walked the length of the porch and back. He stopped near her, but looking into the distance, and said, "New Year's Eve. Special occasion." Then he turned toward her and said, "What do you intend to do about it?"

That's all it took. "Like it's my problem on my own?"

"I'll help pay. Where can you get it done?"

She grabbed his arm and turned him to face her. "It! Say the word. Abortion. What makes you think I'd do that?"

He stepped back and said, "A baby would ruin your life. You're too young."

"Well don't you sound wise. What about you? Are you old enough to feel okay about aborting a baby that's yours?" He didn't answer, his head hung. She barely stopped for breath. It was either that or explode. "Huh, no answer. Well, I know for a fact I don't feel okay about it."

"You haven't been sick. How can you be sure? Maybe it's some other female problem."

"Regardless, it turns out to be a female problem, doesn't it? I know I'm pregnant. I can recite the signs if you need to hear them." Every beat of her heart thrummed in her ears. She sat down on the porch chair, breathed slowly and told herself she'd said all she needed to.

His sigh could have been heard at the barn. "No need. I'm sorry. You took me by surprise. Let's both settle down. We'll figure it out." She didn't move or say anything. He said, "Shouldn't you go to a doctor?"

Aiming for a calm voice, she said, "I've already made an appointment. Two weeks from now in Las Vegas." The words came out almost as a whisper.

He nodded, scuffed something off his right boot. "Okay. Guess we'll find out details then." He nodded again, confirming something only he could hear. Then he started toward the front door. He said, "You hungry? I'll make burgers for supper."

She sat staring at the tiny tomato plants, remembering New Year's Eve, waiting for the roaring in her ears to quiet down.

The doctor in Las Vegas pronounced her a "healthy primipara" and told her the baby would arrive the second week in October, and the nurse said to make appointments for monthly visits and then weekly beginning mid-September.

She expected the weeks and months of pregnancy to seem interminable, different from ordinary time. Instead, the routine from March until August felt much the same as the year before; she helped Cutter when he needed a hand. When she wasn't helping him, the garden kept Marva busy harvesting every vegetable it offered. What they didn't eat, she froze. Neither of them uttered the words *pregnant* or *baby*. But with each week, the fact became more obvious. First, she couldn't button the top button on her Levi's. A few weeks later, she switched to wearing an old pair of his Wranglers, two sizes larger than hers. If there'd been anyone watching they might have thought the two of them were extremely calm and comfortable with the situation.

Marva had intended to make the appointments, but never bothered. Although each day brought some surprise in the way her body looked, her appetite, the changes in her shape, she'd never felt better, so why make the trip? Why take any more silent trips with Cutter if she didn't have to?

The truth was that their conversation on the porch in March had turned them both cautious and nearly silent. Since then, they only talked about their work. No joking, no planning for the next day or week. And the dog no longer ran to the pickup when Cutter left the house. He stuck with her. She wondered if Cutter even noticed.

The ranch owner came out once, alone, in mid-August, and he and Cutter spent several days getting the calves sold. When the man left, Cutter told her it looked like some of the cows would be sold before long, maybe the bulls before them. She said, "Is he going to sell the ranch?"

Cutter shrugged. "It wouldn't surprise me. But he didn't say that."

Marva kept her other questions to herself.

One morning in early September, as he was dressing, Cutter said something. His back was turned, so Marva didn't understand his words. She said, "What?"

He turned to face her as he tucked in his shirttail. "Shouldn't you be going to the doctor?"

"I feel fine and the baby moves around all the time." She'd read about hypertension and eclampsia and rH incompatibility and a ton of other things too frightening to mention. And she didn't let herself utter them or even think the words. Except now. She said, "Why?"

"You said the second week in October." Head down, he slid his belt through his belt loops. "I'm not trying to tell you what to do." He held up both hands, like a man in an old western, the guy with no gun. "Just seems like the safe thing, for all concerned."

"All concerned, meaning who?"

"You, the baby, me."

"You?" If he really meant it, he'd have said "us." Her jaw tightened and she stood. "Yeah, I probably should. I'll call today."

"Okay. I can take you any day." He headed toward the living room. Then he turned around. "We can get a license. Get married while we're there."

She sat on the bed again, her legs suddenly weak. "Who said anything about getting married?"

"I just did."

"A baby's not a reason to get married."

"I'm part of this. The baby should have my name."

"When they fill out the birth certificate and ask who the father is, all I have to do is tell the truth. Just like magic, you're officially the father."

"How do you know that?"

"I read a lot."

He stared at her while he took a deep breath. Then he shook his head and said, "Okay. Have it your way. I offered."

"Yes, you did. No. Thanks." A lot more came to mind, but arguing, getting more upset wouldn't be good for the baby or for her. So, she tried to explain calmly. "That wasn't our deal. Remember? No expectations." She followed him from the room, saw from behind when he nodded. He was walking toward the door when she said, "I'll let you know when the appointment is."

When he got into his pickup and left, Marva, followed by Bullet, went back to the bedroom. Lying on the bed on her right side, her hand on Bullet's head, she let go of the control she'd mustered. Most of the time since she read the books she got in town, she directed that will to avoiding thoughts of all the possible things that could go wrong with the baby or that one or both of them might die in childbirth. Then she'd hid the books under the bed when those possibilities pushed fear into her throat.

But now, it was getting married that frightened her. He'd brought it up, trying to do the right thing. That wasn't enough. She held tight to the notion that being married was supposed to be about love or at least about committing to spend your lives together forever. Why? That voice in her head asked again and again, why when the only marriages she'd seen up close left people miserable, constantly arguing, and hating the person they had once committed themselves to. Finally,

she said aloud, "You don't know what you want, only what you don't."
Then she called herself stubborn and got up from the bed, went to the
phone, and called for the appointment.

CHAPTER 10

September, 1983-November, 1983
Cimarron, New Mexico RFD

Eight forty-five in Las Vegas, New Mexico, on the second
Wednesday morning in September found Marva and Cutter
waiting in the pickup outside the doctor's office. Her
appointment was at nine. They left the ranch at seven. She
remembered some road trips when Cutter hadn't said much for miles.
But that day he surprised her. As he ranged from talking about the
cattle to speculating about the upcoming hunting season, she
wondered if he was skipping around avoiding some topic he'd
eventually get to. All she had to do to keep up her side of the
conversation was to ask an occasional question or comment on the
beautiful morning the way she had seconds before.

He said, "Yeah, it's going to be a pretty fall, with the rain
we've had. The baby will be born at just the right time."

"Right time for what?"

"Sort of in between, when there's not as much ranch work to
do. I'll be able to stick closer to the house for the next several weeks."

She couldn't come up with a reply right away. He actually
intended to help. She had pictured doing it all herself. For a while
before that, she'd thought maybe he was hoping just the same as she
was that it was all a dream. Because she didn't know what else to say,
she finally said, "That'll make things easier."

One thing that had pushed her to accept that the baby was
real was all the movement she felt. Last night and for the past three,
sleep had been hard to find. She'd had to change positions every few
minutes trying to get settled. She'd have sworn that baby was
dragging furniture around in there. Just at the moment she thought
"furniture," a kick told her the baby was a mind reader, knew
everything she thought and felt. So, she concentrated on any positive
idea she could summon. After that last kick, a hard one up under her
ribs on the right side, Marva focused on how nice it would be to sleep
on her stomach again, the way she always had. And she imagined
eating chili and onions and chocolate, all things that gave her

pregnant self indigestion, that she'd had to quit eating for the past four months. Then she told herself to forget that, breast fed babies "ate" what the mother did and got indigestion from lots of things. The books and magazines she'd brought out of hiding and had now almost memorized gave lots of advice about breastfeeding.

Cutter said, "Shouldn't we buy baby clothes, diapers, stuff like that? What if it came tomorrow?"

"Sometimes I wish it would." She paused a second, then said, "We have plenty of dishtowels." She tossed a smile his direction. "And safety pins."

That got a chuckle from him. He said, "After the doctor, we should go shopping."

The thought she'd been having at night during all her wakeful efforts to find a comfortable position—that it would be bad luck to buy baby clothes or a crib; that making ready for the baby might cause something bad to happen—should be kept to herself. No sense causing Cutter to worry along with her. That's what she told herself. And surely part of that was fact, but she also didn't want to hear him ridicule her fears. Which he might, because some of them sounded stupid even to her. But deep down she wondered if that elaborate "might be bad luck" excuse she gave herself was actually her subconscious telling her it was all a big joke, or maybe a test. There wasn't any baby at all. When she was young, her dad had a dog like that one time, looked and acted pregnant. Wanted to be but wasn't, her daddy had said.

There in the daylight, in the doctor's office, she nodded when he said, "This baby's good-sized already, but still floating. It'll be about October 12 best I can tell. You ought to come to town a day or two before and plan to stay. No sense having to make a mad dash in the middle of the night while you're in labor. Never works out. Make an appointment for next week."

Marva recalled something else her daddy had said, "Everything looks worse at night."

She and Cutter ended up at the discount-sells-everything-from-auto-parts-to-baby-bottles store on the south side of town. They filled a shopping cart with two dozen real (not paper) diapers;

two pair of newborn-sized pajamas, one yellow, one pale green; a small crib and sheets for its mattress; four baby blankets; two newborn size cotton knit T-shirts; plus two glass baby bottles, four ounces each, and one plastic bottle, eight-ounce size, with extra nipples. At the last minute she added a diaper bag, a baby seat to use in the house, and a Gerry carrier, thinking she'd wear the baby on her chest or back in the contraption while working.

"Won't we need more bottles than that?" Cutter said.

She didn't hesitate. "I intend to breastfeed. All the books say that's best."

He raised an eyebrow but didn't say anything.

She kept the next appointment and heard the same story, October twelfth. On September thirtieth, two days before the next appointment, Marva, full of energy, spent the morning cleaning the house. Not content to simply sweep, dust, and mop, she scrubbed every counter, laundered everything in the basket, stripped the bed, and changed the sheets. Around two o'clock, she told herself to rest, eat something for lunch. After she seated herself at the table with a ham sandwich, she said to Bullet, "Guess I'd better figure out what to pack. You'll have to be in charge here when we go to the hospital."

About halfway through her sandwich and carrot slices, she stopped chewing and caught her breath. A dull, slow-moving pain crossed her lower back, almost exactly the same sensation she'd felt a couple of weeks ago. She'd read about Braxton-Hicks contractions and decided that's probably what it was. Not real labor. There had only been three of them that other time, all dull, and she'd felt fine since.

Staring at the rest of her sandwich as a second uncomfortable band tightened across her back, Marva said, "Bullet, that means I'm not supposed to clean house ever again. I'll hate giving that up." The dog didn't laugh, but Marva chuckled and waited. After several minutes with no further discomfort, she left her plate on the table and moved to her armchair. Her feet on the hassock, she closed her eyes and let her mind drift. A nap wouldn't hurt. And the few more contractions that followed didn't hurt either. They simply stretched like a band from her back forward, lasted only seconds, and then disappeared. Then she dozed.

When she heard the front door open, she sat up straight in the chair and congratulated herself on the sparkling bar top she could see from where she sat. Cutter ambled in and said, "I think the maid's been here. Smells like furniture polish and bleach." He pulled off his boots and went to the kitchen. From there he said, "Want a beer?"

"A red draw sounds good." She'd craved the beer and tomato juice combo for months and never given in to the urge. Just one now wasn't going to hurt. She said, "I was busy. But now I'm lazy."

"Don't move. Beer on its way. And I'll make burgers for supper."

She leaned back into the chair again, then she caught Cutter looking at her. She winked and said, "I see you watching me." He'd been watching her for the last couple of weeks. Now she knew how those heifers felt last calving season. Always being observed. Annoying sometimes, but she'd admit his attention, even if it was a bit much, was better than being ignored in grim silence.

He laughed and said, "Busted. Didn't think you'd notice."

"I don't mind." She sat up straighter in her chair. "In fact, it's nice."

After they finished supper, they watched television for a little while. Marva's head dropped forward a couple of times, and soon after, she said, "I'm tired. I'll go on to bed." During the night, she made two trips to the bathroom, more than usual, but she reminded herself that as the baby moved down lower in the pelvis before labor, there was more pressure on the bladder. Only so much room in there for baby plus a red draw and a glass of milk.

The next morning Cutter was gone when she got up, but he'd left coffee on the warmer and a note: "I'm checking the cattle and working in the barn. If you need me, come get me." Pressure on her bladder sent her to the bathroom again. But when she got there, the urgent need to urinate had passed. She looked at herself in the mirror as she washed her hands, shrugged in response to her own unuttered question. Bullet stood next to her and tracked behind as she returned to the kitchen.

Midmorning, drinking her second cup of coffee, she felt a

warm, damp sensation on her thighs. In the bathroom again, examining her underwear, she shook her head. Nothing like being incontinent to remind you you're not in charge. As urine dribbled, she waited, thinking another contraction was on the way. But after a couple of minutes, no more urine, no contraction, nothing. She said, "Bullet, let's go get Cutter." At the word, go, the dog rushed to the front door. Marva took it more slowly, moving as if she were suddenly fragile. After several steps, she picked up her pace, told herself she was overreacting. Bullet returned to her side as she changed her plan and went to eat some cereal. Cutter would be in for lunch before long. No sense alarming him.

By the time she heard Cutter slam the pickup door an hour or so later, Marva had packed her bag and was lying on the bed. There had been only three contractions, the same weak ones as before, in the past two hours. Another false alarm.

He stood in the doorway. "Is anything wrong?"

She sat up and said, "No. I thought maybe I was going into labor, but it hasn't happened. I packed. But I think it was just Braxton-Hicks contractions, nothing really."

"Shouldn't we go on to Las Vegas, just in case? We can stay at a motel if it's not labor. Be there when it starts."

"Everything I've read says the first time there's a lot of this before actual labor ever starts. My appointment's tomorrow. Let's just wait and see."

He shrugged. "I'd hate to wait too long. If you were a cow, I'd be able to tell."

She hoped the smile she showed him reassured him. She said, "I'm hungry again."

"Want bacon and eggs?"

She nodded. "And toast with honey and butter."

Revived after the meal, she stood at the kitchen sink, washing their breakfast dishes, looking out the back window. She imagined their child, a boy, playing out there on a swing. She'd guess he was about four years old. Cutter stood behind the swing, pushing the seat gently, but hard enough to make the swing rise, pushing tirelessly, as if the boy was the entire focus of his life. The child's eyes widened in excitement and his giggle rose with each new height, his legs thrust straight out before him.

Cutter eased up beside her. He said, "What are you thinking?"

"Nothing, just daydreaming. Foolish stuff."

"Do you want me to stay here or go back to the barn and work? I've got about two hours more to do."

What she wanted him to do was to lie on their bed with her; hold her; make her feel safe; whisper that everything was going to be fine. She wanted him to understand why she didn't want to marry; understand why she was afraid he would leave or die. But why should he understand? She didn't.

She leaned against him, her belly resting against the cabinet, her right arm hugging him to her. She took a big breath, let it out, and said, "You go ahead. I'm okay."

Less than thirty minutes later, Cutter was back. He was barely in the door when a pain she'd never felt before doubled her forward, holding her abdomen. Before she could catch her breath as the pain ebbed slightly, a gush of liquid splatted against the living room floor. Holding onto the bar, she leaned down to examine the puddle—no blood. Speaking as calmly when she could, she said, "Cutter, come help me. Please."

Bullet beat Cutter to her side. The dog leaned against her and only moved away when Cutter turned up. Marva pointed to the wet floor and said, "Water broke."

"Are you having contractions?"

"Just one and it didn't last long. Think I'll lie down a little now."

He helped her get out of her jeans and brought her a pair of sweatpants to put on. "Just be still a bit. I'll take care of the floor."

Going to Las Vegas seemed like putting a period at the end of a sentence. That would make it all definite. If they were wrong and had to wait, they'd have to spend money on a motel, have to be in a strange place. She wanted to stay there at the ranch as long as possible. The first contraction after she lay down was lighter than any she'd had before. To her that proved nothing was going to happen right away. Tomorrow they'd go to the doctor; he'd know if they needed to stay.

An hour later, she'd marked four contractions on the paper she'd found in the bedside table. They'd alternated twenty minutes apart, then fifteen, then twenty again and the most recent fifteen more. None of them lasted more than thirty seconds. She shifted to her right side, and Bullet jumped up and landed on the bed behind her. Cutter appeared in the doorway. "Is there anything I can do?"

"No, thanks. I'm about to get up."

"I've set your bag by the door and all we planned to take with us. Extra food out on the porch for Bullet. So, we're ready to go whenever you say the word." He turned back toward the living room, then faced her again. "You will tell me, won't you?"

Before she got off the bed, another contraction followed, lasting forty-five seconds. On her way to the bathroom, sure she would wet herself on the way, another contraction followed, harder and longer than the last. In the bathroom, she held onto the wall as she sank to the toilet seat. The contractions before had affected her back, wrapping around her pelvis in a tight embrace. Before she could stand to get back to the bed, another one began. The pressure shifted. It pushed downward, as if all inside her might fall out. She screamed.

Cutter ran in and lifted her toward him. "I'll get you to the bed. As soon as that pain lets up, we're leaving." His words tumbled out as if he might choke on them. She sagged as she tried to walk. He picked her up, carried her to the bed, let her down gently.

Tears streamed down her face as the contraction slowly ebbed. Then in less than a minute, another one began. She grabbed his arm and focused on trying to pant the way the books advised. As that contraction waned, she said, "I won't make it to the hospital. It feels like the baby's already down. Pressure is aw. . ." The last word bit off in a scream. "Do something, dammit! You'll have to do it. Don't just stand there!"

She writhed from her back to her side and back again, but there was no escape, the contraction held her in a grip. Remembering to breathe, she managed a few deep ones. Then she said, "You know what to do. I'll try to help by not pushing until it's time. But . . ." Another contraction grabbed and held her. Panting took all her concentration.

Cutter disappeared, and for a few moments, she didn't care. Contractions followed one on another with little relief between. Then he was back. He said, "I'm putting these newspapers and some clean towels under you." He moved her as he talked. When the next contraction began, he said, "I need to look. See what's happening."

Marva raised her knees and spread them apart, telling herself that her job was to keep breathing. Cutter's hands pressed gently on either side of her lower abdomen. He mumbled something. She didn't ask what. The next contraction began and roared through her. As she panted, Cutter said, "I see the top of the baby's head. I boiled a string and scissors to sterilize them and I'm putting on your dishwashing gloves and soaping them up good. Back in a second. Don't leave."

She knew he meant that to lighten things up. But laughing was beyond her. He was back in seconds and said, "Okay, with the next contraction, go ahead and push." As he spoke, he lifted her head and back to squeeze a second pillow under her. "If you can, when you push, hold onto your knees. Help you get leverage."

He'd no sooner said that than another contraction began, the strongest yet. He said, "Pretend this is weightlifting. Take a big breath, let it out. Then push, push, push."

All the way from the peak of the contraction until it released, Marva did what he said. Then she fell back against the pillows, sweat beading her face. "I can't do any more." As soon as the words were out, the next contraction gripped her. Push along with it or explode, that's what came to her mind.

"You're doing great. I knew you were tough, but not how tough. I think the next contraction will do it." He raised his head to look at her and said, "This baby has a lot of dark hair. I see another contraction coming. Time for you to get it out of there, right now."

Marva focused every ounce of energy she had left and rode the contraction, pushing harder than she thought her body would tolerate. Then suddenly, relief flooded through her. For a few seconds, silence replaced all the roaring in her head and the noise of pain in her body. She opened her eyes and saw Cutter leaning close to her face. He said, "Here, hold this little girl while I take care of the cord."

He placed the baby, wrapped in one of the tiny blankets, on her chest. She hadn't heard a cry, but she could see the baby was breathing, and that all her fingers and toes were present, along with a full head of black hair. She tickled the tiny left foot, which jerked away from her touch, briskly. Then the baby, her daughter, found her voice. A strong, healthy cry prompted Marva to close her eyes, to smile as tears flowed. Then she sniffled. Everything was going to be fine. She moved the newcomer from her chest and cradled her in her right arm, snugging the blanket to swaddle the child after her introduction to the world. The baby's eyes closed, and her crying stopped.

Cutter said, "Amazing. Both of you. Just amazing." He kissed Marva's forehead, then put a kiss on his index finger and applied it to the baby in the same spot. "We'll get organized in a little while and go to Las Vegas, get both of you checked out, other details. Until then, rest a little. The placenta still has to deliver."

Marva closed her eyes, and when she opened them next, startled, she was lying on her side on a pile of blankets and pillows. Then she realized she and baby were in the crew-cab pickup's back floorboard. The baby made a soft snuffling sound, but her eyes stayed closed. Marva gently moved the baby's head toward her breast and squeezed the nipple. She couldn't help smiling when the baby responded with sucking motions. From the front seat, Cutter said, "You girls awake back there? We're nearly to Las Vegas."

She and the baby spent the night in the hospital. Routine, the doctor told her. He checked the two of them and said, "Precipitous births are uncommon with a first pregnancy. But I can't see that either of you were harmed in the process. In fact, you and the baby are both excellent. You did good work. I already congratulated your husband on doing everything right, including checking to see the placenta was whole. You've got a good man there."

By the time they were discharged the next day, they had a list of written instructions about supplemental feeding for breast fed babies, an appointment for the six-week checkup for mother and baby, and a complimentary packet containing samples of baby lotion, no tears baby shampoo, and a tube of something called "Butt Paste." The baby's birth had been recorded and all necessary facts established, including the parents' names. The only difficulty was that neither Marva nor Cutter had any idea what to name her. She admitted she'd never guessed the baby would be a girl. He said he'd always planned to leave the naming up to her. They agreed they should have talked more, about a lot of things, over the past few months. Then an hour later, after discarding the names of all relatives on both sides and after Marva had put a stink eye on Cutter for suggesting Champagne Surprise, they settled on Rose Ellen.

Six weeks later, Cutter suggested they celebrate with a nice meal in Las Vegas after the checkup, said he was in the mood for a celebration. Marva wasn't. Her mind lingered on what the doctor had told her. The baby had gained from her birth weight of six pounds up to seven pounds three ounces. Marva, however, had lost weight, nearly ten pounds since the day she was discharged from the hospital. Her blood work showed she was anemic.

The doctor had said, "Are you having any vaginal bleeding?"

She shook her head. "That stopped after about two weeks."

"Are you still taking your prenatal vitamins."

She shook her head again.

"You should take them for at least six months or as long as you continue breast feeding." While he was talking, he pulled her lower eyelids down, looked closely at something there, then picked up her hand, pressed the fingernail on her index finger. "See how pale? Definitely anemic. "How much sleep are you getting?"

"She cries at night. So, I get up to nurse her, keep her quiet." She didn't bother explaining that Bullet slept next to the crib and alerted her if the baby so much as grunted.

"Not much sleep, then."

"The books say try to nap when the baby does. But. Well, I worry about her not breathing."

"Has she had any problem breathing?"

Marva concentrated on her ragged fingernails. Then she looked up and said, "No. But what if she stops?" Hearing herself say that aloud, she said, "Sounds ridiculous, right?"

"Sounds like a first-time parent." He put a hand on her shoulder. "Do you live near anyone who's made it through a first baby? Some woman you can talk to?"

She thought about Carly. "I could call my sister, I guess." As she said it, Marva knew she wouldn't. She sat up straight. "I'll do my best to figure it all out."

The doctor nodded. "Yes, you will. Make your husband take a turn getting up at night. Give you more rest, if not sleep."

She managed a smile and said, "Thanks for your help."

They left his office with a schedule for the baby's immunizations and an appointment for Marva to return in three months. With the baby asleep in the carrier strapped to her chest, Marva would have been happy to skip eating at a restaurant. Before long Rose would wake up; she'd have to nurse her, then change her diaper. Nothing was simple and none of it lent to a celebration in the Mexican restaurant where Cutter parked.

While Cutter ate and she tried to make a dent in her enchiladas, Marva told Cutter about being anemic. All he said was, "So the vitamins will take care of that. And rest?"

"I guess." It was all she had the energy to say. She fell asleep on the way back to Cimarron. When they got back in the house, she put Rose, who had slept all the way, in her crib, still asleep. She said, "Would you watch her so I can take a nap."

"Weren't you sleeping on the way back?"

"Do you have something to do?"

He heaved a sigh and said, "Nothing in particular, just watch TV. You know, she's not going anywhere. If she wakes up, you'll get up anyway. You don't trust me to take care of her."

"You can't feed her."

"If you'd let me give her a bottle, I could."

"If she cries and I'm asleep, just wake me." She didn't wait for a response.

Lying sprawled across the bed, she dozed, half-awake drifting into images and thoughts of Rose lying still and blue in her crib because no one heard her choking; of herself alone, helpless with a dead baby in her arms; of Cutter off somewhere driving the pickup with the radio playing loud, unable to hear her screaming his name.

"What's wrong?" Marva jumped up, startled. Cutter stood next to the bed, holding the baby against his shoulder like he knew what he was doing. She mumbled, "Was I asleep?"

Cutter said, "Settle down. Nothing's wrong. I changed her diaper. But she wants you." He handed Rose to her. "I'll say this one more time. If you'd let me feed her a bottle, just at night, you could get some rest."

"I'll be fine."

He wanted to say more, she could tell. She carried the baby to the living room, sat in her chair, and nursed her again. It was the best thing for them both.

CHAPTER 11

December,1983-January, 1984
And Then

The last group of hunters left the weekend before Christmas. Marva cleaned the cabin while Cutter turned off the water and cleared the lines to prevent freezing, and then they went back to their house. He made it as far as his armchair where he slumped looking weary and grim. She said, "I'm going to town to get some things for Christmas—food, other stuff. Anything you want?"

His first response was a shake of his head. Then he finally said, "I may not be here when you get back. I have to go see a guy in Springer about a job. No sense waiting for the owner to drop it on us. I'm sure he's trying to sell."

"You know that for certain? The cattle are still here." She wouldn't really mind. Maybe the next place would be closer to a town. Maybe back in Texas. "You have a lead on a job?"

"Not yet. It could take a while. Have to start now."

That made sense and maybe explained his long glum silences for the past several weeks, too. She'd worried he was getting depressed like that time before, and blamed it on all the beer he'd been drinking for the past month. And sometimes she thought he just wasn't man enough to deal with a baby that cried a lot, which she'd admit Rose Ellen did. So at least that day he was trying. She said, "I'll bring you a surprise from the store."

"No need. And don't plan on exchanging Christmas presents. Save your money. You might need it." He stirred like he might be getting out of the chair, but didn't. "Take the ranch pickup."

She went to the bedroom, came back out carrying her purse in her left hand with the diaper bag strap over that same shoulder, the bag banging against her thigh. The baby rode on her back in the carrier. She stopped by his chair and stuffed her purse into the diaper bag. Then she said, "Does it have gas?"

"Enough to get to town. Buy more while you're there."

He didn't offer to get the baby seat out to the pickup, and she'd be damned if she'd ask. Leaving the house for the second time, the baby off her back and in the seat, Marva let the door slam behind her. In town, she took her time stocking up on groceries; she hadn't been to the store in three weeks. In the poultry section she chose a small turkey, added it to her cart. By the time she reached the end of the aisle and turned toward chips and snacks, the anger she'd been ignoring wouldn't let her go another step forward. She wheeled the cart around. He'd said no Christmas gifts, fine. No turkey either. Even though it would have pleased her more right then to throw that frozen bird through the store's front window, she deposited it gently among the other carcasses in the poultry case.

Somehow that action settled her; calm returned, and she managed to haul the four sacks of groceries out to the pickup and return the cart to the space near the grocery store's front door. Rose Ellen slept through the entire episode, resting against Marva's back.

At the Phillips 66, watching the numbers on the pump click as the gas tank filled, she ignored an urge to find a pay phone somewhere and call. . . That's what stopped her. There was no one who'd understand if she called. Her mother would say that "made your bed, now lie in it" line, and Carly would tell her she'd just have to figure it all out same as she had. And Stacey wouldn't rest until she'd said, "I told you so." Of course, Stacey would immediately offer to help but what college senior would want to be a part-time babysitter? And why should she? Marva hadn't done anything to be a friend to her, hadn't sent a Christmas card, didn't know when Stacey's birthday was, hadn't gone to the trouble to make a phone call in all the months since she left Lubbock aiming for adventure. Rose Ellen began fussing, reminding Marva she didn't have time to spend on feeling sorry for herself, and she would have to nurse her before driving back to the ranch.

When Christmas Eve arrived and Cutter hadn't turned up, she allowed herself to think he wasn't coming back. If she had been alone, she'd have probably piled into that pickup, and would have been ended up on Christmas Day somewhere in Texas. In fact, she said that aloud to Bullet. And that's when she reminded herself she wasn't alone. Marva Cope may have been deserted by Cutter, but Rose Ellen Gulley never left, and she depended on her mother. And Bullet did, too. That evening, she put out four stockings on the bar where there had been three last year. As she nursed Rose Ellen late that night, she told her baby girl a story about Santa Claus and hummed a chorus of "Jingle Bells." The full-of-milk baby slept in her crib as her mother cried, Bullet beside her on the bed.

The deadline she set—how long she'd wait before she gave up thinking every sound she heard was Cutter parking out front, or Cutter stepping onto the porch, or that the few occasions when Bullet barked meant he heard Cutter's voice—was January fifth. Their paychecks should turn up in the mail by then, even if Cutter never showed. January fifth would be the day she'd decide what to do next.

Meanwhile, thankful for the sunny, moderate weather without any snow or heavy ice, each day she took care of the chores. The first morning, getting into the thermal underwear the Gulleys had sent the Christmas before, she dithered about preparation she should make for problems she might encounter with the livestock, the equipment, or some lurking, unknown disaster. She laughed about the lurking evil. She hadn't feared anything when Cutter was there. His being gone didn't mean unnamed evil would descend. So, she should cross that off her list of concerns. Easy to think that in the bright daylight. Nighttime was when she put the loaded shotgun under the edge of the bed and double checked the locks on windows and doors.

About the cattle, horses, fences, water, and all the rest, "Take it as it comes," she told herself. Thinking too far ahead to all the bad things that could occur could paralyze her. "Whatever happens, deal with it then. Take along the tools Cutter did. Don't invite trouble."

Five days of sunshine and daytime temperatures in the upper forties with everything on the ranch working as it should encouraged Marva a little. With each passing day, the question of whether Cutter would return became less important. No matter what, she couldn't stay with him any longer. By January fifth, she would make a plan.

But planning required calm, rational thought, which was hard to summon when each day found her kicking at any gate that stuck, screaming "Dammit to hell" the day she hit her thumb with the hammer when breaking ice on the horse trough, and throwing the fencing tool a good six feet when her carefully wrought splice failed.

The night of January fourth she left Rose Ellen in her crib to cry herself to sleep after having tried for over an hour to quiet her. At that point, it was walk away or do something she'd regret forever. Bullet fretted, too, following her from room to room, keeping her in sight, but staying at a distance. She said, "I know, I'm sorry." She patted her leg; he trotted to stand by her chair where exhaustion dropped her. "It's not you I'm mad at."

She woke after midnight, still in the chair. The house was silent except for an occasional soft snore from Bullet. Soundlessly, she got into bed, and Bullet roused and stationed himself just beyond her feet. The next morning, her deadline day began when Rose Ellen fussed enough to wake Marva. She'd slept through the night which surely must mean the baby had, too. Moving quickly, Marva changed the soaked diaper and took her daughter to her breast, both of them under the bed's two quilts. Bullet raised his head but didn't move. She said, "Everything's fine now. I settled down. Promise." The dog's tail wagged and thumped twice as he watched her feed her child.

After finishing the outdoor chores—the words "Cutter's job" came to mind but she managed to ignore them only because anger hadn't been much help the past few days—she drove to the mailbox. Five pieces of Dear Occupant mail, one of them a catalog from a farm and ranch supply store, and one red card-sized envelope addressed to her and Cutter. The owner's checks, one made out to her, one to Cutter, dropped onto her lap when she extracted the gaudy card. A printed message, "Happy New Year," and two handwritten lines, signed by the owner helped Marva decide. The absentee rancher's note said, "I hope to get out there sometime in the next couple of months. Call if you have trouble." Marva read that as a sign to stick it out one more month and collect one more paycheck before leaving. She'd need money to get a start somewhere in Texas.

Six days later, a good night's sleep left her feeling optimistic, capable. Rose Ellen slept without waking almost every night by then. After the early morning feeding, they snuggled under the quilts and Marva talked to her about the things they'd do that day. The pregnancy and childcare books Marva had moved from under the bed to the top of the nightstand agreed that talking to infants benefitted their development. That day she told her daughter about her dream the night before where Chance appeared for the first time in a long time. Maybe it wasn't Chance at all; his features were vague, but the voice was his. Always before, she'd seen herself in those dreams with him. This time he was alone, but his message was clear: she could take care of herself and he'd be there to help if she ever needed him. "You're not alone," he'd said as he waved goodbye. She touched her index finger softly to Rose Ellen's left cheek and said, "We are not alone." The baby turned her face toward the touch, and smiled briefly, just long enough to bring tears to Marva's eyes and spread warmth through her chest. "Sweet baby, I love you."

No big snow, lots of sunny days, commode flushing properly, heater keeping the house warm, washing machine not overflowing, cattle all in good shape, horses, ditto. Marva ticked off all the things that were going her way. So why did this weather forecast for rain or snow someday soon have her counting candles and making an extra trip that day to check on the cattle and the horses? She parked the pickup near the barn, and told the baby she'd be right back as she tucked the blanket across her and beneath the infant seat. One of the horses was down, lying on her side, the other mare and the gelding standing in the grazing pen on the other side of the corral.

"Damn you, Cutter Gulley. Gone when this horse needs you," she muttered as she entered the corral and walked slowly to the animal. At least it was breathing. Marva inhaled deeply and looked around. Cutter had told her about horses getting colicky from an obstruction, a gut twisted, or maybe just constipation. Maybe fewer piles of manure dotted the ground since she'd scooped the pen out the day before. But she couldn't be sure. Call the vet. That's the only thing she could do. What would she tell him? According to her baby books, if you called the doctor you should be ready to report pulse, respiration, temperature, and other symptoms. Surely vets needed something similar.

But forget checking that horse's temperature. She had no thermometer other than Rose Ellen's. She wouldn't even try that.

Marva knelt beside the horse's head, patted gently down its neck. Watching the chest rise and fall, she counted breaths for fifteen seconds ticked off on her fingers. Five multiplied by four equaled twenty breaths. Marva peeled off her right glove and searched for a pulse somewhere near the junction of head and neck—like humans. Sure enough, a strong pulse beat against the two fingers she slid upward from under the edge of the horse's jaw. She counted nine beats in fifteen seconds. Thirty-six. "You'll be okay. I'll get help for you. Just be still," she said, rubbing the neck gently. The horse's upper lip seemed to sneer, but the eye she rolled toward Marva didn't show terror. That's what Marva hoped, anyway. She closed the wire gate between the pen and the corral to keep the other two horses away and ran to the pickup.

Back at the house, she called the number for the vet in Cimarron. She reported her observations, and he accepted the lame excuse she made about Cutter's being gone because of a family emergency in Texas; said he'd be out in two hours or less and not to let the horse eat or drink until he got there. And yes, he knew how to get to the ranch, and oh, by the way, walk the mare around, gently, if she'll get up. Before he hung up he said, "You're doing all the right things."

Marva stopped long enough to change the baby and let her nurse and then bundled her up again. As she started out of the house, she turned and hurried back to the phone. If that horse died, she didn't want it to come as a complete surprise to the owner. Finding his phone number among all the things in the kitchen drawer slowed her down. Her hands shook as she punched his Dallas number.

He, too, didn't press her about Cutter's absence, just thanked her for taking good care of things. She pushed away an urge to tell the truth. She said, "I'll call and let you know what the vet says."

"Sure, call anytime. I'm the only one here, and I'm not going anywhere." His voice sounded sad, like he was somewhere farther away than Dallas.

Her hands quit shaking as she told Rose Ellen that they were two strong women taking care of the ranch, that everything was going to be okay. And she silently gave thanks that the sun was shining.

At the corral, Marva found the horse lying where she'd left her. Nothing changed; pulse and respiration the same. Tugging at her harness did no good. The mare didn't try to rise. So, she left her lying and went back to the pickup. Every fifteen minutes, according to the pickup clock, she went back to the horse, looking for changes, hoping nothing would be different. Between those trips to the corral, she told Rose Ellen a story about Chance, how he always watched out for her at school and taught her to be a sprinter. Then just as she finished telling Rose Ellen how strong and smart her Uncle Chance had been, the baby closed her eyes and sighed. Thank goodness, nap time.

Just then Marva saw the horse try to roll. She closed the pickup door gently and ran to the corral as the mare got to her feet. Hardly able to draw a breath, she grabbed the halter and tugged gently. The horse followed. Marva walked her around the inside of the pen, and she kept walking, telling the horse with each step she'd be okay. It seemed like forever before the horse stopped and passed gas, loudly. Another gentle tug and the mare followed again. Soon after, she halted again and plopped out a large amount of manure. After that, Marva kept the horse moving. A few minutes later a man who looked to be in his thirties, at most, parked a Suburban hauling an empty horse trailer near the corral. By then Marva had stopped shaking. She said, "Are you the vet?"

He smiled and said, "Yes, Ma'am. The only one in Cimarron. Mason Roberts."

She left the horse standing and walked toward the man. She said, "For some reason I assumed you'd be older."

"My dad retired and I came back here to take up his practice after vet school at Texas A & M. Five years ago now. Want to see my license?" He smiled as he said it.

"Sorry, no." She walked back toward the horse, hoping he couldn't see how stupid she felt. "Here's your patient."

After he spent several minutes examining the horse, the vet said, "I believe you cured her. See that pile she dropped? Constipated.

It was the walking that took care of it. Let's keep her on hay and off the sweet feed for another day or two."

Marva shivered as the sun dropped closer toward the mountains. She said, "I could use a cup of coffee. How about you?"

"Sure, that'd be nice. I don't have any more patients today. If you want me to, I'll put the horses in the stalls and be up to the house in a few minutes. I noticed you have a little one in the pickup."

"Yes. And she probably needs a change by now." Marva told herself to shut up about diapers. She slammed the pickup door harder than she intended, and gave a weak nod to the vet watching her as she backed the pickup around and headed to the house.

Twilight waned toward dark. Soon after, the vet knocked on the front door. Bullet barked, once, and shot in front of Marva as she opened the door. "It's okay. Good boy," she said. "Sit." The dog sat briefly, then stood in front of her again as the vet walked slowly past her toward the dining table, then sat.

He said, "That's a good dog. Protective. Did you raise him from a pup?"

She shook her head no, and patted Bullet on the back when he followed her to the kitchen. As she carried their two cups to the table, she said, "Came with the house. Need sugar or cream?"

"Seems like he's yours now. Good coffee, just this way. Thanks."

They each drank and were quiet for a couple of minutes. Then she said, "Should I check on that mare again tonight?"

"I'll see about her once more after I drink this coffee, and if she's okay, you won't need to until tomorrow morning. I think she's going to be fine. Did that ever happen with her before?"

"Not that I know of. We've been here a year and a half and if it had, Cutter probably would have said." His name stuck in her throat, made her eyes water. She took a deep breath and said, "I'm sorry I got you out here for nothing."

"No, you did the right thing. There's lots of reasons a horse can get colicky. Some really dangerous. Same as with a baby."

"Shhh. I don't even want her to hear the word colic. She's finally started sleeping through the night and hasn't been sick. Well, she did cry a lot for a while there, but it might have been something I ate, or maybe too much coffee." She lifted her cup. "That's why this is mostly hot milk."

She stood; Bullet followed her to the kitchen. "I want to give you the owner's name for you to send your bill. It's right here." She wrote the information on an index card she found in the drawer. "More coffee?"

"Better not." He folded the card in half and put it in his billfold. "I'll go check that mare again. I'll honk on the way out to let you know I'm going back to town." He headed to the door, then stopped before going out. "Don't forget to lock up."

"Thanks again for coming."

"Call me anytime."

She stood in the open doorway, looking out the screen as he neared the edge of the porch. She heard him say, "For anything."

She allowed herself a big smile and relaxed a little bit.

After she locked the doors and checked the windows, she reached under the edge of the bed and touched the shotgun. Her safety ritual finished, getting the baby changed again and into her sleeper was the final step that calmed Marva, who wondered why she needed calming. Everything was fine. Rose Ellen nursed noisily and soon fell asleep. A horn honked out on the road just as Marva put her daughter in her crib. The vet. She smiled again.

The next morning, she called the owner's number again. A machine invited her to leave a message. She did, something on the order of "mare is fine; sorry to have bothered you; vet will send a bill." That sad sounding man wouldn't call back. She understood. He probably avoided the telephone the same as she did.

Several busy days passed, days filled with frequent observation of the mare, counting cattle, putting out feed and breaking the ice on the water trough along with tending to Rose Ellen and Bullet and occasionally stopping to rest. Her focus on keeping everything going long enough to collect one more check kept Marva from thinking much past each sunset.

The nights were a different story. When dark descended, outdoor temperature dropped to single digits, and Bullet came right back in after doing his business, his coat and nose cold to Marva's touch. Night sounds, most of them certainly far away from the house, punctuated the silence relieved only by the baby's occasional cries or Marva's speaking in response, telling Rose Ellen stories, or talking to the dog. She could have turned on the radio or television. But she preferred to remain alert for footsteps on the porch, screams of animals in pain, or that pierce-you-to-your-core sound of window glass breaking. She woke each morning with the sun, feeling as if she'd hovered above the bed the entire night.

One morning near the middle of January, after she finished with the livestock, and the baby napped, she stood again at the telephone. Cutter wasn't coming back. But maybe he'd intended to. Angry and hurt, at first she'd assumed the worst; he only cared about himself. Now, not angry, but without a name for how she felt, she knew she should call his parents. He might be dead on a roadside somewhere; they would think he was still here, alive. Before she could talk herself out of the urge, she found the number. A woman answered.

"Mrs. Gulley?"

"Yes."

Marva told his mother that Cutter was gone, hadn't been there since December twenty-third. She said, "I went to the grocery store in Cimarron. He said he might be gone to Springer when I got back. Looking into a job he said." Her voice caught in her throat as she said, "Has something bad happened to him? Do you know?" Then she didn't let herself say more. If she opened her mouth again, no telling what she'd spill out.

For what seemed like a long time, the woman on the other end, the one Cutter had said was the strong one, didn't say anything either. Then she said, "He left and didn't explain? I'm sorry. I didn't raise him to be that way." She made a sound Marva knew was choking back tears. Then she went on. "He called me on New Year's Day and said he was in Colorado. I think he was in a bar. Said he'd call again when he found work. I just assumed you were with him. I hoped you were. He's not good alone."

Again, silence filled the space between them. In a voice that even she could barely hear, Marva said, "Did he say anything else?"

"No, I'm sorry. Just asked if I was okay, told me not to worry about him, then said he had to go. He didn't explain." Mrs. Gulley paused, her breathing ragged. "Please don't hate my son. He has a good heart."

Marva said, "His paycheck came the first of the month. I'll send it to you, in case. Well, if he turns up and needs money. I'm staying here until early February, till the rancher can get someone else."

"Who's doing all the work? You?" Are you okay?"

"Yes. I can handle it. But I'm worried." She'd run out of things she wanted to ask and knew there was nothing else she was willing to tell. "Thanks for talking to me. Bye." She hung up immediately.

She hadn't mentioned Rose Ellen. Telling herself she forgot would be easy, and maybe it was true. She'd wanted more than anything to end the conversation. But if she forgot something as important as letting that woman know she had a grandchild, what else was she forgetting? She stared at the phone, knowing she couldn't call back and say, "Oh, by the way, I forgot to mention our baby, and I forgot to tell you how Cutter saved our lives by delivering her." In her rush to hate him, she was choosing to forget everything good about Cutter. But his disappointed mother, after who knows how many other disappointments, could still believe he had a good heart. Marva forgot everything around her as those thoughts collided. Sitting at the table, her eyes closed and her pulse pounding, she even forgot Rose Ellen for a few seconds, didn't hear her crying until Bullet came and pushed against her.

A few days later Marva stopped the pickup about a mile from the mailbox and walked the rest of the way wearing the baby in her Gerry carrier on her chest. Not really expecting any mail, her purpose was mainly diversion. The sun was bright, the temperature around forty-five, and there was hardly a breeze at all. The only sounds were the crunching of her boots in the damp gravel and the occasional call of a magpie answered by a single bark from Bullet. Rose Ellen's response to the rhythm of her ride was the usual; she lolled her head against Marva's chest, asleep. The mailbox came into view as Marva passed through a gentle curve. Seconds later, a vehicle stopped at the intersection of the gravel road and the pavement where the mailbox stood. She slowed, then stopped, thought of turning and hurrying back to the pickup. Fear could paralyze her if she let it. There was no reason to assume that anyone meant her harm. She clipped Bullet's leash to his collar and marched forward, hoping she looked like a person on a mission.

A woman stepped out of the dark blue Jeep Cherokee, waved in Marva's direction. Then she walked toward the mailbox. When Marva neared, the woman said, "Hi! I'm Carol McQueen. Remember I brought a package to your house December a year ago?"

Marva said, "I do remember."

Carol pointed toward the baby. "Someone new, I see. Congratulations! I was about to take all these things in the box back to the station. Thought you must have moved. Want to come sit a few minutes?"

They sat, left the Jeep's doors open. Marva said, "I haven't come down here for the mail since the first of the month. Been pretty busy."

"Everything all right with this sweetie?" Rose Ellen's eyes opened, then drooped and closed again. "How old?"

"She'll be four months February first."

"I guess she's got her daddy wrapped around her finger. Little girls are born knowing how to do that."

"He's gone." She found herself wiping at her eyes, knew she couldn't be crying. Wouldn't allow it.

"Oh, honey, you're out here by yourself. Are you doing all the work and tending to this baby?"

Marva nodded and sniffed.

"Do you want to talk?"

Looking ahead, measuring the distance to the ranch pickup, she shook her head no. "But thanks."

Neither of them spoke for a bit. Then Carol said, "Just tell me this. Do you have enough food, gas for the pickup? You can get to town if you need to? Call the law if something happens?"

Keeping her focus on the top of the baby's head, Marva nodded yes. "We're okay. You're kind to be concerned. Thank you." She eased out of the Jeep, closed the door.

Carol said, "Not kind. Just a woman who knows how hard it can be on your own with a baby." As she spoke, she wrote on the back of one of the envelopes addressed Current Resident. "Here's my phone number. Call me if you need anything or want to talk."

The night of January twenty-fourth was another of the many when Marva seemed to sleep with her eyes half-open, never quite descending into the place where she let go of the day and of her thoughts of all the days to come. One full month and one day since Cutter left. Rain had fallen that morning, but the day had turned bright later, with full sun that encouraged her to think she might even last on the ranch through February. The possibility of another month's pay for her savings urged her to add to the grocery list before she drove to Cimarron that day. Powdered formula for supplemental feedings for Rose Ellen, cereal, eggs, bacon, bread, two packages of chicken thighs, potatoes, milk, cheese, and treats for Bullet. She'd have enough to last longer if she decided to stay on. She topped off the truck's gas tank, and was back at the ranch in time to check the livestock before dark.

Bullet's routine, which seldom varied, was to ride in the back of the pickup when she went to check the cattle and horses and their feed and water. Then when she stopped to walk around the hunters' cabin, he'd spring over the tailgate and trot off on his own mission. She'd never followed him; it wasn't necessary. He always returned as soon as he did his business, which she suspected involved scouting for rabbits in the low junipers that bounded the edges of the pastures, leaving his scent a thousand places and doing whatever else a fully intact male animal would do. He never failed to race up to the ranch house door within an hour, often sooner, and announce his return with a single bark. He received a treat for his return and she'd lock the door for the night. Reliable, both of them.

That afternoon, because Rose Ellen slept all the way from town, Marva didn't unload the baby or groceries before tending to the animals. She only stopped at the house long enough for Bullet to take his position in the back, and completed the rest of her evening routine as the sun sank below the mountains to the west. Twilight dimmed fast while she put away the groceries. Then she nursed Rose Ellen and told her about the trip to town that she'd slept through. Before she stopped to rest, she filled Bullet's bowl with dry food and put two of the new treats in her pocket. That was when she heard a familiar sound—the loud muffler of a big pickup, throttling toward the house.

Seconds later, Bullet barked several times from somewhere near the porch. She peeked from behind the living room curtain. The big, red, loud, crew cab pickup skidded to a halt near the porch and two of Cutter's friends who'd been there before bailed out of the front doors, each holding a beer can. The one driving was the big guy who'd eyed her too closely for comfort when he'd been there before.

She hurried to the bedroom and returned with the shotgun. Holding it might make her feel better, but Cutter had told her his dad's rule: don't aim a gun unless you intend to shoot it. So, she leaned the gun against Cutter's chair but left the safety off. Boots stomped up the two wooden steps and onto the porch. Deep growling punctuated periods of Bullet's barking. If they had any sense, they'd take their drunken selves off the porch and drive away. Heavy knocking on the single-latch, wood-framed screen door; mumbled speech she couldn't understand; Bullet's frantic barking replaced Marva's impulse to run and hide with something strong and raw. She took a deep breath and shouted. "What do you want?"

"We've got a message for Gulley. Open up!" More banging, now against the heavier, wooden door. They'd jerked the flimsy screen door open. "Shut this damn dog up and let us in."

A different voice said, "Hell, let's just go. I told you he's not here."

"That's why we're here. He owes me for a broken jaw. I'll take what I can get." Scuffling sounds followed, something thudded to the porch. Then the same voice screamed, "My hand! I'll kill that dog."

Bullet began barking again. Then more growling, interrupted again by another scream. "He bit my leg!"

"Get your ass in the pickup."

"Hell no! I'm gonna kill that dog."

Marva clutched the gun and moved the curtain. She saw the smaller of the two men step off the porch, shaking his head. He tossed a beer can to the ground and headed to the pickup. Bullet lunged at the big cowboy with the bloody hand and leg. The guy landed a kick in Bullet's ribs that left the dog flattened on the porch. Bullet didn't move, but the man kicked him again.

Marva jerked open the door as he kicked the unmoving Bullet in the head. She didn't say a word, just aimed the shotgun between the porch and the pickup, and pulled the trigger. Then she said, "Touch that dog again and I'll shoot you. Leave now or I'll shoot you anyway."

The pickup engine roared. The other cowboy yelled, "I'm leavin'." Then he revved the engine.

The bloodied man stumbled off the porch saying, "I'll be back. You tell him that." Then he limped toward the passenger side of the pickup, got in, slammed the door. Gravel spewed as the pickup turned and sped away. Marva fired once more, directly toward the pickup. She wouldn't forget the numbers and letters on that Texas license plate.

Bullet was still breathing, but his eyes were closed. Marva ran inside and came back with a quilt to cover him. Her hands shook and her stomach clenched, making breathing hard. If she called the sheriff, it would be a long time before anyone got there. That might be too late for Bullet. Those kicks surely broke ribs. Moving him could make him worse. She spoke to the dog. "I'm going to get some help. I'll be back. You're a good, good dog." He didn't move.

Jiggling Rose Ellen on her hip as she talked on the phone, Marva explained the situation to the vet—drunk cowboys, shotgun, and all. He said, "I'll be there in thirty minutes. Keep Bullet warm and don't try to move him. I'll call the closest deputy, too." He hesitated, then said, "You have more shells for your shotgun?"

"Uh, huh."

"Reload. It'll make you feel safer."

Marva did as he said. Then she brought two more blankets and the baby in her infant seat out to wait with Bullet. With one hand on the dog, the other touching Rose Ellen, and the shotgun within reach, she listened in the stillness for the sound of a pickup. And when the dark and the silence got too close, she looked toward the stars and said aloud, "Please God, don't let Bullet die, and give me strength . . ."

As abruptly as she'd begun, she stopped. Speaking into the night to a Being that likely, if it existed at all, did not deal in individual personal problems or any of the other things humans pray about, like football games and rain for their cotton crops, was not going to save the dog or get her off this ranch. The vet would do all he could to save Bullet; it was his job, not personal. She and Rose Ellen were a different matter. As much as she hated to admit it, asking people—friends or family or even kind strangers like the postal route driver—to help her was what she had to do. By the time the vet arrived, her pulse had settled, and she knew she had to leave. But she had no idea how to tolerate letting anyone help, even if they were willing. And there was the problem of destination. Where would she go?

As soon as his Suburban came to a halt near the porch, the vet unloaded a large plastic bin and a backpack which he placed on the porch at the same time he said, "You okay now?"

Marva nodded, watching Bullet for some sign that he was conscious. Although he was breathing, his eyes were closed. Her speckled cowdog protector made not so much as a twitch at the sound of the vehicle or the man's voice.

"While I examine him, tell me what happened." He pulled a stethoscope and otoscope from the backpack.

Rose Ellen stirred in her seat, then settled without waking. Marva said, "The drunkest of the two guys, the loud one who banged on the door, tore the screen latch off. At first I didn't have the front door open, so I didn't see. But I know from what he was yelling and then when I did see him, that Bullet got in two good bites. One on his right hand and another on his left thigh. Both bled quite a lot." She pointed toward a trail of blood from near the door to the steps. "From the time Bullet started barking, I think the guy was kicking at him. He kicked him in the ribs at least twice and then twice in the head after he was already down. He's a big guy wearing cowboy boots."

"This is a tough dog. His heart rhythm and rate are fine and his pupils function. Lungs sound clear. I can't say if there's any rib fracture, but right now, I'm pretty sure there's no rib lacerating a lung. I believe he'll come to here in a bit. But he should be watched. I want to give him some anti-inflammatory med and some fluids. If you can give me a little help, we can take him inside and do it there." As he talked, he pulled a dog-sized stretcher and a pet crate from the back of the Suburban. "It'll be better for him than taking him back to town right now."

A sheriff's vehicle pulled in behind the Suburban. The deputy who got out said, "Need some help?"

The vet raised a finger to his lips, then pointed to Rose Ellen, still sleeping in her seat. Marva held the front door open for the men and then followed, carrying the infant seat, which she took to the bedroom.

When she returned to the living room, the vet, squatting to reach the dog now lying in the bottom half of the crate, seemed focused on his work. The top half removed, set on end, held a hook with a small IV bag attached, dripping slowly into Bullet's right front leg. She watched as he injected something into the IV tubing port. The dog's soft snoring breaths were the only sounds in the room.

The deputy beckoned her. Speaking softly, he asked about the incident, and she told him a more detailed version of what she'd explained to the vet, including information about the pickup and its plate number. She wouldn't forget that. The deputy asked some questions about when the two men had been to the ranch previously and their connection to Cutter. Then he said, "Do you think you hit the pickup when you shot?"

"I wish I could say I did, but I doubt it. And to tell you the truth, I don't think they'll be back. It was Cutter they wanted. He isn't coming back, and I'll leave before long. Probably."

"Well, I'd like to find those two anyway. They need a lesson about causing trouble in New Mexico." He handed her a card with his contact information. "I'll be in touch if anything develops." He headed to the door, then turned and said, "Don't hesitate to call if they turn up again."

From across the room, the vet said, "If it's okay with you, I'll stay here for a few more hours to monitor him. Then as soon as it's light, if he's awake by then, I'll take him to the clinic."

Marva's spine stiffened, and at the same time, Rose Ellen began fussing. "There's no couch. You'd have to sleep in that chair." She nodded toward the bedroom. "I'll be right back. She needs changing."

"I have a sleeping bag in that bin I brought in. I'll be fine and real quiet."

"Okay. Thank you," she said as she went to the baby. After she changed Rose Ellen's diaper, Marva made a pot of coffee and sat with the vet, drinking a cup, neither of them speaking. She guessed he had stayed as much to help her as to care for the dog. And she also knew without asking that he'd be embarrassed to have to admit she was right.

She told him to help himself to more coffee or anything in the refrigerator if he got hungry and to call her if he needed any help with Bullet. Then she went to the bedroom and closed the door. As she nursed the baby, she tried to focus on all she needed to do, but when she moved her sleeping daughter to her crib, the only thing Marva could say for sure was that she would call the ranch owner in the morning. The rest would all depend.

At three a.m., according to the bedside clock, Marva woke, surprised that she'd slept soundly that long without the usual feeling she never really settled. She cracked open the bedroom door, she saw that both the dog and the vet were asleep. It was another four hours before anyone in the house stirred again and another thirty minutes, after feeding the baby, before Marva left the bedroom to make coffee.

"About one o'clock, the patient roused and voluntarily opened his eyes, moved his extremities, made a move to stand, but then didn't." The vet, standing away from the topless crate, spoke very softly into a small recorder. "Then he stirred a couple more times, most recently about thirty minutes ago when the baby cried. Seemed to be responding to that sound. I removed the IV. It's clear he's still stunned. I think I should take him to the clinic and observe him at least one more day to be sure he doesn't have a worse concussion."

"You want any breakfast?"

"Thanks for the offer. But I'll just take some of that coffee and then get crate and dog loaded and get back to town. Friday's sometimes a busy day at the office." He shifted from one foot to the other, glanced toward the ceiling, then said, "Not my business, but are you going to be okay out here?"

"Not until I leave for good."

He nodded like that made sense to him. She knew it didn't.

He set the empty coffee cup on the bar. Nodded again. He fitted the crate lid on the bottom half and secured the latches. "I'll open the vehicle. Then I'll need a little help getting the crate in there."

Together they toted the crate, dog on board, still not stirring, to the Suburban, slid it in the back where the vet snugged it in place with two luggage straps. "Call me in the morning before you make the trip to town to get him. Just in case he's not quite ready for activity."

"Thanks for taking such good care of him." Marva backed toward the porch, then stopped. "And thanks for staying here last night. I was able to sleep."

Walking to the driver's side door, he said, "No trouble at all. Glad to help."

She stood on the porch, hands in her Levi's pockets. After he started the engine, he rolled his window down and said, "Anytime." Then he backed up, turned around, and headed toward the road. She hoped he saw her wave goodbye

CHAPTER 12

January 25—January 28, 1984
Another Getaway

Friday morning after Mason left, a second cup of coffee upped Marva's courage to the point where she felt ready to call the ranch owner. He answered the phone after three rings. Telling as few details as possible, she explained Cutter's surprise departure and her realizing that with the baby she couldn't continue taking care of the place alone. She ended by saying, "I'd like to leave right away. When will you be able to get someone else?"

Silence, punctuated by what sounded like a big sigh, was all she heard for several long seconds. Then he said, "Seems like leaving's going around. I don't have any reason to stay here now. I might as well be out there doing something useful."

She waited, thought about the sadness she'd heard in his voice when she'd called about the horse. Then he said, "I'll get things together and be there by Monday." He cleared his throat. "I'm sorry things turned bad for you."

"Me, too." If he kept talking, she'd end up crying for both of them. She said, "I have to hang up. The baby's crying. I'll see you Monday." A few deep breaths later, she cooked an egg and toast and forced herself to concentrate on the food, not on figuring out every next step it would take to get away. Rose Ellen slept on.

Monday. That meant she had to decide where she was going and how she'd get there and she had to decide today. The answer, the simplest one, safest probably, was to go to the only family she had. Her mother and Carly. Or Aunt Violet.

Marva paced from the phone in the kitchen to the bedroom door. She stood watching Rose Ellen in her crib, lying on her back, arms flung out from her sides, blanket pushed off, her breathing smooth and steady. Peaceful. If she went to her mother and sister, there'd never be a minute's peace again. Marva pictured living with her mother in some ratty apartment, her mother spouting hateful words about her having an illegitimate child, taking every opportunity to remind her she'd "told her so." Or worse yet, hearing her mother say on the phone that she wouldn't help; that Marva had to "lie in the bed she'd made." Living with Carly and her two kids wouldn't be much better. Her sister didn't hate her, but she had her own problems and two kids. Marva shook her head. No, she wasn't that desperate.

Marva grabbed the pen and paper she kept near the phone and wrote short phrases, quickly, as if taking notes in class. When she paused, she let herself exhale. Seeing some possibilities on paper helped. Amarillo, Canyon, Plainview, and Lubbock—all in Texas; Cimarron, Red River, Las Vegas—in New Mexico. Staring at the names of the towns, she drew a line through the New Mexico names. Her only connection to those towns was Cutter. He wasn't coming back.

Dimmitt could also be on the Texas list. But she'd left there for good. She didn't bother adding it. Amarillo would be the fastest bus trip from Cimarron, so getting away would be quicker. But Plainview was a smaller town, more manageable without a vehicle, which she probably wouldn't have for a while.

She stared at the page. Violet. Why should she help? Marva had no way of knowing if her aunt had ever tried to be in touch since she sent Marva a graduation gift—that blue suitcase and a check for a hundred dollars in a card with a note saying she wanted Marva to keep in touch. But the distance between keeping in touch and showing up wherever Violet lived now with Rose Ellen on her hip? Way too much.

It became clearer to Marva as she sat still and focused, that Lubbock would be the best place for now. At least she knew she could get work there waiting tables. Until she got situated. And she was familiar with the town. And Stacey might even still be there. Maybe she wouldn't hold a grudge.

Then she remembered—when she came for Dad's funeral, Aunt Violet was living in Jackson's Pond, a small town like Dimmitt. But she had taught school in Amarillo at one time. Maybe she was back there now. Her aunt would understand or at least wouldn't hate Marva and maybe she'd have some ideas about places where Marva could get a job right away.

The information operator she reached had Marva spell

Violet's name. Seconds later, she said, "Sorry, I have no one listed by that name in Amarillo. Would you like to request another number?" Rose Ellen's sudden, loud cry, more frantic than her hunger sound, startled Marva. She thanked the operator and hurried to the crib. As soon as she picked her daughter up, Marva could tell she had fever. She changed her diaper and bathed her quickly with a washcloth.

According to the thermometer, her temperature was 99.2 F. The baby fretted as Marva cleaned and changed and checked her, but quit the frantic-sounding crying. Maybe she'd just gotten overheated by the blanket.

Marva had bottles ready, refrigerated; she knew she had to switch from breast feeding so she could work away from home. She quickly heated one, offered it to Rose Ellen, who pushed it away. She began the insistent crying again and rooted at her mother's chest. And Marva broke into tears. As she opened her shirt and offered her breast, she said, "I know, I'm so sorry. I'm sad, too." As the baby nursed, tugging hard at the nipple, Marva rocked her gently and let her own tears flow.

Soon after she finished nursing, the baby slept again, but when her mother placed her in the crib her eyes opened and the crying began again. Marva stood massaging Rose Ellen's back as she held her to her chest. The baby care book she'd read advised seeing a health care provider if the baby had a temp above 100.4 or if there was difficulty breathing, vomiting, diarrhea, or a rash. None of that applied. So, Mom should relax and continue watching. But she couldn't stand the idea of her baby hurting. And she was tired of feeling helpless. So, she walked slowly through the rooms of the house and hummed and patted her baby's back.

A few minutes later, Rose Ellen settled in the crib sleeping, Marva called the bus station. Regardless of where she decided to go, she needed to know the schedules. It was a short call, as it turned out. There was only one bus a day departing Cimarron heading east, at three p.m. Mountain Time. Its first stop was Las Vegas, and from there, the rest of the schedule depended on whether she wanted Amarillo or Lubbock. The other towns were secondary buses from one of those two. Just before she hung up, she asked, "Are dogs permitted on the bus?"

"Only if they're service dogs, you know, what they used to call seeing-eye dogs. If you want to chance it, you can send it in a crate, as freight. But to tell you truth, I wouldn't do that to my dog. Sorry. Anything else I can help with?"

Marva had all the information she needed and some she didn't want. As she hung up the phone, her baby cried again. Hunger couldn't be the problem. She must be in pain. The crying reduced to fretting as soon as Marva picked her up. Her temperature was still 99.2, no rash. Nothing else. Movement helped the baby and made Marva feel like she was doing something that might help, so she bundled them both and put the baby in her infant seat. The morning chores should have been done two hours ago. After checking water and feed for the horses, driving slowly toward the cattle pasture, she thought how much more difficult leaving was than getting to the ranch had been. So much had happened in between. All that living packed into a handful of months. She refused to let herself think how much of it had been a mistake.

Rose Ellen didn't wake when Marva stopped the pickup at the house, a good sign as far as she was concerned. She had to get more information and then make a decision about where she intended to make her new start. Then tomorrow, she'd clean the house and. . . . Rose Ellen jerked awake in her infant seat, crying loudly, face red, tiny fists waving. She refused the bottle and the breast and stopped crying only to draw in ragged breaths.

Even with her vaccinations, Rose Ellen had never cried like this. Marva remembered the infant ibuprofen that she'd bought and never used. She found it in the kitchen cabinet. But the bottle said consult a physician for children under six months. She called the number for the family doctor in Las Vegas where she took Rose Ellen for her shots. The nurse who answered asked her the same questions she'd seen in the baby care book. Her suggestion was to give a dose half the amount listed on the bottle for a six-month-old. Marva's hands shook as she measured the correct number of drops. Rose Ellen spewed part of the liquid out. Then she commenced crying again.

Nearly frantic, Marva wished for a woman who had experience, someone to tell her what to do. Imagining her mother, she heard her say, "Let her cry it out." No, she wouldn't call her. Carol McQueen had seemed sincere when she offered to help; said she knew what it was like. Marva called the number Carol had given her. A message machine promised she'd call back after 4:30. Marva tried sounding calm when she said, "Carol, please call when you get this. I could use some help with Rose Ellen." Then before she hung up, before she could stop herself, she said, "I've tried everything and she won't stop crying. I'm worried."

She'd left the message around two o'clock. Between then and 4:15, Rose Ellen had fitfully nursed once and had cried almost constantly otherwise. All that time Marva had her either in the Gerry carrier on her chest or held in her arms, except for one brief time when she had to use the bathroom herself. When the phone rang, she was standing near, grabbed it immediately. Carol said, "Marva. You sounded upset. Tell me what's wrong."

Marva started by saying, "I'm sorry to bother you—"

Carol said, "Don't apologize. I offered. Now tell me what's wrong."

So, Marva told her as quickly as possible, speaking loud because Rose Ellen never stopped crying.

Carol said, "That kind of crying sure would make a person frantic. I'm coming out there right away. It's probably teething. The first one's always hard for them. Do you have a carrot?"

"A carrot?" Marva knew she sounded stupid.

"Yes, if you don't have a teething ring or something, you can let her gnaw on a cold carrot. Listen, I'm going to stay there with you tonight it it's okay."

"I don't want to put you to a lot of trouble."

"Not like I'll have to break a date or something." Carol snorted a little laugh. "I'll be out there in about a half hour. Do you need anything from town?"

"I don't have any carrots."

"Put an ice cube in a washcloth and let her work on that. I'll see if the grocery store has any teethers. Otherwise, we'll improvise.

See you soon."

When Marva hung up, at almost the same moment, Rose Ellen closed her eyes and sighed, crying stopped for the moment. Carol had made asking for help easy. Marva busied herself gathering a washcloth and an ice cube.

Carol turned up just as Rose Ellen had started crying again. But this time, it wasn't as loud and her face wasn't all mottled red the way it had been. The ice cube definitely had helped, maybe the few drops of ibuprofen did too. Marva held open the door and Carol hauled in a sleeping bag and a paper sack from the grocery store. "Got us some snacks. No need to cook if it can be avoided; that's my motto." She poked around in the bag, talking all the while. "I got some rice cereal in here somewhere. Your doctor probably told you no solid food until six months. But let me tell you, a little bit of rice cereal at bedtime will help this girl sleep. I'd bet money on that."

Carol's posture and her smile suggested confidence. She didn't give Marva time to feel embarrassed. Next Carol unearthed a ridged, hard rubber ring with a handle. "This is an all-purpose teether and toy. They have those that are freezable, with liquid inside, but I'm concerned they'll break open. Who knows what that liquid is? And what kind of germs grow in there?" She stopped talking, washed the teether with soap and water, and handed it to Marva. "How about you sit down. You look wiped out."

Marva managed not to blurt out that she was close to melting down from relief. She said, "I'm so glad you're here."

Carol pulled two cans of beer from the bag. "Coors okay? We'll split one of these and just sit still for a while, no talking."

Marva nodded, peeked down at the baby, now sleeping in her arms. She took her to the crib. When she returned to the living room, Carol was sitting in one of the chairs, feet on the hassock, a small glass of beer in hand. She put an index finger to her lips, pointed to the other chair, and leaned back and closed her eyes. Marva was happy to follow her instructions.

Silence and stillness worked magic. After a while, Carol said, "If there's anything you need to do—tend animals, whatever, go ahead. I'll be right here if she needs anything."

Marva hesitated, "I don't think I can."

"What, too tired?" Carol said.

Marva said, "I've never left Rose Ellen, not ever."

Carol smiled and shook her head. "I get it. I wouldn't leave my first one either. Not even with my mother."

Marva shrugged. "Sounds silly, right?"

"Not really. We'll go with you."

Rose Ellen fussed when Marva picked her up. But she settled again as soon as she was in Carol's arms in the pickup. As she drove to the barn, her usual first stop, Marva thought about all she had yet to do before she could get away. Nothing was stopping her from deciding where. It was obvious there was no ideal place. Not with a baby and no child care and no transportation and no job waiting for her. Job. She knew she'd have a job at the restaurant where she'd worked before; the manager had said so. That's how she'd decide. If she had the promise of job, she'd go to Lubbock. She breezed through the rest of the chores and went straight to the phone when they walked in the house.

Carol came from the bedroom, Rose Ellen riding on her left hip, while Marva was on the phone. She covered the receiver and said, "Getting a job." Carol nodded, moved toward the front windows, and hummed the tune to "Row, Row, Your Boat" quietly with Rose Ellen cuddled against her.

Marva said, "I'll plan to be there for the day shift beginning Monday, February 4. Count on me. Yes, thanks. I'll be glad to be there, too."

After she hung up, she said, "That's a relief."

Carol, with baby attached, came back near the bar. "Good news?"

"A job in Lubbock. It's just waiting tables, but it's a nice place, good manager."

"Lubbock. Family and friends there?"

Marva held her hands out to take Rose Ellen. "Not really, but I'm familiar with the town, and I worked at this restaurant before."

Carol passed her the baby and the rubber teether, which Rose Ellen reached for. "I checked her gums. Take a look at the top front, on the right. See that swollen part? That's definitely the source of her misery. It should pop through pretty soon." She raised the baby's hand holding the teether, moved it to her mouth. "She'll get the hang of it when she figures out it helps."

Marva watched Carol's gentle touch. She said, "How many children do you have?"

"Two. Grown now. Mothers remember. You'll remember."

While they ate supper, Marva told Carol about the drunken cowboys and Bullet and the vet who was so kind. As Marva talked, Carol stopped with her bacon sandwich part way to her mouth, frowning, shaking her head. "Men. How can they be so stupid? Don't even think it's because they were young. There's plenty of older ones just that ignorant. I hope you hit that truck when you shot at it."

Marva shrugged. "Probably didn't, but I did get the license plate number, told the deputy who came out." She finished the last of the food on her plate. "I never did anything like that. Never even shot a gun until Cutter taught me how." Then she went silent. Soon after, they both went to bed. Rose Ellen slept through the night.

When Marva left the bedroom at 6:30 the next morning, her daughter was still sleeping, her skin cool to the touch, her features placid, looking angelic. It would be easy to think the wailing and tears and the angry face from yesterday had all been a dream. Marva and Carol were drinking their second cups of coffee when baby sounds, not crying, but jabbering and cooing, got their attention. Carol heard her first. She said, "I'll get her. She sounds happy today."

When she returned with the baby on her hip, Carol said, "You'd better watch out if you nurse her again. This girl has a tooth now." She pointed to her own mouth, the top front tooth on the right. "If you have chores to do, I'll tend to her for as long as you need. I don't have anything urgent to do at my place."

As the sun rose and touched the pastures' edges on the west, Marva drove to the farthest pasture, counting cattle as she went. After she turned the pickup and headed toward the east to put out feed for the horses and check their water, she pulled her cap visor down to shield her eyes. She blamed the sun for the tears on her cheeks. There was no other sensible choice except to leave here, but everywhere she looked, she saw something familiar—the horses teasing each other in the brisk morning air; the silhouette of the mountains when she looked west, the now empty vegetable garden that could bloom again. Bits of things that she realized had begun to make this feel like someplace she could belong. A family had begun here—she and Cutter, Rose Ellen, and Bullet.

She stopped at the hunters' cabin, the place where Bullet started his solo rounds each day. She switched off the ignition and sat still, remembering how he'd perch on his hind legs to leap from the pickup bed, then race off into the junipers on his daily expeditions. Leaving him behind would be the hardest part. She opened the pickup door, then shut it again. She'd check the cabin in the evening today. She had to get back to the house and call the vet.

Mason Roberts told her that Bullet was much better and he expected he'd be fine after some more rest. He'd meet her at his office at noon so she could see Bullet, and he'd buy her a burger if she was willing. Carol offered to stay with Rose Ellen if Marva wanted to go to town alone. She said, "Give yourself a break. Let him buy you a burger. He's one of the few young ones in town I'd call an okay guy."

Marva said, "He does seem like a really nice guy. But there's no sense in encouraging him. It wouldn't be fair to either of us." She got as far as the bedroom door, on the way to gather Rose Ellen's bag and her own purse. She turned back to Carol and said, "You sure you don't mind staying here while I go to town? I hate to wake her. I'm going to have to leave Bullet here, you know. I hope maybe. . ."

Carol said, "I'd take that dog in a minute if I had a place with a yard. But I rent. No pets allowed. I hope Mason knows someone who'll take him, love him like you do."

Marva went to the bedroom, came back carrying her purse, pickup keys in her hand. She stood with the front door open, then turned back and said, "I don't know how I'll ever be able to thank you for helping me."

"Just go on and get things taken care of." She followed Marva onto the front porch. "If you're determined to leave on Monday, I can stay till the owner gets here. I don't like you being out here alone with a baby at night."

"I can do it."

Carol said, "We'll see. No need to decide right now."

Marva made it to town in no time, not having to worry about the baby seat sliding even though she always cinched it with the seat belt. Seeing Bullet wasn't as easy. He was standing up in the crate at the vet's office wagging his tail at seeing her. The motion shook his box and the empty one above. Mason said, "Looks like he's ready to go home with you. I think his ribs are sore, but he's fully conscious and eating and all other systems are go." Bullet licked at the vet's hand through the crate and lay down watching Marva.

She said, "There's a big problem. I'm leaving, going back to Texas. There's no way I can take care of him properly in an apartment." As if she already had a place to live. As if she could stand the thought of not taking her best friend with her. "Do you know of anyone who'd take him, take good care of him."

The vet said, "I was afraid you were going to do that." He looked straight at her, more directly than he had anytime before. "I wish you'd stay."

"I have to go."

He nodded. Then he said, "Well, if it's okay with you, Bullet will be my dog from now on."

She couldn't catch her breath for a second. She hugged him briefly and then stepped back. "I can't thank you enough."

"I guess that means no hamburger."

She shook her head and went to the door. She had to leave.

On the way back to the ranch, she decided she'd let Carol stay if she really wanted to. Then she'd spend Sunday packing and when the owner turned up, she'd be ready to leave on Monday. But first, she had to make a reservation at a motel in Lubbock. She chose the only one she knew was clean and safe, the motel where she'd waited for Cutter in what seemed like the ancient past. Packing was the only thing left to do, and she'd leave the place clean, the way it had been when she and Cutter first arrived.

Carol made it clear she'd already decided she was staying, no matter what. So, Marva didn't argue. That night after Rose Ellen was asleep, new tooth peeping through her gum, they talked. Actually, Carol mostly listened, and Marva worried aloud about all the details of getting child care and housing and transportation in Lubbock. Around nine, Carol said, "I'm about ready for bed and I imagine you are, too." She stood and rolled out her sleeping bag. "I have no doubt you'll figure all this out. You're plenty smart. But there's one thing you might overlook if you don't remind yourself every day."

Marva frowned. "What's that?"

"How to ask for help and how to accept it when someone offers."

The next day when she returned from doing the morning chores, the aroma of frying bacon met her at the door, and the phone rang. It was the ranch owner. He said he was packed and ready, so he'd be there that evening. When she hung up, Marva turned to Carol and said, "Good news. Perfect timing." She explained that the ranch owner's day-early return would make it possible to get to the three o'clock bus tomorrow without any rush. "I know you have to get back to your mail route tomorrow. And I'll be fine here tonight with the owner over in the big house. I'm pretty sure he'll be willing to bring us to the bus tomorrow."

Carol said, "Sounds like a plan. But let's see when he gets here." She filled their plates with scrambled eggs, toast, and bacon. "Eat up. I get to take baby duty while you pack and clean. Privilege of age. And I do hate cleaning house."

The ranch owner arrived just after Marva finished her afternoon livestock chores and returned to the house. When she heard the vehicle, Marva opened the front door and stood behind the screen as he got out of the pickup. The sun edged near the mountain tops, casting a long shadow of the man who walked leaning forward like he was accustomed to walking into a stiff wind. Without a speck of wind blowing, Marva knew that walk said something else. Her dad's last couple of years after Chance died, as his sadness grew, he walked just that same way. She opened the screen and said, "Evening, come in."

As he stepped inside, he took off his cowboy hat, glanced at Carol, and said, "Ma'am." Then he turned to Marva. "I don't want to intrude, but I brought your pay. Do you mind that it's in cash?"

"Not at all."

He counted out the amount that totaled her half, then continued until he'd stacked up both her salary and Cutter's. "You've done all the work this month. You deserve all the pay."

She didn't argue. "That will help us get started. Thank you." Rose Ellen complained from her crib, waking after a long nap. Marva said, "Carol, please introduce yourselves." She'd completely forgotten the ranch owner's name. She pointed toward the bedroom. "I'm going to get the baby. Be right back."

When she returned with Rose Ellen, the owner stood again and said, "I'll go on and get things opened up at the other house. If you don't mind my asking, do you have transportation? From what you said about Cutter leaving, I figure you've been making do with the ranch truck."

"Taking the bus. It leaves tomorrow at three."

"Where to?"

"Lubbock."

He flicked with his right forefinger at an invisible spot on his hat. "If it would help any, I'd drive you there."

The offer tempted Marva to hug his neck and say yes. She wasn't looking forward to a long bus ride. But she said, "That's really kind of you. But I have people who'll be waiting for me, so the bus won't be a problem." She told herself the lie was a kindness to him. "But I could use a ride to the bus station in Cimarron tomorrow around one o'clock."

She saw Carol watching their conversation, wearing a slight frown.

As he edged toward the front door, the owner said, "Well then, if you'll give me a call when you're ready tomorrow, I'll come help you load and take you to town. I'll get on up to the house now."

Marva leaned against the front door after she closed and locked it. She said to Carol, "What were you thinking? I noticed."

"I'll feel better if I stay here tonight. Something about him's off."

"Off, how?"

"Did you notice his hat? Hardly ever worn. Same with his boots. Seemed to me like a man in a costume."

"Well, he's the same guy who was here when we started. And he's been paying us."

"Okay, but I could tell you're not sure about him either; you lied about people expecting you in Lubbock."

Marva said, "You're right. I did." She shrugged. "Not because I think he's dangerous. He's just so sad. I can't afford to take on a sad person's misery right now."

The next morning, she and Carol were both up before six. Carol said, "US Postal Service expects me on duty delivering to rural residents today. So, I better get an early start." She talked as she rolled her sleeping bag and then roamed around the kitchen and living room finishing off a cup of coffee. She finally rinsed her coffee cup and then leaned against the bar. "You have my phone number and address. If you run into problems of any kind, please call me. I'll be right here. I'd like it if you'd call me when you get to Lubbock. Just so I know you and my little pal make it okay."

Marva cleared her throat. No words came out. She cleared it again. Then she said, "I can't thank you enough for all you've done for me, for us. I promise I'll call."

Carol, standing at the front door, her sleeping bag under her left arm, said, "I'll count on it. Stay safe, you hear me?"

Carol was out the door in a flash and at her jeep as Marva stood inside the screen. "I hear you."

That afternoon, the bus arrived in Cimarron at 2:30 p.m. Two passengers, a young man and woman about Marva's age stepped off and stood aside while the driver opened the luggage compartment below the bus. The ranch owner stayed parked in front of the grocery store two doors beyond the drugstore/bus station, with Rose Ellen in her infant seat. He'd said he'd tell her a story if she fussed while Marva dealt with the driver and her luggage. She only had her suitcase and two duffle bags to travel as luggage, one of them packed with baby gear. The diaper bag with bottles and all the things a mother carries rested on her left shoulder, her purse on her right. Weighted down with all they had, Marva still felt light.

After he shut the luggage area, the driver told her he would be back and ready to roll in five minutes. She added the infant seat and Rose Ellen to the load she carried, then thanked the rancher again. He said, "I hope things work out for you."

All she knew to do was nod and then get on the bus.

She chose the seat farthest back, glad that there were only six other passengers, all clustered near the middle of the bus. A few minutes later, heading east, the turn to the ranch flashed by on her right. She turned in her seat and watched through the back window as the mountains grew smaller, continued watching until she had to wipe tears from her face with a corner of Rose Ellen's blanket. She was leaving a part of herself back there. And she was leaving Bullet, her best friend, behind.

Rose Ellen fussed for her attention. She took her out of the infant seat, held her close, and laughed when her daughter smiled and showed her emerging tooth.

Marva Cope

142

Jackson's Pond Leader
Thursday, October 5, 2017
It's Your Health
by Claire Havlicek, R.N., Family Nurse Practitioner
Falls in the Fall and Other Times—Prevention is Key

Falls, particularly in those who are elderly or who have chronic health problems, often result in major unwanted changes in people's lives. Often those falls could have been prevented.

One way to prevent falls is to stay strong by exercising. Too often, as we age or deal with chronic illnesses, the first thing to "go" is muscle strength. Prolonged time in bed or seated in a chair while convalescing can rapidly rob muscle strength. Or simply reducing activity because one retires can lead quickly to reduced muscle strength in the legs and in the core muscles of the body's trunk.

If the muscles are soft and a seated leg lift can't be held for thirty seconds, preventive exercise is needed. The same is true if you must use arm rests to rise from a chair. If you seldom walk anywhere except in your home, strength will wane as you age; regular daily walking will improve strength.

If you don't know the best exercise for your stage or condition, ask your health care provider for a prescription to see a physical therapist. Stay healthy!

CHAPTER 13

October 2017

Shirttail Relative

Marva used her key to open the front door. Aunt Violet kept the door locked even in the daytime, and she often was napping when Marva came in from work. Her work ended each day at five, and she liked to let her aunt finish her afternoon rest because they had gotten in the habit of staying up late playing SCRABBLE. These past four months since she'd moved in had been more fun than Marva could recall having in a long time.

As soon as she closed the door, Marva heard Violet's voice. She was talking on the phone. "Willa, I'm sorry to tell you we'll have to cancel our card game this week. I just received warning from Alvin that he'll arrive on Thursday for his annual whirlwind week of *helping his old aunt*."

The tone of her voice when she said those last words suggested Alvin was not Violet's favorite guest. "Would you mind calling the others and making some excuse? I hate to have to explain it to them and hate even worse having them start speculating about what disaster might be afoot with me. Thank God Marva's here. Surely he'll not get into that 'do you have all your affairs in order' and wanting to look at my check register to see if I'm paying my bills on time. Not with her here."

Marva stopped at the door to the den and waved to let her aunt know she was in. As she walked on to the kitchen, she tried to recall Alvin. She couldn't remember any specific occasion, but had a vague image of him as bossy, smelly, a bully with big ears and buck teeth, maybe ten years-old. She would have been much younger. This was the first she'd heard of Alvin's being an annual visitor. But there were lots of things about Violet's life she hadn't learned yet.

The kitchen invited her in every afternoon first thing because her aunt, currently her housemate, loved to bake. Today the aroma of cinnamon and sugar told Marva snickerdoodle cookies were the current creation. A cup sat on the counter beside a spoon and a lemon spice teabag. She turned on the burner under the kettle.

Standing in the doorway, Violet shook her head and said, "News for you this afternoon. I hadn't gotten around to warning you about the visits from your third cousin, Alvin, or maybe he's a fourth. Hard to keep up with what Mother called 'that bunch of shirttail relatives.' Anyway, for some reason, he believes he's in charge of my welfare. I let him think what he wants as long as he keeps his distance. And as long as he turns up only once a year for a week at most, I won't have to set him straight."

"Where does he live?"

"Somewhere close to his mother over in East Texas. Until a few years ago he lived with her. She probably pitched him out, but I never asked him, and I don't even know her, not really." As she talked, Violet bustled around making her tea, and finally lit on the chair opposite Marva's at the kitchen table.

Marva leaned back waiting to hear more.

Violet said, "Without even knowing her, I know her life's been harder than mine, I'm fortunate never to have had the burden of a husband and children, so I'm willing to let her have a rest from her son for a few days every year."

Marva had dithered a little about getting in touch with Violet after her mother suggested talking to her "frail" sister. She finally did call her, and Violet didn't hesitate, said she'd be more than happy to have a housemate, knew they'd get along fine, she'd always thought Marva was a lot like her. Surprised by that comment—what made her think they were a lot alike—Marva concluded it was meant as a compliment. One day she might ask.

"I like these cookies even better than the oatmeal ones," Marva said. "I have to watch myself or I'll put on ten pounds before Christmas, eating your baked goods."

Violet said, "I read recently it's dangerous to eat raw cookie dough. I've never made a batch of cookies in my life that I didn't eat some of the dough. Can't believe everything you read." She sipped at her tea. "You'll notice I seldom eat the cooked ones. It's the baking I enjoy. More than the product. Most I freeze and give away at Christmas."

After a stretch of silence as they drank their tea, Violet said, "I might as well tell you, Alvin's going to be a problem. I'm pretty sure he has his sights on inheriting something from me. Even as a kid he was a sneaky little bastard. Pardon my language. He snoops around when he's here. He'll be surprised when I eventually die and he finds out whatever's left, if there is anything, goes to charity."

"He'll think I have the same scheme?"

Her aunt leaned toward Marva. "Exactly. He'll already have heard, I'm sure, from some cousin somewhere—these are people who have nothing better to do than gossip—that you're living here. He'll start right in trying to undermine you."

Marva said, "I'm not looking for any trouble. I've had plenty to last a lifetime. Let's just wait and see what happens."

"You've been warned. I know you can take care of yourself. Now, let's make a list of things we "need" Alvin to do around the place. He won't do any of the work himself, but he's quite the hand at hiring things done. Of course, I get the bill, not Alvin."

By the time they finished making their list, it was after six. They'd come up with cleaning the gutters, trimming back the hedges around the house, recaulking the windows, and painting the inside of the garage. Violet said, "You're even better at this than I am. I told you we're alike. This is what I mean. We don't play by everyone else's rules."

Now Marva wouldn't have to ask Violet why she thought they were a lot alike. Her aunt's opinion was probably accurate to an extent, but not entirely. Violet had friends, and she seemed to feel at home in Jackson's Pond. She belonged. Marva couldn't recall ever feeling she belonged anywhere, and cultivating friendships took time and effort she'd never had to spare.

She said, "I need to take my walk—work off the snickerdoodles and gather my strength if I'm going to beat Alvin at his own game."

"I rode the exercise bicycle earlier, so I'll sit here and think of more to add to this chore list. He'll be here Thursday."

Marva talked to herself aloud, a lot. She'd gotten in the habit years ago when she lived alone with her baby so far from town that she didn't see another person for days. The sound of her own voice comforted her out there, reminded her that even if no one knew it, she was alive and planning to stay that way. Now, many years later, she'd changed the pattern a bit. Instead of shouting like she had as she trudged down those lonely dirt roads on that New Mexico ranch, letting the universe know she was participating, now she kept her voice to a low mumble. Hearing her thoughts spoken aloud made them clearer to her. And if she came across anyone on the street there in Jackson's Pond, she kept her mouth shut.

It wasn't Alvin's impending visit she mumbled about as she made a circuit around the several blocks of Main Street. Her topics chose themselves. Often she didn't know until days later what propelled a particular stream of her words. She let it flow. *I see so many people every day, but I don't actually know any of them. I take that back, there are a few, like Joyce who forgets to bring her purse when she wants to buy stamps and comes back almost daily, always leaving without being able to buy. And there's Estella, the young one whose dark eyes tell me she's afraid when she's buying a money order and sending it to Mexico every week.*

Mostly I ask, "How can I help you?" They state their business and that's that. No "nice day," no one stopping to ask how I like it in Jackson's Pond. None of that. One day I counted how many said 'thank you' and how many of them sounded like they meant it. Answer: twenty-two, and eight.

At first I thought I liked it that way. Not burdened by people's expectations. But I see Violet, born here, leaving, teaching in several different places, then coming back, teaching high school English and theater to lots of the people still in town. She's ended up living here the majority of her years, fitting in here.

She paused as she checked the street for traffic before crossing in the middle of the block. Then she went on as she headed toward church row. *Little as I know about the people here, I already know more about any one of the ones I see at the post office than they all together know about me. Four months and so far not a single customer has asked my name, or if they read it on my tag, ever called me by my name. But I know their names, addresses, faces, and some of their habits. There's one woman who . . .*

A pickup horn beep interrupted her as she stopped and bent down to retie her left shoe. Pretending she hadn't heard, she stood and continued walking and talking. *Never mind that woman. This is about me. It's not as if I look unpleasant. I practice smiling to make sure. It's as if I am automatic, like a stamp machine might be, if we had a stamp machine* *here. Unless **I** make myself a person to them, most people won't give me any more thought than they would that machine. If we had one.*

It comes down to this. If I'm ever going to fit in anywhere, I have to be the one to make an effort. She walked on silently back toward Violet's house, thinking she might have forgotten long ago how to do that, make an effort.

As threatened, Alvin turned up two days later, Thursday. The tight set of Violet's jaw told her before her aunt even spoke. Violet said, "Let's go in my bedroom. We'll shut the door."

Marva had to hurry to keep up as Violet bustled to her room. Definitely not frail. As soon as they were inside, Violet shut the door and said, "Sit. You're going to love this. He's already told me twice in the four hours since he got here; he plans to move up here. He actually said, 'So I can be close and take better care of you.'" Violet inhaled a noisy breath, sat on the bed next to Marva, and then said, "That's what I get for tolerating him all these years. Should have told him outright I didn't need his supervision." She stood and paced to the window and back. "I can't keep him from living in any town he wants, but I can keep him from moving in here."

Marva said, "Where is he right now? I didn't see a car."

Violet said, "He drives a van!" She shook her head. "A grown man. Looks like something one of those serial killers you see on TV would drive." Then she laughed. "Listen to me, letting him get under my skin."

Her aunt's feisty reaction made her smile. "Did he specifically say he was planning to move in with you? Or did he say move to Jackson's Pond? Could he have been joking about moving in?"

"Sounded serious to me." Violet lifted a slat on the blinds and peered outside. "Come on. We have work to do."

Marva trailed behind as Violet led to the empty bedroom between their two. Her aunt said, "We're going to spread your things out between these two rooms. I'll say we're going to get it renovated, put a door in between the rooms and get rid of the one to the hall. So you'll have your own apartment." As she talked, she scooted a chair into a corner and then opened a closet door. "Move some of your clothes in here. Put your suitcases on the shelf. If you have any papers or other stuff stashed away, lay them out on the bed in here. Make it look occupied."

A few minutes later, the two of them working together had turned the empty bedroom messy—a laundry basket full of dirty clothes took space near the foot of the bed, the closet spewed clothes onto the carpet, and a vacuum cleaner leaned in a corner. Marva's actual bedroom also betrayed slovenly behavior. If Alvin didn't detest her before he arrived, he would soon.

Marva didn't intend to explain to Alvin anything about the arrangement she and Violet had agreed to. The only way she had been willing to intrude on Violet's space was to pay rent. So, before she moved in, they'd settled on a price, and while they were at it, they divided the housekeeping chores so Violet could stop paying someone to come in twice a month. They shared the cooking each evening, with Violet in charge of meal planning. None of that was Alvin's business. And Marva doubted Violet would be inclined to tell him either.

Violet sat on the couch in the den, fanning herself with a Texas Electric Coop magazine. "Before we got carried away creating your apartment, you asked where Alvin went. He marched directly into the kitchen as soon as he got here, opened the refrigerator and inspected it, then said, 'I'm going to the grocery store for provisions. Cooking for you is the least I can do.'" She laughed and shook her head. "He fancies himself an exceptional cook. I've always just stood back and let him since it keeps him from nosing around as much. But there's one word for his food. Inedible. Plus, he probably went out to the county line liquor store to buy beer. Jackson's Pond's still dry."

Marva said, "Aside from the chores he farms out, what else does he do when he's here?"

"Claims he's keeping me company, asking about my health, nosing around in the bathroom cabinets. Oh, and he rests a lot in the daytime because he camps out in the den watching old movies on my TV at night."

Marva said, "Maybe we can tolerate him for a week, just let him stay and then we can shoo him back to wherever he goes until next year."

"It's different this time. He plans to move in. Never leave! No, it's time to set him straight. I'm glad you're here, so I don't have to do it on my own."

The muscles in Marva's neck tightened and threatened a headache. She wondered if there was a baseball bat in the house.

About thirty minutes later, he turned up. The image she'd recalled of Alvin as a child had been a bit repulsive. Adult Alvin had turned into a large man, close to a foot taller than her and obnoxious. Rather than having grown to match his outsized ears and large mouth, as many do over the years, he'd been mistreated by time, rather than improved. He was flat ugly. As they greeted one another, Marva stifled a smile when Violet's serial killer comment came to mind.

Busying himself putting away groceries, he kept silent except for humming occasional snatches of music. "Colonel Bogie March," maybe. Hard to tell. Marva left him alone in the kitchen, and went to her bedroom, leaving the door open. She'd eavesdrop if he remembered how to speak. And eventually he did.

"Aunt Violet?" he said. No response. He raised the volume. "Violet, I'm calling you!" Still no response. He stomped out of the kitchen going toward the den. Marva tracked him by the sound of his footsteps. But the den was too far away for her to hear clearly, so she positioned herself in the hall bathroom. He shouted, "I called to you twice. But you didn't come or even answer. Is something wrong? Do you need new hearing aids?"

"Alvin, it is quite discourteous to shout me up like a dog. If you want to speak with me, come to where I am."

He mumbled something that might have been apologetic. Violet said nothing. Then he said, "I'll move my bags into my room. And I'll need space in the garage for some other things. Later, I'll get us a storage shed for my items that don't need to be in the house. And we can go through your attic, maybe have a garage sale. Years of collected possessions can be a burden."

"What are you going on about, Alvin? I do not need a storage shed. What you do with whatever you're hauling around is up to you, but it won't be stored here. And there will not ever be a garage sale on my property." Violet didn't give him a chance to say a thing. She went right on. "I'm certain you already know Marva isn't visiting; she lives here. The other two bedrooms are hers. That leaves no room for overnight visitors, and certainly not for anyone to move in." Violet brushed past Alvin, and Marva left her post in the bathroom to follow her to the kitchen.

Violet said to Alvin, "The Jackson's Pond Motel is a nice place these days. If you want to go check in and unload there, we can have supper later."

"I haven't had anything since breakfast," he said.

Marva and Violet left him standing in the kitchen surveying something in the refrigerator while they went back to the den. Alvin and his intention to take charge seemed laughable until several minutes later when he stomped in where they were reading. He carried a beer can in his right hand. Apparently it wasn't his first. His voice was at high volume, loud enough for neighbors to hear, if they were interested. "Supper will be fried pork chops, mashed potatoes, and green beans," he announced. "Dessert will have to be the ice cream I bought, the best I could do with the supplies you have here."

Violet, in charge in her own home, sat stone faced and let Alvin roar. Marva watched.

A few seconds later Alvin moved from the den doorway to a few inches from where Marva sat on the couch. She dropped her book, and sat forward. He towered over her, glaring at her between swigs of beer. He took a loud, raspy breath and said, "As for you. I know people like you who take advantage of the elderly. Pretending to be helpful. Your concern is nothing more than the patience of a vulture waiting for an injured animal to die." He paused long enough to turn the beer can up and gulp. Foam dribbled from the right corner of his mouth. "Then you'll strip this place clean of all its treasures."

Her hands trembling, she clenched her fists so the shaking wasn't visible. Her stomach lurched as she stood, her eye level zeroed at his neck and the wattle below his chin. He didn't move, obviously accustomed to backing others down. Not her.

She stepped forward one step, then a second, her shoes pushing flush against the toes of the down-at-the heels oxfords he wore. He stumbled back a few steps, shouting, his face reddening, "I know all about you. Dropped out of college chasing a cowboy. Caught him but weren't woman enough to keep him. No one in this family wants you around. Your daughter hates you, and your mother's ashamed to know you. So, you came here and played on Violet's sympathy." He took a final drink of the beer, then made a show of crushing the can in one hand. "Well, your time here's over. I'm moving in and seeing after Aunt Violet from now on. You've got until tomorrow evening to get out." By then he was breathing fast and gesturing widely, punctuating his pronouncements with the beer can squeezed in his left hand.

Violet slowly let down the footrest on her recliner, then stood. In a calm, steady voice at normal speaking volume, she said, "Alvin. There will be no more of this in my house. I will not have you speaking to Marva that way. You are not welcome here. Leave!"

Advancing another step, Marva said, "You'd better do as Violet says." The trembling in her hands had spread to her arms, but she knew from experience, she could live through that and the urge to vomit, and the pressure on her chest that would next rise to make breathing difficult. Even the roaring in her ears would eventually subside. She inhaled and stood straight. "Now."

By then Violet stood beside her, both of them facing Alvin, Violet with her phone in her hand. She said, "The sheriff's on my speed dial."

Alvin looked at both of them, then shook his head. His volume only slightly lower, he said, "I'm going out to eat now. You'll have to fend for yourselves. I'll sleep in my van tonight. When you're ready to apologize in the morning, I'll be parked in the driveway."

He executed a snappy turn, probably something he saw in an old movie, and strode toward the front door, which he slammed on his way out. Marva waited a few more seconds struggling with her ragged breathing, then hurried to lock the front door.

It took all her strength to walk to the den where Violet had returned to her recliner. Her aunt said, "I think a bowl of cereal will do fine for my supper. What about you?"

Marva nodded. She'd reacted this way plenty of times before. She could manage to be strong until she didn't have to be. Then she'd fall apart. "I'm going to rest a little while. Might have to miss

SCRABBLE tonight if you don't mind." She made it to the door, headed to her bedroom. Then she stopped and said, "Is there a baseball bat in this house? I'd feel safer if I had one nearby." An image of a shotgun under her bed sprang to mind, then disappeared in a second.

Violet laughed and got out of her chair. "I told you we think alike. Not only do I have a baseball bat in the pantry, there are burglar bars we can fit under the front and back door handles. If anyone pushes on the door, it makes a loud, screaming noise. And like I told Alvin, the sheriff's office is on speed dial. That's where they answer 911 calls." She reached the door and gave Marva a quick hug. "Oh, honey, you're trembling. You go rest. I'll bring the bat to your room and take care of the doors."

A phone call to the post office clerk was a must before she'd rest. All it took was a quick mention of a "sick headache; they often last for a couple of days, first one I've had in two years," and the clerk promised she'd handle things fine the next day. Marva wasn't about to leave Violet alone tomorrow to deal with Alvin. Yes, it was a lie, but she could live with it. She told it for the right reason.

Lying down, eyes closed, mind still racing, her heartbeat still roaring in her ears, Marva focused on her breathing. Bits from the many self-help books she'd read over the years flitted through her mind, disrupting her efforts to find calm. "Now" was the word she'd chosen long ago to help her dismiss intruding thoughts—the positive, you-can-be-in-charge-of-your-reactions pep talks as well as the negative you-cannot-breathe-and-you-are-going-to-die panic messages. All those must be erased.

She whispered, "Now." Then she inhaled and exhaled slowly. "Now." And again. "Now." Enough repetitions and her heart eventually settled to a normal rhythm; breaths became deeper and slower. And after a long while, she slept.

Around midnight, she woke, not startled but wary, still in the clothes she'd worn to work. The light was on in the hallway and another in the den. The carpet muffled her steps as she went down the hall, bat in hand, and found Violet asleep in her recliner, a book in her lap. Marva peeked through the blinds. The driveway was empty.

Even though her body had calmed and her thoughts no longer raced, her reaction to the episode with Alvin would recede fully only with time. She knew from experience that the longer she tried to ignore that loss of control, the longer it would be before she'd be able to face the next difficult situation calmly. She watched Violet's steady breathing, her relaxed posture. Then, without opening her eyes, her aunt said, "Marva. Come in and sit. Tell me what happened." Then Violet let down the footrest on her chair and faced her, smiling.

Marva said, "I didn't intend to wake you."

"It's not all about Alvin. Is it?"

Marva shook her head, then sat on the couch angled to Violet's right. "Not entirely. It's me. It's happened before."

"Often?"

"Not anymore. This is the first time in several years."

Violet nodded, left a long silence waiting to be filled.

Marva said, "Panic attack. Feels like I'm dying. The first time was the worst because, well, it was the first time. I was sure it was a heart attack or a stroke. It was worse because Rose Ellen was just over six months old, and she and I lived alone in a garage apartment. If I did die, she'd starve or die of dehydration or maybe hypothermia. But there I was lying on the floor, gasping for breath, my head pounding, my ears ringing. I tried to sit up, but my legs and arms were uncoordinated. I didn't know how I ended up on the floor, but there was a knot on my forehead. It was dark. The phone was off the hook, hanging down from the cabinet, that beeping and then the voice—if you want to make a call, hang up and dial the number—then the beeping again. I couldn't reach it. There was nothing I could do."

"Did you know what started it?"

Marva leaned forward. "A man had followed me from a gas station where I'd stopped on the way home after picking Rose Ellen up at child care. I was tired, working as many hours as I could get, so I didn't notice the pickup following close until I turned into the driveway. I rushed up the stairs and had just gotten in the apartment and locked the door, put the baby on the rug to practice crawling like the books said, and sat down. I told myself I was wrong. He wasn't following me. Then there he was banging on the door, pushing against it. I saw through the peephole he was big, older, dirty. The only thing I knew when it was over was that I had gotten the phone to call the police. But before I could, there I was having a heart attack or stroke or worse."

She held up her right hand, thumb and forefinger an inch or so apart. "I was that close to giving up." Then she was the silent one, looking away from Violet, thinking that she'd heard herself telling that story and feeling as if it were about someone else entirely. A stranger's tale.

Violet said, "But you didn't die, obviously. What happened?"

"When I woke up again—I didn't know if I'd fainted or lost consciousness or just gone to sleep—it was early morning. The door was still locked. Rose Ellen was crying this pitiful little cry as if she'd worn herself out. My head still hurt, but I was able to get up, change her, feed her, and get us both to bed. I was too shaky to work for a couple of days. I felt weak, had a headache, but I'd lived."

"Let me guess. You didn't go to the doctor."

Marva shrugged. "I was afraid I'd be told I was crazy. Or worse, no one would believe me. They'd tell me I had hit my head and imagined the rest. So, I never told anyone. If I had an attack and couldn't work, I used a migraine as my excuse. With the help of the library, I figured out I was having panic attacks. Read a lot of self-help books, some of them actually helpful. Advice about how to interrupt the process if it starts."

"Why now? After all these years? Was it Alvin?"

Tonight, it had been Alvin, a large man, standing above her, threatening, that her body reacted to. Sometimes, it could be the sight of a cowboy with his Stetson cocked at a too familiar angle. Marva shrugged again, "Alvin's big and really ugly. Maybe that's it?" She held her hands out in front of her; they were steady. "No chest pain, no more trembling. Nausea's gone. And Alvin's outside."

She changed into her pajamas, washed her face, brushed her teeth, and said to her reflection in the mirror, "Now." As she turned off her bedside light, she repeated, "Now."

The next morning, she was up before the sun. Alvin's van sat in the driveway, and Violet was in her bedroom, snoring softly. Marva dressed, went to the kitchen, and flipped on the coffee maker. She'd just sat at the small table when Violet said from the doorway, "I woke up and smelled the coffee." She chuckled and said, "It's seldom that a line is both literal and figurative."

Apparently the previous evening's drama hadn't dimmed the retired English teacher's good humor.

Marva said, "I'm happy to say I don't have that sick headache I lied about. Sleep took care of that. But you don't need to have to deal with Alvin alone." She set out cereal bowls and cereal and poured second cups of coffee for both of them.

Violet said, "I predict he'll leave without making too many more waves."

Marva said, "You know him and I don't, but I think we haven't heard the last of him." The words were barely out of her mouth when the doorbell rang several times, followed by banging on the front door.

Violet rose and walked slowly toward the entryway. Marva hurried directly to her bedroom and picked up the baseball bat, then followed Violet. At the front door, Violet said, "Who's there?" She gave a side glance toward Marva and smiled.

"You know damn well it's me, Aunt Violet. Let me in."

"I've told you a hundred times, I am not your aunt. And I told you to leave. If you're not gone within an hour, I *will* call the sheriff."

Alvin said, "Must you shout?"

"I want to be certain you hear me clearly."

He lowered his voice, as if he was suddenly concerned about the neighbors. "I need to use the bathroom. I'll be gone by noon if you'll just let me in now. I have to eat or I'll get hypoglycemic and can't drive. You know I must eat every four hours."

Violet shook her head, rolling her eyes at his plea for food. "I know that's the excuse you use to justify eating all the time." She whispered to Marva, "We could let him in to use the bathroom, hand him the food he bought last night, and tell him to hit the road. What do you think?"

"I have the baseball bat." She wished for a speckled dog and a shotgun.

Violet said, "We'll let you in to use the bathroom. Then you will take your food and leave. No argument. No further discussion. Do you understand?"

Silence, then a sound like the storm door being kicked. More silence. Then Alvin said, "Yes."

Violet removed the burglar bar with the siren attached and opened the door. Marva stood beside her, making no attempt to hide the baseball bat she gripped like a walking stick. As he stalked in, Alvin glared in her direction, but kept moving toward the hall bathroom. She and Violet quickly filled a grocery bag with the items he'd brought in the day before, including the one remaining Lone Star beer.

They stood together near the front door, waiting, as Alvin came out of the bathroom. Violet said, "Here are your groceries."

He took the bag, peered into it, then held it in front of his chest in both hands. "I can't believe you allowed this woman to turn you against me. But when you come to your senses and see her for what she is, all you have to do is call me. That's the kind of understanding relative I am."

Violet didn't respond. Instead, she opened the door to urge him out.

Near the door, he turned and faced Marva. Shifting the groceries to his left arm, and pointing the thick, stubby index finger of his right hand at her, he said, "As for you, I'll do all I can to see that everyone in this town knows the kind of person you are. When I finish no one will care what happens to you." His face flushed and he clutched the grocery bag to his side. "You'll be sorry you crossed me. Mark my words."

In her earlier life, she might have simply bowed her head under such hateful words and waited for the worst. But now—no. She stepped toward Alvin and said, "No matter what you think of me, no matter whether I live here with Violet or in a house of my own, Jackson's Pond is going to be my home. So just bear this in mind: I'll be here and I'll be watching for you."

She rapped the bat against the floor and stepped closer to Alvin.

He didn't look back as he lumbered to his van.

As he backed out of the driveway, Marva cut a glance at her aunt and said, in a voice that mimicked Violet's, "Who's there?" When Violet laughed, Marva said, "You're right. We are a lot alike."

Jackson's Pond Leader
Thursday, October 19, 2017
Good Words
By Sue Jane Goodman

The purpose of this column is to shine a spotlight on individuals, groups, and/or actions in our community that deserve notice or commendation. In some cases, the topic will be an uncommon event that elevates the spirit of others.

Other items that turn up here might relate to selfless individual actions that help others and go otherwise unnoticed. The intention is to encourage all of us to see the good that's all around us every day.

Today's good words are Thank You— to Volunteer Firefighters.

The recent wildfire that burned more than 200 acres of grassland near Jackson's Pond was stopped by volunteer firefighters before damaging any homes or livestock. It wasn't luck; it was dedicated training and action by our neighbors who volunteer on behalf of our community. Thank You!

Sue Jane Goodman is a full-time parent and part-time volunteer in the Jackson's Pond City Hall.

CHAPTER 14

October, 2017
Female in Distress

Chick Talley leaned against the doorframe, waiting, while the woman in charge unlocked the door to the post office business counter that morning. He hadn't been able to remember her name, but he was pretty sure she wouldn't like being called any kind of "mistress." He could tell by that name tag. Postmaster, it said, big as life. He'd made finding out about her his business when she turned up replacing the man who retired. Asked around about her a bit without learning much of anything. She reminded him of someone he couldn't place, and he wasn't ready to ask her directly anything like who her people were let alone her name.

He nodded as she opened the door from the inside and stood back to let him pass. He mustered a smile and, "Ma'am," like it was a title, as he touched an index finger to the brim of his Stetson, his version of a friendly greeting. She said, "Did you need something this morning?"

He reversed direction, saying, "Back in a few minutes." His mind was on the other things he intended to do at the post office, not on messing with the woman who belonged behind the mail counter. He went toward the two walls of mailboxes out in the area that stayed open to the public. Others would be trailing in here soon, and he had news to check out, information to gather.

One thing he would say, if he needed to fill the air with her some morning while he waited for the guys, was that since she'd been there, the post office was cleaner and smelled better than it ever had. That particular day as he put his key in the lock on box 728, he detected the aroma of something like lemon and leather, a scent pleasant to men. From the looks of her, he guessed she'd know about that. He chuckled to himself at that thought as he emptied the box. He sorted through five charity appeals and a farm store circular to find the only two pieces of real mail—a bill from the electric coop and a notice his land and real estate appraiser's license both had to be renewed. He stuffed that one in his hip pocket. Keeping all his licenses up to date was getting to be a full-time job. But doing business out here meant doing lots of different things. That coop bill was something else entirely. His ex-wife hadn't taken his name off the account and it'd been three years now.

Out front Jackie Fred Martin looked like he was having trouble with his pickup tailgate. Chick watched through the glass doors for a few seconds, then pulled a pen from his shirt pocket and scrawled Maxine Talley 1423 Sixth Street, Jackson's Pond, TX on the electric bill envelope. Let them figure out the zip code. After dropping the bill in the outgoing mail slot and disposing of the junk mail in the trash, he opened the front door and yelled, "Need any help?"

"I did. Don't anymore," J.F. yelled back. One final slam and the tailgate stayed closed. "I seen you watching, you lazy SOB."

As soon as he was in the door, J. F. poked Chick on the shoulder, more a tap than a real punch. "Thanks for offerin'." He leaned against the short counter in the mailbox section, right next to Chick. "What's new with you?"

Chick turned so they were side by side both facing toward the door. He frowned a little and rubbed along his jaw at a place his razor had missed. "Let's see—no rain in six weeks, price of cattle down a nickel. But I guess you listened to the markets and the weather reports this morning without my help. You planning to plant wheat this year?"

"It's what dry land farmers do next, ain't it? Hoping for rain before I haul out the wheat drill." J. F. paused, looked off south into the distance. "You?"

Chick gave a noncommittal nod, followed J.F.'s gaze to the grain elevator four blocks away. J. F. pushed back the brim of his gimme cap. He said, "Guess you heard about that plane crash."

"Plane crash? Where?" Chick said.

Being first with the news was always a plus. But letting on you had the information first wasn't always prudent. Even with the Internet, some people just didn't pay attention, not close enough. And getting information was Chick's specialty. That and making deals. He turned toward J.F. and said, "What'd you hear?"

"Private plane, maybe some kind of stunt plane, went down yesterday evening late out north, close to the Jackson Ranch. Maybe on the old Reese place. I was thinking about running out there later on just to take a look."

"He run into one those wind towers?"

"More like he just run into the ground, so I hear. A spray pilot by trade, young one. Not originally from here. Lorenzo, I think."

Both of them went quiet when the Church of Christ preacher's wife opened the door. Wayne Holmes followed immediately behind her. The woman went through the second door toward the business counter. Holmes nodded to Chick and J.F. and said, "Be right with you."

He was back from the mailboxes in less than a minute with a fistful of mail that looked a lot like what Chick had scored. Turned out Wayne hadn't heard about the plane crash. The next three farmers, who came in all together like a band of roving roofers, denied knowing anything as well. Chick looked at his watch and said, "Gotta go. Things to do, people to see."

As they walked out the front door together, J. F. said, "Nice to see you never change, Chick. Full of shit as always. I'll bet you're only going as far as the coffee room at the bank." He gave a tug on his tailgate, then got in his pickup and said, "Don't work too hard today."

His old friend was wrong. Chick turned around and went back inside the post office to the counter. "Need a roll of stamps," he said. Then he laid a fifty on the counter and added, "Please, ma'am."

She didn't actually change the blandly pleasant look on her face, so he'd be hard pressed to call it a smile. But the fraction of an inch her left eyebrow rose told him he'd gotten a little bit of a reaction. Good enough for now.

He left his pickup parked out front and walked slowly two blocks down Main Street to the newly reopened funeral home. About nine months ago the town council bought a piece of land he owned next to the cemetery in order to reopen it for burials. With all the new arrivals in town thanks to Jesko's plant out north, and the six new businesses that had followed, the town had new residents. Some of them were sure to need burying at some point. After selling the town the land for the expansion of the cemetery, Chick had made what he considered his best deal in a long time. It ended up with him as the silent partner in the new Jackson's Pond branch of a chain of funeral homes spreading through small West Texas towns. Went to some legal pains to make sure the silent part would stay that way. Only by a thorough search of county records would anyone ever know Chick owned half of the business, not even the undertaker who ran it.

The new undertaker, who'd coincidentally bought a house from Chick's real estate business, was an employee of the organization headquartered in Amarillo. He'd redone the place so it was all up to date, including a crematorium.

If anyone asked, today Chick was just stopping in to continue talking with the man in charge about making advance arrangements for his own eventual departure. Smart people made plans, he'd tell anyone nosy enough to ask.

The undertaker, who pleasantly corrected Chick by saying "funeral director," proved to be predictable. As soon as Chick said, "I had a few questions about those arrangements I made. Might need to make a change or two. But from what I hear you're probably busy today." He acted as if he planned to leave and let the man get to embalming or whatever.

At that point, the undertaker said, "Well, yes. Perhaps another day would be better. We *are* handling the arrangements for a young man's service, accidental death. I suppose you've heard. Small town." His face suggested he'd been personally acquainted with the departed. Then after a second or two, the sadness disappeared, replaced by a professional smile and a brisk "all business" tone of voice. "I was reading over the facts, about to write the obituary for the wife's approval." He lifted a sheet from his desk, turned the paper where Chick could read it.

- Hezekiah Daniel Burkwalter, age 42, Born January 13, 1975 Died October 14, 2017

- Born in Nazareth, TX, current resident of Floyd County
- Owner of Dan's Ag Spray Service
- Graduate of Nazareth High School, attended West Texas A & M University
- Survived by wife Maricella and daughter Rebecca, both of Floyd County
- Interests included stunt flying, bird hunting, and his home and family
- Service arrangements pending at Jackson's Pond Funeral Home

Chick looked up from scanning the fact sheet. "I thought you said young."

The funeral director said, "It's a manner of speaking, I suppose. Age being relative. And speaking of relative, it seemed interesting to me, him being from Nazareth—all those big German families out there—that she, the wife, didn't list any relatives besides herself and their one child. And from the looks of it, she's pregnant with another. But that's not my business." He picked up the piece of paper and turned a professional smile toward Chick. "Will you be able to drop by Thursday afternoon?"

"Sure, I'm in no rush." He headed toward the door, noticing as a proud owner would, the thick, plush carpet. "By the way, when's the visitation? I have a feeling I may know some distant kin of his."

"I'll be suggesting tomorrow evening, subject to her approval."

Chick assured him he'd be back Thursday assuming nothing came up.

Before the day was over, he'd located the two farms the deceased operated in the northeast corner part of the county and as a bonus had managed to get historical information on those farms from the woman in the County Clerk's office. Some generations past, that land had belonged to a couple of brothers, both Burkwalters. What he hadn't been able to get was a notion of whether Dan owned the property outright or had big debt on it. Chick wasn't worried; he'd get it.

So, the next evening, some soft instrumental music which sounded faintly familiar played in the visitation room. Mrs. Burkwalter sat on a couch across from the door, flanked by a young girl Chick presumed was Rebecca, and a man who appeared to be around thirty-five. He had a farmer's tan, blond hair, and blue eyes. Both of the Burkwalter females had dark hair and dark eyes. When Chick introduced himself, the wife's response, "Thank you for coming," carried a bare hint of a Spanish accent.

"Please accept my condolences, Mrs. Burkwalter." He nodded at the girl and said, "You're Rebecca?"

Tears in her eyes threatened to spill over as she said, "Yes, sir."

"Mind if I sit?" As he said it, he pulled a folding chair up close to the couch, facing the wife. He continued standing and introduced himself to the man, the only other person in the room, and for all Chick knew, a mute because he only looked up at Chick and gave a single nod. No offer of a handshake, no mention of his name.

Since no one told him not to, he sat on the chair and said, "Being a spray pilot's a dangerous business. I guess you always worried about Dan when he left the house."

The daughter frowned and turned toward the silent man. Her mother said, "My husband didn't do much of the spraying, not since we married. He has, had, two pilots who did that. Mostly he farmed and worked on his stunt plane."

He kept his mouth shut, waiting to see if she'd say more. She was now a widow who probably just inherited land. And if what she said about the farm was true, there was probably a cotton crop already growing and winter wheat might soon be coming up on some part of that land. Although she was pretty, in her pregnant way (give the undertaker credit for understatement—the woman was surely at least six months along), it wasn't her looks that caught Chick's interest. It was her situation.

"I didn't know he was going to fly that plane. Not yet. He'd been working on it in that barn for months, at least seven months."

Her voice changed, thickened. Chick reached for the box of tissues on the nearby end table, handed it to her. "He never told me he was, never said goodbye or anything." Then the tears flowed.

Still no other visitors. Chick had pretty much run out his string. He patted her hand one last time and wondered at the same moment why the daughter seemed so detached. There but not there. He stood and said, "I'm sure you have family and friends who'll help you with your farm now that Dan's gone. But if there's anything I can do, well, here's my card. I know quite a bit about farming and dealing with land. I'd be happy to advise you. Help any way I can."

She took the card and said, "Tell me how you knew Dan."

He hesitated, then sat on the chair again. "Tell the truth, I'm not certain I did. It was a long time ago. I had some cotton needed spraying, defoliation, and I'm pretty sure he was the one who did it. Must have been ten or fifteen years ago." If he was lucky, that would be before the man had married her. The daughter looked about twelve, kind of coltish, teeth still too big for her face. No need to raise suspicion, so he went on. "I'm not sure. Might have been from the coop meetings, some time back. When I heard, and the name rang a bell, well, it seemed like the right thing to do for a fellow farmer to come and offer condolences. Offer help."

She looked at the card in her hand. The daughter stared into space. The silent man squinted at him. Chick left.

Driving to his farm, two things came to him. First, the only way a dead person was sure to have funeral home visitors was to be a church member. He had as little family as Dan had. So when Chick talked to that undertaker again, he was going to tell him when his time came, don't schedule any visitation. Just get the funeral done.

The second thing was he needed to see what he could find out about Dan's Ag Spray Service. Maybe he had a partner. Maybe it was that silent guy. Didn't matter a whole lot, Chick wasn't in the market to own a spray service.

Thursday afternoon Chick presented himself at the funeral home again. He'd come up with a couple of items about the plans for his burial plans to justify the visit. He'd almost crossed the whole spray pilot thing off his list. There were plenty of other opportunities he could poke around in. But something about that silent fellow at the visitation bothered him. So he'd spent the evening before sipping at a glass of bourbon, thinking about dying. Not exactly the dying or what from, but the what after. Turned him sort of grim. He woke up without his usual vigor. Blamed the whiskey, but knew better. He told himself he needed a new project. Acquiring land never failed to improve his attitude.

The funeral director focused on the open file on his desk. Without looking up at Chick, he said, "Are you familiar with the ancient custom of using moirologists?"

"Can't say as I am." He tried making light of a limited vocabulary by saying, "Must not have been in the Spelling Bee list the year I won."

Without displaying a trace of emotion, the funeral director said, "Paid mourners. It's a respectable occupation, very important in some cultures."

"Well maybe some countries ...but around here? Wait, are you suggesting that might be something to plan for my funeral?" Chick couldn't help laughing. He leaned back in his chair and said, "You know, thinking about my funeral had kind of made me gloomy. But you just fixed that. Hadn't heard anything as funny in a while."

"Suppose you live to be ninety-nine, have no living children, no classmates, no surviving family except the children of a few cousins you haven't seen in more than eighty years. If not for paid mourners it would be you and the preacher and the gravedigger." He paused as if considering that scene, his face displaying sadness at the very thought. Then as if it just occurred to him, he said, "And what if it's a cremation? Not even a gravedigger present. Push a button and the deceased slides into the . . . well, that's irrelevant because you've said you want burial."

Chick straightened up in his chair. "Well, before we change the subject, which I want to do, I have one more question. Say a person wanted one of these criers, where would you find them?"

That actually bought a smile from the man across the desk. He said, "I have a list."

Chick nodded and pondered that. Then he said, "Well, you've given me more things to think about. There's no hurry, so I'll come back another time so we can finish this up." He stood and headed toward the door, then turned back and said, "Speaking of funerals, how did that one yesterday go? I felt bad being the only person at the visitation. For the wife and daughter, I mean."

"The word I'd choose is odd, to say the least. It's what made me think of professional mourners." The funeral director nodded like he was pondering what else to say. "She asked me to conduct a simple service, no minister. The only people present were the wife, the daughter, and that man, the one who never said a word. I had my people carry the coffin. Aside from her having a service rather than just a burial, when it was only the three of them, the other odd thing was that man's attitude. I had the impression she didn't want him there, but he sat right next to her between her and the girl. All the time, his eyes shifting from one to the other and then around the cemetery. The place was deserted except for the man who drives the backhoe. And he was clear over by the gate."

"Never said anything?"

"Not to me." After funeral director said that, he was quiet a few seconds. "Took maybe fifteen minutes, start to finish." Then he shrugged. "A couple of professional mourners could have come in handy."

"Takes all kinds, I guess."

The funeral director shrugged again. "Maybe I shouldn't say, but I had the feeling she was afraid of something."

As Chick left, he wondered if Mrs. Burkwalter would call him. Maybe he shouldn't wait too long to find out.

The post office counter closed at four, so he made it in with ten minutes to spare. No other customers in sight—maybe he could waste a little of the postmaster's time. She appeared from someplace he couldn't see. And this time there was a trace of an actual smile when she said, "How can I help you today?"

"Three postcards, please, ma'am."

That eyebrow again, and the smile didn't disappear. Inspiration struck Chick just as she handed him the three postcards.

He said, "I know it's close to time to lock the doors. But until then, since there's no one in line behind me, could I ask a question that's not post office business, not related at all?"

She cocked her head to the right a fraction. "You can ask. I don't know if I'll have an answer."

"Fair enough. You heard about the pilot who crashed and died?"

She nodded.

"First off, I admit I got interested, even though I doubt if I knew him, thinking his widow might plan to sell their place. I'm a land appraiser, always scouting for work."

The postmaster wrinkled, just a tiny bit, between her eyes. She said, "I hear you also have quite a bit of land. Always looking to buy or sell."

His turn to nod. He told her she'd heard right, then quickly explained that right now he was less concerned about land than he was about the widow.

"Looking for a land-rich widow to marry?" That came with a playful look that suggested she might be kidding, or might not.

"Not anymore." He hesitated, then said, "Decided a while back I wasn't much good at marriage."

She waited, giving away nothing with that pleasant professional expression she was wearing.

He said, "I went to the visitation. I was the only person there the whole time except for her, the daughter, and some man who never spoke a word. Maybe he doesn't do English. But I got the distinct feeling she was afraid, and maybe the daughter was, too. I thought I'd ask if you know her. You see lots of people every day."

"I have seen her, but don't know her. What made you think she's afraid?"

He shrugged. "I know it sounds dumb, but it's just a feeling."

"All I can tell you is they have a mailbox at the house, way out on the north rural route. But she sometimes comes in and mails packages. And before you ask, I can't say where or who to."

"I understand. I was hoping maybe she went to the same church you do or some women's group."

"You're asking the wrong person about church. And the only women's group I'm part of is the little two person one—me and my seventy-nine-year-old aunt." She looked at her watch. "Got to lock the door now."

He aimed himself toward the door. Then she said, "Wait a second." She disappeared and reappeared at another door set back in the wall opposite the counter. "My office," she said, nodding her head backward at the small door. As she went to lock up, him tagging behind, she said, "What did the man look like?"

He gave a quick description as he stepped into the mailbox area.

"Sounds like a guy who works on a farm out north. Came in here a couple of times. Maybe he worked for her husband. He does speak; it's English, but sounds a little different, like Australians do." She looked at her watch again.

"I'm going to keep asking around, but if you hear anything, would you give me a call?" He handed her his card. "Or if you just want to talk sometime."

As she locked the door, he noticed she was prettier when she smiled. He still couldn't remember her name.

Several days later Chick found a message on his machine at his office. "This is Maricella Burkwalter. I need to talk to you." A long pause followed. He heard a few rapid breaths. Then the voice said, "Privately. Please call this number." She reeled it off, and finished by saying, "Speak only to me. Do not leave a message." After another pause, a final word, "Please."

He'd read a few spy novels, and when he played the message twice more, the same sensation he imagined a covert operative felt crept up the back of his neck—adrenaline powered hyper-alert wariness. He scrawled the number she'd given on a notepad, tore off the sheet and folded it into a one-inch square, intending to hide it and call back after he'd given the whole thing some thought. Then he sat still with his eyes closed until the pulse he heard in his ears disappeared. It only took a couple of minutes. When he reopened his eyes, he felt pretty sure she didn't want to talk about land appraisal. The square of paper in his left hand felt like a rock. He opened it, copied the numbers off onto the inside of his khaki shirt cuff, and tore the paper into confetti. Then he erased the phone message.

In the bathroom he scattered the bits on the water in the toilet and flushed, telling himself as he watched the water swirl that it was for her protection. Back at his desk, he said aloud, "And you're a fool, Chick Talley." He confirmed that by tearing off and shredding the notepad sheet under the one he'd written on.

Later that afternoon, he stood alone inside the laundromat operated as a service by the Give Praise Church. Housed in a long-abandoned building one block off of Main Street, the enterprise had been one of his no-profit sales. Now and then he reminded himself that civic duty demanded that everyone share the burden of keeping commerce alive in their small town. And on those occasions, he'd been known to go the other side of break-even on a piece of property right on into taking a loss. The best part of finishing off one of those deals was never uttering to anyone that he'd done the town a good turn. Just kept it to himself. Virtue is its own reward. His grandmother had drilled that into him.

He wondered what his grandmother would think about this urge that impelled him to go to the payphone at the laundry to return that phone call. No one would bother to bug his office phone, but there was such a thing as caller ID and Mrs. Burkwalter's message suggested she was concerned about privacy, so no message. He lifted the receiver, then replaced it. Feeling in his pockets, he came up with four pennies, a dime, and one nickel. The instruction on the phone stipulated twenty-five cents.

In his pickup, a search of the center console and both cup holders netted only three more pennies. He sat with the driver side door open, reminding himself once again that he was a fool. A pickup pulled in perpendicular behind his. With his motor still running, Jackie Frank yelled, "Need some help?"

Chick shook his head. His pal said, "Washing machine broke at home?"

"No. I just pulled in here to hunt for a CD I thought I had. Willie's latest. Not in the console, or the side pockets. Guess I left it at the house." As he reeled off that excuse, even he thought it sounded lame. But there it was.

Jackie Frank was out of his vehicle by that time, walking toward Chick. "Missed you at coffee this morning. Feelin' okay?"

"Fine, just slept a little late. Hear any news?"

Chick's friend and high school classmate pretended to ponder the question. "Let's see. Helicopter was called last night to take Nancy Dickson. Stroke. Doing okay at St. Margaret's in Lubbock. You know she's younger than we are."

Chick said, "We aren't all that young, if you haven't noticed."

"Must be a burden on you, pointing out the obvious to me all the time." Jackie Frank stepped back, then said, "Oh. Tag Butler said the spray pilot found that wife of his on the Internet. They just been married maybe four years."

"Hmmm. Internet, huh. I heard most of those brides came from Russia. Course I never looked for a bride on the Internet, so I don't know." He hadn't mentioned to Jackie Frank that he'd met the woman. Didn't intend to now. But still. He said, "Butler know anything else?"

"Only what his wife told him about feeling sorry for the woman cause she stayed on the place all the time, home-schooled her daughter, didn't come to town much, even to church. No friends. His wife took a cake over after the funeral and said the widow seemed real upset, maybe afraid. Didn't even invite Miz Butler in."

Chick pulled his door shut. "Thanks for checking on me." He pointed to his watch. "I've got an appointment in a few minutes." He intended to thank him for the news, too, but Jackie Frank was already back in his pickup pulling away by then.

At his office, which comprised two rooms in a storefront facing Main Street, where he'd installed one-way glass in the large windows across the front, Chick sat at the desk nearest the front so he could see out without being seen, not the one he usually occupied at the back of the room. This desk stood unused on the days his bookkeeper and woman-of-all-work was off. Although she had no formal job description, she basically took care of every detail of his business without having to be told. It was her nature to be nosy, so she knew about most of Chick's deals before he even put them on paper. So far the only exceptions were the funeral home arrangement, and the shameful details of the settlement he'd agreed to in order to get rid of that last wife. He'd have chewed off his foot if that was what it took to get out of that trap of a marriage.

A single room with a bathroom and storage in a separate back space completed his unsumptuous office. There was no sign outside. Private. He liked it that way. He'd have been happier keeping his business on scraps of paper in his back pocket, but he'd long ago passed the point where that was practical. He'd done very well for himself over the years business-wise. Records must be kept.

He turned on his assistant's computer, thinking he'd do a search of sites introducing single men to Spanish-speaking women. As soon as the browser started up, he turned the machine off, whirled the desk chair around, and stood. Any seventh-grade kid knew that every computer search left tracks. The next time she opened her computer, his helper would be greeted by offers to connect her with Spanish-speaking women eager to meet foreign men. He stalked to his own desk. Using his own computer he searched for information about citizenship status of foreign women who marry U.S. citizens. Just as he thought, Maricella would have permanent residence status, the green card, even though Dan had died. She didn't have to sell out and leave if she didn't want to, at least not because she'd be deported.

He grabbed the phone off its hook when it rang. Maricella's voice, urgent, breathless, said, "Meet me at the clinic. I am bringing Rebecca for a flu shot this afternoon at two. If he is with me . . ." After a pause, she said, "I will leave a magazine in the chair where I sit. After I leave, find the letter inside. Do not talk to me."

What the hell?

At 1:45 p.m., Chick stepped into the clinic waiting room. He scanned the room and didn't see Maricella or Rebecca anywhere. From the desk several feet away, a receptionist said, "May I help you?"

He ambled across the room, and eased up to the counter in front of the woman who'd hailed him. "Thinking I ought to get a flu shot this year. Are they available yet?'

She explained that there would be a wait, maybe thirty minutes. "We're very busy today." A big smile, and then she said, "If you don't mind waiting, you can go ahead and sign in."

"Be right back. I have to check on a business appointment, see if I can make it if I wait for the shot."

She nodded and repeated her offer of help to a woman who had stepped up behind him. The toddler on her hip coughed and started whining. That kid needed the doctor more than he did, for certain. Besides, he never took flu shots. He turned to scout the room again before leaving—it was already ten after two. Just then Maricella and Rebecca came out from the door to the exam rooms. Maricella carried a magazine in her right hand. As she passed him, she said, "Something to read while you wait?"

He took the magazine without glancing at her, thinking she'd seen too many James Bond movies. By the time he seated himself, she and Rebecca were exiting the clinic. He was careful not to stare. A couple of minutes later he stopped by the counter and explained he couldn't wait and would be back another day. The magazine, a year-old *Texas Co-op Power* rolled into a cylinder, stuck out of his hip pocket, but no one stopped him from leaving with it.

Parked outside the post office, Willie Nelson singing "Last Man Standing" as mood music, Chick held the envelope he'd found in the magazine. So far he hadn't opened it. What reason did he have to get mixed up with that woman's troubles? With the unopened envelope still stuffed in his pocket, he got out of the pickup and made his way into the post office. If she was at the counter and no one else was there . . . well, he'd see when he got inside. No mail in his box; no line at the counter; no postmaster in sight. He leaned forward, getting close enough to the counter to peer into the back, and just then he heard her say, "Did you need some help, Mr. Talley?"

He turned toward the sound. The door to her office was open a crack, just enough for him to see her sitting at a desk inside. "Not post office business. I'll let you get back to your work. I just. . ."

"Hold on." The door shut and seconds later she stood at the counter. "Paperwork," she said. "Something on your mind?"

Now that she was there, he wasn't sure what he wanted to say. He'd been thinking about getting a second opinion about the letter. Even though he hadn't read it, he had a feeling that opening it was taking a step that would be hard to turn back from. Hell, he didn't even know the Burkwalter woman. Her problems weren't his to solve. At the same time, it had been his own greed—yes, he admitted it to himself—that had sent him to that visitation in the first place. And greed is one of seven deadlies, right? He said, "You have the advantage on me, knowing my name. But I don't know yours. Mind telling me?"

"Marva Cope." That wrinkle showed up between her eyebrows again. "That all you wanted?"

"Recall I asked about that widow?"

"Yes, I do. And no, I haven't heard anything else."

Then, since they were the only ones in the post office, Chick gave her the short version about Maricella's message on his machine and the stealthy delivery of the envelope. Then he pulled it from his pocket.

Marva said, "You haven't opened it."

"Points to you." He shifted and leaned on the counter. "Now that I'm older I've figured out something about myself. I'm a sucker for a woman in distress. Not always a healthy way to be. I hoped you might be willing to give me a woman's opinion on whatever's in here, and what, if anything, I ought to do."

The Postmaster said, "She'd be easy to be a sucker for. Real pretty."

More points to her. Lots of women won't compliment another female. Hearing her say that confirmed what he thought. With no basis whatever, he already trusted Marva Cope.

He said, "It's not so much that, it's the fear in her eyes. I think it's real." He waited to see if she might volunteer. If he was smart, he'd probably tear up the letter right now and get back in his pickup, stay home for about a month until he talked himself out of getting involved with any females, no matter how exceptional he thought they were.

"Why me?"

He laughed and shook his head. "I don't really know. But I figure if the post office trusts you to handle mail, you must be okay. And women understand other women better than most men can."

After a long look that suggested she could read his mind, she shrugged and said, "Okay. But not now, not here." Then she gave him an address. "Six o'clock. My aunt will be watching TV in the den. She won't bother us."

Later, sitting side by side at the dining room table at her aunt's house, they opened the letter and read silently. They both finished the third and final page about the same time. Marva moved to sit across from him. She said, "What do you think?"

"I think she has reason to be afraid. She needs a good lawyer. And the sheriff needs to know."

Marva said, "I agree about the lawyer. Her husband's will may make her owner of the land and business. That needs to be seen to right away. So far the hired man hasn't actually done anything he could be arrested for, if this is the whole story. And he's told her she'll be deported because she's not a citizen yet. That's not true. I know that for a fact."

Chick thought a few seconds, then said, "Sounds as if he won't let her out of his sight, and he won't leave even though she told him to. But a lawyer could get a restraining order, arrest him if he bothers her."

Her frown was back. "If it's like she says, that he wants the daughter, he might just take her and run. Or worse, kill Maricella to get the daughter. He sounds obsessed to me, crazy." She took a deep breath. "I think you ought to talk to the sheriff right now. Not some deputy, the sheriff."

"Without telling Maricella?"

After about thirty more minutes of trading what ifs, he said he'd go to the sheriff's office in Calverton first thing in the morning and take the letter. And he would try to get in touch with Maricella after that. He thanked Marva for her help and stood to leave. She said, "In case you're wondering, I won't tell anyone anything about this. And if you talk to her, tell her I'll help her if I can, if she needs a friend."

"If you don't want to get involved in this mess, I'd understand."

"I'm offering. I wouldn't if I didn't mean it. Just tell her."

That night, at home, Chick left off the drink before supper, which ended up being a bowl of raisin bran, and reread Maricella's letter.

To: Señor Talley

I am writing this to you because you are the only person who has offered help.

My husband was a good man. I admit I looked for someone to save me and my daughter by using a dating site on the Internet. I spent hours searching at a public Internet shop near the place I lived in Caracas. This letter is not about my sad life before I found him.

It is true that my daughter and I would not have survived long if he had not rescued us. We corresponded for months before he made the trip there and brought us to Texas where we married nearly five years ago. Immediately, I was grateful. Soon, I loved him with all my heart. He adopted Rebecca and treated her as his own. And I intended to give him the son he wanted so much.

Chick didn't doubt any of what he was reading. He knew about wanting a son. And although he didn't know from personal experience about the kind of life she might have had before, imagining gratitude turning to love was easy. He blinked to clear his vision and read on.

I could not believe the fine house he had and the farm. He told me the house and barns were all he owned. The land belonged in his family who live in another town. I didn't care. We had food and shelter and clothing and Dan loved us both.

Then seven months ago Jacob Hogner came wanting work. He was in Texas because he had come from South Africa to work at a dairy in a town many miles from here. But his visa had run out and they fired him. Soon I could see why they would not want him. The man is evil. Dan's good heart would not let him believe that Jacob is dangerous. He would come to the house when Dan was away, asking questions about Rebecca, calling me names, and every day reminding me that if I told Dan, he would kill us all.

I did tell Dan. He only said Jacob was a big joker. When I told him Jacob said he was going to marry Rebecca and take her away with him, Dan said, "He's only joking. After all, she's a child." I even told him about men in my country who take children like Rebecca and sell them for evil purposes. He would not believe Jacob could be that sort of person. But he said, "Soon as he gets his visa straightened out, I will tell him to move on if that will make you feel safe." He was treating me like a child.

Having Jacob for farm work gave Dan more time for his plane and he promised he would have it finished soon and wouldn't need Jacob. But the day after the crash Jacob told me he was going to leave and take Rebecca with him, as soon as I got my money. Until then, he was taking charge, he said. He said I would need him because now that Dan was dead I would be deported. He shouted at me, "You are not a citizen here. Before long they will come after you, too."

He was red in the face and waving a gun when he said all this. The last thing he said was that if I got in his way at all, he would kill me.

I cannot call the police. I cannot tell anyone. He watches me constantly. Rebecca is so afraid that she has not been able to eat, she barely sleeps, even though I have her in my bed as when she was a baby. I fear also for my unborn baby, Dan's son.

I do not know what to do.

Maricella Burkwalter

Chick couldn't think of a reason in the world for her to have made up the story. Staring at the letter left him too sad to do anything but go to bed.

He woke in the night thinking about his first wife, Kara Ann, his only wife as far as he was concerned—that second one didn't count. Kara Ann would have told him he had to help that woman. He could hear her voice, the same way he often did here at the house. He hadn't changed a thing in the thirty-two years since the cancer took her, never moved the furniture, left all the paintings on the walls just where she'd hung them. Her dying young almost killed him, too. If it hadn't been for work, he'd have given up. But she wouldn't have approved of his giving up. So, he worked and kept going and yes, he was a sucker for a woman in a jam.

Kara Ann hadn't thought that was a bad trait, but had often reminded him to analyze a situation before jumping in. The only time he forgot that caution, he ended up married that second time to a woman he later realized was a perpetual victim, and who enjoyed all the drama she could stir up. Thank God he had bought a house in town for them when they married. He couldn't stand the idea of her changing Kara's house.

Early the next morning, getting ready to go to the sheriff's office, he stopped to look at the last picture taken of Kara Ann. Sort of a ritual; he stopped every day to say good morning to her. That morning, he noticed something in the photograph he'd never been consciously aware of before. Even though she was smiling, she had a little frown wrinkle between her eyebrows, and the right one was cocked up just a bit, as if she'd asked a question. It was a fixture in her expression, something that told anyone who knew her that along with good humor and kindness, she carried curiosity and wisdom usually reserved for those who have lived many years.

Dealing with the sheriff took longer than Chick thought it should. He showed the lawman the letter and then had to put up with being questioned like a suspect himself: How did you know Mrs. Burkwalter? Why would she turn to you for help instead of calling the law? Do you know this Jacob Hogner from any other encounters? Did you consider the possibility that the widow sabotaged the plane so she could inherit, and that this letter and all her accusations are a way to get rid of Hogner, who only wants to help and who was loyal to Dan?"

That last question made him sit up straight in his chair. He said, "No, that never occurred to me. But I can't imagine her being able to manufacture the fear in her eyes. I asked myself already, why get in touch with me rather than your office. I came up with this. I'm the only person who turned up at the visitation." By then he was leaning across the desk toward the sheriff. "But the biggest part is that immigrants, legal or not, have reason to be worried if they are noticed by any police, that they might get in trouble. See, I've never lived in another country, never had to prove I belonged. But I think it's the case here. You saw in the letter where she says Jacob told her she'll be deported now that Dan's dead? He was using that fear."

The sheriff said something like, "See what you mean. I'll think about this a little bit, and then I'll personally go out there and talk to her and to this Jacob character. By the way, does she have a lawyer? Cause if she doesn't, well I think it's a good idea that she get one."

Chick said, "I'll try to get in touch with her this morning, tell her to expect you."

The sheriff stayed seated. He said, "Just wondering—so she got in touch with you, not the other way around. But what's in all this for you?"

"You mean money? Yes, I went to the visitation thinking there might be an appraising job, but we never talked about it. I offered her my card and said she could call if I could help. I've got plenty of business without chasing hearses."

"I hear she's pretty. Maybe you'll get a ready-made family out of the deal."

Chick told himself to stay calm, lean back out of the sheriff's face. "You have my number if you need anything from me. Thank you for your time." He waited until he was halfway to his pickup before he yelled at the top of his lungs to the empty parking lot, "It'll be a cold day in hell before I vote for you again."

Alone at his office, he piddled around reading ads for land sales and checking the Lubbock newspaper online. Mostly he was waiting to see if the phone would ring. It didn't. He'd called Maricella's number and left a message saying, "Mrs. Burkwalter, Chick Talley, we met at the funeral home. Just following up to see if there's anything I can do to help."

Around five o'clock, he gathered his briefcase and pickup keys and headed toward the door. He'd just turned the key in the lock from the outside when he heard the phone. When he got back inside and answered, Maricella said, "The sheriff took Jacob away. I don't know what will happen, but I thank you for your help."

"Can I come out after a while, and bring a woman friend? If she can come, that is."

"I will prepare a meal. Come whenever you can. And yes, bring your friend."

On the way to Marva's aunt's house, Chick realized his breathing was more like panting. He told himself to settle down. She'd said she'd help. Just knock on the door and ask her. But this time it was the aunt who answered the door. She said, "You again? Come on in. Marva's changing clothes. I'll get her."

Hearing her voice was all it took—this was Miss Steele, his tenth grade English teacher, in person. He said, "I just realized who you are, Miss Steele. I'm Chick Talley."

"I remember you, Chick. Glad you didn't forget the person who made you rewrite your themes until they were perfect."

"It was good practice. I knew you still lived in town, but I had no idea you were Marva's aunt."

"Now you know. Welcome. She'll be here in just a minute."

Marva was true to her word about helping. They ate supper with Maricella and the suddenly talkative Rebecca. Maricella described the sheriff's arrival and Jacob's belligerent reaction. "He ran into the little house Dan let him stay in out by the barn and came out with a gun right after the sheriff and his deputy arrived. He must have thought they were coming for him."

Marva encouraged her to come to town and stay at the Jackson's Pond Motel until things settled down. But Maricella said, "I am no longer afraid. And I have to be here when the aviation accident investigator comes tomorrow morning."

After leaving Maricella and Rebecca with instructions to lock all the windows and keep the cell phone charged and near at hand, Chick and Marva rode for a few miles in silence. Then she said, "I didn't call you before because I didn't think we had anything to talk about, had no idea what you wanted, why you were being friendly. Yeah, suspicious, I'll admit. But I'm over that. You helped her without expecting anything in return."

He could tell she was looking at him, but he focused on the windshield and beyond. She said, "If you don't mind, I'll give you my number in case you want to call me sometime."

He wasn't sure what to say, so he drove with one hand and with the other reached in his pocket, got two of his business cards. "Why don't you write your number on the back of one of those." He handed her a pen from the console. He glanced over and noticed a tiny wrinkle form between her eyebrows as she wrote. Then he said, "And on the back of that other one put my cell number and home phone." He recited the numbers and she wrote them on the card.

Jackson's Pond Leader
Thursday, November 10, 2017
Cooks and Cooking
By Stephanie Jacobson,
City Manager of Jackson's Pond.
Sweet Potato Casserole
Ingredients
2 28 oz. cans of sweet potatoes
½ c orange or pineapple juice
½ c brown sugar
½ tsp cinnamon
marshmallows enough to dot the top of
the of the casserole
1/4 pound butter
Preparation
-Preheat oven to 350 f
-Mash the sweet potatoes with ½ of the
liquid they are canned in.
-Add fruit juice, mash until mixture
is thin but not too soupy.
-Stir in brown sugar and cinnamon
-Grease the bottom and sides of a 9x13
baking dish with butter.
-Spread potato mixture in the dish.
Dot with the rest of the butter.
-Heat in the oven until bubbly, about 20 minutes.
-Remove and top with marshmallows.
-Return to oven until marshmallows are
tan. Serves 5 or 6, depending. Double
recipe and size of dish for more. ENJOY

CHAPTER 15

November, 2017
Words from the Past

Marva had just taken off her work clothes and put on jeans and a T-shirt when she heard the phone ring. Seconds later, Violet called to her from the kitchen. "Phone for you."

When Marva answered, Rose Ellen said, "Mom, it's Dad. He died." She sounded as if she spoke through tears.

"Oh, Rose Ellen. I'm so sorry." It was all she could say. The nausea and clutch in her chest came without words. She leaned against the kitchen counter, eyes closed.

Her daughter said, "Memaw didn't know what happened exactly. He'd been sick with a urinary infection. He had those. Being paralyzed." Sobs interrupted her words. "They thought he was getting better."

"Are you with your grandmother now? This will be hard for her. Taking care of him all these years."

"On the way there. I wanted to tell you." Rose Ellen sniffled and took an audible breath. Then she said, "I didn't know if you'd care. But …"

Finding any words, choosing the right ones took a few seconds. Marva said, "I'm glad you did. Thank you. Please tell your grandmother I'm very sorry. Are you okay to drive?"

Rose Ellen said, "Yes, I'm okay now. I will be. It's not much farther to San Antonio."

"Please call to let me know you get there okay."

"Yes. I promise." There was a pause. Then Rose Ellen said, "Mom, wait, I want to tell you something he said not to tell you."

Marva waited.

Rose Ellen said, "I promised not to tell so I never did. Now …Well, I think it's okay. He always asked about you. Wanted to know if you ever talked about him. I told him you said he was kindhearted and sad and he had to leave us. He told me how strong you were, said you deserved better than him." She sounded choked when she said, "Mom, you were right. He was good-hearted. And even when he smiled, I could see he was always so sad."

"Honey, thank you for calling. We'll talk again soon. I love you." Marva stood with the phone in her hand, dial tone humming until it beeped and didn't quit.

From the doorway, Violet said, "She sounded upset."

Marva nodded, hanging up the phone. "Her dad died. Cutter."

Violet steered Marva to a kitchen chair. She said, "Would you prefer tea or wine this afternoon?"

"Wine might be right."

Violet poured them each a glass of white and sat across from Marva. "I imagine a lot of things come to mind right now. Don't worry about making sense. Just say what's comes to you."

How could Violet know that was just what she needed, permission not to make sense?

After a minute or so she spent staring at the wine before taking a drink, Marva said, "All those years ago . . . I called his mother after he left. Worried something had happened to him. She only knew he was looking for work. Colorado. He had called her on New Year's Day. She thought I was with him. I never mentioned Rose Ellen. That was 1985. She was close to four months old. I waited there on the ranch, hoping he'd come back. Doubting it. Then . . . well, something happened. Convinced me I wasn't safe there all those miles from town. Soon after that I moved us back to Lubbock. More concerned about finding work and figuring out how to . . . survive without asking for help, I guess."

Violet said, "You didn't tell your mother or Carly?"

Marva shook her head. "Not until I had a steady job and a place to live. Reliable child care. And, oh yes, something drivable. That took several months. I don't really recall. There's a lot I don't remember."

For a brief second, Marva thought about stopping right there. Violet wouldn't press for more. And the more she talked, the more likely Violet would think she was, at least, unbalanced. Or more likely completely nuts. Then that thought passed, discarded.

Marva said, "Later, after Rose Ellen left for college, I had time to think. Alone. Nothing else to occupy me. More time than I'd had in years. Hard as I tried, there were only a few things I could remember about those eighteen years from the day she and I arrived in Lubbock. Not the names of her school teachers, whether I went to any of her activities, signing report cards, immunizations, how old she was when she started her periods, nothing. I told myself it had been like being under anesthesia for all that time. But I did remember the day she asked why she didn't have a daddy. She was four, too smart for her age."

Violet refilled their glasses and sat without saying anything.

"I told her about Cutter and that he'd had to leave. And I told her he loved her. That had to be true. He'd delivered her into the world and had kept us both alive." She paused and closed her eyes again. "He was strong and something about him felt magnetic. And he was often funny. We laughed a lot. Rose Ellen looks like him. That was when I finally called Mrs. Gulley and told her she had a granddaughter."

Her aunt said, "I can imagine his mother was shocked if he hadn't told her."

"He hadn't told her and hadn't ever come home, even when his father died, heart attack, which had happened not long before I called her. Cutter was making sort of a living rodeoing and working for a rodeo stock company. She'd hear from him a couple of times a year—Mother's Day and New Year's. As soon as I told her, she wanted to meet Rose Ellen. So, we arranged it. After that, even at long distance, she was a presence for her granddaughter. More than I remember, I'm sure. Later, Rose Ellen spent a couple of weeks each summer with her."

The phone rang again. Marva answered—Rose Ellen again. She said, "Mom, I made it. There won't be a funeral. Cremation. I'll stay for a while, and I'll let you know before I start back."

After she hung up, sat again at the table, Marva said to Violet, "One of these days, maybe I can tell you more about those missing years. I still wonder why I don't remember."

"Grieving?" Violet said.

Marva raised her eyes from the ring the wine glass had made on the table and looked at her aunt.

Violet smiled and said, "Or coping."

"Made me forget?"

"Maybe didn't leave room for anything else to make an impression. Grief's powerful."

Marva shrugged. "I worry I might have lost something important with all that forgetting."

Violet stood and said, "I'll cook tonight. Don't argue. It will be my specialty, scrambled egg sandwiches." She assembled eggs, a loaf of bread, mayonnaise, and dill pickles on the counter.

Marva said, "Cutter was probably ready to die. Being paraplegic, wheelchair bound. He'd have hated it. All those years not able to be free, on horseback."

She went quiet, back to staring at her now empty wine glass. "Twenty-two years since that accident. Bull riding injury—severed his spine. Rose Ellen probably knows more about it. I wanted to remember him the way he was. So, I didn't ask. He'd have been fifty-seven this year." When she closed her eyes she saw him at twenty-five.

Violet got out a skillet, butter, plates, and silverware. "Many people who are paraplegic live full lives, work, so on. Wonder why he didn't."

"That's one more thing I'll never know." Marva got up and set the table. She said, "If you don't mind, after we eat, I think I'd better skip SCRABBLE tonight."

That night in bed, not even trying to sleep, she thought again about a brief time in her life that she knew now had set in motion so much of the rest of it. Cutter didn't cause everything bad that had happened to her. There had been good times with him when she laughed and learned and enjoyed doing things she'd never imagined before she agreed to that summer adventure. She'd been miserable long before she met him, when she was busy trying to just make it to high school graduation, to get away from home and her mother. Cutter had nothing to do with Chance and her dad dying; he had no part in making her a person who wouldn't let herself make real friends. She focused on the glow cast by the bathroom night light across the hall and whispered, "I'm so sorry for you, Cutter. I hope you can be at peace now." She closed her eyes and saw the little silver heart necklace he surprised her with that Christmas. Crying silently, she fell asleep.

The next morning before she dressed, she lifted the silver necklace in its the tiny box from the bottom of her jewelry case, put the box in her handbag. She'd give it to Rose Ellen soon, when she knew exactly how to explain what it had meant to her.

That morning, it happened again. Often, when Marva showered, in the comforting warmth of the enclosed space and water gently massaging her into wakefulness, she remembered dreams from the night before. Disjointed bits from the tales her mind told her in sleep surfaced. Most were scenes she recognized from the more than two years she and Cutter were together, and she was in them, not observing, but participating. They reminded her of a time when she'd felt most alive, when every emotion was raw, acute.

A change in the water temperature signaled she'd soon be shocked by loss of warmth. She'd used nearly all the hot water. The montage of dream pieces she'd been viewing disappeared when she turned off the faucet. She covered herself in one towel and wrapped another around her wet hair. Then she stopped, remembering last night's final, just-on-the-edge-of-waking image; Chance. Her brother was no longer young as in all the other times he'd come to her through the years. In the dream, she said, "You've grown up."

He said, "We all do." Then he edged away, leaving. A dog, she was sure it was Bullet, walked beside him. Chance waved to her and said, "Remember this. Now is what you have, all you have."

She slowly dried herself, then squeezed the towel on her hair and released it. Still moving slowly, she repeated the single word. "Now."

Jackson's Pond Leader
Early Holiday Edition
Wednesday, November 22, 2017
Letters to the Editor
Dear Editor,

I enclose payment for two subscriptions, one for myself and the other for my sister who lives in Colorado, but who still calls Jackson's Pond home. Your editions so far have been informative and interesting, representing topics that reflect good reasons to be proud of our town. Keep up the good work.
Mamie Kelly

Editor,

I don't need a local rag like this published by a liberal. Yes, I know you for what you are, always have been even back in ninth grade, nothing but a bleeding heart. We don't need your kind in our town. (No signature provided.)
Editor's note: The policy of the Jackson's Pond Leader is to publish only signed letters. An exception is made in this case.

Also of note, as of this printing, subscriptions total 432. We pledge to continue providing local news and items of interest. Further, this editor pledges to present all views on any issues reported, in order to remain fair and unbiased.

CHAPTER 16

November, 2017
No, This is Not a Date

At noon on Wednesday, November 15, 2017, Marva wrapped a wool scarf around her neck and zipped her down jacket. No matter that the wind was gusting to thirty miles per hour; she'd promised herself she'd start her walking again today. Days were shorter and darkness fell soon after her work day was over at five. That had given her a good excuse back in September to stop her afternoon roaming around Jackson's Pond. Now, six weeks later, she was starting all over again, five pounds heavier than at the end of September. No more excuses. Each day at noon, wind, rain or shine. She'd hoof it around Jackson's Pond until those pounds were gone. It would be easier than giving up Violet's cookies.

She was in her second lap around the blocks she usually walked when she slowed before crossing the main street. From the corner of her eye, she saw a pickup behind her, on the same side of the street. She moved to the sidewalk and kept walking,

The pickup continued moving along on the street behind her, following her, keeping pace but not passing even though she'd given whoever it was the street. When she slowed before crossing at the next intersection, a quick beep of a horn told her she was correct. Chick Talley was following her. She reversed direction. The pickup stopped. She marched to the driver side door and rapped on the window. He opened it an inch or two. She said, "Broad daylight, accosting a citizen walking for her health? I memorized your plate number. I *will* report you."

Chick lowered the window the rest of the way, pushed his hat back off his forehead, and laughed. "I surrender, Ma'am. But I plead not guilty. I was just enjoying the sight of a person engaged in serious walking. A person with a purpose, it appeared to me. Want a ride?"

She pointed across the street and one block down. "My work's waiting for me. I'll be glad when winter's over so I can walk in the evening."

"It's barely started."

"Yeah, I know. Must go." She hustled off toward the post office imitating a race walker, certain Chick was still watching.

Violet was cleaning away a chip bowl and drink glasses from the game table in the den when Marva walked in soon after five. Violet said, "The card game went a little longer than usual. One of the girls won't let us quit until she wins a pot."

Marva said, "Gambling is a dangerous thing. Do you check for weapons at the door?"

Violet said, "Always. Oh, Rose Ellen called and asked for you to call her."

"I'll do that right now. Thanks."

Her daughter answered on the first ring. "Hi, Mom," she said. Then she rushed out the words, "Mom, will you be busy on Thanksgiving? I wondered if I could come and visit."

"Of course, I'd love it. I have to work that Friday. But if you could stay until Sunday we could have more time to visit. And you'd have a chance to get to know Aunt Violet. You'll love her."

"Will you bake a pumpkin pie like you used to do when it was just us?"

Marva's chest felt full, not open for a good breath. She said, almost a whisper, "I did? If that's what you want, of course." She hesitated briefly, then in a stronger voice she said, "You know, the first pie I ever made was for your dad, before you were born. Pumpkin."

"Then it's even more special for me. Okay then, I'll be there on Wednesday evening. We have early dismissal."

Violet returned from the den carrying three empty glasses and four dessert plates on a tray, set them on the counter, then sat in a kitchen chair. "Everyone was talkative today, eager about Thanksgiving plans. I think Lucy used it as an excuse to cheat. She won the pot. $4.25."

Marva sat opposite Violet, folding and unfolding a napkin. Violet said, "Is everything okay with Rose Ellen?"

Marva leaned back in the chair. "She sounded good, maybe a little excited. She's coming for Thanksgiving. I'll cook if you'll make the menu. It must include pumpkin pie. A special request."

Violet said, "My favorite pie." She got up and rinsed the plates and put them in the dishwasher. "Do you think there's something else that made her want to come out? Maybe lonely?"

"She sounded happy and eager to come out. Why?"

"Something your mother said about Rose Ellen one time. It was something like, 'She's too much like her mother to ever get married.' At the time I didn't respond, didn't ask what she meant."

Marva shrugged. "More likely it was one more chance to say I wasn't the person she thought I should be. Mother didn't, doesn't really know Rose Ellen that well. Never spent that much time around her. Mrs. Gulley has far more of a connection to her." Marva left the chair and opened the pantry. "Looks like I'll need to pick up some more groceries. Even though she's over thirty, she still snacks like a teenager. She'll be here Wednesday afternoon. Seymour's about two and a half hours from here. And she'll stay until Sunday."

Violet said, "We'll give her Alvin's room."

Marva turned from staring at the pantry shelves and saw her aunt smiling at her own joke.

Thursday afternoon, around three, Violet took the rolls from the oven and said, "It's all ready now." She didn't have to call them to the table. Marva and Rose Ellen had set the table earlier and claimed their places, waiting, inhaling the aromas of the pumpkin pie, turkey, dressing, and other side dishes as the rolls browned.

Rose Ellen said, "Let's agree, no judgment or use of the word gluttony here today. I *will* eat seconds. It all looks and smells so good." For a few minutes, little was said, other than the occasional request for a dish to be passed. Then Rose Ellen spoke again. "Thank you both. I love being here and this is the best meal I've had in a long time."

Marva said, "I guess it does beat Luby's. Would either of you like more dressing?"

"I believe I'll save myself for the pie," Violet said.

Rose Ellen shook her head. "I'll stop now and reserve the right to return late tonight for more of everything." She finished the last of her second buttered roll, then leaned back from the table. "I have a question. What is the best holiday meal you ever had, no matter what your age, what year?"

Marva said, "Before either of you answer, would you like more iced tea, or some coffee, or a glass of wine and are you ready for me to serve pie?"

Violet took a small glass of white wine. "I'll delay my dessert in favor of focusing on this excellent question."

Rose Ellen said, "Me, too."

Marva poured a glass of iced tea for herself and waited to see which of the other two would answer Rose Ellen's question first. A tiny frown followed quickly by a smile suggested Violet had isolated a memory. "I'll go first—my most memorable holiday meal."

Her aunt painted a verbal picture of an Easter dinner. "I was eight; it was 1946. The war was over and people were trying to get back to normal. But there were several families in town who had sons or fathers killed or badly injured. Nothing for them would ever be normal in the way it had been before. I only knew that because my mother explained why we were having the biggest Easter dinner we ever had. She said, 'We are more fortunate than many. Your father was too old to go to war and we had no sons. We have you two girls and chickens and geese and we have plenty of fruit and vegetables we canned. So we are inviting neighbors and family for a feast. And there will be food left over for anyone who will to take some home.' Then she said, 'Some are embarrassed to accept help, whether it's a kind word or a shared meal or something more. So make no mention of any of this to any of your friends.'

"Ordinarily there would have only been the four of us for Easter dinner. That year, there were three tables spread and twenty-one others joined us. Mother told me that among them, they had lost twelve to the war. I don't really remember the food as much as the event. The deaths in their families would certainly explain the sorrow some of them wore like heavy capes. For a while that day, I think some of them felt lighter, felt understood." Violet paused. "But I will say that the turkey here today is better than any I recall ever eating."

Rose Ellen sat forward, took the last remaining bit of roll from her plate. She said, "I remember several memorable holiday meals, most of them with Mom, a few with Memaw and Dad. But the one that stands out was when I was nine, fourth grade. Our teacher at Wheatley Elementary in Lubbock asked us to invite our parents for lunch the day before Thanksgiving. We would eat in our classroom with all the parents and other students plus the teacher. She told us we could dress up if we wanted. I wanted to. I wore my new plaid, pleated skirt and a navy blue blouse. When the lunch bell rang, the parents waiting in the hall came in and the cafeteria ladies rolled in a cart. I don't recall that the food was particularly good—who likes turkey roll? What made it memorable was how proud I was to introduce my mother. She was the prettiest one there. She was wearing a red sweater and skirt with a red and black checked scarf. I knew that all the others must be jealous of my beautiful mother who had taken the day off work to come to my school. The next day on Thanksgiving, she cooked for the two of us, a whole turkey and all the trimmings, which tasted so much better than what we had at school. And best of all, she baked a pumpkin pie and said I could eat as much of it as I wanted, have it for breakfast, too. 'After all,' she said, 'pumpkin is a vegetable.' Our apartment smelled like spice and pumpkin for days."

As her daughter told of that visit to her school, Marva remembered the sweater and skirt, the scarf. And she could almost hear that part about pumpkin pie for breakfast. She hadn't lost that memory, after all. Her throat tightened as Rose Ellen's "she was the prettiest" replayed in her head and her heart.

"Do you remember that, Mom?"

"I do. Thank you for reminding me." Marva hesitated a second, then said, "My most memorable holiday meal was Christmas 1982, the only Christmas Cutter and I celebrated together. The day turned beautiful when it snowed. We were both excited to be having an adventure there on that ranch in Cimarron, New Mexico. I cooked turkey for the very first time and it turned out fine. And that was the day I made my first pumpkin pie." If she allowed herself to take her eyes off of Rose Ellen, tears would fall and spoil this nice dinner. So Marva said, "Cutter and I had some great times together." She took a drink of her iced tea and then a deep breath.

After a few seconds' silence, Violet said, "All this talk of pie makes me hungry again. If you're ready, I'll serve." She cut and served generous pieces, offered whipped cream, an addition no one refused. After her first bite, she said "Rose Ellen, how are you at SCRABBLE?"

Without any hesitation, Rose Ellen said, "I am called rabid by those I can still get to play with me. Why?"

"Your mother could use more practice," Violet said. "I'm trying to help her improve, but . . . well, perhaps three-handed would work out better for her."

Marva could see Violet hiding a smile. "Perhaps, if you'd tell me the secret of drawing all the best tiles, I'd have a chance." Marva said to Rose Ellen, "I checked the backs of the tiles to see if she'd etched braille on them. No luck."

Rose Ellen shrugged. "Practice is the key, I think. By the way, Mom, you bought me a SCRABBLE game when I was about twelve, taught me to play."

"Apparently that was a mistake. Okay, go ahead and bring out the board."

After their long weekend together, Marva sat on the bed watching her daughter packing to leave. She said, "Wait just a bit before you close your bag. I have something for you. Be right back."

She returned with the small necklace box. "I think you should have this. Go ahead. Open it."

Rose Ellen touched the tiny heart as if it were precious. "It's beautiful. So delicate. Have you had it a long time?"

Marva sat beside her daughter on the bed. "Your dad gave it to me on that Christmas we celebrated together. It was a complete surprise. I wore it all the time for years." She took a deep breath and said, "Want to try it on?"

Rose Ellen said, "You'll have to work the clasp." She turned her back and Marva fastened the delicate silver chain around Rose Ellen's neck. When Cutter's daughter turned and faced her mother again, she said, "I'll wear it all the time. I love that you wanted me to have it." She hugged Marva. They sat without speaking for a couple of minutes.

Then Rose Ellen said, "Well, I have to get on the road. Tomorrow's a school day. My fifth-graders will be hard to corral after their short holiday. I promised Dwight I'd go out for a burger with him when I get in this evening."

After the hugging in the driveway, Marva and Violet stood and waved goodbye as Rose Ellen drove away. Back in the house, sitting in the den, they congratulated one another on an excellent Thanksgiving dinner. Violet said, "I think she liked the baked goods best." She had included homemade dinner rolls on the menu. As the main baker, she had made two dozen rolls, and Marva did the pie. By Sunday Rose Ellen had eaten five rolls beyond the two she had with Thanksgiving turkey. She'd said she didn't want to see any go to waste. Violet sent six of the remaining ones home with her.

"That's where it's true she's her mother's daughter. But somehow she manages to work it off and stay slim. I have to walk miles to compensate for one piece of pie." Marva leaned back, closed her eyes. "I'm glad she was here."

Violet said, "Who's Dwight?"

"I chose not to pry. All she told me was that he's a 'very close friend.' He's the high school band director in Seymour, a year or two older than she is, never married."

Violet said, "She mentioned the names of several other friends, most females. And she did drop in Dwight's name when she and I were talking, too. Said she'd first known him when they were both at Texas Tech."

"So, I guess if my mother should ever mention Rose Ellen again, we can assure her that the girl is nothing like her mother. She knows how to make friends."

Violet said, "I'm sure you know how to make friends."

"Let's just say it's something I'm working on." Marva picked up a *Smithsonian* magazine from the end table. She leafed to a story about Chaco Canyon and read briefly. Then she said, "Speaking of friends. Would you be willing to have Maricella Burkwalter and her daughter to dinner some evening? She cooked dinner when Chick Talley and I went to visit her. I thought returning the gesture would be a friendly thing to do."

Violet said, "I think you're right. Certainly. And I suppose you ought to invite that rascal Chick, too."

"You think so?"

"Sure, why not? A woman can have men friends without it meaning anything romantic if you don't want it to. I've had lots. I still keep in touch with some of them."

"Really?"

"Yes, really." Violet raised an eyebrow. "I could entertain you with some tales. In fact, one of these days you and I will drink wine and tell random stories to one another. Like friends do."

Monday at noon, Marva stepped out of the post office into a sunny, warm-for-November day. A light breeze stirred the flag in front of the post office. Marva knew not to trust a beautiful day in November. A norther could roar in and remind everyone how little they had control of most things and that they had none over the weather in the Texas Panhandle. She intended to make the most of every minute of her lunch hour soaking up the beautiful day. She whispered a single word as she walked east toward the several residential blocks off of Main Street. "Now."

She passed two city employees huddled next to a truck with an extendable bucket holding a third man. He was installing a Christmas decoration on a utility pole—a flag with Santa and a sleigh full of toys. The next pole she passed held an already installed flag showing a brightly decorated Christmas tree. She picked up her pace, wearing a smile. The post office busy season would make the next few weeks pass quickly. Fine with her. It was too easy to be sad at holiday time. At least this year, she wouldn't be alone.

A large SUV approached her heading west. The driver waved, a real wave, not the couple of raised fingers that West Texans used to acknowledge other drivers, almost as a reflex. Marva waved in return, even though she had no idea who it was. As the car passed, she registered it was Willa's granddaughter Claire. They'd met a couple of times. According to Violet, Claire was trustworthy, highly competent as a nurse practitioner, and known for her special dedication to the elderly. And apparently, she was outgoing and friendly. They had only met twice that Marva could recall, both times when Claire brought packages to mail at the post office.

She roamed the east side of Main until 12:30, then crossed Main and started down church row. About the time she reached the Catholic church, the final one on the street, she heard a horn honk behind her. She was on the sidewalk, so anyone who actually wanted to pass needn't honk. It must be Chick again.

She stopped and he pulled up beside her. She said, "Are you free for dinner Thursday evening?"

She'd never seen him look surprised before. But that's what showed on his face. He said, "I'm free every evening for dinner. And lunch, too. Why do you ask?"

"I invited Maricella Burkwalter and her daughter, repaying her kindness for feeding us. Violet said you should come, too."

"She did? And that's okay with you? Who's cooking?"

"Would it matter?"

"Not really. As long as it's not me making an egg sandwich, I'm happy. Just let me know what time and I'll be there." He pushed his cowboy hat back off his forehead, watching her from his driver's seat. "Something I need to know; are you asking me on a date?"

"Would it matter?"

He laughed. "Okay, you got me. No, it wouldn't. I just wondered."

"The answer's no. I've had all the dates I need in this life. I'm planning on making friends from here on out." She backed away from his pickup, about to walk on. Then she said, "Six-thirty."

He nodded and revved his motor, then winked at her when she rolled her eyes and shook her head.

At dinner that Thursday, Maricella and Rebecca both seemed transformed from the frightened pair they'd been before. Maricella told about making friends with a couple of women who'd invited them to attend Mass, and who both had children in Rebecca's grade at school. "I am happy that I decided to stay here," she said. "I am no longer fearful. The Sheriff let me know Jacob was deported because his visa was long expired. I contacted my husband's relatives who own the farmland. They will do the farming, and because I own the house and a few acres, I will not have to move. Soon the legal details will be settled and there is a buyer waiting to purchase the spray business. So,

I will have money to live until I decide what I will do for work. All that is later, after the baby comes."

Marva watched Chick, who seemed at ease being the only male there. Rebecca engaged him in a long conversation about her school and how much she liked art class. He told her about a donkey that lives on his farm, and that she could come out and visit Old Jess, and draw his picture if she wanted.

The three guests ate heartily. Chick had a second helping of fried chicken. And cherry pie baked by Violet was a big success with everyone. Because it was a school night, Maricella and Rebecca left just after eight. Chick offered to help clear the table. Violet let him while Marva made coffee. By eight-thirty, the three of them agreed it had been a nice evening and that they were pleased for the recently-widowed, soon-to-be-a-mother-again Maricella and her steps toward becoming part of Jackson's Pond. Violet said, "She's obviously intelligent and I think brave. I can't imagine how I'd have coped if I had been in a foreign country in such a situation." She sipped at her coffee, then said, "I hope you two don't mind, but I think I'll retire for the evening. The book I've started is calling me."

Chick stood as Violet left the table. He said, "Thanks for inviting me, Miss Steel."

"Thank Marva. Her idea."

Chick said, "I'm sure glad she and Rebecca are safe now."

"So am I. I'm glad you made me part of helping her."

He said to Marva. "Well."

"Well what?"

Chick turned to face her directly. He said, "Well, it's time for me to go, too. I guess. Thanks for inviting me. And thanks for an excellent dinner. The next one's on me."

She followed him to the front door. He said, "I grill a pretty mean steak. Sometime, if you're willing, you could come see my place, meet Old Jess, my donkey. Have dinner."

"Are you asking me on a date?"

"Oh, no. Just friends having dinner."

"Right. Okay. We can do that sometime."

She waved to him as he backed out of the driveway. It couldn't hurt to have dinner. If anyone knew about making friends, it was probably Chick Talley.

Jackson's Pond Leader
Thursday, February 8, 2018
The Arts and Literary Scene
<u>Art Exhibit Opening at RBJ
Education Center</u>
An exhibit of watercolors on the theme "Texas Panhandle—A Frontier Evolving" is slated to open with a gala reception on February 14, 2018. The reception provides a first look at the show and an opportunity to meet the artists and invited guests from across the state. Contact the RBJ Visitor Reception Center for ticket information.

Robert Stanley, Professor Emeritus of Art History at U. T. Austin, curator for the show, said, "Paintings by various artists from throughout Texas reflect interpretations of the show's theme. Visitors will appreciate the quality of the work and the variety of styles."

Following the opening, the exhibit will be open to the public free of charge at the RBJ Education Center 9 a.m. to 6 p.m. Saturday and 1 p.m. to 6 p.m. Sunday each weekend through March 31, 2018.

CHAPTER 17

February, 2018
Chili Weather

"I never have liked February, no matter where I lived," Violet said. "If a person's not hoping for a heart-shaped box of chocolates or an engagement ring, this month offers nothing to look forward to in my books."

At that moment, Marva was inclined to agree. They were sitting at the kitchen table, both facing the two large windows on the back of the house giving a view of the back yard. The remainder of summer grass was brown and brittle; the elm trees, stripped to bare branches by the winter team of freezing temperatures and wind, stood staring upward like pitiful supplicants. She said, "At least it's not raining and freezing. I hate driving on ice."

A silent few seconds passed before Violet said, "Maybe it's because I never yearned for an engagement ring, and I figured out that I could buy my own candy if I really wanted any." She smiled, a sort of conspiratorial expression that told Marva her aunt had a story ready to tell. "Although there was one man I did think might turn up with an engagement ring."

Marva said, "Tell me." Her aunt never forced her reminiscences on Marva, and early on had suggested that they were not meant to go further. She needn't have worried. Marva avoided gossip. Always had.

In the months since Marva had moved in with her, Violet had told bits of her interesting life several times. Her skill as a storyteller made them not only vivid in detail but also entertaining in content. Maybe she embellished; either that or she had an encyclopedic memory. That didn't matter to Marva. She knew there was at least a kernel of truth in each of them. What she wondered was how Violet could remember so much. More than twenty years older than Marva, her aunt seemed to have no trouble recalling far more of her life than Marva could of hers. She'd promised herself she'd put aside worrying about her vacant years, the ones she referred to as under anesthesia. But she couldn't help wondering.

Violet nibbled a bit from a cookie. Then she said, "We were college seniors and had dated quite a few times. Campus activities— his fraternity events, plays, the occasional movie. He was handsome, came from some money—probably oil—grew up in Fort Worth, but came to Tech for his degree, not TCU. Full of plans for the future. He had it all mapped out. Or maybe his parents did and he'd agreed. He'd have a finance degree, and in a few years, take over the family business.

"My acquaintances kept telling me he was a great catch. I laughed it off. I was attracted to him, very. But I had some plans of my own; I would teach subjects I loved, influence young minds, and I'd travel the world during my summers off. I'll admit I was flattered by his attention. After all, I wasn't in a sorority. A small-town girl. Came from a comfortable, but not wealthy, family. I might not have been rated as a "catch" but I spoke intelligently and knew which forks to use, so I wasn't an embarrassment socially. And by the time I was twenty-one, I had blossomed from a rather plain, bookish youngster to a young woman who turned some heads. He wasn't the only person who asked me out.

"So, when that February came and he hinted he had something important we should talk about, I took a hard look at what I knew of him, what I felt. I realized, to my surprise, that I'd be relieved if he didn't have a speech prepared and a diamond ring in his pocket. And more than that, if he did, I'd have to say no."

She stopped talking and ate some more of the cookie. That was Marva's cue. She said, "Don't keep me in suspense."

"Well, he took me out to a restaurant, and when the dessert arrived, the waiter offered him an extra plate. He placed a ring box on the plate and had the waiter place it in front of me —a bit of a dramatic flourish. Then he dismissed the waiter and made a proposal speech. I have to say he did appear earnest. I heard him out, hoping my expression suggested a suitable level of surprise. Then, with my own delicate little maneuver, I slid the plate back to him. Switching from the surprised appearance to a slightly sad, sincere one, I said, 'I'm flattered, but I'm not the one for you.'"

"Besides the different backgrounds, was there some other reason?"

"We weren't friends." She looked directly at Marva and continued. "I'd realized I wanted someone who was my friend that I'd come to love rather than someone I'd been dazzled and infatuated with whom I would have to learn to like and have as a friend. Even then, young as I was, I thought that real friendship lasts, but infatuation, even some kinds of love, might not."

Marva said, "Sounds very wise for a twenty-one-year-old."

"Some have called me self-centered, my sister, for example." Violet shrugged. "There's some truth in that, I guess."

"I have to ask, what did he say?"

"Ha! That's the best part. He had that ring box back in his pocket as fast as a sleight of hand artist. Then he signaled the waiter for the check, and he said to me, 'Well, I tried. Your loss.'" She chuckled, then said, "And thus endeth this lesson."

"Wait, not yet," Marva said. "You rejected this great catch because you weren't friends. But you'd dated. How would you have known if you were friends? When I think of friends, nowadays social media friends come to mind. I'm not on social media, but I know how people get to be friends on there. Just a couple of clicks sends a friend request. Often the person accepts, a couple of more clicks, and they've never even actually met in person."

Violet said, "My definition is different. Layered. There are acquaintances, people I would recognize if I saw them, people I might know a few facts about, someone I've seen at social gatherings. Might have worked with them." She demonstrated with one hand flat, palm up. Then she placed her other hand, above the first. Then she said, "Next there are acquaintance you've known for a long time in that same way, just longer, my second layer. Real friends, close friends are something different for me. Put a hand here, above mine, closer to me, metaphorically speaking. These are friends, not simply acquaintances. Willa is an example. People who know things about my life, either because they were there or because I have told them about my experiences. We have experiences in common, or similar interests, or we are committed to the same values. They know what's important to me; they are people I trust. Only a few fit here." Violet moved her hands back, clapped them. "Sorry for being such an English teacher."

Marva said, "Don't apologize. That was interesting, gave me lots to think about." She moved from her chair to the kitchen stove. "One more cup of tea, and I'll find something useful to do on this Saturday. If the sun comes out, I'll bundle up and take a walk. More tea?"

Violet shook her head. "You're more ambitious than I am this morning. I'll be in the den reading."

As if on cue a few minutes later, the sun burst from behind the clouds. Before she could lose her resolve, Marva pulled on a pair of Levi's and the thermal shirt she'd had since that Christmas in Cimarron, thick socks, and her cowboy boots. On top of the thermal shirt, she layered a sweater and her insulated jacket. A wool scarf, knit hat, and gloves topped off the winter garb. On her way out, she stopped at the doorway to the den and said to Violet, "I'm off. I'll have to walk at least an hour to make it worth getting into all this gear."

When she opened the front door, a blast of frigid wind struck her face and made her eyes water. She headed south, away from the gusts and had no trouble picking up her pace; she had a tailwind. The gusts soon settled down to a steady wind of twenty or so miles an hour. She slowed, no longer concerned about being downed by a gust, and allowed her mind to rove back to Violet's levels of friendship. A minute later, she was muttering to herself.

Quite a few people call me by name now when they come in the post office. Adding that name tag to the Postal Service-issued neutral one, Postmaster, was a good idea. Compared to six months ago, I now have quite a few acquaintances. Many even stop to visit a few seconds after they do their business if there's no one in line. Of course, the conversation is nothing of substance. 'Think it's going to rain? How was your weekend?' That's progress. But I'd agree with Violet; those are acquaintances, not friends. I'm one step above an automated stamp machine.

Marva came to the end of the sidewalk. Almost walked right out of town with her head down. Instead of turning back toward the house, which would mean facing directly into the wind, she turned right, crossed Main Street and continued west on the newer street leading to the RBJ plant. She'd zigzag her way back-two blocks west, then one north into the wind, then another turn and head east a couple more, then north, and so forth. This wasn't her first encounter with cold winter wind.

Why do I care? Because I want this to be home. I think that means fitting in and that probably means having friends, at least one or two. Well, Violet and I are becoming friends. Something she said—trusting a person is part of what makes them more than an acquaintance. Trust them for what, with what, to do what?

I'm tired of thinking about myself.

Her phone rang. Jammed down in her pocket, it sounded choked. By the time she pulled off a glove and got the phone out, it had stopped ringing. Chick. She texted a quick message, "Too windy to hear, walking, will call in a bit, M."

He texted right back with, "It's important."

She had been gone nearly an hour when she opened the front door at Violet's. Her aunt's voice, from the direction of the den, said, "I thought you might have been blown to Central Texas by now."

"Stiff wind, but I outwitted it. Zigzagged my way back. Everything okay?"

Violet came from the den. She said, "Chick called. I told him to try your cell phone. Want some tea to warm you up?"

Marva nodded as she pulled off her gloves, then her hat. "Glad you reminded me. He called. I couldn't hear in the wind. I said I'd call back. I'll change clothes and do that and be there for a cup in just a minute."

After shedding her cold weather garb, Marva called Chick, then returned for the tea. Violet had set out cups, saucers, and a small plate holding four cookies. The teapot sat on the stove. "It's ready. Have a seat. I'll serve." As she poured tea, something fragrant with cinnamon, into Marva's cup, Violet said, "After he called, I was thinking about Chick, and how he was as a boy. Do you recall he said I made him rewrite his themes until they were perfect? I did. That's because he was the best writer in the class, and the essays he wrote for assignments always showed thinking one would have expected of a much older person. I wanted to urge him on, make him dig deeper."

"Did your method accomplish what you hoped with him?"

"I never knew. That was when I was teaching here after I finished college. Even though my parents lived right here, I rented a house over on Pecan Street. Live my own life, you know. That was 1960. My plan was to get my Master's degree and then teach in some larger schools. I did the graduate degree mostly in the summers. Then when I finished in 1965, I just stayed put. But I spent my summers traveling—Europe, the British Isles, I even went to Australia one summer. Then later South America, Mexico, Canada. I enjoyed every minute, so by the time I bothered leaving here, it had been nine years since I got my BA. Then after teaching in Amarillo and later Austin, I came back here, taught until I retired when the district consolidated the high school with the one in Calverton. Junior high and elementary were not for me. Chick was in my 10th grade class in '70 or '71.

"Because we were talking about friends, and then Chick called, I remembered one of the book reviews I assigned to the class he was in. *Leaving Cheyenne*, by Larry McMurtry. You may know the story. I thought because it was set in West Texas and had three characters of equal weight, two male, one female, the students might actually read it. Apparently most of them did; they turned in some decent analyses of the book. But Chick's stood out. He actually identified a major, often overlooked, point of the book, which was that friendship binds people together through some terrible things. Most of the other students were focused on the love triangle."

Marva said, "Interesting." She sipped her tea. "The reason he called was to tell me he was making chili and would pick me up if I wanted to come out and have supper with him."

Violet smiled across her teacup brim. "What did you say?"

"I told him I'd be ready at six. Do you have a copy of that book? I've never read it."

"I do. I'll find it and leave it in your room. I'll probably be in bed when you come in, so be sure to take your key."

Later, on the way out to Chick's place, he said, "I'm glad you didn't blow away in that wind today. It'd be a shame for you to miss my homemade chili."

"I'm looking forward to it." She didn't mention she was curious about his house. Since October when they'd joined forces to help Maricella Burkwalter, they'd spent a fair amount of time together—the meal with Maricella and Rebecca at Violet's house, a couple of drives around the county on Sunday evenings, another up to Palo Duro Canyon, a Sunday meal at a café in Matador. But she'd stuck to the "not a date" description of their get togethers and he'd never brought the subject up again. And until that day, he'd never shown her his place.

Leaving Jackson's Pond, he drove south a few miles, then east where the road made several curves as it dropped down off the flat cropland that marked most of the rest of the county and entered rolling grassland. Occasional clusters of mesquites dotted the pastures where cattle stopped their grazing to watch them pass. As he turned right and crossed over a cattle guard, he said, "It's just another half-mile. It's only nine miles to Jackson's Pond but seems farther because it's not as flat, has some trees."

He stopped the pickup in front of the house, a single-story ranch house with a red metal roof surrounded by six tall elms that had to have been there a very long time. Marva could see a few more cattle clustered at an earthen tank not far from the barn behind the house. As he opened the front door, Chick said, "Welcome. You're the first visitor here in a very long time. Kitchen and den are straight ahead. Bathroom's down that hall to the right, first door on the left. Come on in and make yourself comfortable."

Onion, comino, cilantro, and red chiles scented the air in the entry, encouraged her toward the kitchen.

She said, "Can I help with the chili?"

He shook his head. "I'll just turn it back on and let it cook down a little. Started it this morning early."

"Smells great." She took her time getting out of her coat, taking in the homey scene; the brightly colored pottery on the table set for two; the furnishings; the neat condition of the den.

From the kitchen, he said, "Some people like beer with their chili. Others prefer margaritas. The faint-hearted take milk, water, or iced tea. Which would you like?"

"Whatever you're having." She moved to a bookcase close to the glass patio doors. Several Larry McMurtry books along with some by John LeCarre and some others she didn't recognize, all in hardcover, filled the shelves. Two photographs in silver frames occupied the top shelf. One showed a young couple standing near one another on the porch of a two-story, yellow-painted brick house. She leaned closer. That was young Chick Talley, smiling an adoring smile toward the dark-haired, hazel-eyed, slender, young woman. A beauty. The second frame held a studio portrait of the same woman, a few years older, still beautiful. Her smile was the same, the kind that would have cast light in any room she entered. Something about her seemed familiar, and something about her eyes suggested sadness.

Chick came into the room carrying two open beers with lime slices clutching their rims. He said, "Let's start with a Corona. Might switch to margaritas later." He nodded toward the photographs. "My wife."

"Beautiful."

"Inside and out." He nodded toward two leather chairs, with matching ottomans. They sat. He took a drink of his beer. Then he said, "That other picture was taken right after we got engaged."

Marva said, "You both look happy, ready to take on the world."

Chick leaned his head back against the tufted upholstery of the chair, closed his eyes. He soon opened them and said, "That day I was sure we would live happily ever after. Nineteen seventy-four. Less than ten years later, I felt like there was nothing left to live for at all."

Marva examined the lime slice, then squeezed juice from it into the beer and pushed rind, pulp, and all into the bottle.

Chick said, "Sorry, I didn't mean to get maudlin. I seldom tell people about her anymore. But I think about her every day." His sigh reached toward Marva. "After we were situated out here, her working with me part time at the office, me full-time hustling to get a good reputation established as an appraiser, and both of us getting out and having fun together, we had a great time for about three years. Pretty soon after that, we decided it was time to start a family. When pregnancy didn't happen, she went to her gyn doctor. He found the reason. She had a rare kind of ovarian cancer. So, it was surgery right away, radiation, chemo. They thought they'd caught it in time."

He pushed the hassock away and leaned forward, elbows on his knees. He shook his head, then straightened up and had another swig of his beer. "For a couple of years after that, she felt good. Sad about not having a baby, thinking we might adopt, but good otherwise. Then she started having what she thought was a stomach problem. Well, the short version is that she died right after starting the newest chemo, a last-ditch effort down in Houston. She was just thirty-one."

There didn't seem to be any right thing to say, so Marva wiped the sweaty bottom of her beer, then took another drink.

He chuckled, "Sorry, Marva. I brought you out here to have a good time, eat chili, maybe watch a movie. Then I bring on the gloom. I sure know how to show a girl a good time, don't I?"

She said, "Don't apologize. It's hard missing someone you love." That was all she meant to say, but words kept coming. "I still dream about my brother, talk to him, and it's been more than forty years since he died." She'd never told anyone else.

Chick stood, headed toward the kitchen. "You're a good listener." A nod of his head beckoned her to follow. "I could use some help in the kitchen now. How are you at grating cheese?"

He diced onions; she grated cheese. Then she stood back and finished her beer, watching him chop cilantro, every move precise and steady, as if he had only that one task to do and all the time in world to do it. Without looking her way, he said, "I can hear you thinking. What is it?"

"The way you work suggests you're not in a hurry, not now, not ever. I think it might be good to feel that way."

"Tell you one thing, I'm in no hurry to eat. Rather drink and visit a while longer. What about you?"

She pointed toward the package of tortilla chips lying on the counter. "I'd munch on those and drink beer all evening as long as the conversation's interesting."

They each finished off their beer, and Chick brought two more. Marva said, "The smell of that chili reminds me of Cimarron, New Mexico."

"In a good way?"

She nodded. "The first time I made chili." A long pause filled the space between them.

Chick said, "Cimarron. Really pretty up there, soon as you head uphill from Springer. Vacation?"

"My dad was a farmer. I don't recall he ever took a vacation. No, I was on an adventure." She tried taking her time like Chick. After several long seconds, she said, "I can tell you about it if you're interested."

"I am. Hope it's not all sad, like mine."

Marva exhaled a long breath. Then she told him about her time in Cimarron, about Cutter, about Rose Ellen's birth, about Cutter leaving, holding off an attack by drunken cowboys, and Bullet. Couldn't seem to stop after she got rolling. Then she looped back and explained about what might have encouraged her to step off the cautious path toward a college degree into that time at high altitude. "I'd never had a boyfriend, not even a date. If I wasn't born a loner, I'd become one. Then at Tech, I actually did have a friend. She's the one who introduced me to Cutter. Maybe I was just ready to try out being someone else. Someone who had an adventure. And Cutter was a cowboy, charming, troubled, intense—all the things that appeal to a girl at that age."

All the time she was talking, Chick watched. Even when she wasn't looking at him, she felt his attention, his eyes on her. She finished off her beer, said, "Any questions from the audience?"

Chick laughed quietly, shook his head. "I'd never have guessed. Interesting what we all carry around, isn't it?" He hoisted himself from his chair, headed toward the kitchen, then turned back and held out a hand to her. "Come with me to dish up chili. I do have questions, best asked with warm food."

Sitting at the dining table, they both ate a few bites before Chick said, "Actually, it's only one question, two at the most."

Marva said, "Before that, let me say this chili is excellent. Never had better."

Chick said, "Practice. It's one of four things I cook—over and over. Thanks."

She aimed her spoon in his direction and said, "Okay, question one."

"Your story stopped at the point when you left Cimarron. Any particular reason?"

"In fact, there is. Mostly I don't recall those years nearly as clearly as the ones I told you about. Don't recall them much at all. And before you ask, yes that bothers me a little. But I did notice when Rose Ellen was here at Thanksgiving and she told something I'd done one time when she was a child, I did recall. So maybe I just hadn't had any reason to remember. Or maybe it doesn't matter." She considered a second helping of chili. When Chick mentioned another beer, they went to the kitchen and returned to their seats, each with another beer and more chili.

Chick said, "The only other questions is do you have many regrets about your life so far?"

Marva raised an index finger, piled grated cheese on a tortilla chip, and guided it to her mouth. Forming an answer took a bit longer than polishing off the chip. Chick didn't interrupt or prod. Finally, she said, "Maybe at times I have had regrets, but most of the things I thought I regretted I realized later were things I experienced to learn lessons. I could choose to regret that adventure, but if I hadn't taken that leap, then I'd have missed learning so much about so many things. And I would never have had Rose Ellen." She smiled at Chick. "You'll have to meet her. She's quite a woman." She picked up her beer, about to drink, then lowered it. "I do regret one thing."

"What?"

"Leaving Bullet behind."

By the time Marva put her key in the lock at Violet's, near midnight, the wind had laid and the nearly-full moon revealed Chick to her even more than their conversation had. She stopped before turning the key. Chick's sad-eyed smile touched her, urged her to hug him close. She said, "Thanks for good company and an excellent meal." Her words muffled against his coat because he hugged her in return, for a long time. Finally, he stepped back and said, "Thank you. I haven't had as good an evening in years." Then he smiled again. He said, "The donkey will be worried about me, late as it is. Better go." He made the few steps to his pickup. Holding the door handle, he said, "Thanks again."

Jackson's Pond Leader
Thursday, March 8, 2018
Chamber of Commerce Banquet
The annual Chamber of Commerce banquet is only 9 days away. The March 17 event will be held in the all-purpose room at RBJ. Tickets are available at City Hall--$25 per person, $45 per couple. Dress is western and the theme is A Year of Renewal for Jackson's Pond.

The evening will include a catered buffet meal of barbecued brisket, beverages, and all the trimmings including peach cobbler for dessert.

Awards will be presented to the Citizen of the Year, Man and Woman of the Year, and Volunteer of the Year.

Live music will encourage dancing following the meal and a raffle for door prizes will reward the lucky in the crowd.

In order to assure adequate food and seating, tickets will be available until 5 p.m. March 15, 2018. None will be available at the door.

Editor's Note: Let's all support this celebration of Jackson's Pond. We hope to see you there. Photos of attendees will appear in the March 22, 2018 edition of The Jackson's Pond Leader.

CHAPTER 18
March, 2018
Chamber of Commerce

Violet waited in the kitchen for Marva to come in from work. She moved the full teapot from the stove to the trivet on the table and situated a plate of the chocolate chip cookies she'd made earlier next to their two cups and saucers.

She didn't have to wait long. Marva came straight to the kitchen as soon as she was in the house. She said, "Chocolate chip, right? I smelled them in the driveway." She sat across the table and filled her cup. "It's such a fine day, I want to get in my walk right away. Not without one of these cookies and this tea first, but before I lose my enthusiasm. Do you mind?"

"Not a bit. I'll be right here." She sipped her tea as Marva selected two from the plate of six chocolate cookies. Marva was at the doorway when Violet said, "I have some news. But it will hold until you get back. And a question." That should keep her niece from dawdling.

Marva gave her a raised eyebrow and a shrug. "Sure you want don't want to tell me now?"

"We'll need to discuss it. It'll keep till you get back."

Marva reappeared a couple of minutes later, wearing a sweatshirt, jeans, windbreaker, and a Texas Tech baseball cap. Violet knew she'd come back from a recent outing with Chick sporting the cap. "I'll be back soon. By the way, I counted the cookies on that plate."

Less than an hour later, Marva sat across from her at the table again. She'd taken off the windbreaker, but still wore the cap. She finished the last bit of her current cookie, pushed the plate away, dusted invisible crumbs from her hands. She said, "Okay, ready now for the news."

Violet started right in. "Every year, except for the years when they gave up and decided not to bother because business was so bad, the Jackson's Pond Chamber of Commerce has had an annual banquet. A fundraiser and a way to encourage community pride. The Man and Woman of the Year are named; Citizen of the Year; and Volunteer of the Year. Food, entertainment and so forth. Years back, it was well attended. But that slacked off as business declined. It was sad seeing a town dying by inches." She paused, thinking that decline had been inevitable given all that changed in agriculture, transportation, successive generations of families with less commitment to the rural life, and other factors.

"But for the moment, things have changed course from that downward trajectory, plateaued at least, and the Chamber started up again last year. This year they're having the first celebration and fundraiser in a long time. Three weeks from now. How do you feel about double dating?"

She managed not to laugh at the look on Marva's face, a mixture of wonder and concern, as if she thought her aunt had slipped around the bend, gone completely nuts between that morning and early evening. She watched Marva straighten in her chair, then look directly at her.

Marva said, "Sorry, Violet, I think I missed something. I don't know how double dating is connected to the Chamber of Commerce."

"It wouldn't be a true double date. Three people, not four. It's Chick's idea. He called and asked if we would be his *dates* for the Chamber event. Said he knew how you feel about dating, so it might end up being him and me." Violet paused, a long, teacher's pause, waiting for the student to catch up. "So how *do* you feel about dating?"

Marva shook her head. "I might have known Chick had something to do with this. I told him a long time ago that when he and I go places together, it's not a date, just friends."

"Joking or being cautious?"

"Maybe both . . . or neither." Marva focused on her empty teacup. "I have almost zero experience with dating and none as an adult."

Violet said, "I'd like to go to the event. Would you?"

Marva leaned back from the table. "I don't have anything to wear."

Violet gave her the "over the bifocals" look she long ago perfected with students who evaded in order not to admit they hadn't done their homework. "Three weeks is plenty of time to find something." Seconds of silence later, she said, "I'm going to tell him yes, I'd love to go and that you'll speak for yourself." She stood, took her teacup and the cookie plate to the sink.

Still at the table, Marva said, "I'm probably overthinking this."

"No doubt. Asked yourself why?"

"Pretty sure I know why."

Violet said, "Well then. I believe you're ahead 35 games to 33 in our ongoing SCRABBLE tournament. Shall we snack for supper and go right to the next game? I plan to win twice in a row."

"If you'll put out the food, I'll get the game."

A few minutes later, Marva returned to the table with the game. She said, "I just called Chick. Told him we'd be pleased to go to the Chamber event. A double date is great. He said the theme is western. I guess you know that means I'll need to go shopping. And you'll have to go along to encourage me."

Violet smiled, hoping it looked angelic. "I may buy boots. I hear there's going to be a live band and dancing." She opened the game and shook the bag of tiles. "Two in a row, I said, I intend to win. It's actually disturbing me a little that you have upped your game, as they say. Tell the truth, were you holding back to begin with? Are you actually improving, or am I losing my grip?"

"Could be a combination. You're not the only crafty one here in Jackson's Pond," Marva said. "We could switch to dominoes if you prefer."

"Nope," Violet said, chin up, "This is *my* game." On the fifth play, she moved her right hand with the grace of a hula dancer as she moved each of the seven tiles from her holder onto the board, making the word *extruded* ending in a d in the middle of the first word played, including both a triple word score and a double letter on the r. "Bingo! Ninety-eight points. Count 'em and weep." Then she let out a stage laugh that was more of a cackle.

Marva said, her chin at the same snippy angle as Violet's, "Gloating is so unseemly." Then she played a word that scored three.

The all-purpose room at RBJ was far larger than Violet had imagined. The three of them, Chick in the middle between her and Marva, arrived about fifteen minutes after the doors opened. There were already at least fifty people mingling inside. A bandstand at one end and buffet tables at the other, and at least twenty-five, eight-person tables between filled the space not occupied by the dance floor. Along one side of the room, a beverage area four tables long featured iced tea, soft drinks, bottled beer, and wine. The wall behind that area held a banner proclaiming "A Year of Renewal for Jackson's Pond." Recorded music, mostly western swing, played at low volume, and the hum of conversation suggested good spirits abounded.

Chick suggested they claim a table and wait to see who would join them. "See an empty one you like?" he said. Then he offered an arm to each of them and headed toward the bandstand. They reached the first row of tables bordering the dance floor. "This one look okay to you ladies?" When they agreed, he leaned the top of his chair, then each of theirs, against the table and said, "That'll show these are occupied. Now we can get out and visit a bit. Show off my two dates."

She was surprised to see Marva smiling as they edged toward the beverage tables through the increasing crowd. After all the time Marva spent deciding whether to wear Levi's or the ankle-length denim skirt she'd bought, Violet worried that she dreaded meeting Jackson's Pond's citizens as a herd rather than one at a time at the post office window. She'd finally chosen the Levi's and dressed them up with the western-style shirt and silk scarf. After that, she spent a lot of time shining the red, high-topped, cowboy boots she produced from the back of her closet. Without looking up from her polishing chore, she said to Violet, "I bought these that summer when Cutter taught me to ride. I was so proud the first time I wore them."

Violet waved at Willa and Robert Stanley who were standing with the rest of the Jackson Ranch clan and left Chick and Marva on their own. She eased in next to Willa and said, "I came with a date, did you notice?"

Her weekly card partner said, "Your idea or Chick's?"

Violet said, "All his. I was a little surprised Marva agreed to a double date. Or any date. Just friends, she assures me."

"Either way, good for them both," Willa said. They turned to watch the growing crowd fill the tables.

Aiming to take along a glass of wine on her return to their table, Violet moved toward the beverage area, then halted. A large man stood near the table at the far end. He was speaking in a loud voice, gesturing broadly with one hand, holding an open beer bottle in the other. Surely that couldn't be who she thought it was. She eased along behind a man who appeared to be slow at deciding between sweet iced tea and plain. No question about it. Alvin was definitely holding forth right there at the Chamber of Commerce celebration. She startled when she heard Chick say, "Ready to take our seats? Marva's at our table. I got to talking over near the wine with the mayor and the city manager. Anyway, we both lost sight of you."

She said, "Keep an eye on that loud man over there." She nodded in Alvin's direction. "I think we may have told you a little about Alvin. Well, there he is. He may cause trouble."

"Got it," Chick said. "I'll see what he's up to if you'll let Marva know." He took a couple of steps, then turned back. "Violet, I don't remember you saying anything about anyone named Alvin. But that same guy stopped in my office yesterday. I intended to ask you about him. Said he's your nephew and was looking for a place to live. I didn't have any rentals listed, so he didn't stay long. Struck me as odd at the time."

"Nephew? No way. Trust me, he wants to make trouble, especially for Marva." Then Violet made a beeline for their table where Marva was talking with Claire Havlicek and Melanie Banks and a woman Violet didn't recognize.

Halfway to the table, Violet heard a loud voice, words slurred, obviously Alvin, say, "I guess you've heard about Marva Cope, that woman who shouldn't be trusted to run anything, much less a post office. Has her reputation from Plainview made it here? Let me just fill you in."

Another voice, one Violet didn't recognize, said, "You're not from around here, are you, pardner? We don't need you starting trouble. I suggest you settle down."

"You people need to know what kind of woman she is."
Obviously Alvin again.

Violet fought against her urge to elbow her way toward his voice
and shout, "What people need to know is what kind of person you are—
shiftless and greedy among other things."

But she didn't turn around, and right away she heard a man's
voice say, "Sir, you have to step outside with me. You're causing a
disturbance. Outside. Now." She willed herself to head straight on to
their table. So far, Marva and the other women at their table hadn't
looked up. Violet hoped they hadn't heard. Alvin shouted, "I bought a
ticket. I'm staying. I belong here as much as Marva Cope does."

Violet turned at the sounds of scuffling, saw three men walk
away from the table, one of them shaking his head, and saw two other
men in blue uniforms hustling Alvin out through the entry door. Several
other men from the drinks area followed behind the security officers
until Alvin was no longer visible. Then she continued her trek to their
table wearing an everything-is-just-fine smile she beamed directly at
Marva. Just as Violet took the last few steps, Chick joined her and
whispered, "Security took care of him. Handing him over to the sheriff
for public drunkenness, disturbing the peace, all that. Before the night's
over, I'll pass a tidbit along to Jackie Frank about that drunk man
escaping from the mental unit at the prison in Plainview. Jackie Frank
can't stand to see a rumor rest unrepeated."

Violet whispered in return. "There's a mental unit at Plainview?
I had no idea."

Chick shrugged and said, "If there's not, there probably should
be."

Marva didn't ask and Violet didn't offer any comment about
the fracas. Seconds later an announcement asked all attending to
stand and bow their heads for the invocation, and then make their
way to the buffet promptly. "Don't dawdle folks, there's lots more
on this evening's agenda—awards, door prizes, music, and dancing."

The barbecued brisket and ribs were a hit with everyone at
their table—they'd been joined by Willa and Robert Stanley, Chris
Jackson and Andrew Mullins, and Stephanie Jacobson, the city
manager—and the beverage area incident wasn't mentioned. As far

as Violet could tell, Marva was enjoying herself, getting acquainted with lots of folks. After the awards, loudly applauded by all, winners' gratitude expressed appropriately, names were drawn raffle style for winners of door prizes. Chick ambled to the podium when he won the final prize—two round-trip airline tickets and hotel accommodations for three nights in Las Vegas, Nevada. By the time he made it to the front, several men had made loud comments giving him a tough ribbing, the way friends will—"rigged raffle," "Chick only bets on sure things," "we'll do anything to get him out of town." He was blushing by the time he took the envelope from the emcee.

Immediately after that final prize, the band took the stage and began playing a lively two step. The first people on the floor were Richard Jesko and his wife. Their initial steps fetched applause. Mayor Ray Banks and his wife Melanie joined and other couples followed.

About half of the crowd straggled out the door in the next few minutes, but the rest of them stayed, talking, dancing, applauding the band at the end of each piece, and making return trips to the beverage area. Aside from crowd watching, Violet kept an eye on Marva, who actually table-hopped to one nearby. She spent time there chatting with Melanie Banks, Claire Havlicek, and Dolores Montoya. Then she joined Maricella Burkwalter and Dwain Goodlow at another table. Violet smiled thinking about those two as a couple. Dwain was a nice man, but one who seemed resigned to loneliness. There must have been a heartbreak sometime. But he and Maricella both looked happy, and Marva was right there with them, looking for all the world like she was enjoying herself.

So intent was Violet on watching her niece, she startled when Chick appeared at her side and said, "Miss Steel, would you dance with me? I've always wanted to dance with my favorite English teacher, the one I had a crush on in tenth grade."

"You may have had one too many beers, Chick. But I'm flattered; I'd be pleased." With that, she and Chick joined the dancers doing western swing to a Bob Wills oldie. As soon as they returned to the table, Violet fanning herself, Chick said, "I need to find Marva. Double dating can wear a guy out."

Violet watched him survey the room for a few seconds. He said, "She's taken up with another guy. Just my luck." He sat on the chair next to Violet. "It's almost too much excitement for me—winning a door prize, trying to keep up with two women, protecting everyone from an escapee. By the way, what's the story on him?"

Violet gave a condensed version of Alvin's last appearance, mentioning his threat to smear Marva's reputation. Chick said, "Just in case, I hope you'll keep your doors locked even when you're at home. I'll check with a friend tomorrow and find out what happened with the sheriff's office and let you know." About that time, Chris and Marva returned to the table. Before she made it to her chair, Chick said, "Next dance is mine."

Violet watched them dancing, Marva looking relaxed and happy. When that song was over, they stayed on the floor for the next one, as well. And then the band struck up "Cotton-Eyed Joe." The emcee announced, "Last dance. Everyone on the floor!" She and the others at their table joined Marva and Chick in one of the lines radiating from the center of the floor. They all danced the schottische-like steps with only a few stumbles. To her surprise, no one shouted "Bullshit" at the usual points in the song. Perhaps that was the result of the invocation earlier or the fact this was a civic event. Lots of hugging and laughing followed the final flourish by the fiddler. And then the emcee thanked everyone for attending and encouraged them to put their beer bottles in the recycling barrel on the way out.

In Chick's pickup on the way to her house, Violet said, "I haven't had as good a time in a long while. Thanks, Chick."

"My pleasure, Ma'am."

Marva said, "I enjoyed the evening. Double dating is a fine idea. And just because I'm smiling, don't think I missed Alvin's display. I chose to ignore it."

Chick drove on, no comment. Violet said, "There will be some who didn't. I can hardly wait to set them straight."

Chick spoke up then. "Well, he livened up the evening a bit. People always need something to talk about. Only thing is, my winning the door prize will cause a lot more speculation than any gossip about Marva. Trying to guess the answer to 'Who will he take to Las Vegas?'

will surely be the main topic for the farm store coffee group for at least a week."

When Chick parked in front of her house, none of them made a move to get out of the vehicle. Sounds of breathing were the only sign of life for a minute or so. Then Violet opened the pickup's back door. In a flash, Chick made it around to the passenger side and opened the front door as well. He offered Marva and Violet his arms and ushered them to the house. "Thank you both. We must do this again."

In the house, she and Marva sat at the kitchen table, each sipping wine. They chatted briefly about the people at their table and the band. Violet said, "That episode with Alvin reminded me of something I intended to do. Stay here, I'll be right back." She went toward the den and returned a few seconds later. She handed Marva a key. "After that visit from Alvin back in the fall, I did what I should have a long time ago. I reviewed my will and the medical directive and then took those and the deed to this property and put them in a safe deposit box at the bank. More than once I had found him snooping through my desk and asking too many questions for good manners. I'm giving you this key to that box. If he managed to come in here and pilfer around again, he'd never think to look among your things."

Marva took the key and promised to hide it. She said, "Do you really think he'd try to find your legal documents?"

"I wouldn't put anything past him. You saw him tonight."

Marva sat back, sipping again. Violet said, "You look a little sad. Was it that business with Alvin?"

"No, not really."

"What, then?"

"I think it's that I had a really good time, and I had nearly forgotten how until recently. I've probably missed out on a lot."

"Does Chick have anything to do with that?"

Marva smiled and nodded. "Probably. Remember what you showed me?" She put one hand out, then another above it nearer to her. "About the difference between acquaintances and friends?"

"I do."

Marva said, "I'd say he's moved out of the acquaintance category into friend." She finished her wine and stood. "I'm locking the doors and putting the burglar bars under the handles. The baseball bat's in my room. Just in case." She stopped in the doorway and said, "I wish I hadn't given away that shotgun I had back in New Mexico."

Jackson's Pond Leader
Thursday, March 23, 2018
Law Enforcement Report
Jackson's Pond deputies of the Floyd County Sheriff's Department investigated a burglary and theft at the Jackson's Pond laundromat which occurred sometime between 9 p.m. on March 19th and 8 a.m. March 20.

The lock on the front door to the building had been secured on March 19 by the minister of the church that sponsors the laundromat, and was found to have been forced and the door opened at 8 a.m. when he ordinarily opens the facility.

A change machine with at least $100 in coins in it had been torn from a wall near the door. Two washers and a dryer were damaged in an apparent attempt to extract coins from them, also.

Deputies recovered fingerprints from the doorway and the machines, and are investigating further. There were no citizen reports of suspicious individuals on Bond Street where the laundry is located during the night of the burglary.

The Sheriff's office requests that all citizens report any suspicious person near their property. They also encourage that all parked vehicles be locked and any outdoor storage sheds be secured.

CHAPTER 19

Late March 2018
Finding Stacey Farris

id-morning on Saturday, Marva stared at her computer screen. She'd expected that after more than thirty years, finding Stacey might be impossible. But there she was on Facebook. Marva had spent some time signing up for the site after searching on the web for Stacey Farris, the same name as when they lived in the Tech dorm. No surprise, since apparently everyone in the world except Marva was already on Facebook, the first listing that popped up for Stacey was for one on Facebook.

So, Marva had gritted her teeth and joined the social media world. Now she wasn't sure what to do next. It looked simple enough, send a friend request. According to her page, Stacey had 287 friends. Again, no surprise. She was the one who engineered group dates, could talk to anyone, and did, and called everyone by name. She never forgot a name. Her profile picture showed her astride a beautiful black horse. She was wearing jeans, a red and black western shirt, and a barn coat, and her smile was as bright as Marva remembered. Probably still an indiscriminate hugger. There was nothing listed under the personal information and no pictures of a husband or kids. Marva clicked friend request.

She sat on the back porch drinking coffee, thinking of what she'd say if Stacey responded. How to explain thirty plus years' absence. A couple of hours later, she gave up thinking about how to make sense of something she didn't really understand herself. She returned to her computer and Facebook. Stacey had accepted the friend request and sent a private message in which she offered her phone number and asked Marva to call, AS SOON AS POSSIBLE. Marva had read somewhere that using all capital letters online was like shouting, not a nice thing to do. But the Stacey she had known would shout because she was excited. Regardless, Marva put Stacey's number in her phone's contact list, noticing it had an 806 area code, same as hers. Then she returned to Facebook and answered: *I'll call at 1 p.m. today, if that works for you.* She had nothing else urgent to do—it was her Saturday off. Seconds later, the reply to her message blinked: *1 is great! Can't wait!*

At one o'clock, Marva's hands shook as she pressed the numbers on her phone. *What am I nervous about? It's Stacey. But she'll have questions. I won't have answers, not ones that make sense. She'll be a successful ranch owner, married with three kids. A handsome husband. They'll have two adjoining ranches and own all of Uvalde, Texas. She'll remember every conversation we ever had, will want to know what happened that summer.* Her finger poised over the red end-call button, then she took a deep breath and waited.

Stacey answered, her voice the same as always—enthusiastic, happy. "Oh, Marva, I'm so glad you found me. I've looked for you. You can't imagine how many times."

"Well, here I am. I'm sorry I haven't been in touch. Thought about you often." She didn't say she couldn't recall any specific time in the past thirty years she'd had that thought. "Tell me about yourself. How's life treated you? So far, I mean."

Stacey didn't respond immediately. Finally, she said, "It's been interesting. I'll say that. Nothing like I planned, though." Marva waited. Knowing Stacey, she'd say more, fill the silence. But it took a while. Finally, Stacey said, "Maybe you remember the plan, well, my parents' plan, was that I'd come home and move into running the ranch. My dad, for sure, was counting on that. My mom, maybe not so much. But I was to carry the name on. Only child. Turned out after I graduated from Tech, my ideas and his about running a ranch in dry country were miles apart. I tried really hard to work with him, do things his way."

Marva settled back in her chair. Stacey barely took a breath, kept on talking. Not long after she returned to Uvalde after graduating, her mother was diagnosed with ovarian cancer. So she stayed and helped take care of her. Her dad went to pieces. Wanted her to "just take over." But he didn't mean take over her way. Anytime she actually tried to make ranch decisions, they bickered and he won. For two years, as she watched her mother go through surgery and chemo and get sicker and sicker, he was either out buying up more land so they could "enlarge the herd" or sitting in his chair staring straight ahead. "You'd have thought mother getting cancer was a personal affront to him. I was too busy being the caregiver to stop and think much about what would happen in the long term. And then the doctor put her on hospice care. There were nurses coming regularly. She wasn't in pain any longer. All of a sudden, I had time, and I could see I'd be left there with him, both of us frustrated."

Marva could tell from her voice that the memories were still fresh for Stacey after all this time. She said, "That must have been really hard for you. I can't imagine." She paused, then said, "That was a long time ago. What happened next?"

"Let's just say I disappointed my father by taking a job at the bank in Uvalde, moving into town. They made me the ag loan officer. Truth is, I thought my dad was going to live on forever, and no matter how much I loved him, I wasn't going to live out there with him and end up being his bookkeeper and cook."

"You still live in Uvalde?"

"You and I need to see each other, have a real talk, for days. I live most of the time in Lubbock. How far is that from you?"

"Not far. Sixty miles. Jackson's Pond."

"What? This is ridiculous. Let's get together right away. Can you come and spend next weekend here? I know that's selfish. You probably have family, or work or both. Obligations. But I really want to see you. There's so much to talk about."

Marva's first thought was to make an excuse, invent a family or some local friends relying on her for an important party that would keep her from leaving town. But that would never work with Stacey, she'd just volunteer to come to Jackson's Pond. She'd offer to help. Marva said, "I can't see why not. You name the time and place and I'll be there." She was shaking her head as she said that, thinking she'd made a huge mistake by ever signing up for Facebook.

Before they hung up, they agreed to meet at noon the following Saturday at the restaurant where Marva worked all those years ago. Same name and still located on Broadway a few blocks from campus. She'd stay at Stacey's Saturday night and they'd decide later about any other plans. After they ended the call, Marva went to the den and said to Violet, "I can't believe what I just did." She explained briefly about searching for Stacey and wondered aloud why she now felt so anxious about agreeing to see her, to stay with her in Lubbock.

Violet shrugged and said, "Maybe it's easier to let everyone and everything from the past stay there?"

Marva said, "She'll probably be successful, have handsome grown sons, an adoring husband, and a gigantic house in Lubbock as well as owning a massive ranch near Uvalde."

"Maybe. Or she could be like most of the people in the world—have had some successes and failures, joys and regrets. If she was worth knowing back then and remembering until now, she's probably still worth knowing." Violet hesitated, then said, "You may not have a clear notion of why you got in touch with her. But you did it, so something in you thought it was worth doing."

Marva felt her aunt watching her. Violet said, "Would a cup of tea help?"

"A walk would help first. I'll be back in time to help with dinner."

Her route took her up and down each of the blocks in Violet's neighborhood, then past the Methodist Church heading west three blocks to Main Street. As usual, the wind gusted occasionally, but the sun was shining. Eight large elm trees across the street from City Hall, planted decades ago and sustained by the care of generations of settlers' descendants, had begun leafing out. Grackles haggled in the high branches as if annoyed by her muttering in their territory.

She'll be pretty and successful and . . . she'll ask about that summer and she'll say she told me so. She'll want to know about the years between. Do I have children, did I ever marry? I won't lie. I'd never deny Rose Ellen. What will I say about that and all those years between?

Marva stopped, stood still as if her path were blocked. Alone on the sidewalk near the only remaining empty store front on Main, she closed her eyes, leaned against the dusty window of what had once been a dry-cleaning service. Behind her closed lids, the image that stopped her was one she'd seen many times when she was near sleep, weary from a day at the post office. Other times it simply appeared vividly when sadness rolled over her like a cloud of springtime dust. Each time, she knew without knowing why, not until today, that it was a scene from where she lived when she left Cimarron until she found a place with more space for the baby. It was the only apartment in Lubbock she could afford, and those glimpses of that image made her want to cover her eyes.

It was a place sandwiched between two of five identical apartments lined up along a side street. One bedroom, a claustrophobic little bathroom and a living room/kitchen, each two steps apart, fit for a doll house or a trailer. But it was safe and quiet. In the six months she lived there never did she ever meet any of her neighbors. Now she knew it was her fault. She'd closed herself up when she waved goodbye in Cimarron to Carol McQueen, that woman who treated her like a friend. More than once in those six months she had thought about finding Stacey. But she hadn't tried. *Because I was ashamed.*

She straightened up and headed back toward Violet's house.

When she joined her aunt in the kitchen, Violet was already cooking, so the only thing for Marva to do was sit and watch while Violet peeled potatoes. She pointed with her paring knife to a plate on the countertop and said, "I already ate my piece of gingerbread. There's yours." Marva slid the plate near and bit into her the spicy treat immediately. Violet said, "Did the walk help?"

Wiping crumbs from her chin, Marva said, "It did. I'm ready to see Stacey, actually eager. I think everything will be fine. And if she's anything like the Stacey I knew, she won't let me get away with evading questions. I'm glad I called her." She poured a cup of tea and then cut another square of gingerbread. "I don't think one more small piece will hurt my appetite."

On her way to Lubbock the following Saturday, Marva forced herself to focus on the drive, not on what the afternoon in Lubbock would hold. She kept her speed below the limit. Her ten-year-old Chevy—low mileage because she seldom drove anywhere but to work—would probably benefit from some road miles. She might, too. That last thought made her smile. There was no reason at all that she couldn't travel some. Maybe this weekend's little trip would be the first of many. Central Texas, the Hill Country would be nice this time of year. Bluebonnets would already be blooming down there. Or she could load up Violet and go all the way to South Padre. She hadn't ever managed to get to a beach. Not yet. For that matter, she didn't have to limit herself to Texas. New Orleans would be . . . or maybe the Grand Canyon . . . or San Francisco. She slowed and made the turn in Calverton that would take her on into Lubbock.

Marva entered the restaurant and saw Stacey standing near a table at the back of the restaurant. She half expected Stacey to rush to her, but she didn't; she stood still, wearing a big smile the way she had all those years ago. The only obvious difference was her hair, still the chocolate brown she recalled, but now there were gray streaks at her temples that emphasized her cheekbones. The effect was a grown woman's classic beauty. When Marva reached the table, she opened her arms and Stacey wrapped her in a tight hug. She said to Marva, "You haven't changed a bit."

A young woman, about the same age Marva had been when she worked in that restaurant, offered menus and brought water. "This place has changed, but not much," Marva said. She considered her menu briefly, snuck a look at Stacey who had pulled out a pair of readers and still squinted a bit studying hers. "Want to split some nachos to start?" Stacey nodded and continued focusing on the menu. Marva said, "Descriptions are fancier—must have had a menu consultant—but basically the food's still pretty much the same as when I worked here."

Stacey closed her menu, looked up at Marva. Her smile was sadder than before, a bit wistful, Marva thought. Stacey said, "The last time I saw you, more than thirty years ago, was when I dropped you off right out front here. You were picking up a couple of shifts before taking off with Cutter." She shook her head a bit. "I shouldn't admit it, but I was a little jealous. You were going to have an adventure. I was stuck here doing exactly what my parents had planned for me."

Before Marva could respond, the server returned. They placed their order, and Stacey spoke again. "After we talked on the phone, I was thinking about all the things we might tell each other, filling in the gaps, how one weekend surely won't be enough. I decided one thing I want us to do this weekend is to only tell about the good things that have happened to us so far. If you're like me, like most people, I think, there's plenty to regret, ways to get stuck, losses, all that. But I don't want to be a person who sees someone they care about after a long time and all they end up talking about is their health problems, disappointments, and other miseries." She peered at Marva intensely, seriously, over the lenses. "Are you okay with that? There'll be time for all the rest later."

Marva said, "Sure, that's definitely beats a litany of bad dates and bankruptcies." Making certain she smiled, she said, "While we're waiting for nachos, here's something you probably don't know; when I came back to Lubbock, I worked here for close to four years, taking classes part time, and finally ended up with a degree in sociology." As the words came out, she realized she hadn't even told Violet how proud of herself she'd been to finish that degree with a baby on her hip.

"I was long gone before that. I finished my degree in ag eco in three and a half years and went right home," Stacey said. "In fact, I'm sure I was gone before you came back. Otherwise, I'd have seen you here or on campus."

Their food arrived. They bumped hands reaching for nachos at the same time. Marva knew she'd turned clumsy because she was thinking of how to explain the time it took getting that degree. No sense saving it for another time. Thankful for the seconds required for them to consume one nacho each, she reached for her iced tea and said, "Here's something good, and it explains why it took me so long to finish that last thirty credit hours for my degree."

She plunged right on after the tiniest pause. "My daughter, Rose Ellen Gulley, was born October, 1984. I came back to Lubbock in January of '85. Rose Ellen is thirty-two now, a teacher. I read a lot to her from my sociology books when she was a baby. So, she's quite intelligent. And she's good-hearted and kind." She blinked several times and reached for another nacho.

Stacey pulled off the half-glasses and said, "Wow! I had no idea."

Marva said, "Really?" Maybe Stacey actually hadn't heard from someone in Uvalde. Maybe the Gulleys were already living near San Antonio by the time they were aware of Rose Ellen's existence. No sense trying to figure that out. If she ever knew, she wouldn't remember. Back then, it had been hard enough keeping up with daily responsibilities much less being concerned about gossip in a distant, small town in Texas.

Stacey said, "No, I didn't know. I heard the Gulleys moved not long before I got back home. So I never knew what happened to Cutter after you two left here. High school friends scattered, and lots of those guys from home were more than eager to get away and never come back. Like most twenty-year-olds, I was more concerned with my own life than anyone else's."

They ate silently for about a minute, then Marva said, "Get to many rodeos these days? You know, I give you credit for explaining the event scoring to me that first time you invited me out with your gang."

That brought a smile from Stacey. "That's something I haven't ever let go of. Now I volunteer with the Tech rodeo team, just helping them with practice, and I have a few horses at my place, one really good barrel horse I still like to work."

Finding it wasn't hard at all to talk about the good times, especially after having told of Rose Ellen, Marva said, "Here's another good thing. I learned to ride. Cutter taught me and I was okay at it."

Stacey said, "We should plan to go trail riding sometime."

After their meal, left half-finished because it got cold while they talked, she followed Stacey to her house where, according to her, she lived about three quarters of the time; the rest she spent in Uvalde seeing to the place her folks left her when they died. She had a manager and his wife living on the place which she'd turned into a hunting "resort," which she called a fancy way of saying she took tidy sums of money from hunters who came mostly from the metroplex and Houston to pretend they were better shots than they were. "I go down and meet any new ones and lay out the rules, tell them to leave it better than they found it or they won't be allowed back, things like that. In between my visits, the couple take good care of the place."

That sounded familiar to Marva, too familiar.

Stacey lived in a medium-sized, older, well-maintained house just south of the university. Marva remembered the neighborhood, several blocks of substantial houses with beautiful yards, home to many faculty and other professionals in the 1980s. It faced a city park full of trees, some picnic tables, and a jogging path. A large elm shaded the front yard and pansies bloomed in two giant pots on the wide front porch. The inside of the house had obviously been remodeled—all up-to-date features but the hardwood floors looked like the original, now vintage, pride of owners from mid-twentieth century. She followed as Stacey led her to the guest room, passing a home office next to it. "Make yourself comfortable. The bathroom's connected, that door over there. I'll be in the kitchen." As she left Marva to unpack her overnight bag, Stacey said, "Do you drink wine or prefer iced tea?"

"Whatever you're having will be great."

Marva found Stacey in the kitchen, opening a bottle of wine. "From a Lubbock winery," Stacey said. "Want to sit out back since the wind's not blowing?"

'Out back' was an understatement. The yard was a landscape designer's dream. Plus, a covered patio extended across the entire back of the house. They sat in lounge chairs on either side of a wrought iron table. Stacey said, "We'll order supper delivered from somewhere when we get hungry if that suits you. That way our visiting won't be interrupted with cooking."

They eased from making comments about the birds the yard attracted back to a story about the house's former owners, the original ones who'd had the house built and promptly planted mature trees at no small expense. Then Marva said, "Do you still work? Or have you retired early?"

"Some might say I have, those who envy my being my own boss. I deal in real estate. After my dad died, I left the bank in

Uvalde. I'd had enough of that. It wasn't all that difficult, just sort of sad to me, people borrowing money, dreaming of making it big in ranching down there. They didn't want to hear my advice about their ranching practices' not fitting the reality of the situation. Reminded me of gamblers wanting just one more stake because their luck was sure to come back." She refreshed both of their glasses and pointed to a squirrel running from a branch to the back fence. "So I got a real estate license. I don't sell many houses and list very few. I mostly represent people selling land in the area around Lubbock. But I've picked up some good rental properties along the way. Before you ask, no, as far as the tenants know, I'm not their landlord. I pay a manager to handle the properties, keep them in good shape, deal with tenants." She held up her glass admiring the wine's color in the sunlight. "Say, you remember that house I moved into with a roommate? You were right. It was a nightmare. I moved back into the dorm my last semester just to get out of there."

Marva shook her head. She remembered that day. "I should apologize. I might have been a little harsh. You were good natured about my being so blunt, as I recall."

"Speaking of retired, what about you? I would have bet you were a teacher."

"It's too early for me to retire. After twenty-four years in the USPS, I'm postmaster of Jackson's Pond, Texas. Since last summer."

"Sounds impressive. Do you like your work?"

"It's not all that impressive. Small town. But yes, I like it. There's variety, some interesting folks. Only a couple of people to manage—a clerk and one in-town route driver and a part-timer who does rural route delivery. Next step up would be a larger post office. But I've worked in a couple of those, and I'm happy to stay where I am. At least for now. Maybe for good." Admitting that surprised her.

In the course of a couple of hours, they wandered through a few more topics, all fitting the "good things" rule Stacey proposed, and finished off the wine. Pizza delivered to the door made switching to beer sound like a good idea.

The day was still warm, so they ate on the patio, and by the time the sun dropped low, leaving long shadows across the yard, conversation changed course. Beer will do that. From the particulars of job function and marital status—each declaring one near miss and neither pressing the other for details—to general, almost philosophical questions, the sort where answers are often gray and tentative.

Surprising herself for a second time that day, Marva said, "Here's a personal observation, about me. I tell you this with the purpose of asking if you've had any similar thoughts." She straightened up on the lounge chair and turned to face Stacey. "Do you ever have the feeling that you should be able to remember things that have happened at times in your life and you can't? In my case, there's a lot of blank space between when Rose Ellen was about one up until the last couple of years."

Stacey didn't hesitate before she said, "Sure. And I've thought about why. I think it's because we don't remember the chronology of our lives, we remember events. I don't only mean events in the typical sense, like a big party, a graduation, a birth, but also interpersonal things that were BIG to us for a reason. I can give you an example. I don't remember anything about the actual ceremony, about walking across a stage receiving a diploma when I graduated from Tech, even though it was an important event at the time. But I do remember my dad and mom leaving for home afterward, him saying, 'No more partying for you girl. Now's when life gets real.' That seemed unjustified, even hateful. I remember what he said, but nothing of my own big moment." She nodded as if confirming something. "Maybe we're all that way. The day-to-day disappears pretty quickly, the things that hurt us last a long time."

"So you don't think it's odd that I couldn't answer Rose Ellen when she asked me if I was a member of the PTA at her school?"

"Why would you? Maybe you would if you spilled the punch at some PTA ceremony or you stole the funds for the kids' end of school party." Stacey laughed and snorted. "I bet you'd remember that if you got caught."

Marva laughed with her. "So it's not surprising I can remember big firsts, like the first time I had sex, or that first rodeo you made me go to, but not what kind of car I drove in 1995?"

"Exactly." Stacey sipped at her beer, then after a long pause said, "Seriously, I think when we're busy doing everyday life, particularly if we feel under pressure, like I did with the ranch, or you probably did being a single parent, then it's easy for only the best, the worst, the scariest to be the only things we recall." She shrugged, then squinted for a few seconds. Marva nursed her beer and felt the evening chill settle. Then Stacey said, "Here's something I've been thinking about: what am I supposed to do with the rest of my life? Does that ever come to your mind?"

Marva said, "Not in those exact words. But it has occurred to me that when I was twenty, I never reckoned with the fact that being a woman was different, something more, than being a girl. Hadn't realized a woman should be more than the surface; there has to be substance. Otherwise she'd wake up at forty-five and be an old girl, not a woman. I was only concerned with being 'not-my-mother.' To be truthful, I'm not sure if I ever got past that surface, gathered the necessary substance. It seems like it's time I figured that out." She watched Stacey turning her gaze, following the path of an airplane gliding above. "Have you answered that question for yourself, what you'll do with these next years?"

Stacey laughed, "I only recently accepted that fact that I'm over fifty. And I swear, it's beer and good company that made me even bring that up. I guess I'll just have to wait and see what turns up and try in the meantime to do some kind of good, somewhere." She stood and said, "I don't know about you, but I'm about ready for bed. We could go out to where my horse lives tomorrow morning if you'd like to. I usually go out and feed him early. Then we could come back, have lunch somewhere before you have to go."

As soon as she stood, Marva knew she could do with a good night's sleep, too. She said, "Sure I'd love to meet your horse. And I agree, it's bedtime." Even though the day had been full of laughter and positive things, she needed the shelter of time alone.

Early Sunday morning, they drove to the south edge of Lubbock, past the new houses that dotted what once had been cotton fields, and turned onto a dirt road that dead-ended at a gate. Before she got out to unlock it, Stacey said, "The cotton farmer that owned these two sections listed his land for sale with me. Before I put it on the market, I offered him a good price for 160 of the 1280 acres." She pointed toward a barn about a quarter mile away. "I got that in the deal, along with the well that he irrigated from." She returned, drove through, then got out and locked the gate behind them. Driving to the barn, she said, "He was thrilled with the money he ended up with. I made sure the developer who bought it planned to build ranch-style houses, not a bunch of two-story, zero lot uglies, and each lot would be no less than ten acres. So far, only a couple of those have actually materialized, so this still seems a little like the country."

When they stopped at the barn, three horses trotted from the pasture toward Stacey's pickup. She said, "The black one's Pal, my horse. And those are his two friends, Ace and Slick. They belong to the family that lives down there." She pointed east to a small house with a red metal roof. "Horses are social. So, sharing this pasture is good for them, and it's a good deal for me and Pal. Having someone who'll keep an eye on him, water and feed when I'm not here."

Marva had no trouble pitching in to help Stacey finish tending to the horses. The barn's scent brought a brief image of the New Mexico ranch and a sorrow-tinged memory of a constipated horse. When the chores were finished, Stacey drove around south Lubbock, then the university campus, and finally returned to her own neighborhood, narrating the entire tour with tales of changes in the city since 1985.

Before they got out at her house, Stacey said, "I have to ask one thing, Marva. Why did you never in all those years get in touch with me? I thought we were friends."

Concentrating on the flowers on Stacey's front porch, Marva hesitated, then sighed. "I can only say I was probably too busy feeling sorry for myself, and probably punishing myself. You were a person who would have succeeded. I was the one who screwed up her life."

Stacey shook her head. Marva turned to face her. Stacey said, "You were important to me and then you were gone."

Marva said, "I'm sorry. Sorry if that hurt you."

"It did."

"You have every right to be angry with me. I wouldn't blame you if you never spoke to me again."

Stacey's voice was barely above a whisper when she said, "I'm not angry; just sad. I've missed you."

Neither of them moved for a long minute. Then Stacey said, "That's all behind us now. We're starting over." Then she reached across the pickup console and hugged Marva. "I'm hungry. Let's go in and find food."

They ate a leisurely salad lunch at her house and set a date in April for her to come to Jackson's Pond for a stayover. "We still have lots to catch up on. Next time we'll trade regrets and discuss what to do with the rest of our lives," Stacey said.

On the drive back to Jackson's Pond, Marva focused again on spring's effect on the countryside—fields green, some pivot sprinklers circling their slow march through the planted acres, cattle pastures dotted with black angus cows and their calves—but unlike the day before, no dread traveled with her. Instead, she thought of Carol McQueen, another person who, like Stacey, had been a friend to her, even though she hadn't been a real friend in return. Not until now. Carol would be in her seventies by now. It might take some searching, but she intended to find her.

When she made the turn in Calverton toward Jackson's Pond, she slowed and tried to form a coherent thought she could keep to remind her of that weekend.

Rose Ellen was seven when Marva first gave her a large, five-hundred-piece jigsaw puzzle. Until then, the puzzles in her daughter's Christmas gifts were for children, and they spent hours working them together. When she unwrapped the new one, Rose Ellen said, "A grown-up puzzle! Will you show me the rules?" Stacey was right, those firsts do stay in memory. That puzzle, Rose Ellen's asking for the "rules" were a sort of first. And she recalled telling her there were lots of ways to fit the puzzle together, but that she always started with the borders. Marva knew why this came to mind. She and Stacey were fitting together the borders of their lives, the more difficult parts would come later, learning about each other, more of the pieces fitting. That could take a long time, maybe the rest of their lives.

She opened the door at Violet's. The usual aroma of recent baking didn't greet her. She looked into the den and saw her aunt lying on the couch, not in her usual chair. A book lay open on her chest. Marva took her bag to her room. When she returned, went to the kitchen, she found Violet standing at the sink, filling the teakettle.

"Don't think you can sneak in on me, Missy. How was your visit?"

"Good, really good. Stacey's coming out next month. You'll like her." She snuck a look at Violet. "Everything okay here?"

"Oh, fine. I skipped church today, and as you probably noticed, I was napping when you came in."

Marva waited. Violet would explain if she wanted to, only if she chose.

"I let my ambition get the best of me. I'd planned for a while to clear out things in my closet. That wasn't the problem. But after that, I tackled those shelves in the garage. I swear, I even wished for a minute that Alvin was here. At least I could occasionally get him to carry out accumulated junk. Anyway, I knew better than to lift and drag and haul stuff. But I went right on and did it. Osteoarthritis, you know. Entirely my own fault for overdoing."

"Are you okay now?"

"I am. Rest is the answer. That and Tylenol. And remembering to stay within my limits. Now, let's sit down, and you tell me all about your friend."

Jackson's Pond Leader
Thursday, April 19, 2018
Youth Soccer in Full Swing

Jackson's Pond Tadpoles won their division in the first soccer tournament played at the new Soccer Complex. Twelve teams competed in this first tournament at the new facility. Towns represented in addition to Jackson's Pond were Matador, Calverton, and Lockney.

The Tadpoles, a girls' team ages 4-6 played a 3 versus 3 game, no goalie. They scored 2 points to their opponent's 0 in their first game, 3 to 1 in their second, and won the prize with a tight 3-2 over a team from Matador. (see photos page 4)

Other Jackson's Pond teams competing in the tournament were age 9-10 boys Rockets and age 9-10 girls Amazons.

Coaches and parents deserve thanks and congratulations for their dedication to supporting this youth sports league in Jackson's Pond.

Editor's Note: I am new to soccer, completely. So the sight of 4-year-olds racing up and down the field perhaps in pursuit of the ball, but more often of each other, is more comical than athletic. But watching the older players, it's evident that as they progress, they learn athletic skills as well as the rules of the game.

CHAPTER 20

Late April, 2018
Rose Ellen

The first surprise for Marva that day was Rose Ellen's call. She was sitting on the patio watching a sparrow build a nest. When the phone rang, she thought it was Stacey, who was supposed to arrive in Jackson's Pond around noon; maybe she'd changed her mind. So, when Rose Ellen said, "Hi, Mom! How is this sunny Saturday for you?" Marva said, "Uh . . ." Then she laughed and said, "It's great so far. I'm glad to hear your voice. What's happening for you this weekend?"

That was her way of disguising the bit of worry that any call from her grown daughter brought. Her first thought was always that something bad had happened. She hated being that way, too much like her mother's lifetime of negative expectations. But Rose Ellen had called only a week ago—talking about the teaching assignment she was looking forward to next year and a bookshelf she found at a garage sale and refinished. Then she'd emailed a picture of her handiwork. So, Marva inhaled and exhaled slowly, working to avoid any doom embellished prediction.

"I couldn't wait any longer to tell you. Dwight and I are engaged, as of last night at dinner! Do you have time for me to tell you about how he proposed?" Then without a pause, she launched into describing a romantic dinner in Wichita Falls—an excellent meal, fine wine, and beautiful chocolate soufflé for dessert. Then the waiter produced champagne and Dwight flourished a napkin to the floor near her chair. He knelt on it on one knee and asked if she would do him the honor of being his wife for the rest of time and beyond. "I could barely get out the words 'Yes, I will.' " Rose Ellen finally took a breath. Then she said, "You have to see the ring. I'll send a picture. And you have to meet Dwight."

"Of course. Have you set a date for the wedding?"

"We're thinking June ninth. That's a Saturday and school will be out. But if that won't work for you, we can choose another date. It's not like we've already sent out invitations or booked a church. Not like it's an urgent matter, actually. To tell the truth, I was surprised, completely surprised."

"You two hadn't discussed marriage before?"

Marva heard a deep breath from Rose Ellen. She waited. Rose Ellen said, "Only in vague terms, about marriage in general. He probably would have proposed earlier if I hadn't told him I wasn't sure marriage made any sense, was basically a property arrangement. We'd talked about love, specifically, though. I do love him. He's a really good, decent person. I believe he loves me. He's said it plenty of times."

"June ninth will definitely work for me, and if you decide on another date, just let me know. I'll make certain to be there."

"Part of why I called is that I want you to meet Dwight, you know, before. And I'll need your advice about wedding arrangements. Can you come to Seymour one weekend soon?"

Marva couldn't help chuckling. "I doubt I'll be much good offering wedding advice."

"Please, Mom, it's important to me."

"Oh, honey, I was just joking. Sorry. Of course, I'll come." They agreed on the following weekend. Before they hung up, Marva said, "I want your wedding to be everything you've hoped for. I'm happy for you." She hesitated, then said, "Just for the record, I believe in marriage when it's based on love."

Rose Ellen said, "Thank you. I love you, Mom."

A picture of a wide platinum band set with a hefty solitaire diamond appeared on Marva's phone. She went to show it to Violet but saw her resting on the couch, her eyes closed. Seeing that reminded her. Before the weekend was over she'd ask Violet if she had seen her doctor recently. Her naps were definitely more frequent. As far as Marva knew, her aunt only took one or two Tylenol a day for the aches of arthritis and one small dose of blood pressure medication. But she'd never actually asked. Leaving the doorway quietly, Marva stopped in her bathroom to put out clean towels. Stacey should arrive any minute.

The two of them were sitting on the back porch drinking iced tea when Violet joined them. Marva did the introductions and then said, "I have news." On her phone, she opened the picture of the engagement ring and turned it so they could both see. "Rose Ellen called today to announce she's engaged. This picture arrived right after we talked."

"You had no idea?" Violet said.

"I knew she and Dwight were dating, but no. She said he surprised her last night with a formal proposal after a romantic dinner. Sounds like he has a flair for the dramatic—down on one knee in a fancy restaurant."

"Well?" Stacey said. "What's your reaction?"

"Surprised. Happy for her if that's what she wants. To tell you the truth, I don't think it should matter to her what I think."

Violet said, "That's a good point. What would any of the three of us, all never married, know about what is right for her?"

For a few seconds, they all drank tea and stared at the recently leafed elm trees. Then Marva said, "I wonder if I am supposed to go shopping for one of those mother-of-the-bride dresses. Pastel, I guess."

"Perhaps trimmed in denim, to go with your red boots," Violet said, then laughed. "I think it's time we opened a bottle of wine."

A bit later, after they settled the question of what to do about dinner by deciding to forage in the kitchen for snacks and call it a meal, they opened the bottle and toasted to Rose Ellen and her intended. Stacey said, "I'd like to continue the topic of marriage, and trade 'why I didn't and/or how many times I chose not to' stories. I'll go first."

Marva listened as Stacey admitted she had thought she'd probably never hear a proposal because she was twenty-eight when it finally happened. The way she made a joke of thinking she was the oldest virgin to ever graduate from Texas Tech gave Marva the feeling Stacey had perfected that tale by telling it before. Then Stacey explained why she'd said no to the proposal. "We didn't really know each other and had very few experiences in common. His close friends were already married, had kids. I met them and their Junior League wives and that cinched it. I wouldn't have fit in."

Violet said, "Did you regret turning him down?"

"Nope, not then and certainly not when I saw him a few years later. Fat and bald." She winked when she raised her glass after that.

She sped through stories of two more proposals, the most recent a couple of years back. That last one she called a near miss.

Violet asked, "Did those three have anything in common aside from wanting to marry you?"

Stacey didn't hesitate. "I thought about that just now as I was telling about them. They were completely different types—young banker, a not much older rancher, and a middle-aged Realtor—but they all asked me without really knowing me. I was worried, I think, that they had an idea of someone they'd turn me into."

Marva had been quiet, listening, remembering how Stacey could lift everyone's mood when they'd been young. She still had that quality, but that last comment told her Stacey would only choose to marry someone who saw past her ability to elevate others, would want to stand with her during her own tough times. She refreshed their glasses.

Violet cleared her throat, lifted her chin, and said, "I have in my lifetime received a total of six marriage proposals. I accepted two of those, one of which I quickly recanted. The other resulted in, as you called it, Stacey, a near miss. I am less than proud to say I left him standing in front of a Justice of the Peace in Austin, Texas. But it is important to note that in both of those cases, I did return the rings." She glanced at Stacey and Marva, stretched the pause, then said, "Why? Surely you . . ."

Marva waved a hand, interrupting. "Stacey, I warn you, my aunt taught English, and she also taught drama. I'm not sure we should trust this performance. Violet, swear what you've said so far is true."

"Okay. I'm busted. There were actually seven proposals, and I did keep one of the rings. But let me finish. As I said, you ask why? In every case, I knew that they would want to hold me down, expect me to go where they wanted to go, live an ordinary life."

Marva leaned forward, elbows on the patio table. "Unlike others here. Let me repeat, unlike others here, I feel bound to tell the truth. So, I have only a single proposal to report. The only thing that would have made it any less cartoon-worthy would have been a parent standing by with a shotgun. To give the man, actually the boy, credit, he thought he was doing the right thing by saying that if I wanted to, we'd get married. He couldn't have been more wrong. So I have no engagements nor any other proposals to offer, and as far as I can recall only a handful of dates." After a bit more wine, she said, "I may have made those dates up."

The other two laughed, Violet pointing at her nose. "Your nose is growing. I vote we choose things to snack on and come back out here for more fascinating true stories of three Texas spinsters."

Marva led the way from the kitchen, arms full. Potato chips, corn chips, grocery store onion dip, carrot strips, a bowl of leftover-from-the-day-before chicken salad, all stacked atop three dinner plates. Violet followed with a plate of sliced cheeses and thinly sliced ham and a box of saltine crackers. Stacey followed, carrying two bottles of wine and two of water. Marva surveyed the table. She said, "Silverware. Napkins. I'll be right back."

After they filled their plates, Stacey said, "One follow-up question. Some people would feel sorry for us. Do either of you have regrets about those decisions?"

Marva said, "Once in a while, years ago. I felt sorry that Rose Ellen didn't have a dad on site. But I knew he and I were both too young and weren't equal to helping each other grow up. Hard enough doing it for myself." She sipped the last of the wine in her glass. "But now I'm glad I didn't marry Cutter. And I never have wanted to marry anyone else." She glanced at Stacey. "What about you, regrets?"

"I sometimes think it would be nice if someone was waiting for me when I come home."

Violet said, "That's what dogs are for."

Stacey laughed, then coughed and spewed bits of the cracker she'd just bitten into. "Don't make me laugh like that again! But seriously, you are absolutely right. And if I could find a dog that could bring me coffee in the morning, I'd never have another regret."

"I apologize. I'd hate to have to call the EMTs on your first visit here." Violet patted Stacey's shoulder. "You okay? Need some water?"

They snacked for several minutes, then, first Marva, then Stacey, sat back, nursing their glasses of wine. After a bit, Violet said, "There have been times in my life I've wished to have someone I loved to wake up beside. But I can truthfully say that after a fling or two that involved that waking up next to someone experience, I realized I was soon eager for whoever was beside me to take his leave. I knew I was too selfish and too fond of the excitement of romance and adventure to be limited to one person long term."

She nodded toward Marva and said, "But I will say, having a good SCRABBLE companion suits me fine."

Marva leaned forward, reached for a bottle of water. "I have one more question for tonight. Have either of you had health problems—long illnesses, broken bones, chronic problems?"

Stacey said, "Until I was forty, I was sure I was bulletproof, except for a broken arm and that was my own fault. Helping out in a rodeo alley, I got banged against a chute and had a fractured humerus. Then forty arrived and a breast lump gave me a good scare, especially with mother having died with cancer. After a lumpectomy, no recurrence. I've had annual mammograms. And for the past two years, I've had to take a small dose of blood pressure medicine. No big problems, but I did have to accept that I'm not invincible. So, annual checkups. Routine screening."

Violet nodded and said, "Maybe we're all that way when we're young. Bulletproof. It was hard for me to accept when I was around thirty-five that I needed some counseling. Well, more than some, quite a lot. It helped; I learned a lot. Then after I turned sixty, my blood pressure rose. I have medicine for that. But I admit I have neglected the regular checkups. In fact, I have an appointment next week to see the doctor. According to her office person, I have to come in or there'll be no more refills."

Now she wouldn't have to ask. Marva said, "I can drive you to that appointment if you like."

Violet shook her head. "Not necessary, but thanks. Willa has lined Robert up to drive us. She and I will do a little shopping after."

Marva said, "My turn, I guess. I admit it took a scare to get me to pay attention, too. Getting anemic, feeling awful, and having extremely heavy menstrual periods sent me to a gynecologist. The bleeding was perimenopausal hormone problems, but she discovered suspicious endometrial cells. So I had a hysterectomy. No cancer, though. Now I do have regular screenings. And one more thing. I wish now I had been as smart as you Violet, to get counseling." She stacked their plates together, moved the scraps of cheese and crackers to the one on top. "Seems we three have some things in common. It's nice to know we're all more human than otherwise. I'll clear these dishes."

Violet said, "If you girls don't mind, I'm going to take this nice glow and head on to bed. See you in the morning."

The two of them sat without speaking, sipping occasionally at the wine, Marva's thoughts roved, rested a second on fitting together borders, moved on, then settled. She heard Stacey say, "What are you thinking?"

"What I'm supposed to do with the rest of my life."

"Me, too."

Marva said, "I think we'll be okay."

Monday after having a quick lunch she brought from home, Marva looked out the post office window. The flag hung limp against the pole. The weather site on her computer declared the temperature a tolerable 84 degrees F. Perfect conditions for her walk. She told the clerk she'd be back before one, and left by the back door.

After Stacey left the afternoon before to get home in time to feed her horse, Violet had napped and Marva had pretended to be cleaning the kitchen and clearing the refrigerator. In truth, that was busywork, mindless chores she chose to give herself time to think. Her main concern was how to make certain Rose Ellen's wedding didn't become an opportunity for her mother to . . . actually she couldn't quite express what she thought her mother might do that would ruin Rose Ellen's day. For that matter, she had no real reason to believe her mother would want to spoil it. And by the time Marva went to bed, she still hadn't managed to name the dread she felt.

When she shut the post office door, Marva walked quickly back toward Violet's house, staying on residential streets rather than on Main. Right away, she began speaking aloud, softly, *Don't give your mother any more thought. Rose Ellen will invite her, knowing it's an obligation. She'll also invite her other grandmother, because she loves her. Your daughter is a grown woman who doesn't need you worrying on her behalf. Tell the truth, it's you you're worried about, having to see your mother in person after so many years of occasional phone calls and holiday cards. Focus on something you're actually in charge of, like what to wear when you meet Dwight, something that won't embarrass Rose Ellen and that won't require a shopping trip between now and Friday.*

The clothing question didn't occupy much time. Marva knew exactly what clothes hung in her closet. Slacks—black, navy, brown, and white, tailored shirts—mostly white, a few blouses in bright prints, three dresses that fit nicely, three blazers—white linen, navy blue linen, and red poplin, and several pair of Levi's 501s. She'd come up with three casual combinations and one dress for the weekend. And she promised herself she'd go shopping before the actual wedding. This weekend was supposed to be mother and daughter planning a wedding. She imagined herself driving east, heading for Seymour, then the image changed. There she was standing by her stranded old car, no traffic in sight. Marva stopped in the middle of the sidewalk. *I knew there was something else. My car needs an oil change and tire rotation.*

A horn beeped behind her. She didn't turn, but did quit lecturing herself aloud. She kept walking until she reached an intersection. A turn to the right would let her identify the honker, most likely Chick. Might as well stop because if it was Chick, he'd tag along until she finally did. A patient man who enjoyed kidding her about her walking and talking to herself. Marva turned right, then stopped. The pickup wasn't Chick's. Then the driver lowered his window.

Chick said, "Need a ride, lady?"

"Might as well." She got in the passenger side of the 4-door, red Chevrolet pickup. "Smells mighty new."

"It is. Well, new to me and less than a thousand miles on the odometer. I wasn't looking for a new ride, but the people in Plainview made me a good deal on mine and a good deal on this one, so . . ."

Marva looked at her phone. "I have to be back at the P.O. in ten minutes. Were you just out looking for women on foot or me in particular?"

"You. I thought we might make a day-long road trip this weekend to put some miles on this. Start early and come back late, head anywhere you want in a 300-mile radius. Your choice."

She said she'd like to go, and then explained why she couldn't. He drove slowly as she talked about Rose Ellen and the fancy proposal. He asked how she felt about her daughter getting married. Then he pulled to the side of the street and parked. "Here's an idea. I'll drive you to Seymour and drop you off. Then I'll go on to Wichita Falls and prowl around, then pick you up on Sunday."

"I hate to put you to that much trouble. I don't mind driving alone."

"Don't take this wrong, but your car's seen its better days. Ought to be retired from road trips. Nothing personal. Just an observation."

Her first inclination was to bail out and say, "Observe this. Me walking away." She was already holding the door handle. But her better sense told her he was correct. "You're right."

She turned to face him. "You'd be so easy to take advantage of, Chick Talley. But I'm not a female in distress. No rescue required."

"Don't worry, I know you can take care of yourself. But think about this. Maybe it's me who needs rescuing. I don't like spending all my time alone. I enjoy your company. Makes perfect sense, you do me a favor and have an easy trip in the bargain."

"In that case, it's a deal. Let's talk later about details. I have to get back to work."

As he started the vehicle again, he said, "I didn't mention one thing. The passenger does have some responsibilities. Like reading the operator's manual and helping figure out how to set the clock and get the radio stations on automatic, stuff like that. It's a full-time job."

Jackson's Pond Leader
Thursday, May 10, 2018
It's Your Health
by Claire Havlicek, FNP
More About Fall Prevention

This column offers more advice on preventing falls, particularly for the elderly and those with chronic illnesses.

Another preventive action is reorganizing the home to reduce hazards. At the top of the list of hazards is throw rugs. If a person's gait is impaired, a throw rug is a snare waiting for an already unsure foot.
*Remove all throw rugs.

Another hazard is inadequate lighting or dangerous light fixtures. If vision is impaired, shadows invite missteps. Floor lamp cords can tangle with feet.
*Increase wattage in light fixtures.
*Remove floor lamps or move them to corners with cords tucked away.

Reaching to get dishes or utensils on high shelves or items on high closet shelves can cause imbalance and falls. The same is true of bending to get articles from low cabinets. Barns, garages, and sheds are also sites of falls from overreaching and imbalance.
*Reorganize shelves and cabinets to reduce danger of imbalance.

Finally, recall the adage—"Pride goeth before a fall."

CHAPTER 21

Early May, 2018
Plans for the Future

Chick stowed a handful of his favorite CDs in the console in his new pickup and pushed up the back seats to leave floor room for suitcases and a cooler. Next he brought the cooler from the kitchen to the garage. He'd already stacked in a package of sliced ham and one of sliced turkey, a couple of oranges, a bag of Fritos, and a loaf of whole wheat bread. When he slid it into the back floorboard, he realized he had no condiments. What kind of ham sandwich had no mustard? Back through the garage to the kitchen. His plan was that he and Marva could picnic on the way to Seymour. He'd pick her up as soon as she got off work and be out of town just after five. The drive to Seymour should take no more than two and a half hours.

Just as he stepped back into the garage from his trip to the kitchen, the container of mustard he had under his left arm fell to the floor. Thank God it wasn't the jar of pickles. He retrieved the mustard, stowed it and the mayonnaise and the pickles in the cooler, then stood still. It never failed, he forgot something. His wife had been the organized, ready-for-any-trip-no-hitches person at their house. Next time he'd make a list, probably save some boot leather.

He'd forgotten to put in the blue cooling blocks from the freezer. And the drinks. No room for them in that cooler anyway. At this rate, Marva would be standing in her driveway tapping her foot by the time he got there. He jerked a small cooler off a shelf and crammed in six canned Coors beers and four Dr Peppers with two more icy blocks. Finally, his suitcase was all he lacked. Four-thirty. If he didn't have a blowout on his fancy new pickup, he'd make it to town before five. A quick tour of the house, suitcase in hand, checking locks and stove burners, a stop to load the luggage, and he was out of the garage, on the road to Jackson's Pond. Helping Marva seemed like a good idea. He had no idea it'd turn into such an ordeal.

Her daughter was expecting her around eight, so a short stop for sandwiches somewhere around the Four Sixes ranch shouldn't be a problem. But getting packed shouldn't have caused him trouble either. Thank goodness, Marva wasn't outside pacing when he pulled into Violet's driveway. In fact, he was greeted at the front door by Violet who said Marva was running a little behind, so would he like a cookie while he waited.

A few minutes and three cookies later, Marva stood in the doorway to the kitchen. He let himself relax when she flashed a big smile and said, "I'm sorry I kept you waiting. Had a few things to do before I left work. I let Rose Ellen know I'd be there later. Turns out that's fine with her. She can grade papers this evening and not have that to do on Sunday."

Violet handed him a zip bag full of oatmeal cookies. "In case you get stranded. I expect you'll call or text to let me know when you get there."

Once they were on the road, Chick said, "So . . ."

Marva said, "So, I'm in no big hurry. And I'll tell you right now that your driving me over here makes everything easier for me. Thanks again." She patted his shoulder. "You're a pal."

Chick nodded, pretty sure he could take that as a compliment. Kept his mouth shut. Willie Nelson's *Red Headed Stranger* CD entertained them as they descended from the Caprock to the Rolling Plains. Marva occasionally hummed along, and other than that, they rode in silence until they made a turn in Dickens toward Guthrie. Chick said, "If you're interested, we can picnic somewhere around Guthrie, pretend we own the Four Sixes ranch out there. I brought sandwich makings."

"Sounds good to me." A few miles later, she said, "Did you have time to visit much with Violet while you waited? Did she seem okay?"

He shrugged. "I think so. Why?"

"Seems to me she's not quite her usual perky self. Not since she went to the doctor a few weeks back. May be nothing."

"You asked her?"

She shook her head. "She's pretty private about some things." She turned, watching something out her window. She said, "Did you see that?"

He slowed the pickup. "Something wrong?"

"Something odd. Mind going back a mile or so?"

The road was bare of traffic in both directions, so he made a quick U turn. Soon he saw what had caught her interest, and made another U. He'd barely stopped before she had her phone out, snapping pictures. There on the south side of the road, impaled like Monday's laundry on a five-strand barbed wire fence, fluttering in the wind, were a white nightgown, a pair of woman's underpants, and a large-cupped woman's bra, all three cotton, it looked like. Marva jammed her phone in her Levi's pocket and bailed out of the pickup, heading toward the fence. After a bit of fumbling, Chick found the switch for the hazard lights. Then he followed her into the ditch and up to the fence. He said, "See any blood on them anywhere?"

She shook her head. "I don't see any footprints on the other side of the fence, either. That's good. I imagined a woman, running." She bent and slipped between the second and third strands of fence wire and crossed into the pasture. He watched and waited while she paced several feet in each direction along the fence line and out into the pasture. "Nothing seems disturbed over here." She slipped back between the wire strands, stood beside him. "Makes you wonder, though." She stared at the array a bit longer, then said, "Looks more intentional than accidental. Art, maybe." She shrugged and said, "Thanks for stopping."

They stopped at a roadside park beyond Guthrie to picnic. Chick apologized for not having lettuce and tomatoes for the sandwiches. Marva told him her turkey was just right. He noticed she had seemed focused on something in the distance for a while before they stopped. "Something serious on your mind?"

She finished the last of her sandwich and opened the cookie bag, took a drink of her Dr Pepper. He wondered if she'd heard him. Then she said, "More curious. You imagined laundry back there. I imagined a woman running away. We must imagine things based on experience. A long time ago, I ran away." She put the cookies down without taking one. Then she told him about Chance's death and how getting away from home was her only goal for a long time after her dad died. He listened, not interrupting.

She said, "Remember I told you about my brother who died in an accident? For a very long time, I dreamed Chance took care of me, helped me get away, go to college, all that. I imagined him talking to me, giving advice. I know now I also felt guilty, that the accident was my fault. Then not too long ago, I dreamed he told me I was grown now, and I could take care of myself." She opened the cookie bag again. She smiled at him and said, "I'm not sure why I told you that."

"I'm glad you did. Can I have one of those cookies?"

A while later, when they passed a sign that said Seymour 24 miles, Chick told her it was time for her to start earning her keep. "Remember I said you'd have to read the Operator's Manual? It's in the glove box. This vehicle has a navigation system, according to the salesman. If you have Rose Ellen's address, and if you understand the instructions, then we'll find her. Okay?" He waited until she found the manual. He said, "All right, any time now, I'm ready for your orders."

She located the page, stared at it for a bit, then cut her eyes his direction. She said, "Seymour's not that big. We can just stop at a 7-Eleven and ask where Harrison Street is."

"What fun would that be?"

"Right." Then she commenced reading the instructions aloud.

Soon after they entered the city limits in Seymour, directed by the map shown on the dashboard screen, Chick pulled into the driveway at 715 Harrison. Marva's daughter came out to the pickup. "I heard you drive up. Great timing. I just finished grading papers." Marva introduced them, and Rose Ellen invited him in. He tried not to stare at her as he thanked her and said he needed to get on over to Wichita Falls. The two of them could have been sisters. Same curly hair, same inquisitive eyes, same voice, same smile—the daughter's a little quicker to appear.

He handed Marva her suitcase, and started the pickup. He started raising the window. Rose Ellen said, "Wait. Would you come for brunch Sunday before you two have to go back?" He lowered the window, looked toward Marva standing behind her. He said, "This is

Marva's trip. I'll do whatever she says." He said to Marva, "Call or message me and let me know when to turn up. You two have a good visit."

Chick was at the outskirts of Wichita Falls by nine-thirty and checked in at a La Quinta a few minutes later. He thought about eating another sandwich, but decided on finishing off the Fritos with a beer. Soon after, he turned in and slept better than he had in a long time, without waking, until seven the next morning. A text from Marva waited on his phone: "Lots of discussion—I'm clueless about advice. Come Sunday around eleven. Meet the groom to be. I'm trying to remain calm." He laughed at that last part.

He entertained himself with in-room TV, reading the local newspaper focusing on the real estate ads, then checking out a couple of the places listed to see what a 300-thousand-dollar house in Wichita Falls looked like. Then he kept on driving, ending up out in the country around Holliday, looking at land, mentally estimating the value. A real estate appraiser's holiday. After a chicken fried steak dinner, he hit the sack early again. If pressed, he'd admit he thought a lot of random thoughts about how it would be having a daughter getting married. The last thing he recalled was wondering if Old Jess would have sense enough to find the food he left out for him.

Sunday morning, as he dressed in clean, starched Wranglers and a good shirt, he wished he'd brought slacks and a dress shirt. It would be nice if Rose Ellen thought he was good enough to be her mother's friend. He made it to Seymour and found Harrison Street again just in time to park out front behind another 2018 model pickup. Maybe he wouldn't embarrass anyone after all.

The groom to be was a tall, slim, dark-haired man who had a firm handshake and a genuine-seeming smile. He'd be hard not to like immediately. He chatted easily with them about growing up in Seymour, working summers on his parents' farm, and his job as band director at the high school. Rose Ellen busied herself in the kitchen while they sat at the nearby table in the dining area. She wouldn't hear of anyone helping. "I want y'all to get to know each other," she said. But it was clear she was following the conversation as she glanced at them frequently. Once she said, "Dwight won't tell you, but I will, that his band has won State the past two years. And the marching band wins every competition they enter." Chick was certain that Dwight actually blushed when she said that.

They left, full of omelets, fresh fruit, and coffee cake, around one. Marva was quiet for about forty miles. Had a lot to think about, he imagined. After a restroom stop in Guthrie, they broke out the cookies and the last two Dr Peppers and continued west. He had figured out the cruise control on the new pickup, and set it at 65. If she was in a hurry, she'd tell him. When they were back on the road, she said, "This wedding's going to be quite a production. Thank goodness they decided to delay until July rather than try to get it all together by early June. July twenty-first, to be exact. Part of the reason for the delay is that Dwight was asked to be faculty for the band camp at Tech for two weeks in June. Big honor for an alum, they assured me. Plus, once the band kids heard about the engagement, they 'demanded' to be allowed to play at the wedding. And the reception and dance afterward. He and Rose Ellen are just oblivious to any possible problems with the event. As far as they're concerned. It will be great fun."

Chick said, "Sounds like they have a good attitude. That'll go a long way."

"Oh, I have no doubt they'll pull it off. It's all kind of amazing to me—how was I so lucky to have a daughter like her?"

She pulled a notepad and pen from her purse and wrote something brief, snapped the ballpoint in and out a couple of times, then sighed and stowed the pen and pad in the purse. "The ceremony isn't going to be in a church, but they'll have a minister. Methodist. Someone Dwight went to high school with. Two attendants each. Her colors are two shades of purple. Wedding dress already purchased. It's a calf-length ivory satin—I told her I liked it, but to tell the truth, wedding dresses leave me cold."

He didn't ask any questions. She'd tell him whatever had her stirred up if and when she wanted to. But after several more miles, he thought a nudge might help. He said, "Have you been assigned a job or two for this affair?"

"I agreed to walk her down the aisle and give her away. And there'll be a rehearsal and a dinner the night before, plus the reception and dance afterward." She tapped a random beat with on the console with her left hand's fingernails, then halted and shifted in her seat. "I had money set aside, saved for years, to be able to give her something—a car for high school graduation, a big trip after college, a down payment on a house, I don't know, whatever she wanted.

"But every time there was an occasion, she'd say no, she wanted me to do nice things for myself. Said I had done everything for her for eighteen years. Even in high school and ever since, she's always had a job. Traditionally, the bride's parents pay for the wedding. Finally, I thought, this is something I can do. She won't have to feel bad about having only one parent. But when I got out my checkbook and told her I was going to pay, she said no." The fingernail tapping started again, then stopped. "I think she feels sorry for me."

He drove several miles before saying, "Did you tell her that?"

She shook her head.

He said, "My guess is she's proud to be independent, like you. Proving to herself she's competent, like you. That's not feeling sorry for you; it's being proud of you, wanting to be like you."

He heard her inhale a long breath, then exhale. "They won't even need a down payment. Dwight has a nice house and she's already started redecorating it."

"Sounds like she's got things handled."

"Better than I do. Rose Ellen told me her grandmother Gulley is excited for her and will be there. And she plans to let my mother know by sending her an invitation when they're printed. I was worried she would call to tell her and Mother would say something awful. You're right she does have things handled."

"Looks to me like you're free now to do what you want to do, be who you want to be."

"Scary thought."

Around five o'clock, he pulled into Jackson's Pond, poking along on Main Street. Marva had turned quiet again. He said, "It's early. Anything you want to do before I deliver you to your doorstep?"

"That beer still cold?"

"Sure."

She said, "Let's park somewhere, have a beer. I want to tell you some things and ask you a question."

Chick drove west past the road to the Jackson Ranch, then north on a county road, then turned off on a service road to one of the wind turbines. "How's this?"

Marva said, "Just right." She unbuckled her seat belt and reached into the back, pulled two beer cans from the cooler. She popped hers open and raised it toward Chick. "My thanks to an excellent driver and companion."

"You're more than welcome. Any time."

She said, "There's something else I want to tell you." She took a drink of her beer, worked on getting her thought straight before she spoke again. "Your remark about being able to do what I want now woke me like a slap in the face. I've avoided thinking about that. See, the problem is I know what I *don't* want to do, but what I do want is not entirely clear."

She looked away, out the window, then shook her head and said, "My list of 'don't want tos' includes going to church, gossiping with women, watching soap operas, going shopping, going places to meet men, and quilting. My ideas of what I want to do are still a little fuzzy. But I do know I want to feel at home someplace, and to have at least a couple of real friends." She stopped and inhaled, noticed a smile pass across Chick's face. She said, "So, your comment about being free to do what I want reminded me I have to keep working on myself."

He'd finished off a good portion of his beer when he said, "You said there was a question."

"Yes. Would you go with me in July to the rehearsal dinner and the wedding? I'll pay for your gas."

"Not necessary. I'd love to."

"You sure? It'll take up the whole weekend."

"Right. I'll let Old Jess know in advance."

She pushed the Willie Nelson disk in to play, leaned back in her seat, drank more of the beer. "Rose Ellen said she liked you as soon as she met you."

He patted her hand. "You made that up, I'll bet. Sweet of you to wait till I agreed to take you back to Seymour."

Jackson's Pond Leader
Thursday, June 14, 2018
Around Town

Next week's edition of the Leader will feature local yards and gardens. Photos and interviews will spotlight planting and maintenance activities that promote plant health and conserve water.

Touring town and talking with residents, we saw projects underway and other complete with results including emerging vegetable gardens in containers, pallet plantings attached vertically to fences, xeriscape areas or entire yards that combine low water use with beautiful design, and many other horticultural activities that enhance homes and Jackson's Pond as a whole.

Another, somewhat related project, is the development of a "seed library" sponsored by our local library. The old practice of seed saving is being revived, and a group meeting at the library plans to promote the practice. The end result will be that residents will be able to use the library as a source of sharing seeds from their gardens with other interested gardeners.

CHAPTER 22
June 18, 2018
Now

That Monday morning had been quiet at the post office, so Marva had eaten the salad she brought for lunch and was tying on her walking shoes when the clerk tapped a timid couple of knocks on the office door. When Marva let her in, she saw a tear dribble down the young woman's face. She told her to sit and handed her a tissue. "Tell me what's wrong."

The story, which took a while to piece together between the sobbing that followed and the clerk's frequent, "I'm so sorry to cry, but there's no one I can tell," was that she'd just learned that morning she was pregnant. The third pregnancy test she'd used before she came to work showed positive, the same as the previous two. Her husband, recently unemployed would kill her.

Marva abandoned hope of getting in a walk and spent the rest of the lunch hour helping the girl settle down. She finally confessed that the problem wasn't her husband. That was an excuse. He loved kids and he loved her. Actually, she was afraid of being pregnant because having a baby had been the end of her sister's marriage. "We were doing so well. This will ruin everything."

Marva listened without commenting until the crying and blubbering stopped. Then she said, "What can I do to help?"

The girl sniffled once more, then sat up and said, "You already did it. You listened to me. I just had to tell someone how scared I am. Please don't tell anyone."

Marva told her she could trust her; their talk was confidential. She urged her to take the rest of the day off, get some lunch, rest, and then talk to her husband. "If you need someone to listen again, let me know. You're a grown woman, and I know you're smart. I think you'll be able to handle this."

After the clerk left, the afternoon sped by—intermittent post office business punctuated during the lulls by Marva's thinking about how panic inducing an unplanned pregnancy could be. She knew.

At five, she locked the back door, then hesitated at her car, finally deciding she'd get in her two miles before heading home. The sun wouldn't set for hours yet. So she had no excuse. She locked her purse in her car and walked east, pretending she was being pursued, which was true in a way. Ten extra pounds lurked behind her, ready to make the mother of the bride look matronly and dowdy, a replica of her own mother. That extra adipose would overtake her the moment she stopped exercising and started enjoying too many of Violet's baked creations.

Rose Ellen's formal wedding invitation arrived the day before. That had sent Marva online for a couple of hours the night before, searching for a dress suitable for the occasion and something else to wear to the rehearsal dinner. Frustration stopped her—finding something in a shade of purple limited the selection; finding something she could imagine wearing reduced the possibilities even further. Stacey convinced her, when she called her for advice, that she should come to Lubbock to shop. Come Friday evening, they'd start early Saturday and get that chore over with even if it took the whole weekend.

She turned left and headed north, the still-bright afternoon sun glinting in her left eye. Her sunglasses were in her purse back in the car. The vision of those extra pounds in pursuit banished the thought of stopping her compulsory exercise. It also started her talking to herself. _Pick up the pace._ A rain earlier in the week had refreshed the grass in the neighborhood she entered, perfuming the air, encouraging clumps of iris foliage in a flower bed she passed to thrust blossom spikes that would soon bloom. _Purple, Rose Ellen's bridal colors. Mother would have gotten her invitation today. No sense thinking about that, planning what to say. Remember to focus on now._ She repeated the word. _Now. Now._ And she kept on walking.

Her supervisor had called her early that morning and reminded her it was her anniversary, one year as Postmaster. He complimented her work and then surprised her. He'd recommended her for promotion to postmaster at a larger facility, a job opening in Central Texas. He was sending her the information and hoped she'd consider it. "It would be good for your career in the Postal Service," he'd said. "Even if you're looking toward retirement in the next five or ten years, no sense just marking time. This promotion would increase your pension. Think about it."

Marva had said, "My clerk is ill today so I need to go. Work the counter. Thank you for calling." That excuse about the clerk's being ill, well, she considered that an acceptable lie.

Recalling that now, she told herself that acceptable or not, avoiding her supervisor's meddling was justified. She didn't need or want advice from him. A few more blocks later, when she ran out of paved street, she made a right turn and headed east again. Ten more minutes, a few more blocks, and she'd be back to her car. She needed to get to the house; Violet wanted to pot the tomato plants this afternoon.

What makes him think advancing my career is the thing I want to do, now, in my mid-fifties? More money, more responsibility, a different town. But I can retire in two years, with twenty-five years in the Postal Service. I'll admit it, I want to stay here. She stopped at the intersection with Main Street, looked both ways. *Now. Now, now.*

As she neared her car, Marva answered a question she hadn't allowed herself to consider before. *I will spend my time until retirement helping that young clerk learn as much as she can; help her advance in the Postal Service. I won't be marking time. I'll be productive until my final day as Postmaster.*

Her car welcomed her with a wave of hot air when she opened the door. Marva lowered the windows and blotted perspiration from her upper lip while thinking whether she needed to stop at the grocery store. No. She'd eat light again tonight; there were plenty of salad vegetables in the refrigerator.

The aroma of peanut butter cookies met her as she opened the front door. Violet, baking as usual. After changing from her work clothes into jeans and a T-shirt, Marva went to the kitchen. Two teacups, each with a fresh teabag, sat on the counter next to the SCRABBLE box, unopened. It wasn't like Violet not to call out to her when she came in. She'd promised she'd wait for Marva and wouldn't lift the heavy pots they planned to fill that afternoon. Some would hold the tomato plants—they'd grow their own and not run out of salad vegetables, others multicolored petunias. Marva had brought three twenty-five-pound bags of potting soil into the garage Saturday afternoon. "Please don't try to lift these either," she'd said. Violet had nodded, which Marva knew meant maybe.

She opened the back door, pushed open the screen. She saw Violet on the grass, in the shade just off the left side of the patio. She lay prone, her face turned to the left, her left arm at her side, her right arm reaching above her head, a pose for a swimmer's crawl stroke. Marva couldn't catch her breath for a second. Then she rushed to her aunt, shouted, "Violet, do you hear me?"

Marva knelt in the grass beside her, knowing that calling to Violet was useless. Motionless, pulseless, cold to the touch, even on this summer day, she was dead. Marva pushed back a strand of hair that had fallen across Violet's cheek, noticed a garden trowel on the ground near her waist, an overturned pot of petunia plants just beyond that. Marva forgot again how to breathe, and when she couldn't inhale properly, she lay down beside Violet, her left arm stretched across the woman who always had understood her, even when she didn't understand herself. Seconds later she gasped, then strangled out the words, "No, Violet, please don't go!" Sobbing, she tried to think, knew she couldn't think until she could breathe. Breathing, crying, remembering her father and Chance, working at breathing steadily, slowly, and crying more than she'd cried in years, she didn't stir from Violet's side. And finally after what seemed a very long time, she sat up and did the only thing she knew for sure she should do. She called Chick.

He answered. She breathed, but couldn't say words. Chick said, "Marva, what's wrong?"

She choked out, "It's Violet."

"Are you at home?"

"Yes. Oh, Chick. Violet's dead."

"Stay where you are. Don't move. I'll be right there."

Marva didn't move and she didn't hear Chick until he touched her shoulder and said, "Let me help you stand." She made it to her feet, then he hugged her, and she sagged against him as he walked her to the lounge chair. He went to Violet, touched her arm, felt for a pulse at her neck. Then he returned to Marva and said,

"Here's what has to be done. Tell me what happened. After that, I'll call the sheriff's office. They'll send the local deputy, and he will notify the Justice of the Peace. They'll come and investigate and then they'll decide whether an autopsy is required or whether to take her to the funeral home directly."

She said, "I left work at five, took a walk for thirty minutes, and then I came home. I changed clothes and then I called out for Violet. We were going to plant those pots this evening. So I looked out here and saw her right there. She had no pulse and wasn't breathing, was cold to touch. I was useless for a few minutes, couldn't breathe or do anything but cry. Then I called you." She shrugged, then sighed. "I should have been here."

He said, "When you came in, was anything odd, any sign of disturbance, anything missing?"

Marva tried to recall, then said, "I wasn't looking to see if anything was missing, but I would have noticed if things had been disturbed in the den or kitchen or my room." She rubbed a hand across her forehead. "You could look in her room, but nothing seemed out of order to me."

"Has she said anything about being sick?" He shook his head. "Never mind, I remember we talked about her seeing a doctor for high blood pressure."

"Right. She mentioned she went back for follow-up. The doctor had changed her medicine. Wanted to be sure it was effective. But nothing else."

"Has Alvin been around?"

"No."

Chick spoke slowly and clearly, as if she might be confused or hard of hearing. "Do you think she'd have talked to Willa? Not wanting to worry you?"

"I wouldn't be surprised. Chick. I'm okay."

"Are you okay to call Willa, let her know, ask if she told her anything?"

Marva nodded.

He said, "I'll call the Sheriff's office while you do that." He got as far as the back door, then said, "I'll stay with her."

She nodded again. Then she said, "She baked sometime today. The oven was off, but I smelled cookies." She fumbled in the kitchen drawer, looking for the phone directory, gave up, and called Claire's number on her phone's contact list. Without asking any questions, Claire gave her Willa's number. Marva congratulated herself on having a speck of sense to thank Claire.

She had difficulty saying the word "dead" to Willa when she explained the reason for her call. Willa must have understood because she said the doctor had made a referral to a cardiologist, and she and her husband, Robert, were supposed to take Violet to Lubbock for the appointment Monday. "Atrial fibrillation is what she said. I wrote it down. Violet was going to tell you after she'd gotten it taken care of. She's stubborn that way. Are you alone? Do you need help?"

"I called Chick. I didn't know what to do." Her voice failed her for a few seconds. "He's getting the deputy, called him."

Willa said, "I'll be there in thirty minutes. Do you mind if I tell Claire?"

"That's fine, thank you." Her voice trailed off as she said, "I'll hang up now." She didn't move. She needed something she didn't know the name of right then, didn't know how to ask for.

Chick came inside. She said, "Did you call the Sheriff."

He nodded, said, "He's on his way." Then he went in the den and came out with the fuzzy blanket Violet used when she rested. He patted Marva on the shoulder as he walked by, then went out and covered Violet where she lay.

Marva wandered around in the kitchen, turned on the burner under the teakettle, then went outside and sat with Violet and Chick. He said, "The deputy will be here in a few minutes and the JP will come shortly after. I alerted the funeral director to expect a call for transport sometime in the evening."

The kettle whistled. Marva didn't move. Chick brought the two teacups with their bags to the table, then returned with the kettle and poured. He said, "Is there anyone you'd like me to call?"

"Stacey." She dipped the tea bag up and down. "I should have been here."

"Give me your phone, I'll call her." She handed him the

phone that was lying face down on the table, picked up the teacup, then set it down.

She said, "I don't know what to do next."

"Nothing right now. When the deputy comes, just tell him what you told me. He'll take it from there. I'll go inside, let him in when he comes. And I'll call Stacey. You can stay here with Violet."

There was a lot she wanted to say to Violet, but speaking any more was beyond her. So she closed her eyes and thought about how safe and loved she felt in her aunt's presence, always had. And how selfish, she thought, that she wanted Violet to live forever, selfish because she wanted her there to be wise, to sometimes be funny, to cheat at SCRABBLE, and to help her know how to live the rest of her life.

Marva opened her eyes when she heard the screen open. Chick led out a stocky, forty-something man wearing a deputy sheriff's badge and a baseball cap with Floyd County S.D. embroidered across the front to her. Chick introduced them and then stood aside. The deputy said, "I'm sure sorry, Ma'am. I know this is hard."

Marva followed him to where Violet lay. She watched his every move as he removed the blanket, then squatted next to her aunt, felt for a pulse, nodded to himself, then gently turned her to her back. Her telephone fell from the patch pocket of the loose smock she was wearing with her shirt and denim pants. He checked the phone and made another note on his pad. He looked at her and said, "Phone's working. No calls in or out all day." He stood, replaced the blanket, and said, "Let's sit over there. I have to ask some questions."

After a deep breath, she managed to respond promptly to his what, when, where questions. Over his shoulder, she saw Willa and Claire looking out from the back door. Chick left her with the deputy and went to talk with them. The deputy made notes on a narrow pad he took from his hip pocket. Without looking up, he pointed to the bags of potting soil, the tomato and petunia plants, "Looks like she was doing some gardening."

Marva said, "We were going to pot those when I came in from work. She promised me she'd wait and not lift the pots. I told her not to carry those bags." She wiped her shirt sleeve across her eyes. "I expected her to live forever."

He asked about Violet's health. Marva told him she knew she took medicine for high blood pressure, and had been to see the doctor recently. "Her friend Willa went with her. You could ask her." She pointed toward the back door.

The deputy said, "I'm going to confirm about the doctor, and then I'll get the Justice of the Peace over here to certify death. I believe she'll agree it's natural causes." He took a step toward the back door, then returned. "I knew Miss Steel. My mother told me she was her favorite teacher when she was in school. I sure am sorry for your loss."

Marva tried for a smile, but a nod was all she could manage.

He said, "After the JP's finished, the body can be removed. I expect Mr. Talley can help you get that taken care of."

As if the lawman's coming inside was his cue, Chick turned up sitting next to her a few seconds later. He handed her phone to her. "Stacey will be here by eight. Willa and Claire will be here until then. I'll take care of the funeral home after the JP finishes. Do you want to talk to Rose Ellen?"

Marva nodded. "I'll call her in a few minutes."

"There's no rush. Not for anything. No need to make any decisions tonight."

Willa and Claire came out. Claire said, "The deputy's outside waiting for the JP. We'll wait here with you, if that's okay." She, and then Willa, hugged Marva, then sat with her at the table. None of them said a word. For Marva, the silence brought calm.

Before long, the other necessary procedures were complete. Violet's body was on the way to the funeral home; Stacey arrived and smothered Marva in an embrace, then moved her bag into the extra bedroom and took charge in the kitchen. Willa and Claire chose clothes for Violet, in case there was a funeral. Willa said, "That doesn't have to be decided tonight. She may have left instructions. But I know the clothes she liked best. It's something I can do for her." Claire brought a pen and paper and placed them on the table next to Marva's elbow. "When you think of things that need to be done or questions or anything, just write it down. We'll all help." Chick warmed her tea and set a plate of peanut butter cookies on the table. He said, "I think Violet intended these to be eaten." Silently, they each ate two.

Through it all, Marva didn't leave her place near the tomato plants and petunias. At some point before dark fell, she couldn't recall exactly when, she called Rose Ellen. When her daughter asked if she wanted her to come, Marva said, "You have plans to make and students to teach."

"I only have one mother, and I don't want you to be alone to deal with all of this."

"I love you for saying that. When arrangements are made, I'll let you know. Until then, I'll be fine. I'm not alone. I have good friends helping me."

Stars peeked between the elm leaves; the crescent moon rose; the wind settled to a faint whisper. Stacey appeared at the table carrying two glasses of wine. "I thought this might be time for a bit of nourishment." She made a second trip inside and came back with a tray of cheese, crackers, and sliced apple. She said, "Willa and Claire will be back tomorrow. Willa promised they will handle all the necessary things about accepting the gifts of food that people will bring. They'll note the source for thank-you notes, all that. You know small town people always bring food. Chick called your clerk and told her you won't be in tomorrow, and why. He went to feed his donkey, said call anytime if you need him, but regardless, he'll be back in the morning. Said he'd help you with some of the details. And I'm here to do whatever you need for as long as you need. I won't burden you with talk, but I'll sure listen."

Marva said, "Right now, I'm okay with just drinking this wine, eating a little something."

Several quiet minutes later, her phone rang. Rose Ellen said, "I need to tell you something. I was thinking about what you said earlier. That you have good friends to help you. I want you to know how happy it makes me to know that. You deserve good friends. It's time."

Marva hesitated, didn't answer. Rose Ellen said, "Night, Mom. I love you."

After Marva hung up, Stacey said, "You okay?"

She took another sip of wine, nodded. Then she said, "I am. Sadder than I've been in a long time. But okay. Rose Ellen just told me something. It makes me know that now I'm probably better than I've ever been."

Made in USA - Crawfordsville, IN
55415_9781626770379
02.21.2023 1822